THE MARKED

VOLUME ONE: FRESH INK

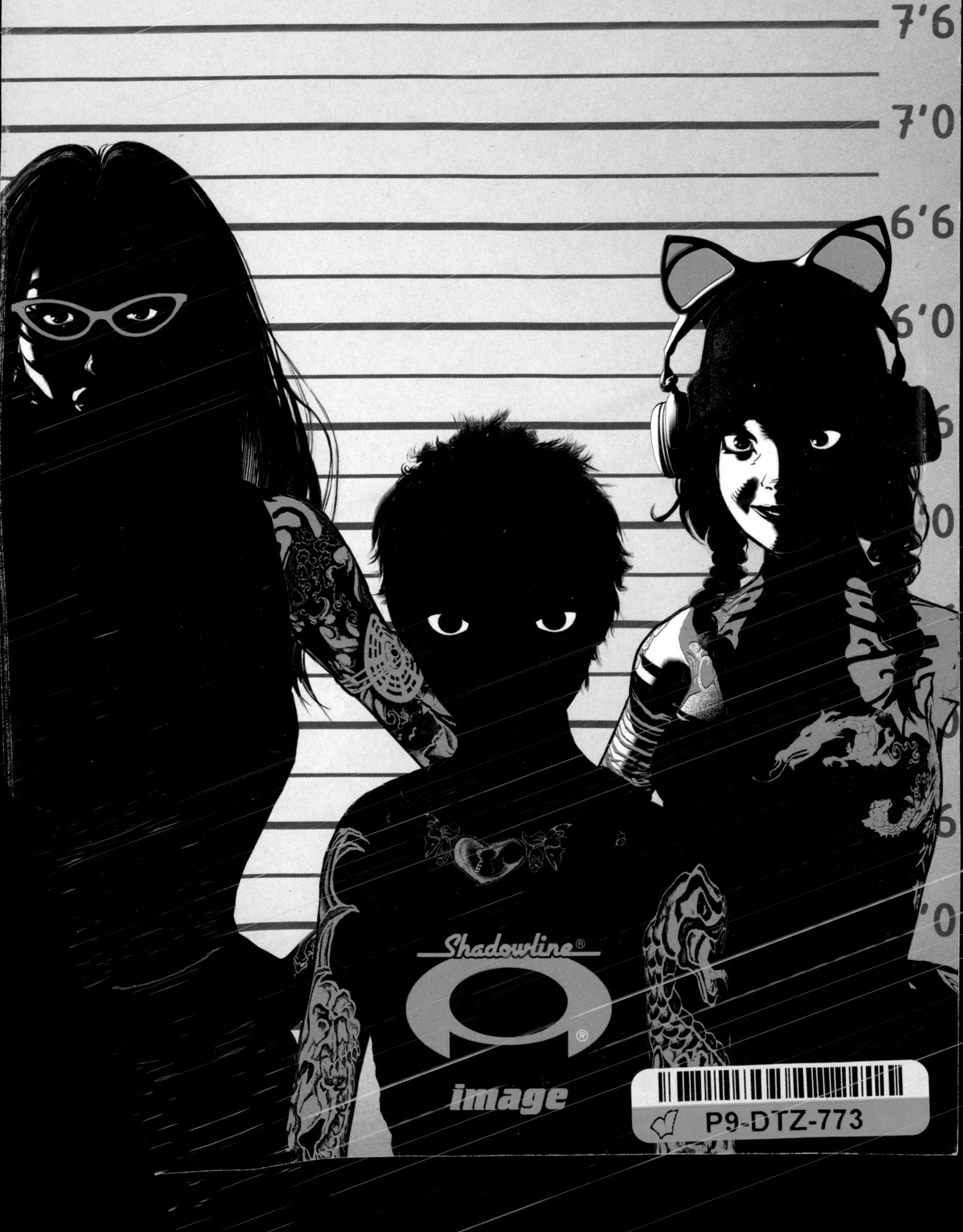
7'6
7'0
6'6
6'0
Shadowline
image

First printing: July 2020

ISBN: 978-1-5343-14

THE MARKED, Vol. 1. Published by Image Comics, Inc. Office of publication: 2701 NW Vaughn St., Suite 780, Portland, OR 97210. Copyright © 2020 ANOMALY PRODUCTIONS, INC. All rights reserved. Contains material originally published in single magazine form as THE MARKED #1-5. "The Marked," its logos, and the likenesses of all characters herein are trademarks of Anomaly Productions, Inc., unless otherwise noted. "Image" and the Image Comics logos are registered trademarks of Image Comics, Inc. Shadowline® and its logos are registered trademarks of Jim Valentino. No part of this publication may be reproduced or transmitted, in any form or by any means (except for short excerpts for journalistic or review purposes), without the express written permission of Brian Haberlin, or Image Comics, Inc. All names, characters, events, and locales in this publication are entirely fictional. Any resemblance to actual persons (living or dead), events, or places, without satirical intent, is coincidental. Printed in the USA. International Rights/Foreign Licensing: Christine Meyer at christine@gfloystudio.com.

image COMICS PRESENTS

THE MARKED™

FOR

STORY
**DAVID HINE &
BRIAN HABERLIN**

ART
**BRIAN HABERLIN
JAY ANACLETO**

COLORS
GEIRROD VAN DYKE

LETTERS
FRANCIS TAKENAGA

LEAD DEVELOPER
DAVID PENTZ

PRODUCTION
**HANNAH WALL
DIANA SANSON
J.P. JUPITER
MADDIE HUANG
DEVON RAE
CRISTIAN PRECIADO**

A
Shadowline®
PRODUCTION

MELANIE HACKETT
EDITOR

MARC LOMBARDI
COMMUNICATIONS

JIM VALENTINO
PUBLISHER/BOOK DESIGN

IMAGE COMICS, INC.
Robert Kirkman—Chief Operating Officer
Erik Larsen—Chief Financial Officer
Todd McFarlane—President
Marc Silvestri—Chief Executive Officer
Jim Valentino—Vice President
Eric Stephenson—Publisher/Chief Creative Officer
Jeff Boison—Director of Publishing Planning
& Book Trade Sales
Chris Ross—Director of Digital Services
Jeff Stang—Director of Direct Market Sales
Kat Salazar—Director of PR & Marketing
Drew Gill—Cover Editor
Heather Doornink—Production Director
Nicole Lapalme—Controller

IMAGECOMICS.COM

FOR
image®

ERIKA SCHNATZ
PRODUCTION

PREVIOUSLY UNPUBLISHED ART

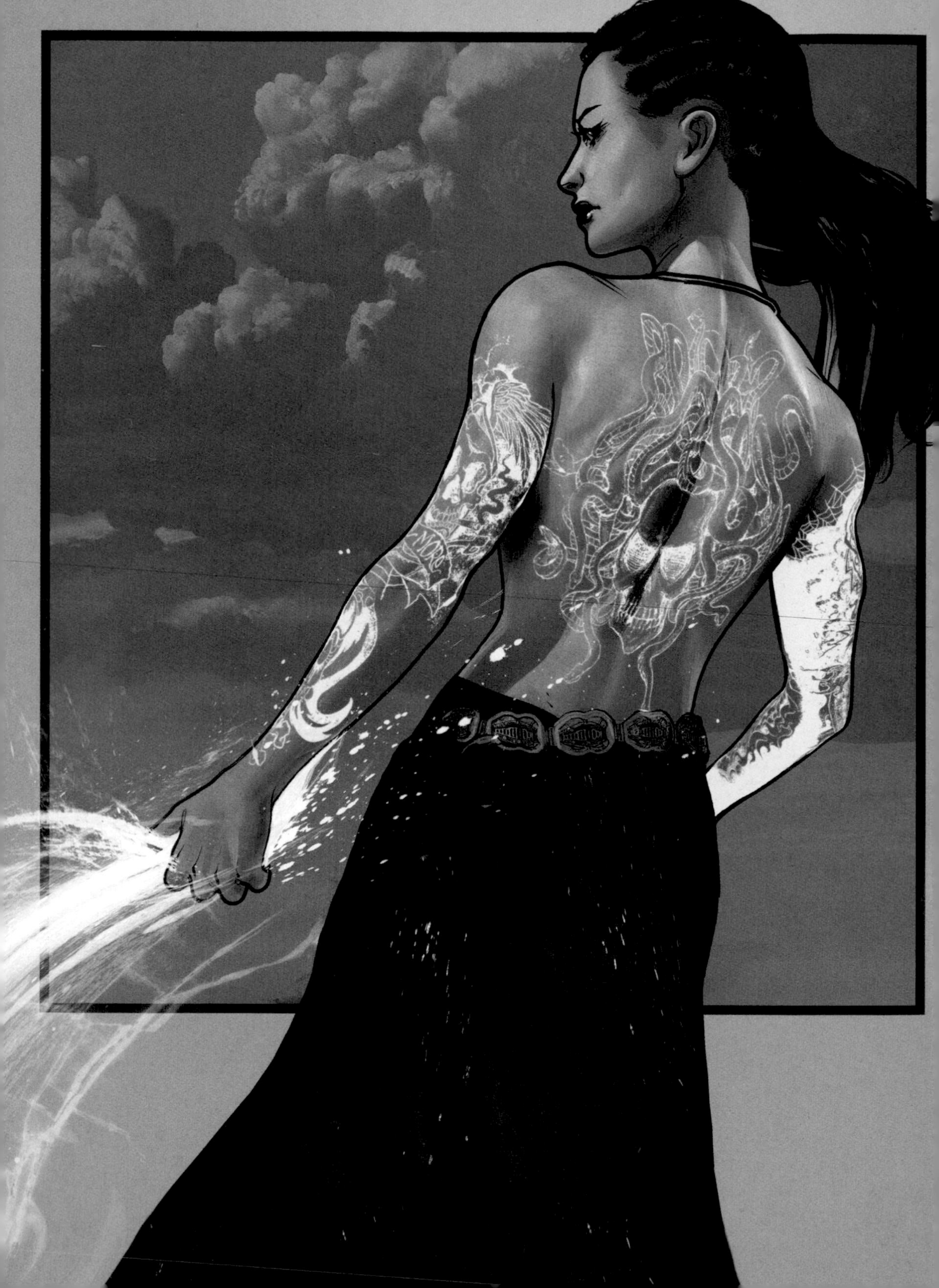

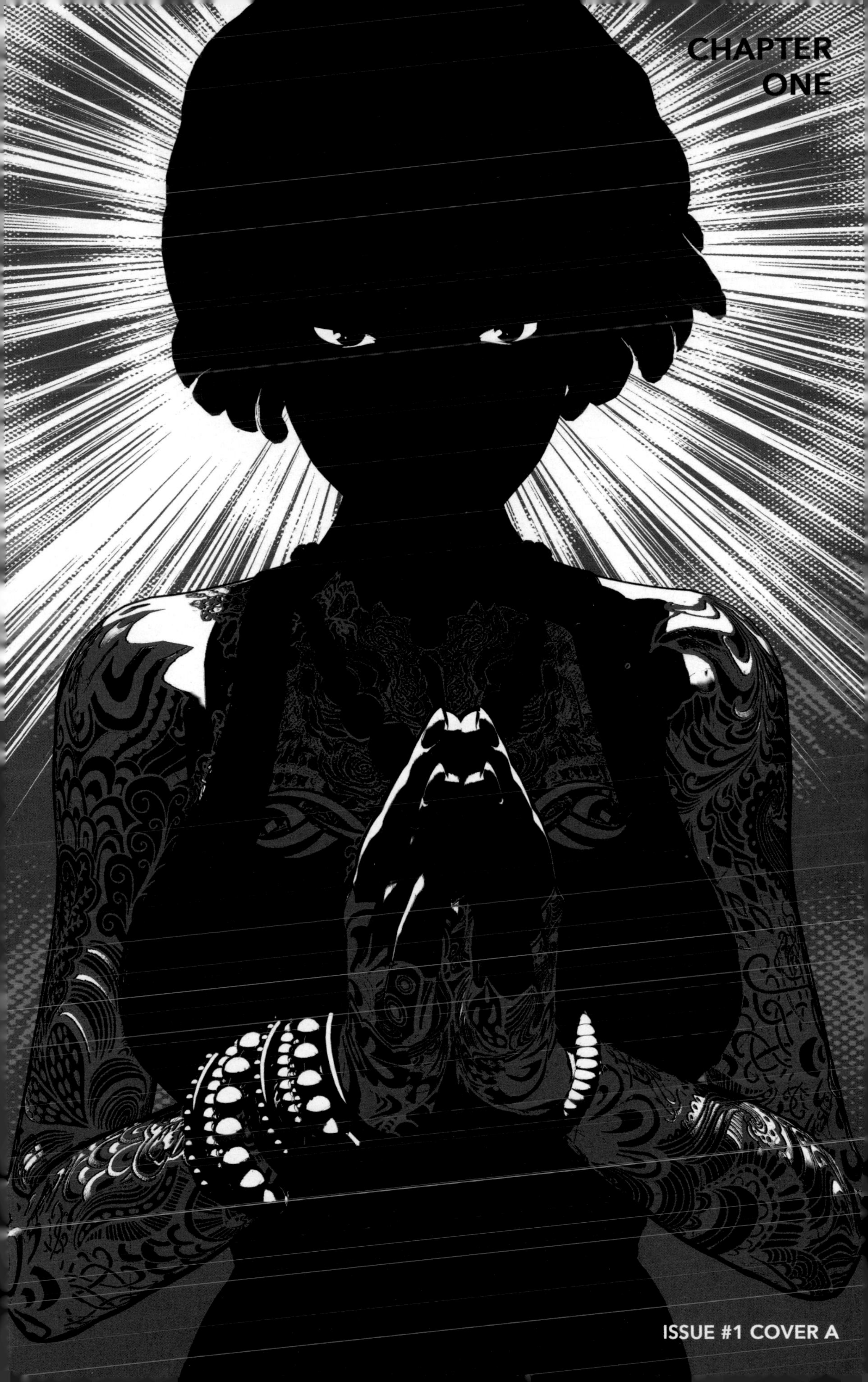
CHAPTER
ONE
ISSUE #1 COVER A

ISSUE #1 COVER C

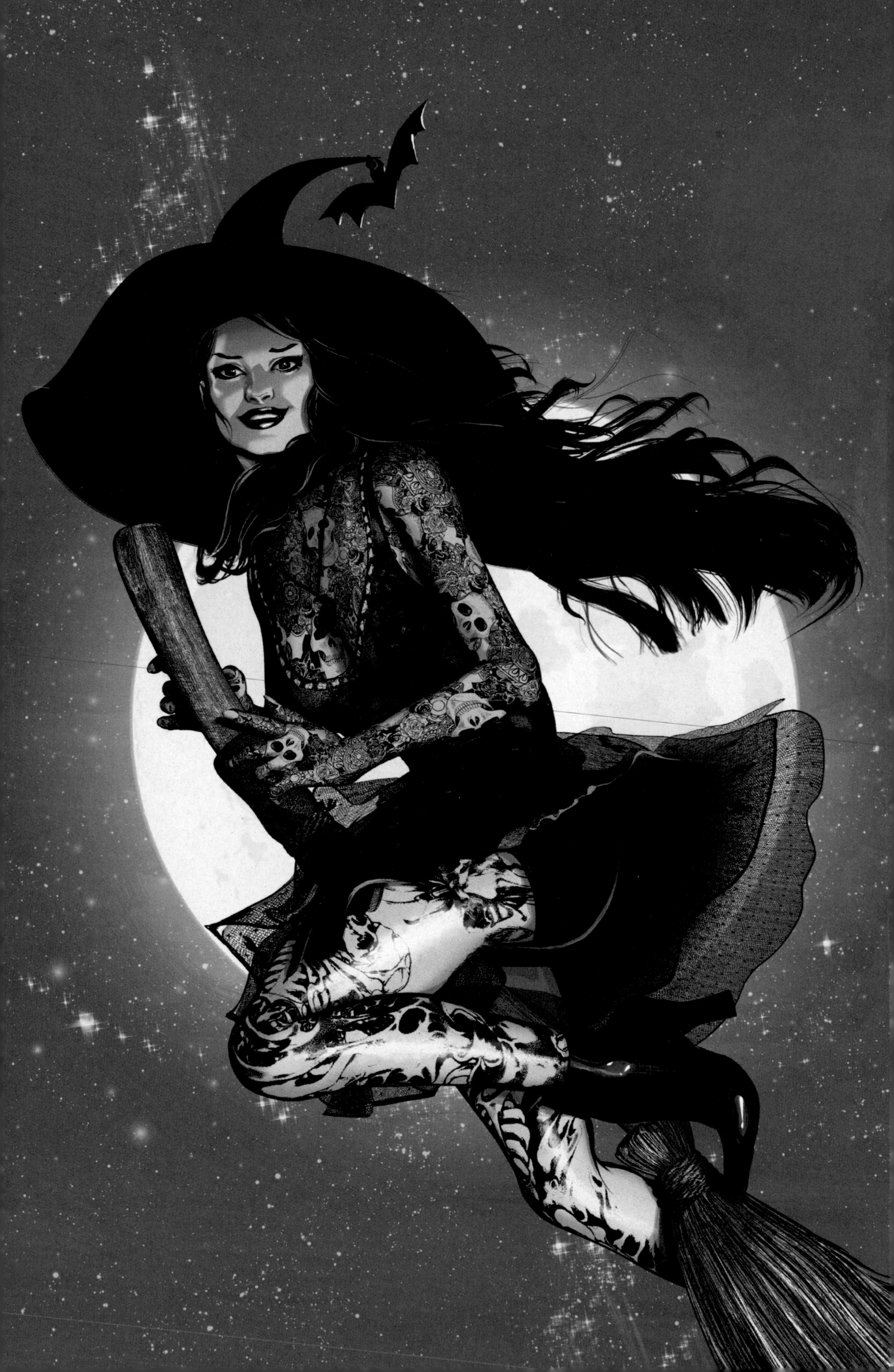

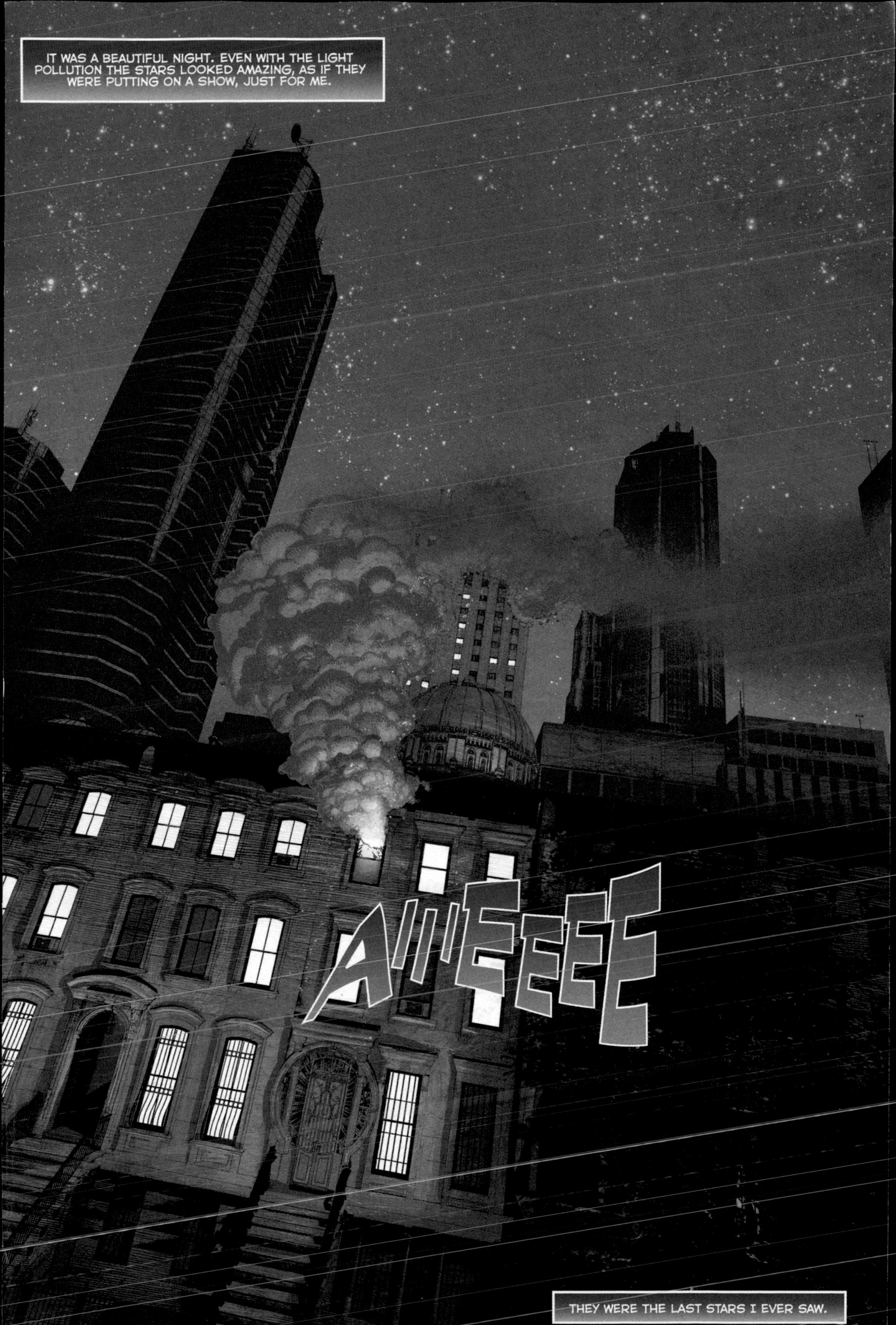
IT WAS A BEAUTIFUL NIGHT. EVEN WITH THE LIGHT POLLUTION THE STARS LOOKED AMAZING, AS IF THEY WERE PUTTING ON A SHOW, JUST FOR ME.
AIIIEEEE
THEY WERE THE LAST STARS I EVER SAW.

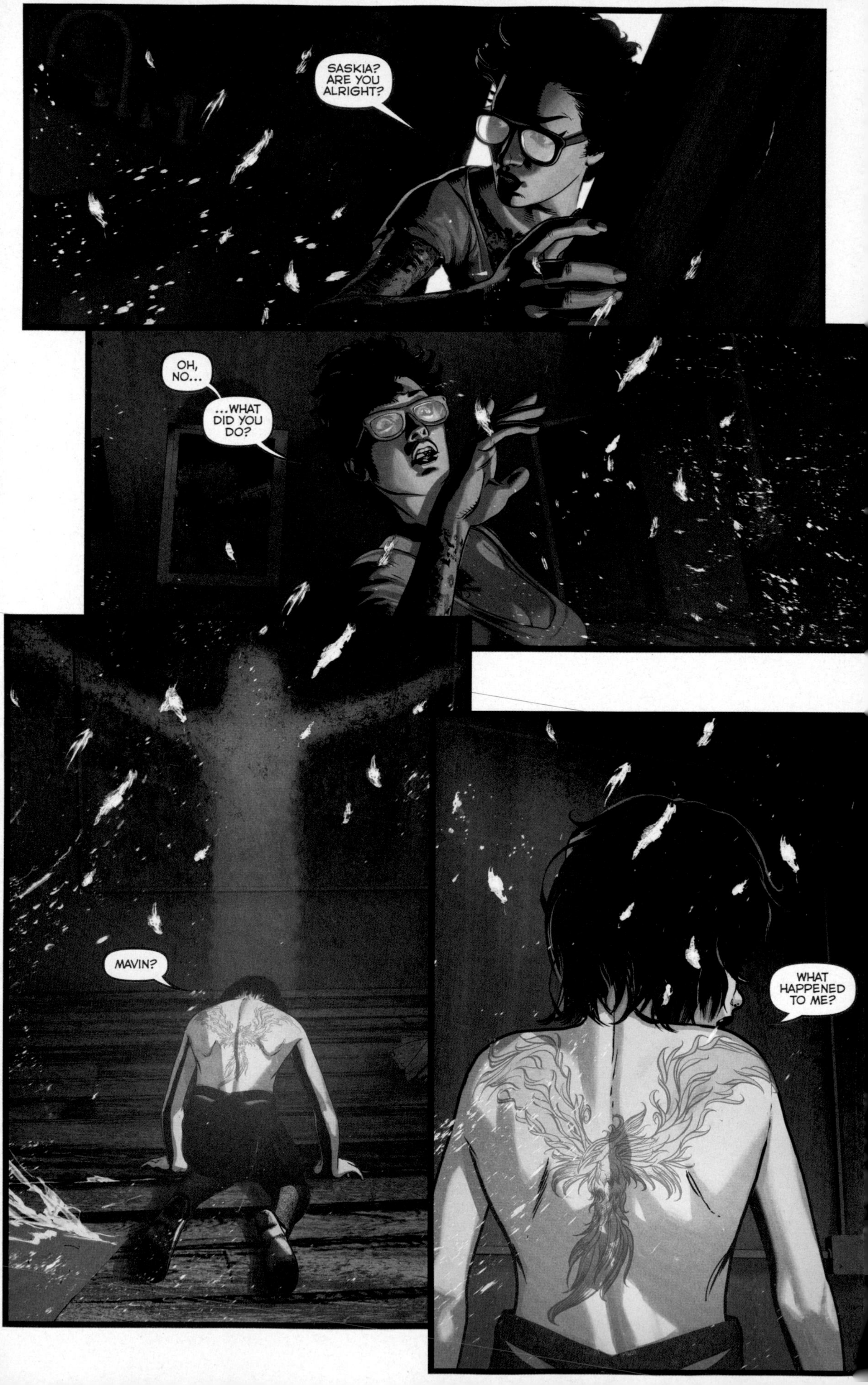
SASKIA? ARE YOU ALRIGHT?
OH, NO...
...WHAT DID YOU DO?
MAVIN?
WHAT HAPPENED TO ME?

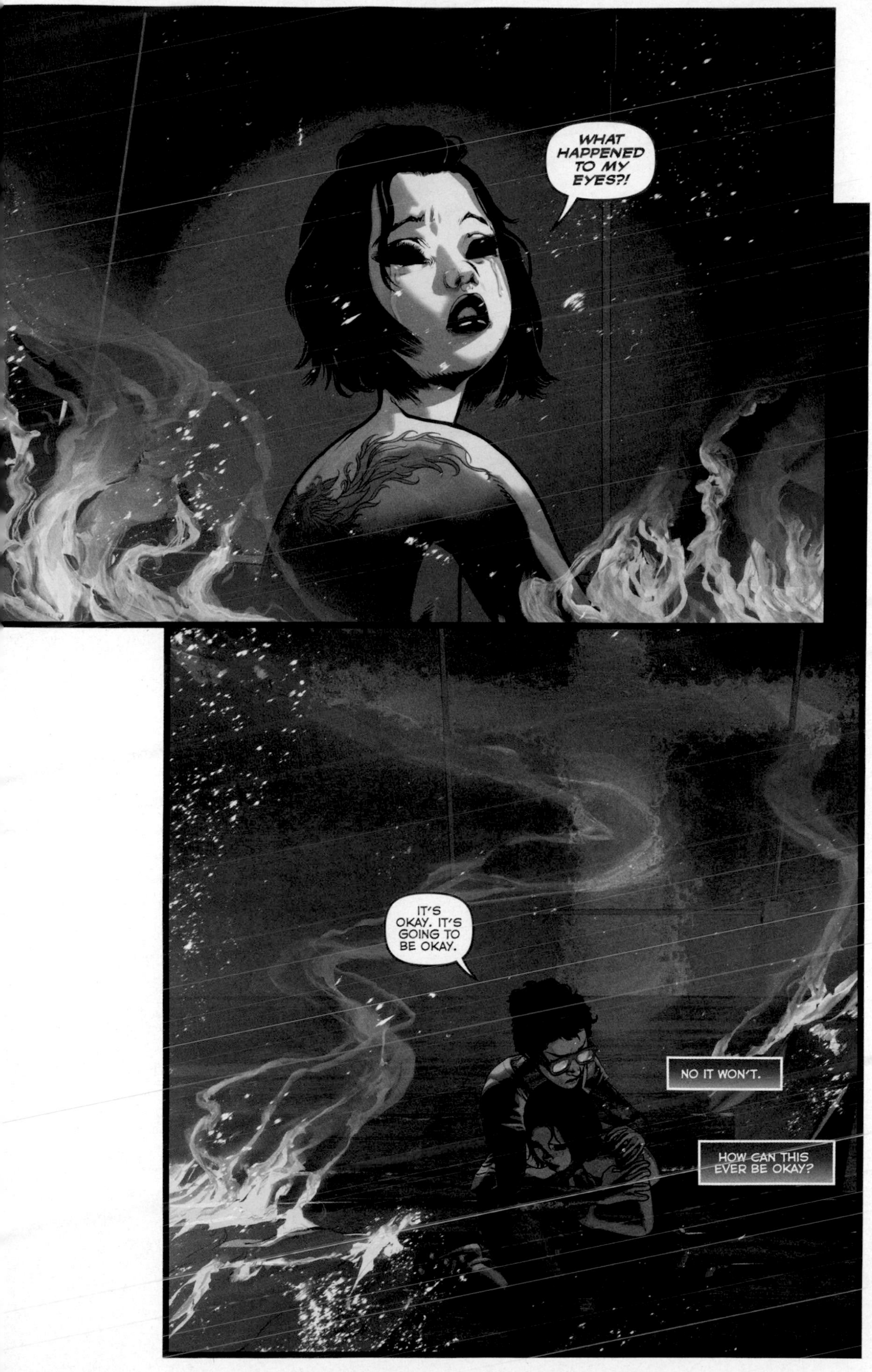
WHAT HAPPENED TO MY EYES?!
IT'S OKAY. IT'S GOING TO BE OKAY.
NO IT WON'T.
HOW CAN THIS EVER BE OKAY?

I NEVER ASKED FOR ANY OF THIS SHIT. ALL I EVER WANTED WAS A CHANCE TO MAKE MY ART.

BLACK BREW COFFEE HOUSE

CULLEN'S

1250   1252

PASTRIES AN

HI, CYREESE.

HI, SASKIA. YOU WANT YOUR USUAL?

OH, HEY, I HAVE SOMETHING FOR YOU TO CHECK OUT.

00:30

SOMEONE LEFT A STACK OF THESE FLIERS ON THE COUNTER.

YOU DRAW, RIGHT? I MEAN, PRETTY MUCH *ALL* YOU DO IS DRAW AND INGEST SATURATED FAT AND CAFFEINE.

DO YOU HAV

DRAW WHAT YO
IN THIS PICTU

EMAIL A DIGITAL SCAN OR PHOTO
ING TO THE ADDRESS BELOW FO
TO WIN A $20,000 ONE YEAR SC
OUR COURSE IN CREATIVE
THEARTSCHOOLTEST@GM

DO YOU HAVE THE VISION?

DRAW WHAT YOU SE
IN THIS PICTURE!

EMAIL A DIGITAL SCAN OR PHOTO OF YOUR D
ING TO THE ADDRESS BELOW FOR YOUR CH
TO WIN A $20,000 ONE YEAR SCHOLARS
OUR COURSE IN CREATIVE DESIGN
RTSCHOOLTEST@GMAIL.C

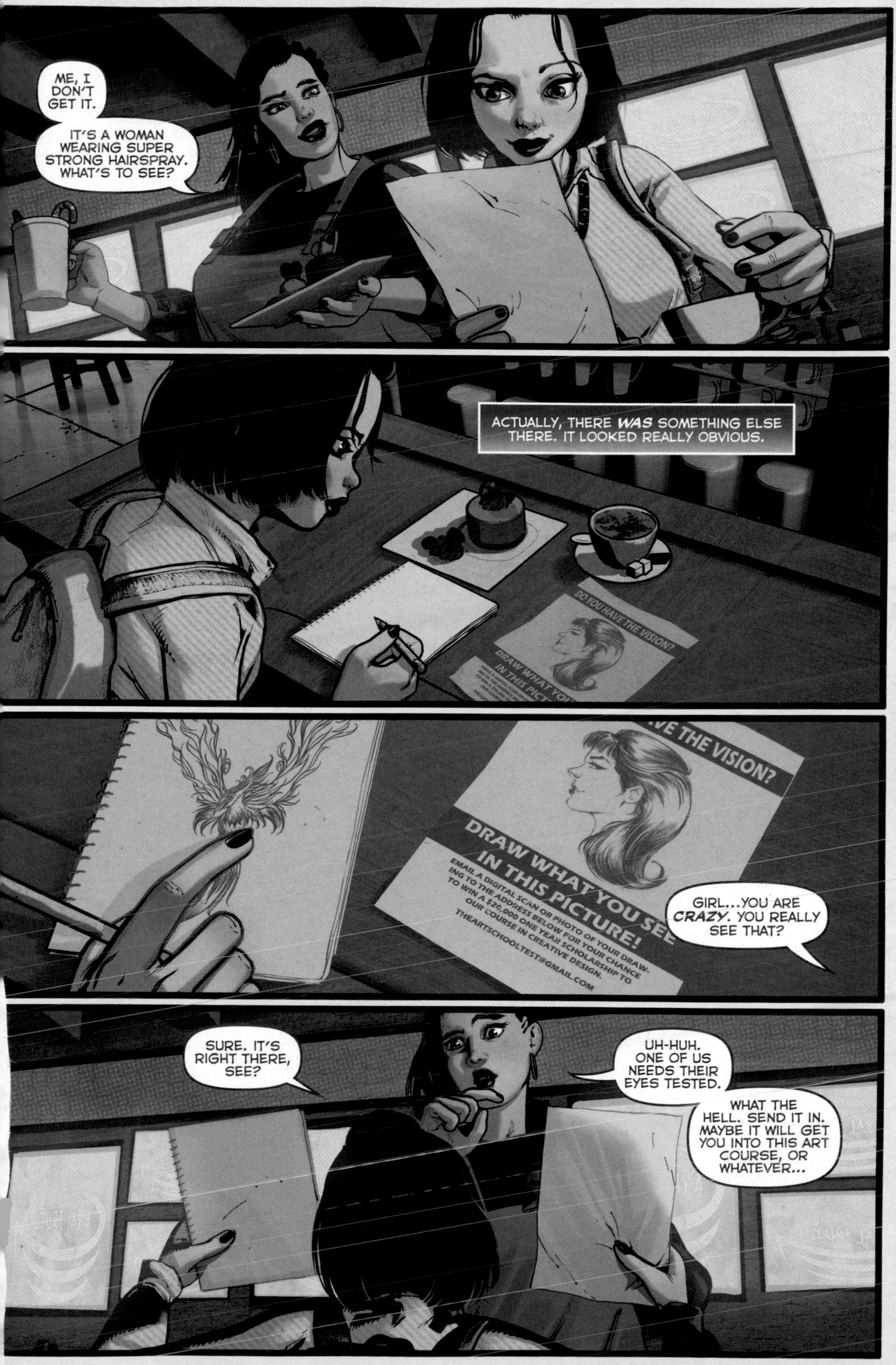
ME, I DON'T GET IT.
IT'S A WOMAN WEARING SUPER STRONG HAIRSPRAY. WHAT'S TO SEE?
ACTUALLY, THERE *WAS* SOMETHING ELSE THERE. IT LOOKED REALLY OBVIOUS.
DO YOU HAVE THE VISION?
DRAW WHAT YOU SEE IN THIS PICTURE!
EMAIL A DIGITAL SCAN OR PHOTO OF YOUR DRAWING TO THE ADDRESS BELOW FOR YOUR CHANCE TO WIN A $20,000 ONE YEAR SCHOLARSHIP TO OUR COURSE IN CREATIVE DESIGN.
THEARTSCHOOLTEST@GMAIL.COM
GIRL...YOU ARE *CRAZY*. YOU REALLY SEE THAT?
SURE. IT'S RIGHT THERE, SEE?
UH-HUH. ONE OF US NEEDS THEIR EYES TESTED.
WHAT THE HELL. SEND IT IN. MAYBE IT WILL GET YOU INTO THIS ART COURSE, OR WHATEVER...

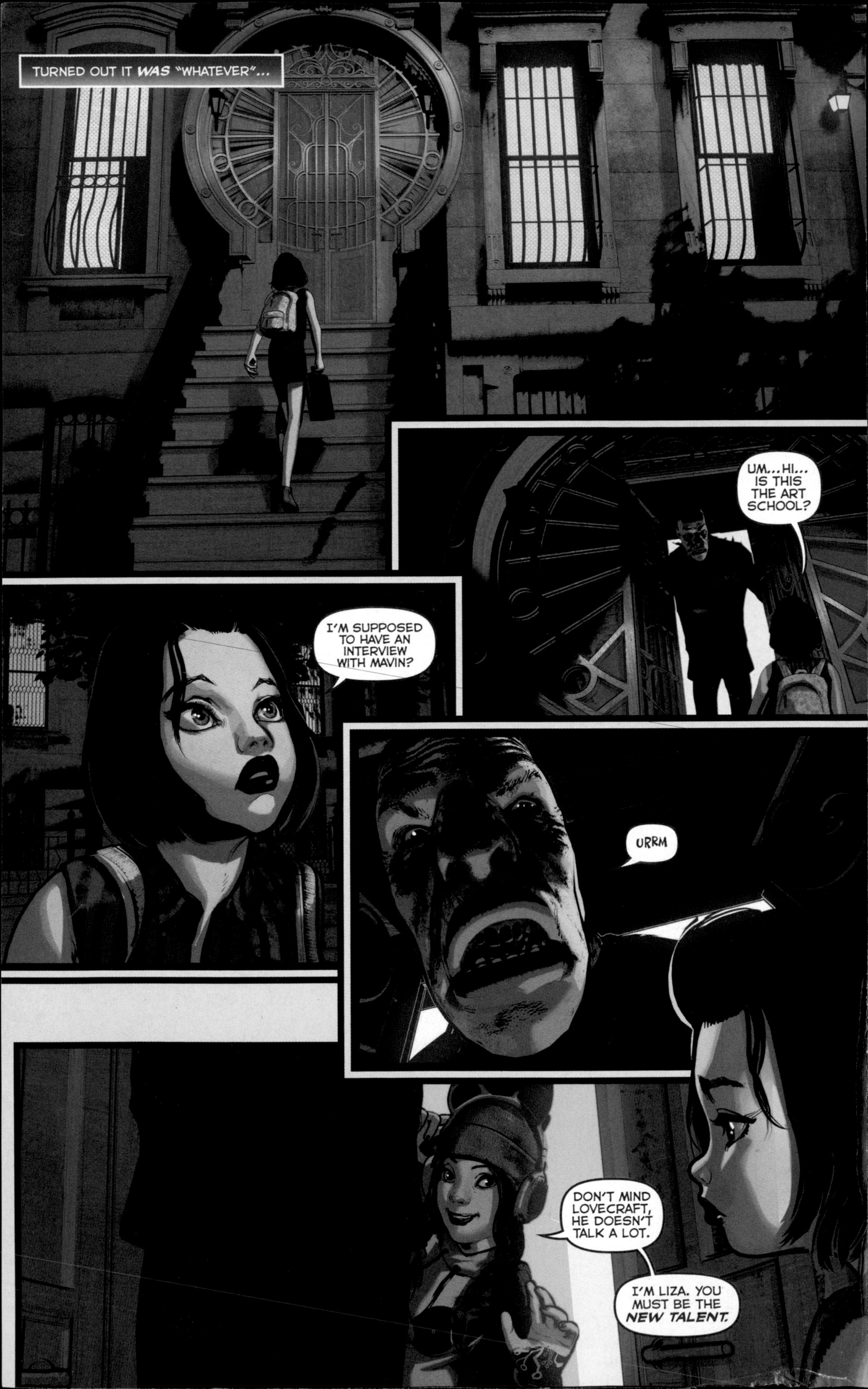
TURNED OUT IT WAS "WHATEVER"...
UM...HI... IS THIS THE ART SCHOOL?
I'M SUPPOSED TO HAVE AN INTERVIEW WITH MAVIN?
URRM
DON'T MIND LOVECRAFT, HE DOESN'T TALK A LOT.
I'M LIZA. YOU MUST BE THE NEW TALENT.

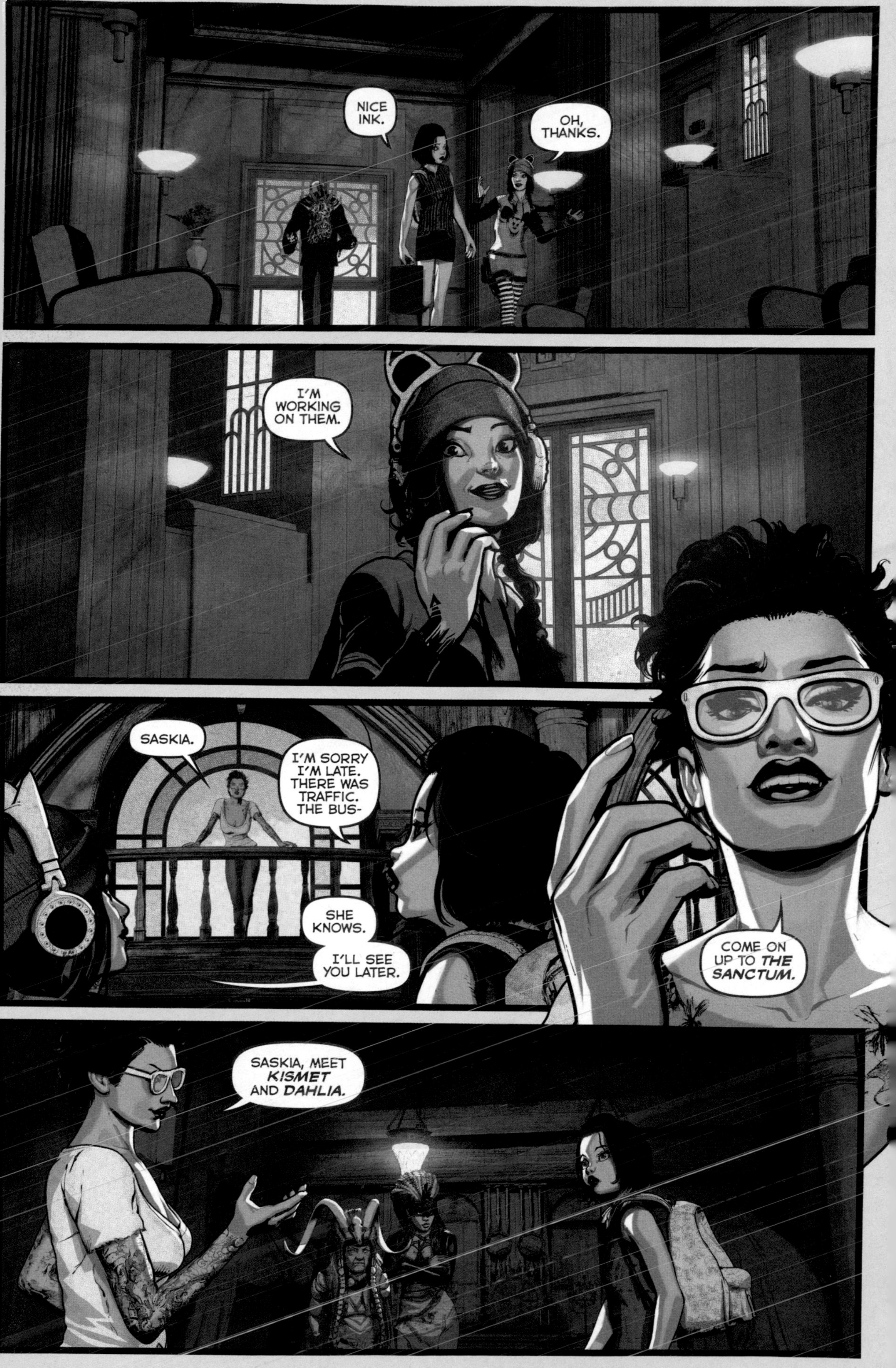
NICE INK.
OH, THANKS.
I'M WORKING ON THEM.
SASKIA.
I'M SORRY I'M LATE. THERE WAS TRAFFIC. THE BUS-
SHE KNOWS.
I'LL SEE YOU LATER.
COME ON UP TO THE SANCTUM.
SASKIA, MEET KISMET AND DAHLIA.

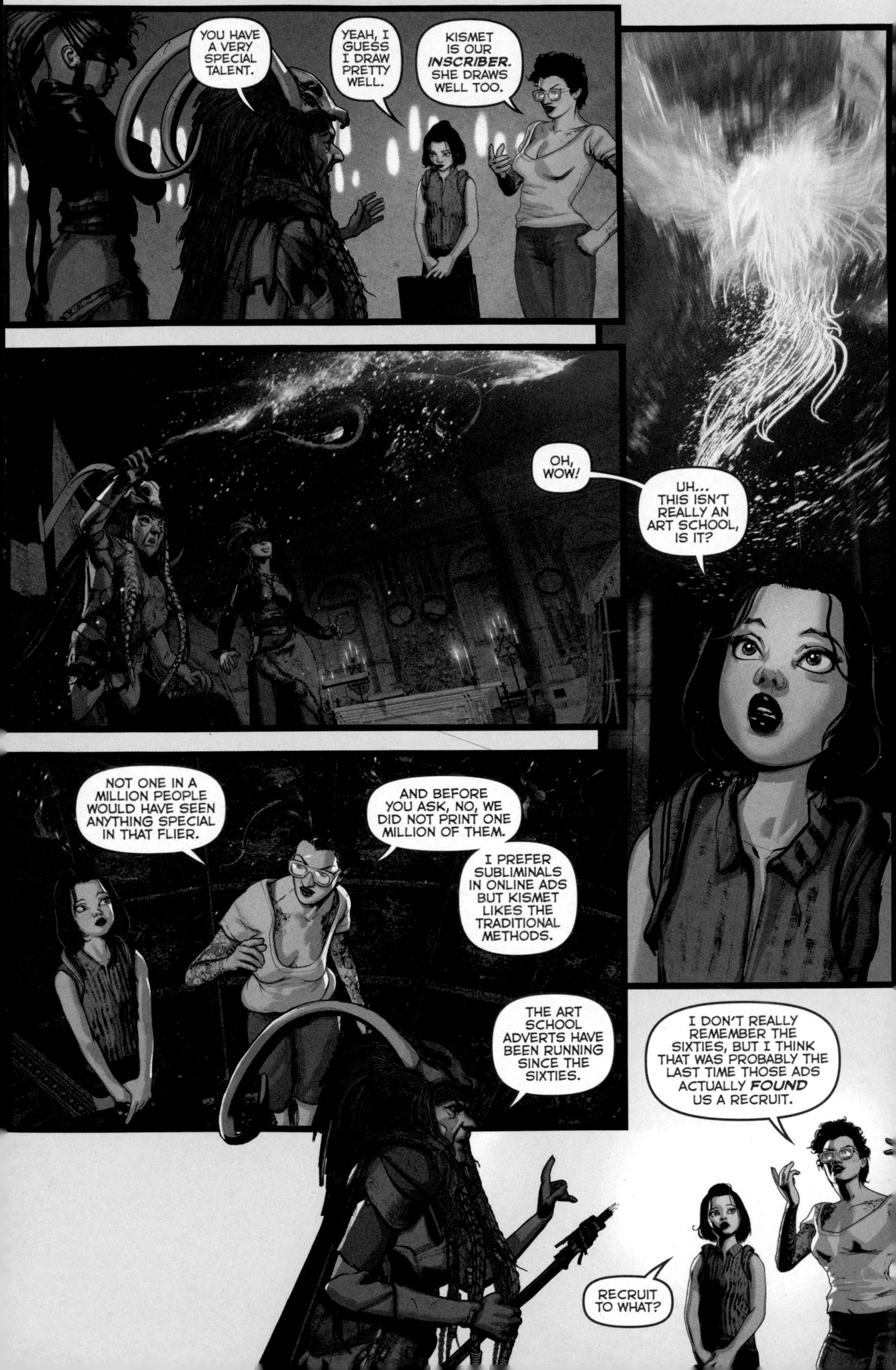
YOU HAVE A VERY SPECIAL TALENT.
YEAH, I GUESS I DRAW PRETTY WELL.
KISMET IS OUR INSCRIBER. SHE DRAWS WELL TOO.
OH, WOW!
UH... THIS ISN'T REALLY AN ART SCHOOL, IS IT?
NOT ONE IN A MILLION PEOPLE WOULD HAVE SEEN ANYTHING SPECIAL IN THAT FLIER.
AND BEFORE YOU ASK, NO, WE DID NOT PRINT ONE MILLION OF THEM.
I PREFER SUBLIMINALS IN ONLINE ADS BUT KISMET LIKES THE TRADITIONAL METHODS.
THE ART SCHOOL ADVERTS HAVE BEEN RUNNING SINCE THE SIXTIES.
I DON'T REALLY REMEMBER THE SIXTIES, BUT I THINK THAT WAS PROBABLY THE LAST TIME THOSE ADS ACTUALLY FOUND US A RECRUIT.
RECRUIT TO WHAT?

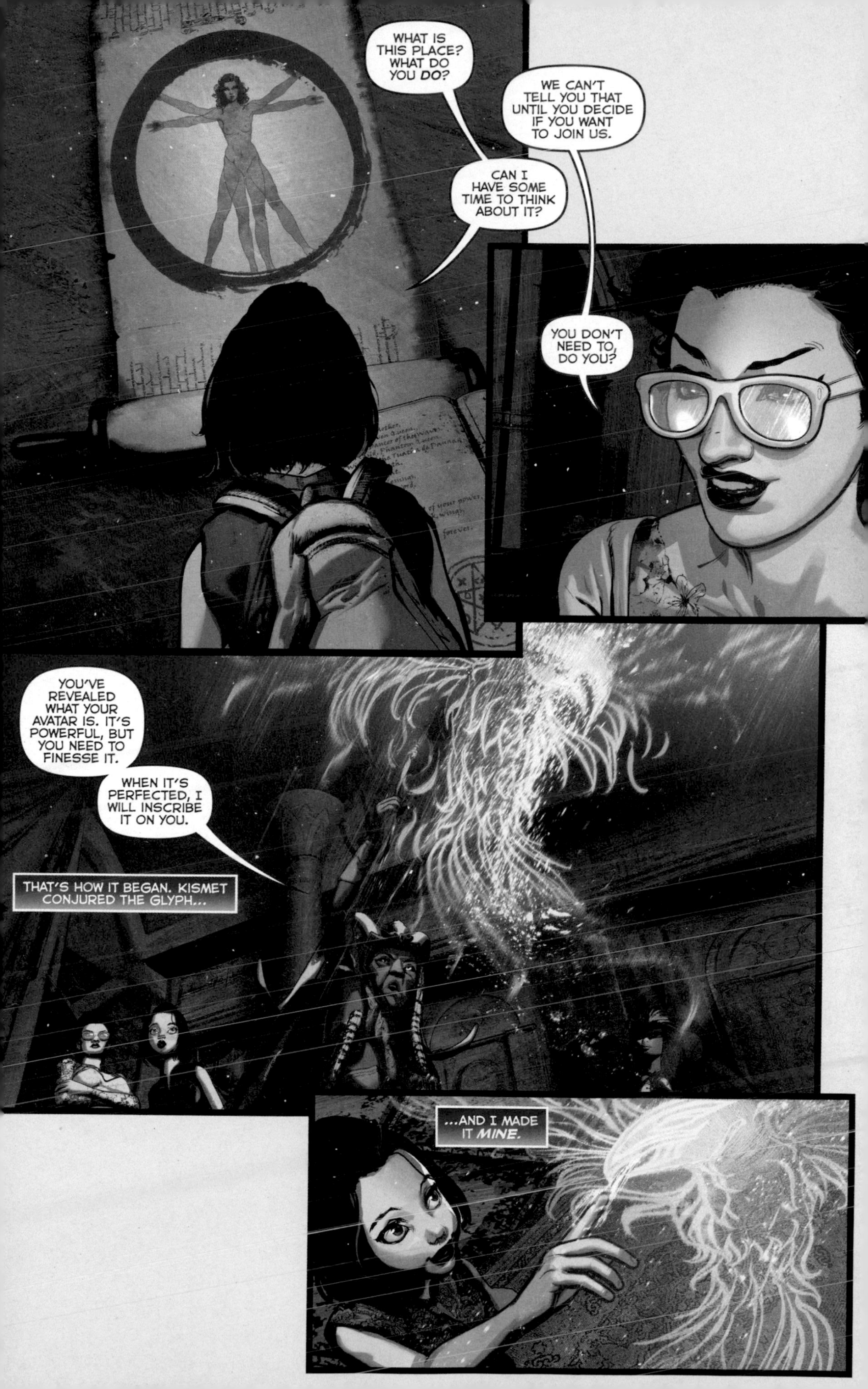
WHAT IS THIS PLACE? WHAT DO YOU DO?
WE CAN'T TELL YOU THAT UNTIL YOU DECIDE IF YOU WANT TO JOIN US.
CAN I HAVE SOME TIME TO THINK ABOUT IT?
YOU DON'T NEED TO, DO YOU?
YOU'VE REVEALED WHAT YOUR AVATAR IS. IT'S POWERFUL, BUT YOU NEED TO FINESSE IT.
WHEN IT'S PERFECTED, I WILL INSCRIBE IT ON YOU.
THAT'S HOW IT BEGAN. KISMET CONJURED THE GLYPH...
...AND I MADE IT *MINE.*

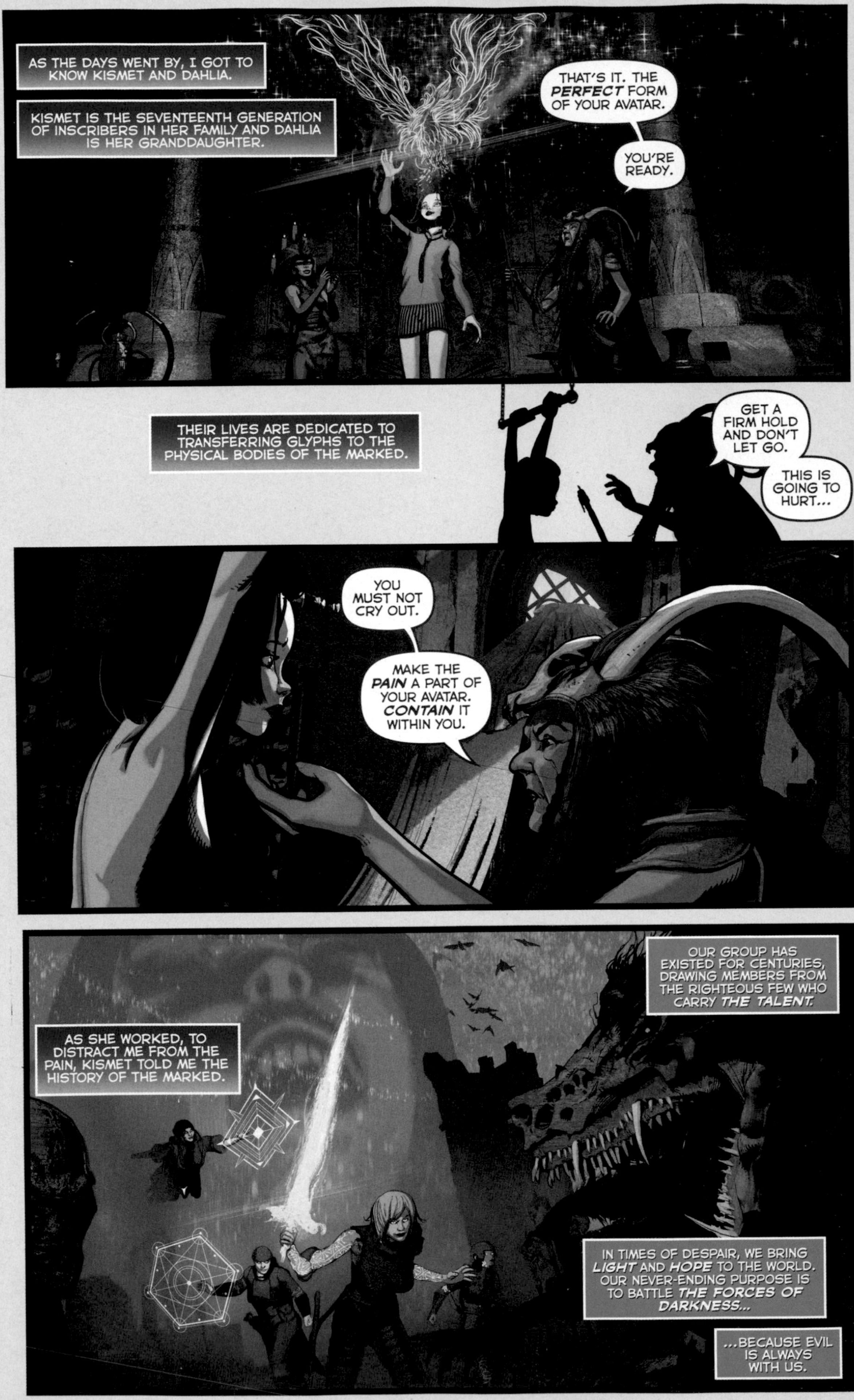
AS THE DAYS WENT BY, I GOT TO KNOW KISMET AND DAHLIA.
KISMET IS THE SEVENTEENTH GENERATION OF INSCRIBERS IN HER FAMILY AND DAHLIA IS HER GRANDDAUGHTER.
THAT'S IT. THE *PERFECT* FORM OF YOUR AVATAR.
YOU'RE READY.
THEIR LIVES ARE DEDICATED TO TRANSFERRING GLYPHS TO THE PHYSICAL BODIES OF THE MARKED.
GET A FIRM HOLD AND DON'T LET GO.
THIS IS GOING TO HURT...
YOU MUST NOT CRY OUT.
MAKE THE *PAIN* A PART OF YOUR AVATAR. *CONTAIN* IT WITHIN YOU.
AS SHE WORKED, TO DISTRACT ME FROM THE PAIN, KISMET TOLD ME THE HISTORY OF THE MARKED.
OUR GROUP HAS EXISTED FOR CENTURIES, DRAWING MEMBERS FROM THE RIGHTEOUS FEW WHO CARRY *THE TALENT.*
IN TIMES OF DESPAIR, WE BRING *LIGHT* AND *HOPE* TO THE WORLD. OUR NEVER-ENDING PURPOSE IS TO BATTLE *THE FORCES OF DARKNESS...*
...BECAUSE EVIL IS ALWAYS WITH US.

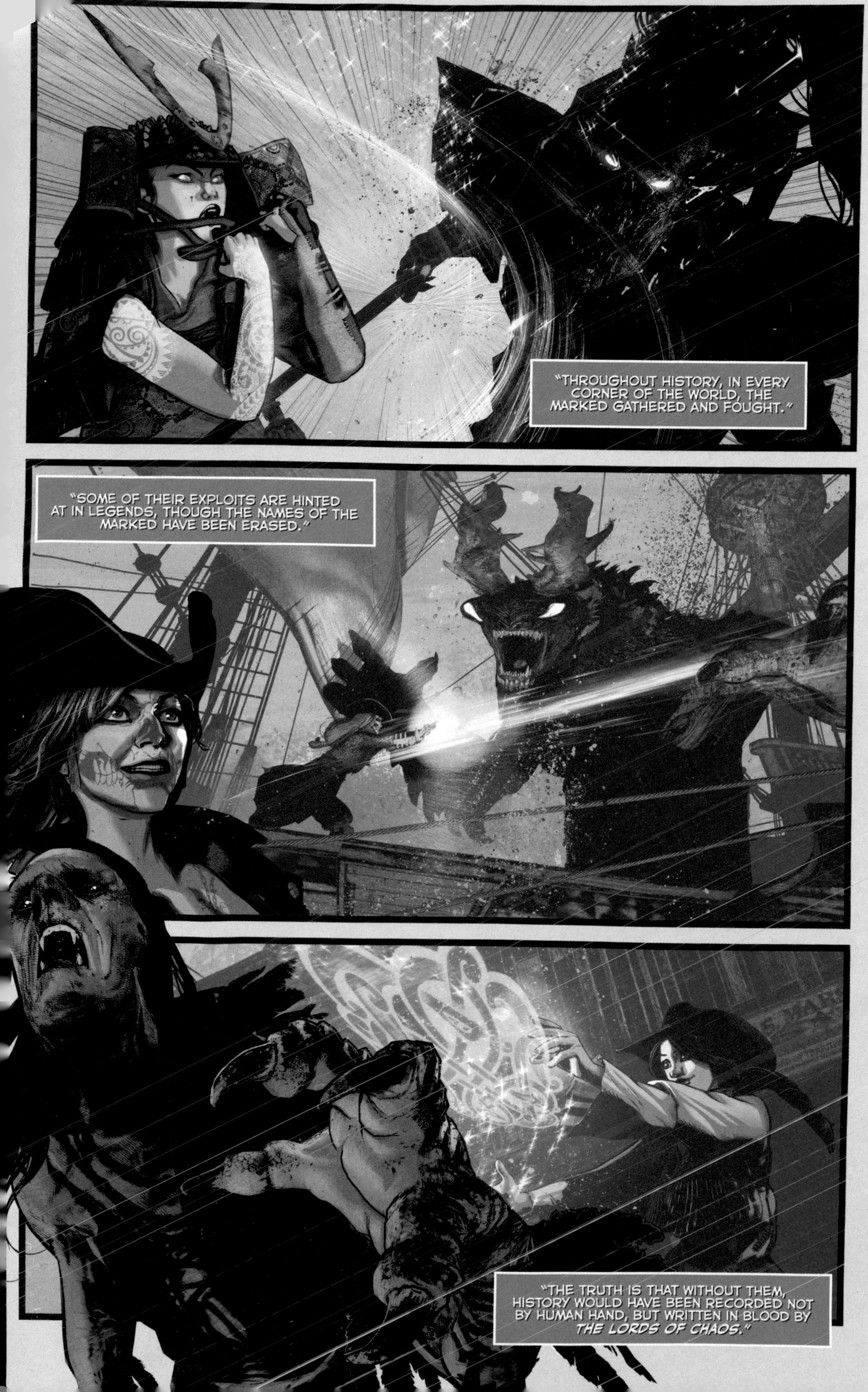
"THROUGHOUT HISTORY, IN EVERY CORNER OF THE WORLD, THE MARKED GATHERED AND FOUGHT."
"SOME OF THEIR EXPLOITS ARE HINTED AT IN LEGENDS, THOUGH THE NAMES OF THE MARKED HAVE BEEN ERASED."
"THE TRUTH IS THAT WITHOUT THEM, HISTORY WOULD HAVE BEEN RECORDED NOT BY HUMAN HAND, BUT WRITTEN IN BLOOD BY *THE LORDS OF CHAOS.*"

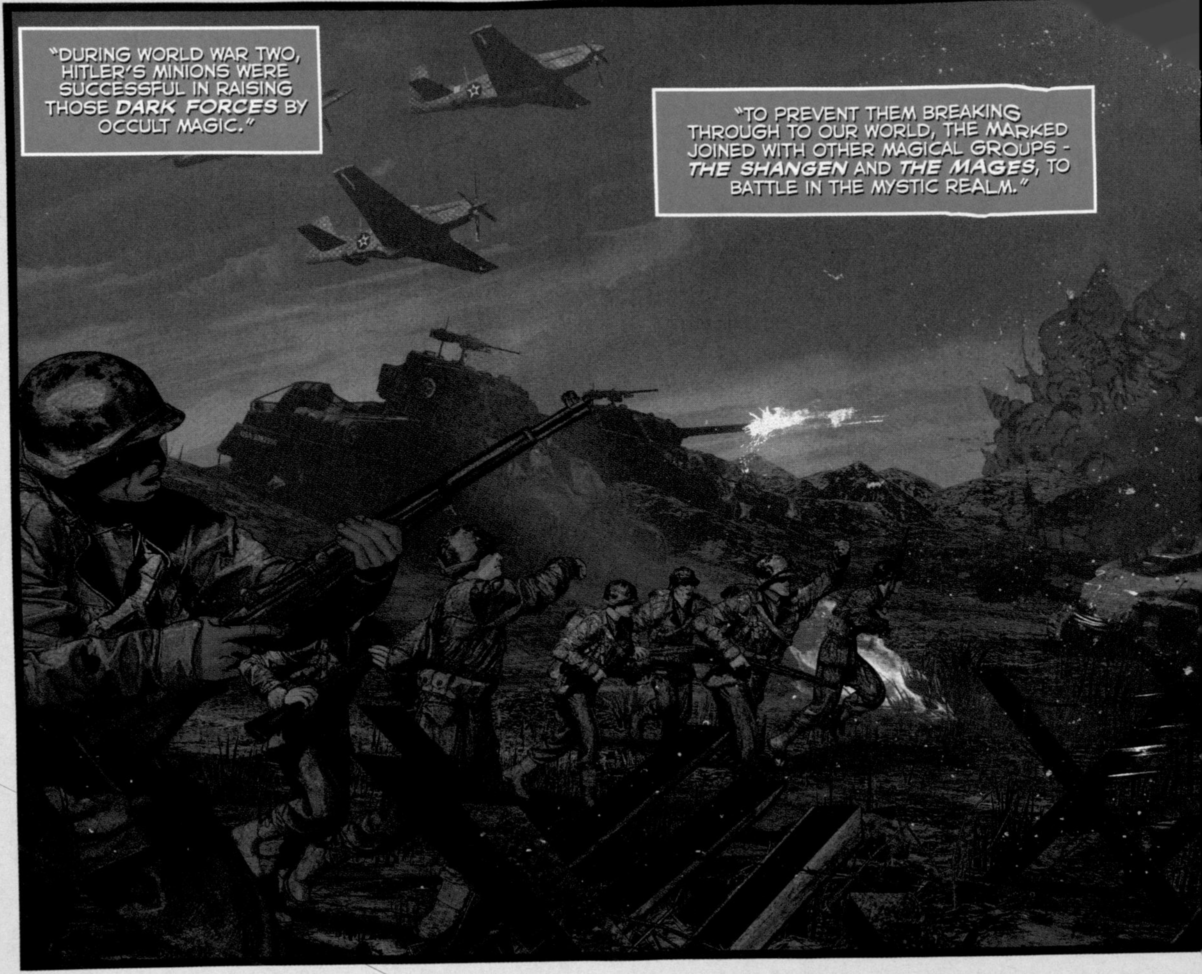
"DURING WORLD WAR TWO, HITLER'S MINIONS WERE SUCCESSFUL IN RAISING THOSE DARK FORCES BY OCCULT MAGIC."
"TO PREVENT THEM BREAKING THROUGH TO OUR WORLD, THE MARKED JOINED WITH OTHER MAGICAL GROUPS - THE SHANGEN AND THE MAGES, TO BATTLE IN THE MYSTIC REALM."

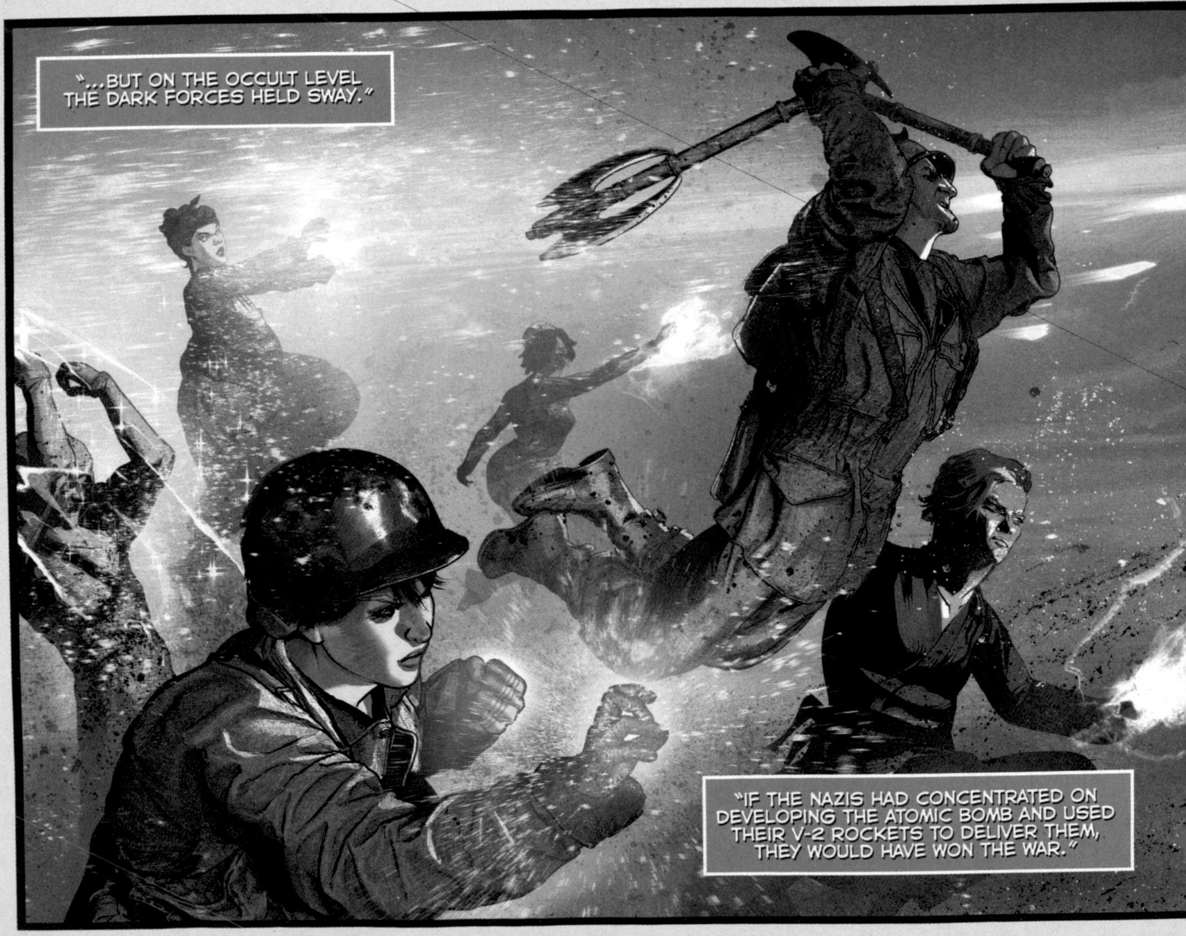
"...BUT ON THE OCCULT LEVEL THE DARK FORCES HELD SWAY."
"IF THE NAZIS HAD CONCENTRATED ON DEVELOPING THE ATOMIC BOMB AND USED THEIR V-2 ROCKETS TO DELIVER THEM, THEY WOULD HAVE WON THE WAR."

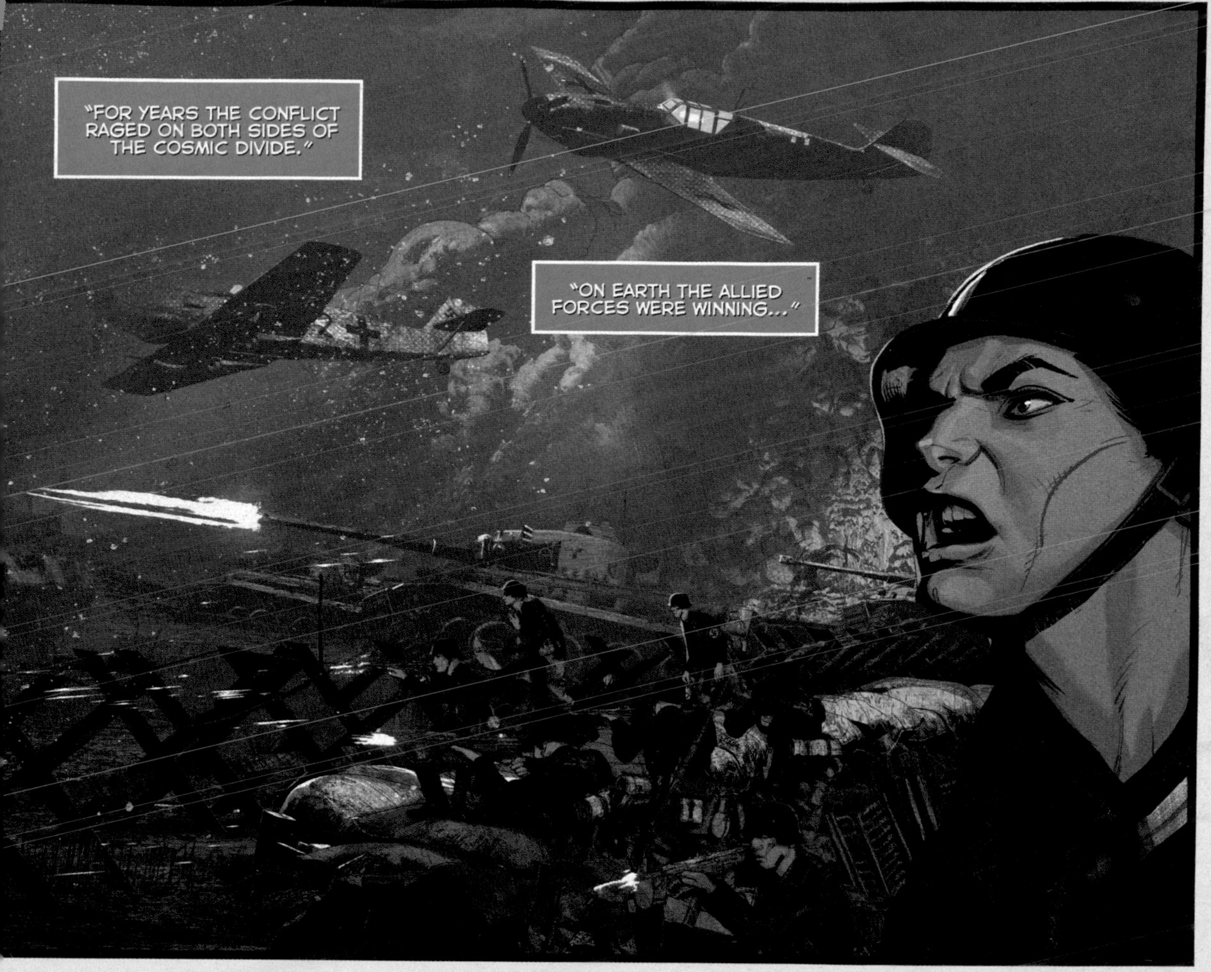
"FOR YEARS THE CONFLICT RAGED ON BOTH SIDES OF THE COSMIC DIVIDE."
"ON EARTH THE ALLIED FORCES WERE WINNING..."

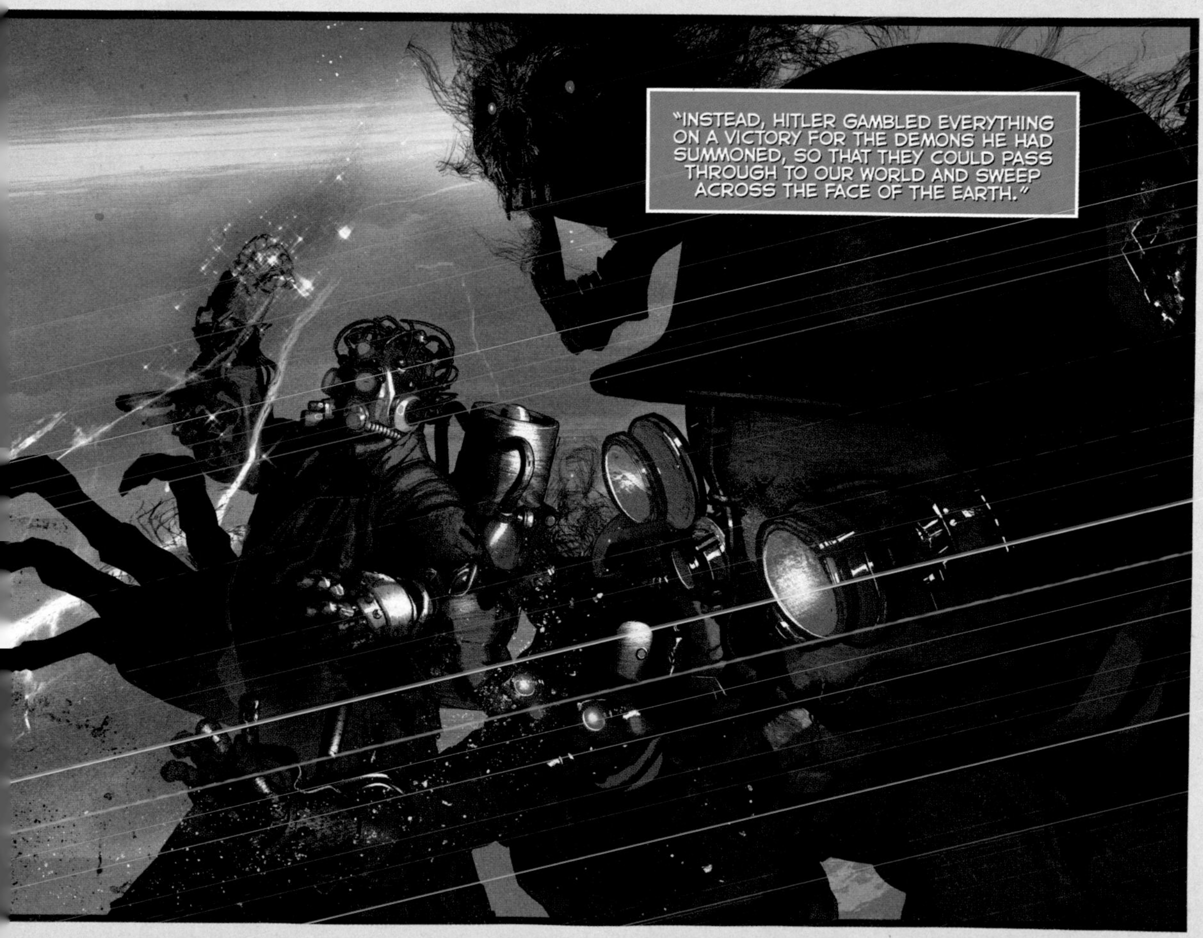
"INSTEAD, HITLER GAMBLED EVERYTHING ON A VICTORY FOR THE DEMONS HE HAD SUMMONED, SO THAT THEY COULD PASS THROUGH TO OUR WORLD AND SWEEP ACROSS THE FACE OF THE EARTH."

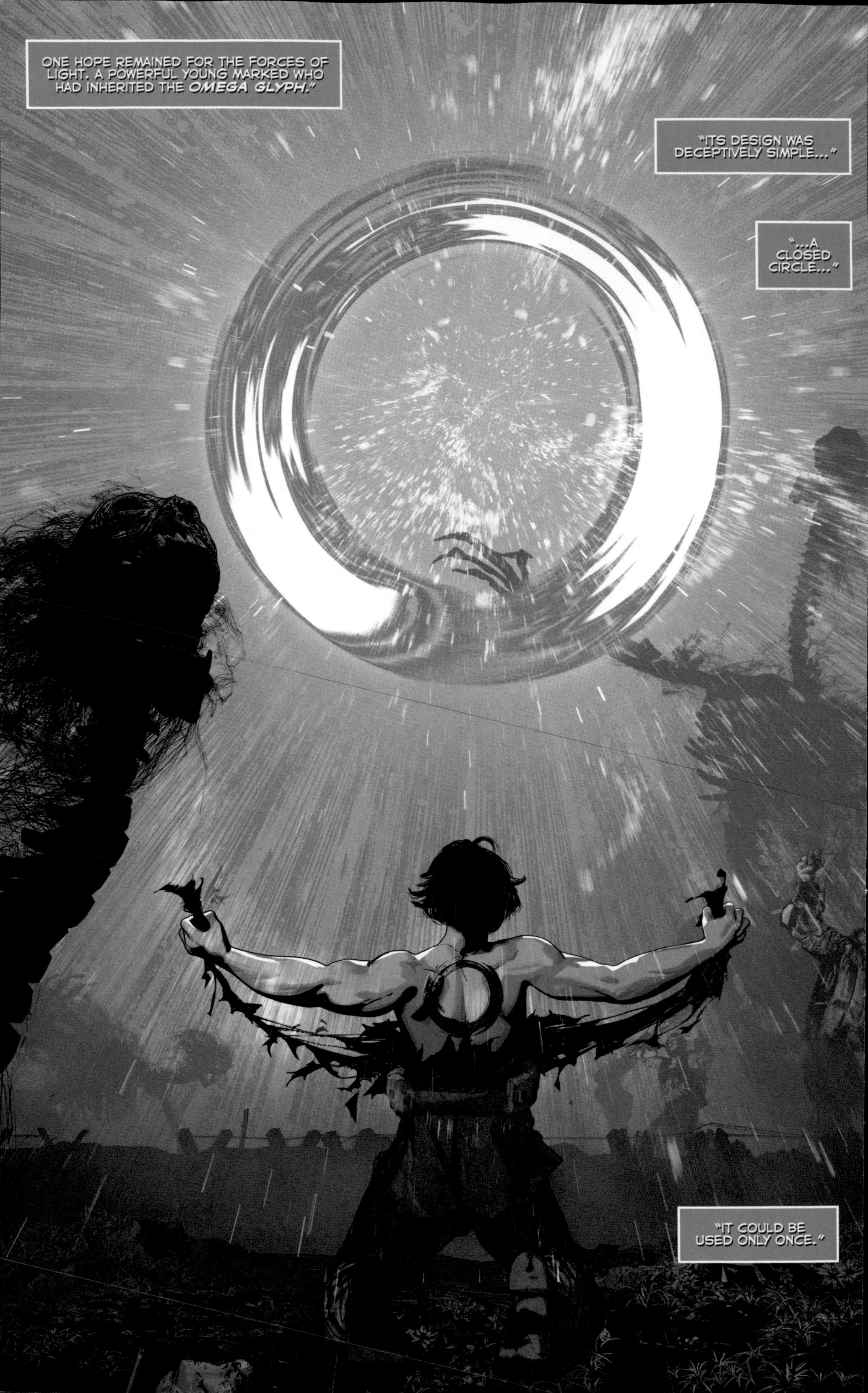
ONE HOPE REMAINED FOR THE FORCES OF LIGHT. A POWERFUL YOUNG MARKED WHO HAD INHERITED THE *OMEGA GLYPH.*"
"ITS DESIGN WAS DECEPTIVELY SIMPLE..."
"...A CLOSED CIRCLE..."
"IT COULD BE USED ONLY ONCE."

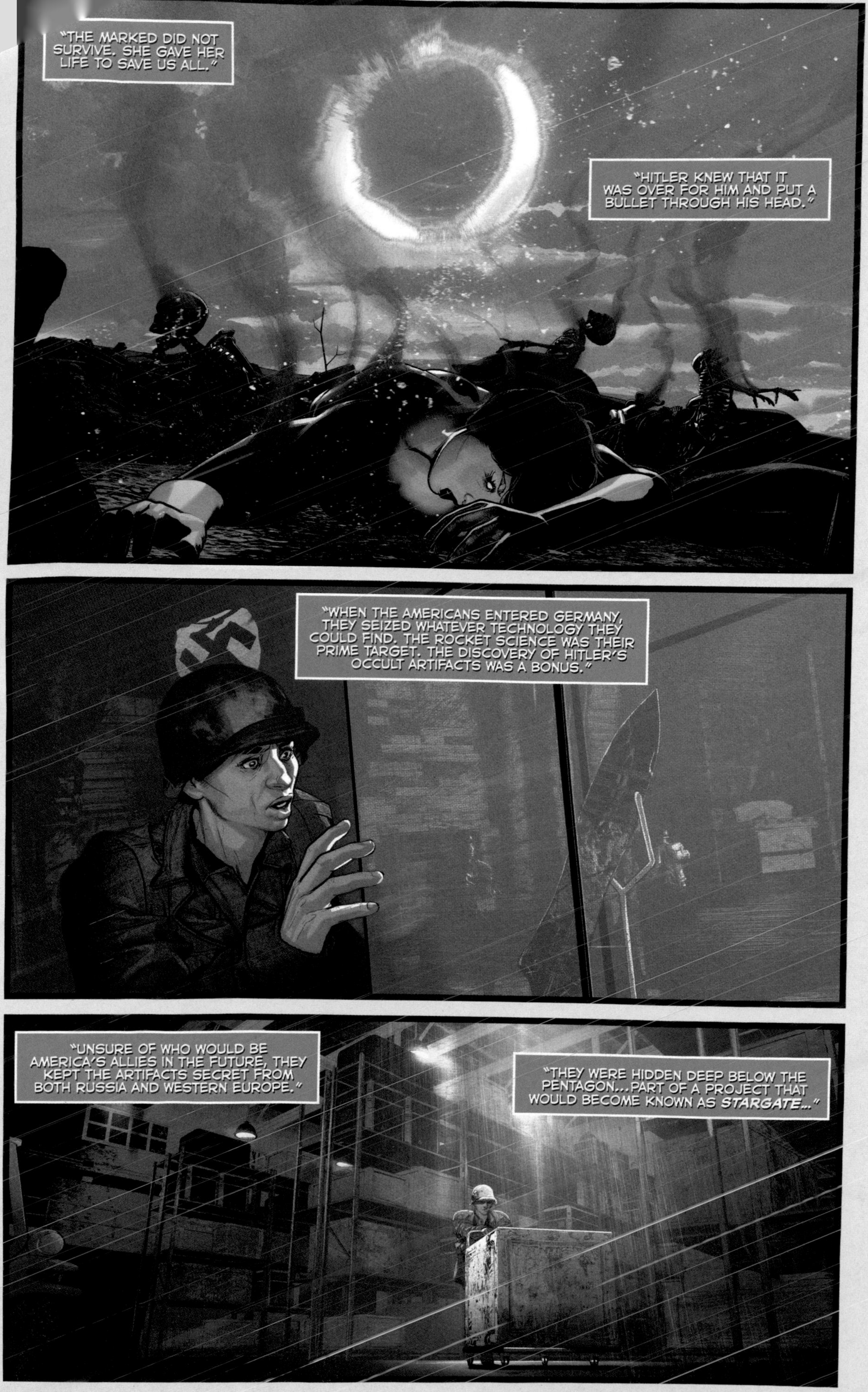
"THE MARKED DID NOT SURVIVE. SHE GAVE HER LIFE TO SAVE US ALL."
"HITLER KNEW THAT IT WAS OVER FOR HIM AND PUT A BULLET THROUGH HIS HEAD."
"WHEN THE AMERICANS ENTERED GERMANY, THEY SEIZED WHATEVER TECHNOLOGY THEY COULD FIND. THE ROCKET SCIENCE WAS THEIR PRIME TARGET. THE DISCOVERY OF HITLER'S OCCULT ARTIFACTS WAS A BONUS."
"UNSURE OF WHO WOULD BE AMERICA'S ALLIES IN THE FUTURE, THEY KEPT THE ARTIFACTS SECRET FROM BOTH RUSSIA AND WESTERN EUROPE."
"THEY WERE HIDDEN DEEP BELOW THE PENTAGON...PART OF A PROJECT THAT WOULD BECOME KNOWN AS *STARGATE*..."

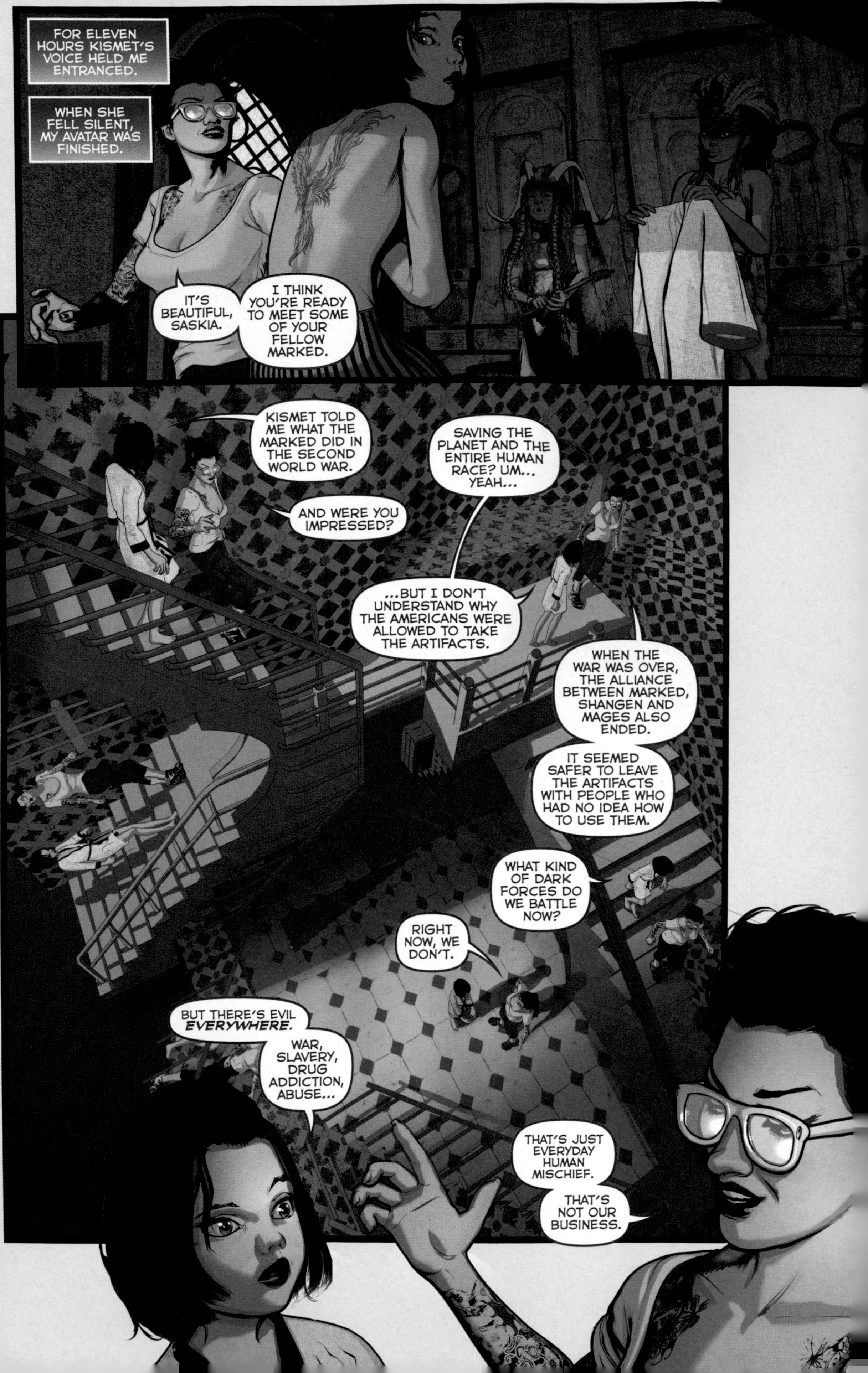
FOR ELEVEN HOURS KISMET'S VOICE HELD ME ENTRANCED.
WHEN SHE FELL SILENT, MY AVATAR WAS FINISHED.
IT'S BEAUTIFUL, SASKIA.
I THINK YOU'RE READY TO MEET SOME OF YOUR FELLOW MARKED.
KISMET TOLD ME WHAT THE MARKED DID IN THE SECOND WORLD WAR.
AND WERE YOU IMPRESSED?
SAVING THE PLANET AND THE ENTIRE HUMAN RACE? UM... YEAH...
...BUT I DON'T UNDERSTAND WHY THE AMERICANS WERE ALLOWED TO TAKE THE ARTIFACTS.
WHEN THE WAR WAS OVER, THE ALLIANCE BETWEEN MARKED, SHANGEN AND MAGES ALSO ENDED.
IT SEEMED SAFER TO LEAVE THE ARTIFACTS WITH PEOPLE WHO HAD NO IDEA HOW TO USE THEM.
WHAT KIND OF DARK FORCES DO WE BATTLE NOW?
RIGHT NOW, WE DON'T.
BUT THERE'S EVIL *EVERYWHERE.*
WAR, SLAVERY, DRUG ADDICTION, ABUSE...
THAT'S JUST EVERYDAY HUMAN MISCHIEF.
THAT'S NOT OUR BUSINESS.

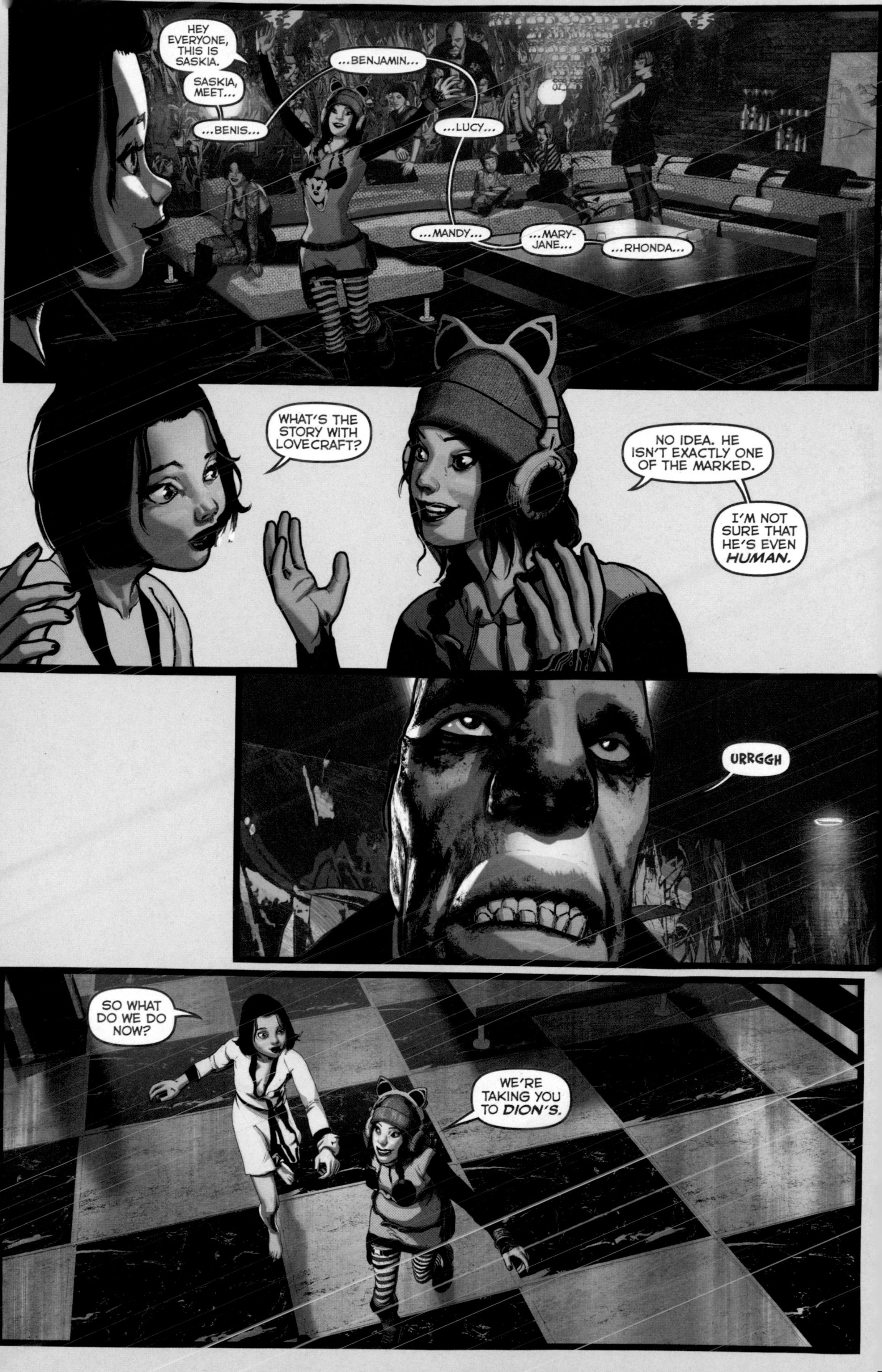
HEY EVERYONE, THIS IS SASKIA.
SASKIA, MEET...
...BENIS...
...BENJAMIN...
...LUCY...
...MANDY...
...MARY-JANE...
...RHONDA...
WHAT'S THE STORY WITH LOVECRAFT?
NO IDEA. HE ISN'T EXACTLY ONE OF THE MARKED.
I'M NOT SURE THAT HE'S EVEN HUMAN.
URRGGH
SO WHAT DO WE DO NOW?
WE'RE TAKING YOU TO DION'S.

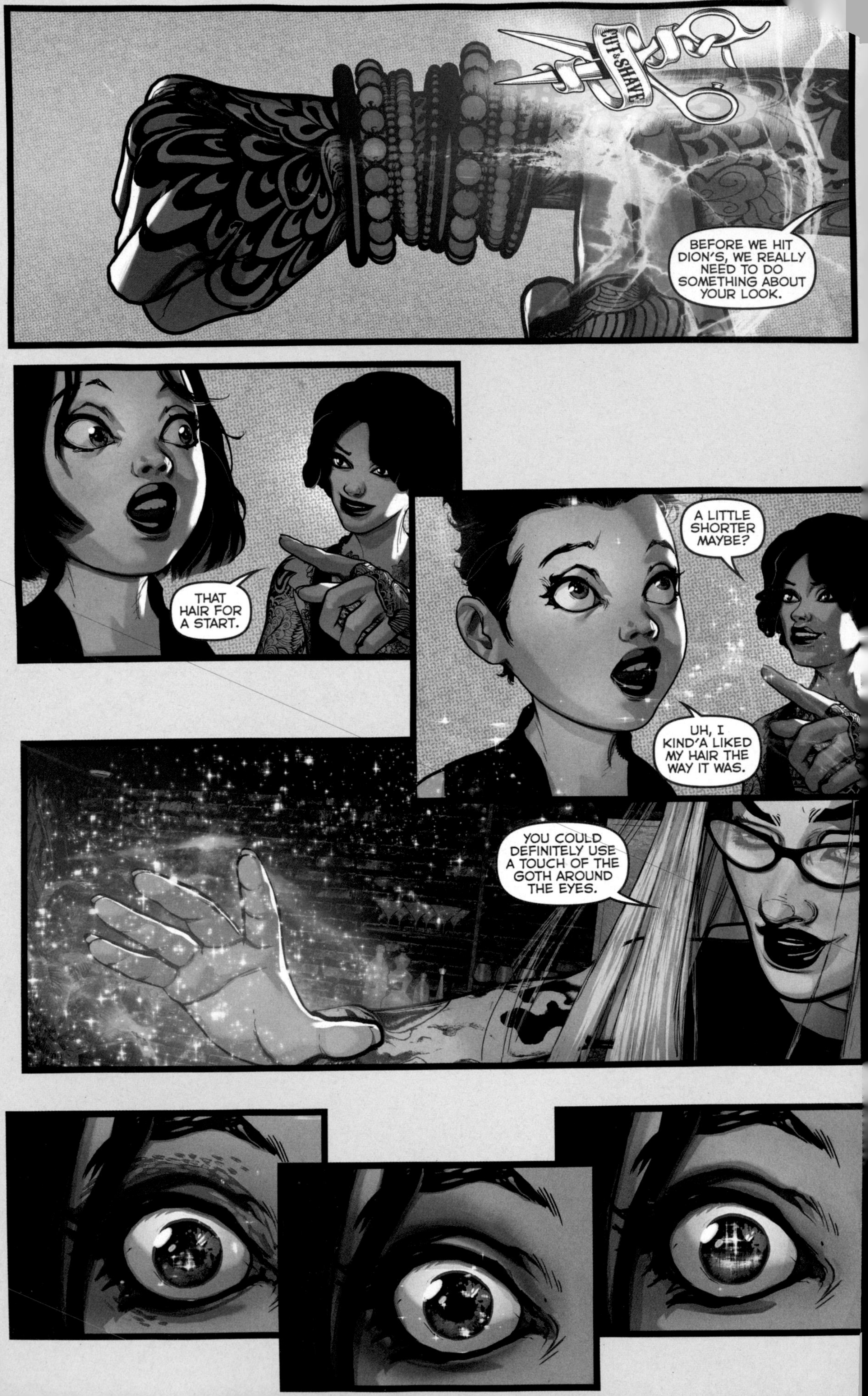
CUT & SHAVE
BEFORE WE HIT DION'S, WE REALLY NEED TO DO SOMETHING ABOUT YOUR LOOK.
THAT HAIR FOR A START.
A LITTLE SHORTER MAYBE?
UH, I KIND'A LIKED MY HAIR THE WAY IT WAS.
YOU COULD DEFINITELY USE A TOUCH OF THE GOTH AROUND THE EYES.

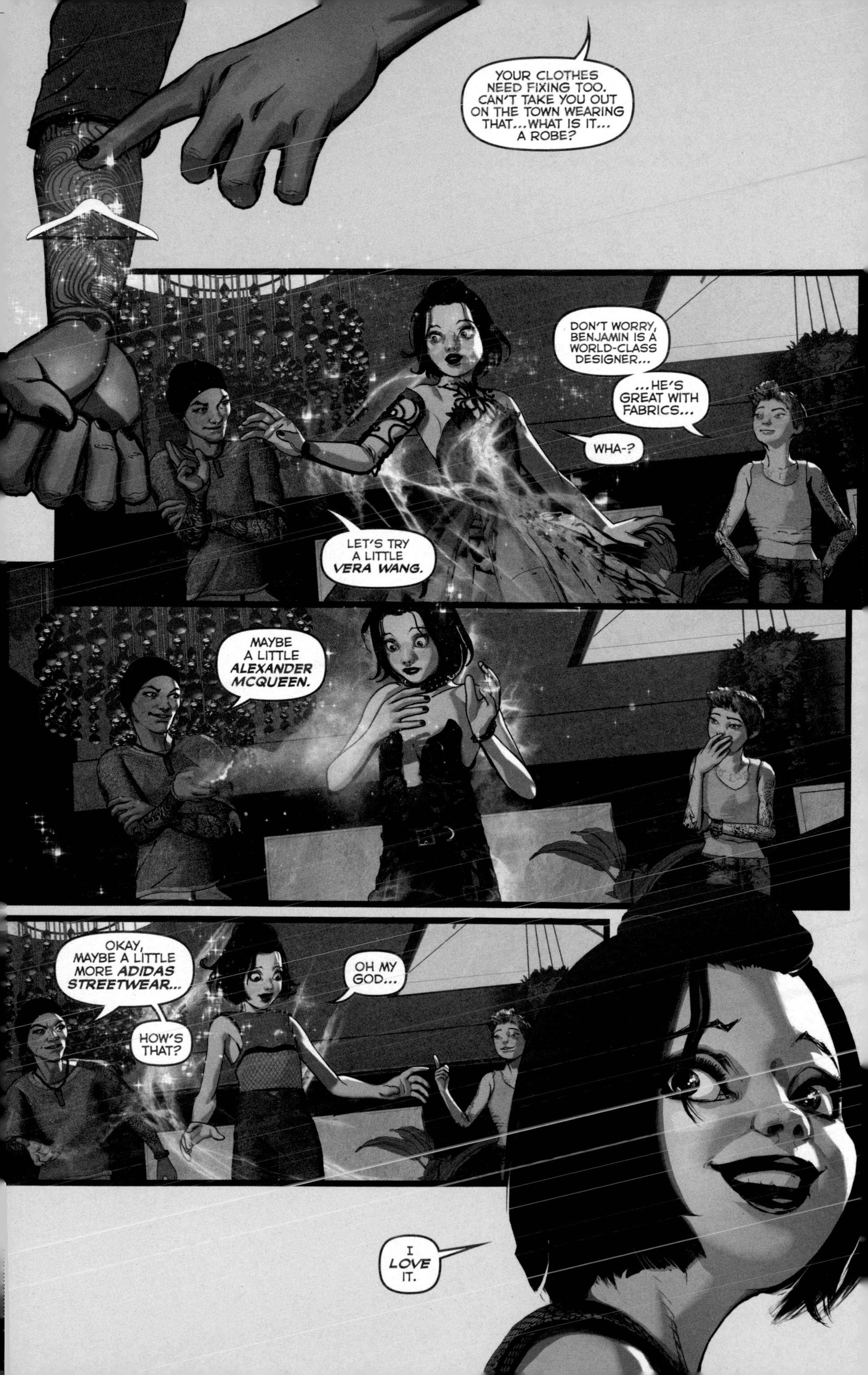
YOUR CLOTHES NEED FIXING TOO. CAN'T TAKE YOU OUT ON THE TOWN WEARING THAT...WHAT IS IT... A ROBE?
DON'T WORRY, BENJAMIN IS A WORLD-CLASS DESIGNER...
...HE'S GREAT WITH FABRICS...
WHA-?
LET'S TRY A LITTLE *VERA WANG.*
MAYBE A LITTLE *ALEXANDER MCQUEEN.*
OKAY, MAYBE A LITTLE MORE *ADIDAS STREETWEAR...*
HOW'S THAT?
OH MY GOD...
I *LOVE* IT.

THAT WAS PROBABLY THE BEST DAY OF MY LIFE.

RED LIGHT AHEAD!

LET ME GET THAT.

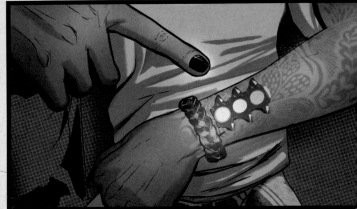

DION

IS SHE *UP?* YOU KNOW THE RULES.

SHE HAS TO BE OVER TWENTY-ONE AND UP OR SHE DON'T GET IN.

SHE'S COOL. SHOW HIM YOUR MARK, SASKIA.

LIZA! HEY, LIZA!

OKAY, WELCOME TO DION'S.

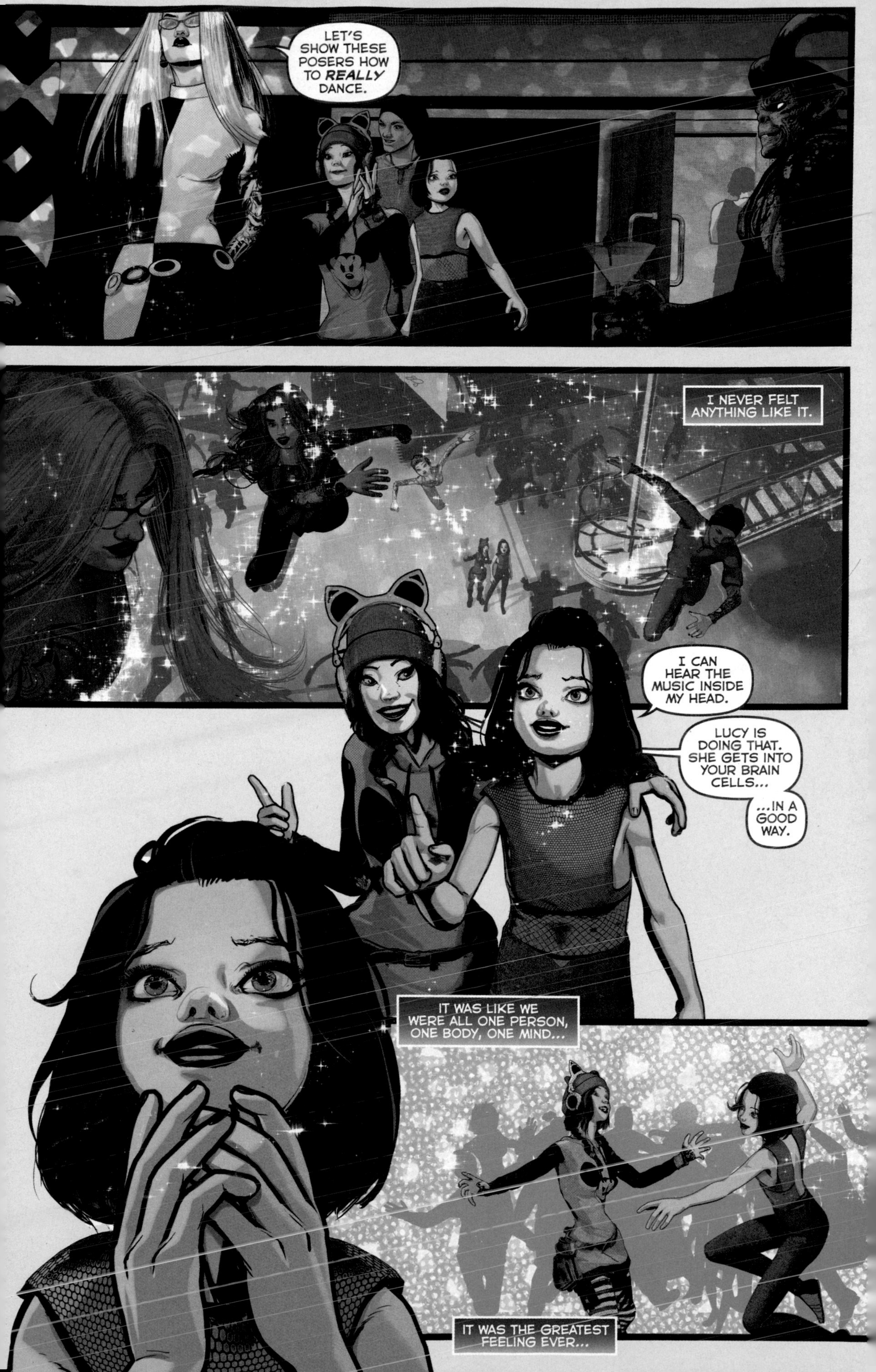

LET'S SHOW THESE POSERS HOW TO *REALLY* DANCE.
I NEVER FELT ANYTHING LIKE IT.
I CAN HEAR THE MUSIC INSIDE MY HEAD.
LUCY IS DOING THAT. SHE GETS INTO YOUR BRAIN CELLS...
...IN A GOOD WAY.
IT WAS LIKE WE WERE ALL ONE PERSON, ONE BODY, ONE MIND...
IT WAS THE GREATEST FEELING EVER...

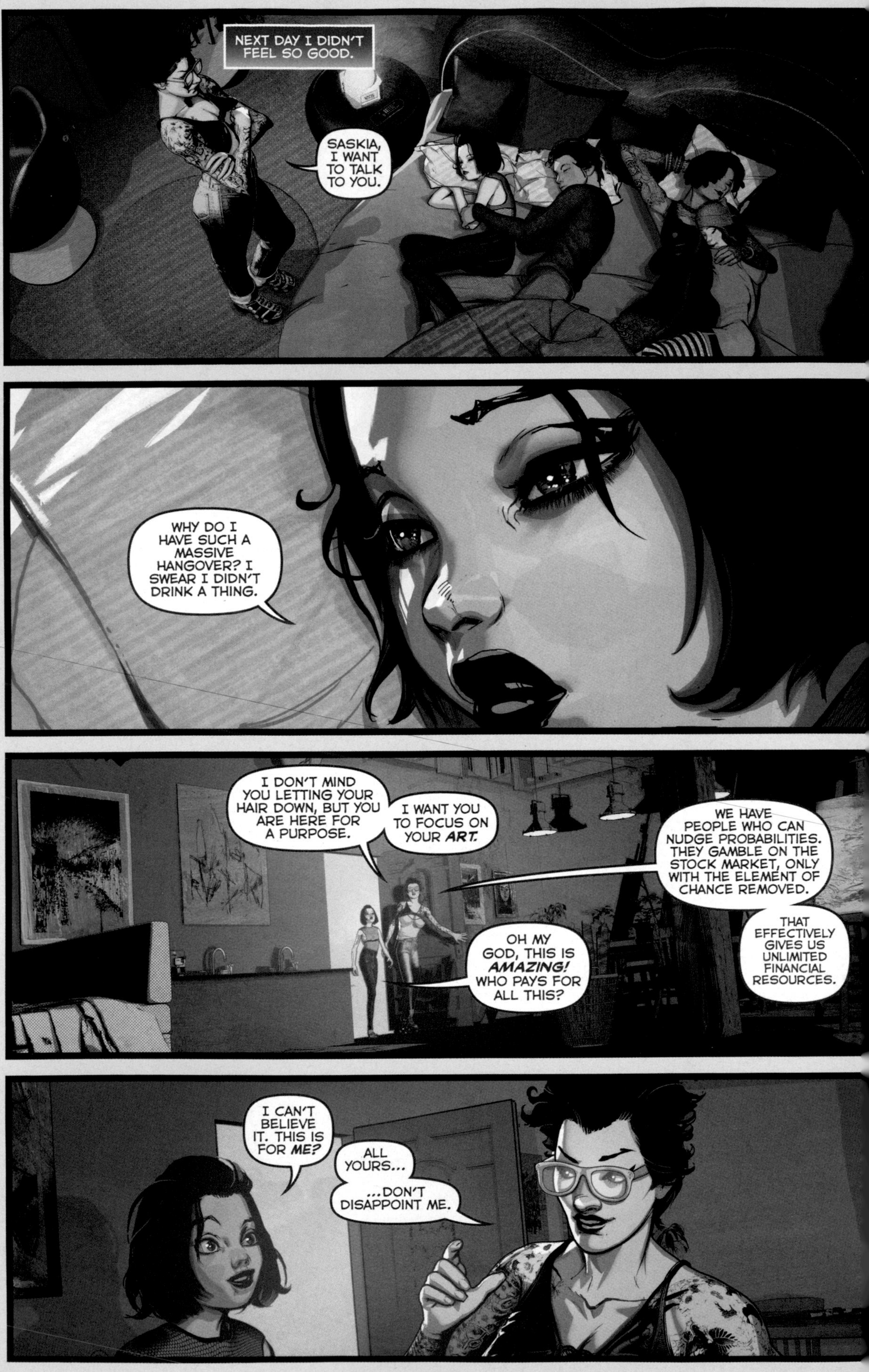
NEXT DAY I DIDN'T FEEL SO GOOD.
SASKIA, I WANT TO TALK TO YOU.
WHY DO I HAVE SUCH A MASSIVE HANGOVER? I SWEAR I DIDN'T DRINK A THING.
I DON'T MIND YOU LETTING YOUR HAIR DOWN, BUT YOU ARE HERE FOR A PURPOSE.
I WANT YOU TO FOCUS ON YOUR *ART.*
OH MY GOD, THIS IS ***AMAZING!*** WHO PAYS FOR ALL THIS?
WE HAVE PEOPLE WHO CAN NUDGE PROBABILITIES. THEY GAMBLE ON THE STOCK MARKET, ONLY WITH THE ELEMENT OF CHANCE REMOVED.
THAT EFFECTIVELY GIVES US UNLIMITED FINANCIAL RESOURCES.
I CAN'T BELIEVE IT. THIS IS FOR *ME?*
ALL YOURS...
...DON'T DISAPPOINT ME.

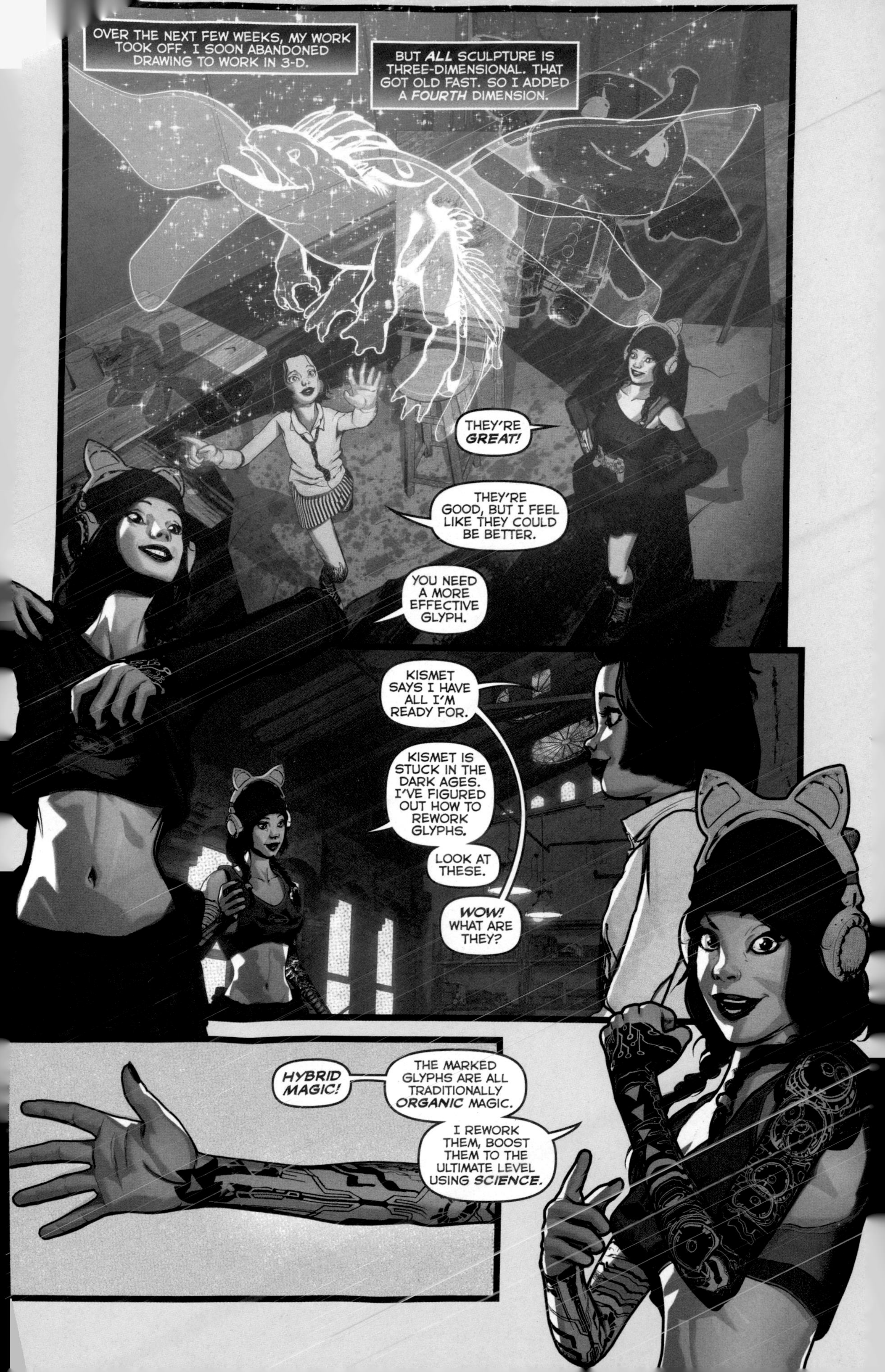

OVER THE NEXT FEW WEEKS, MY WORK TOOK OFF. I SOON ABANDONED DRAWING TO WORK IN 3-D.
BUT ALL SCULPTURE IS THREE-DIMENSIONAL. THAT GOT OLD FAST. SO I ADDED A FOURTH DIMENSION.
THEY'RE GREAT!
THEY'RE GOOD, BUT I FEEL LIKE THEY COULD BE BETTER.
YOU NEED A MORE EFFECTIVE GLYPH.
KISMET SAYS I HAVE ALL I'M READY FOR.
KISMET IS STUCK IN THE DARK AGES. I'VE FIGURED OUT HOW TO REWORK GLYPHS.
LOOK AT THESE.
WOW! WHAT ARE THEY?
HYBRID MAGIC!
THE MARKED GLYPHS ARE ALL TRADITIONALLY ORGANIC MAGIC.
I REWORK THEM, BOOST THEM TO THE ULTIMATE LEVEL USING SCIENCE.

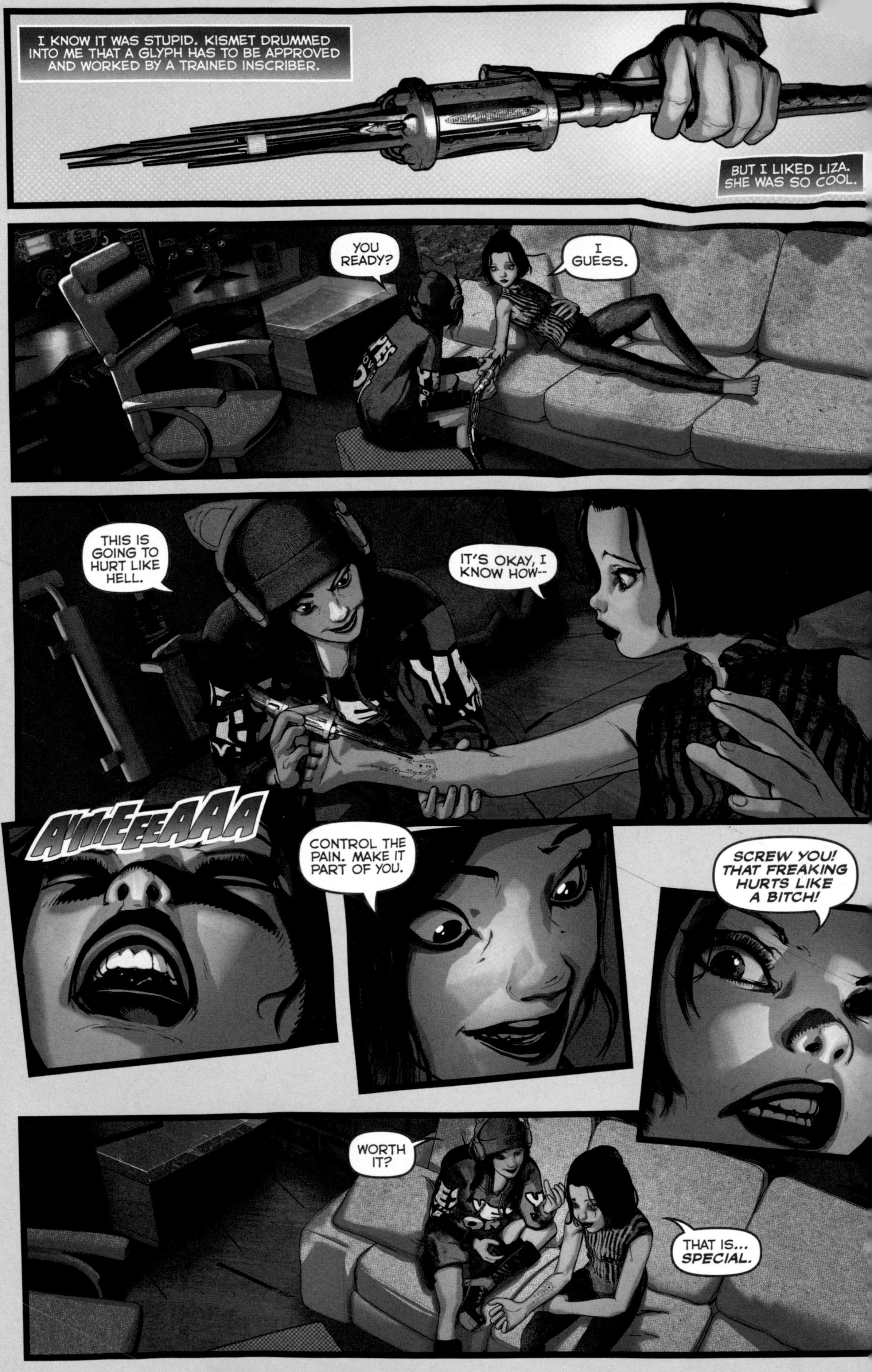
I KNOW IT WAS STUPID. KISMET DRUMMED INTO ME THAT A GLYPH HAS TO BE APPROVED AND WORKED BY A TRAINED INSCRIBER.
BUT I LIKED LIZA. SHE WAS SO COOL.
YOU READY?
I GUESS.
THIS IS GOING TO HURT LIKE HELL.
IT'S OKAY, I KNOW HOW--
AIIIEEEAAA
CONTROL THE PAIN. MAKE IT PART OF YOU.
SCREW YOU! THAT FREAKING HURTS LIKE A BITCH!
WORTH IT?
THAT IS... SPECIAL.

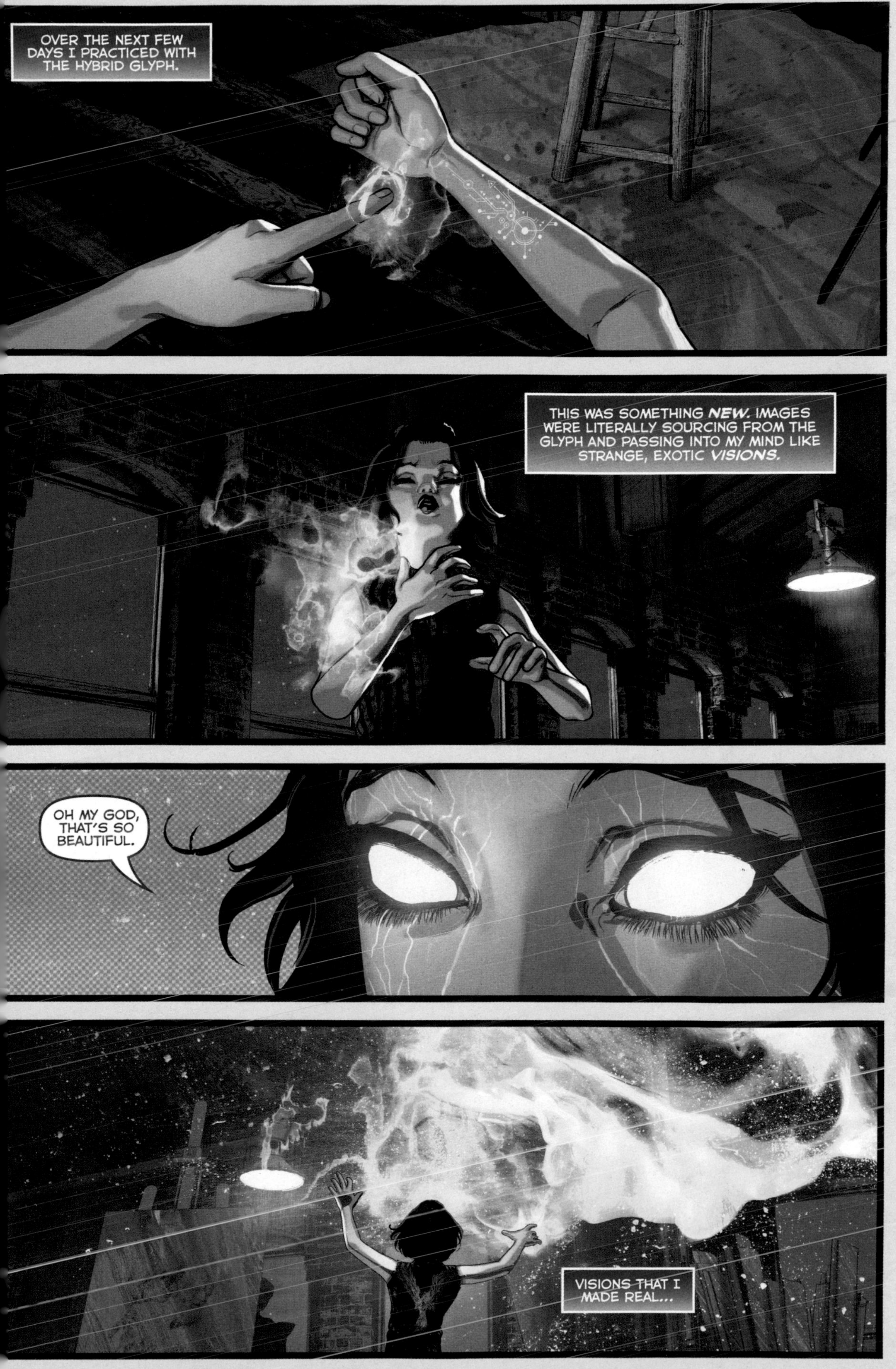
OVER THE NEXT FEW DAYS I PRACTICED WITH THE HYBRID GLYPH.
THIS WAS SOMETHING NEW. IMAGES WERE LITERALLY SOURCING FROM THE GLYPH AND PASSING INTO MY MIND LIKE STRANGE, EXOTIC VISIONS.
OH MY GOD, THAT'S SO BEAUTIFUL.
VISIONS THAT I MADE REAL...

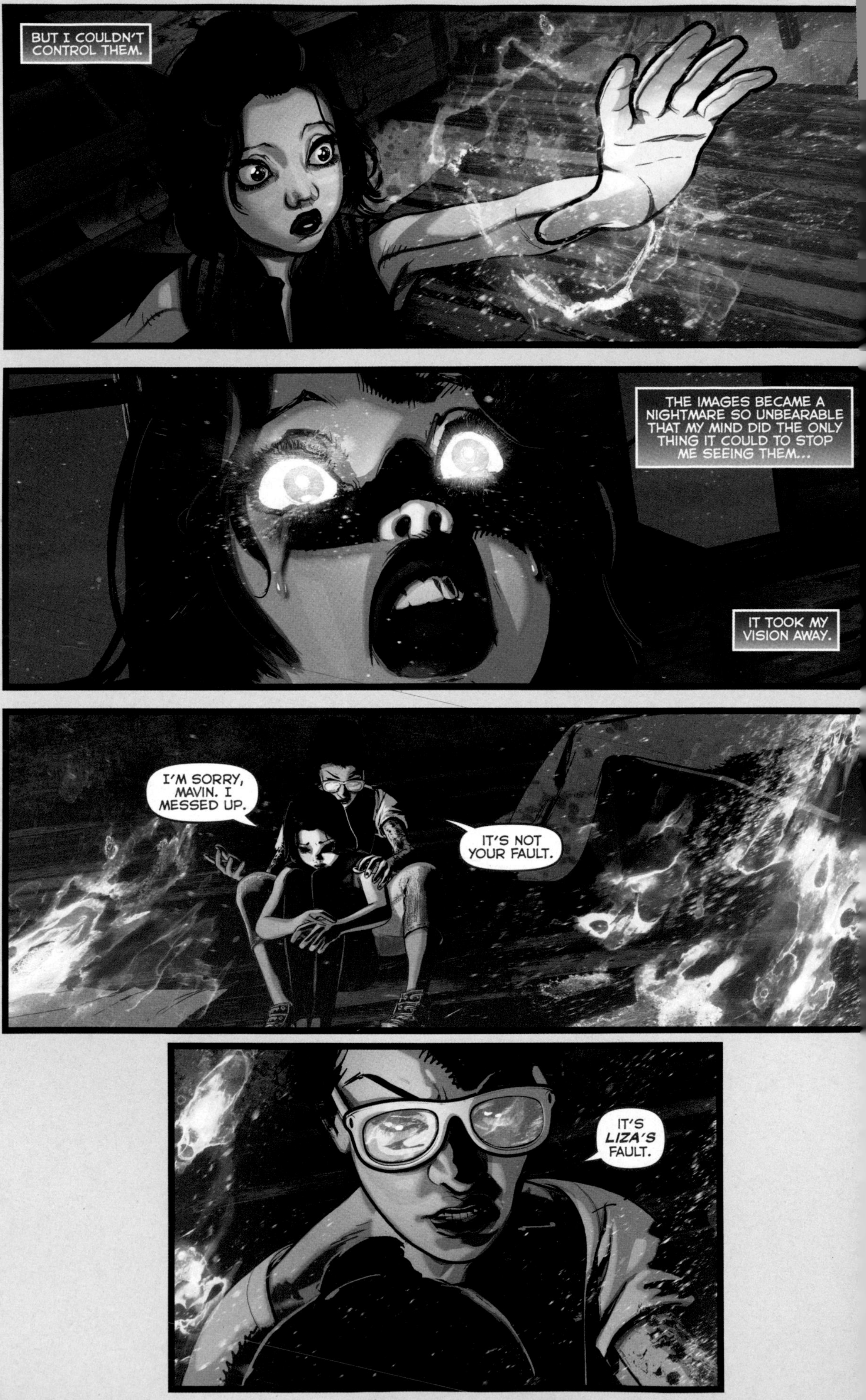
BUT I COULDN'T CONTROL THEM.
THE IMAGES BECAME A NIGHTMARE SO UNBEARABLE THAT MY MIND DID THE ONLY THING IT COULD TO STOP ME SEEING THEM...
IT TOOK MY VISION AWAY.
I'M SORRY, MAVIN. I MESSED UP.
IT'S NOT YOUR FAULT.
IT'S LIZA'S FAULT.

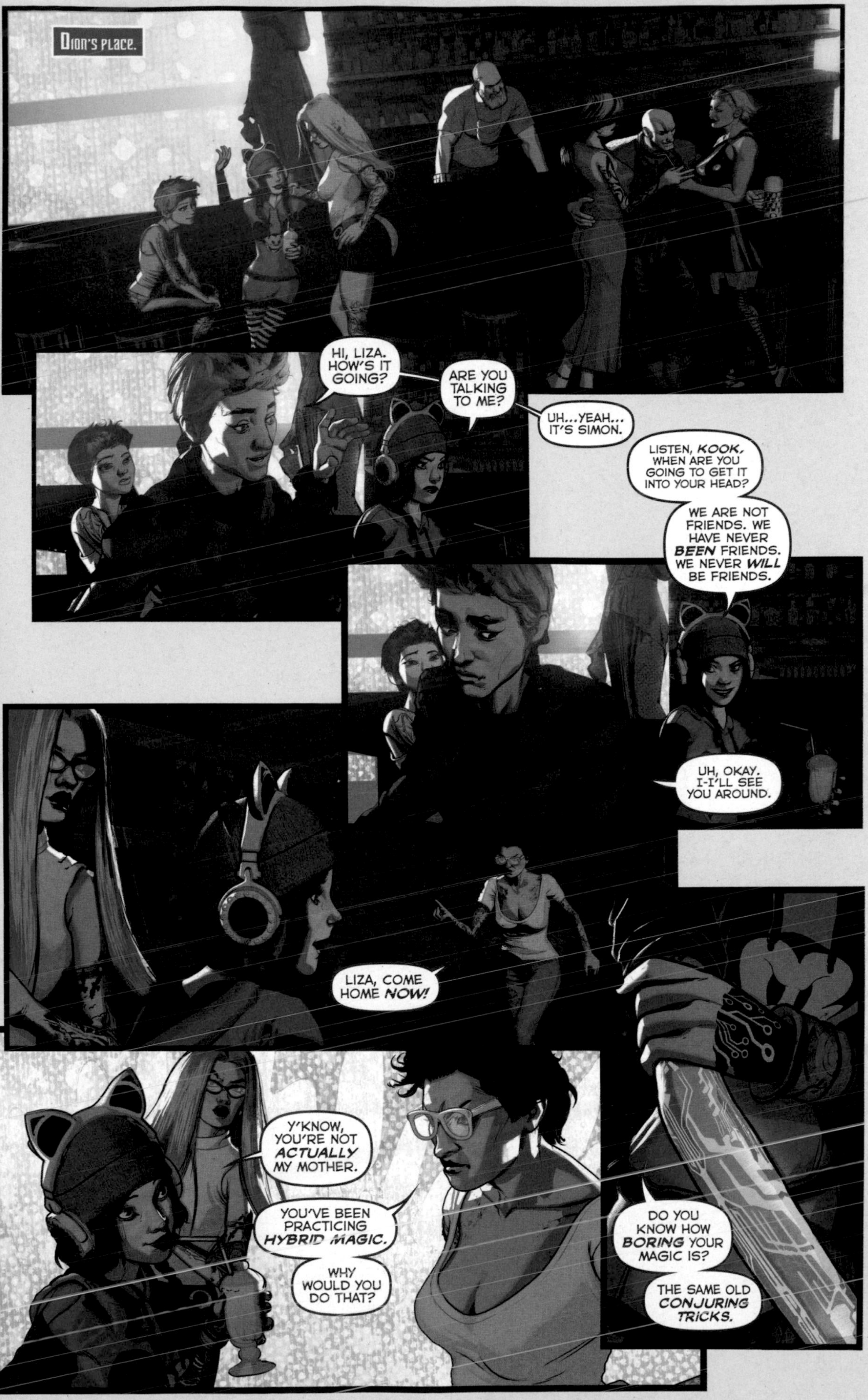
Dion's place.
HI, LIZA. HOW'S IT GOING?
ARE YOU TALKING TO ME?
UH...YEAH... IT'S SIMON.
LISTEN, KOOK, WHEN ARE YOU GOING TO GET IT INTO YOUR HEAD?
WE ARE NOT FRIENDS. WE HAVE NEVER BEEN FRIENDS. WE NEVER WILL BE FRIENDS.
UH, OKAY. I-I'LL SEE YOU AROUND.
LIZA, COME HOME NOW!
Y'KNOW, YOU'RE NOT ACTUALLY MY MOTHER.
YOU'VE BEEN PRACTICING HYBRID MAGIC.
WHY WOULD YOU DO THAT?
DO YOU KNOW HOW BORING YOUR MAGIC IS?
THE SAME OLD CONJURING TRICKS.

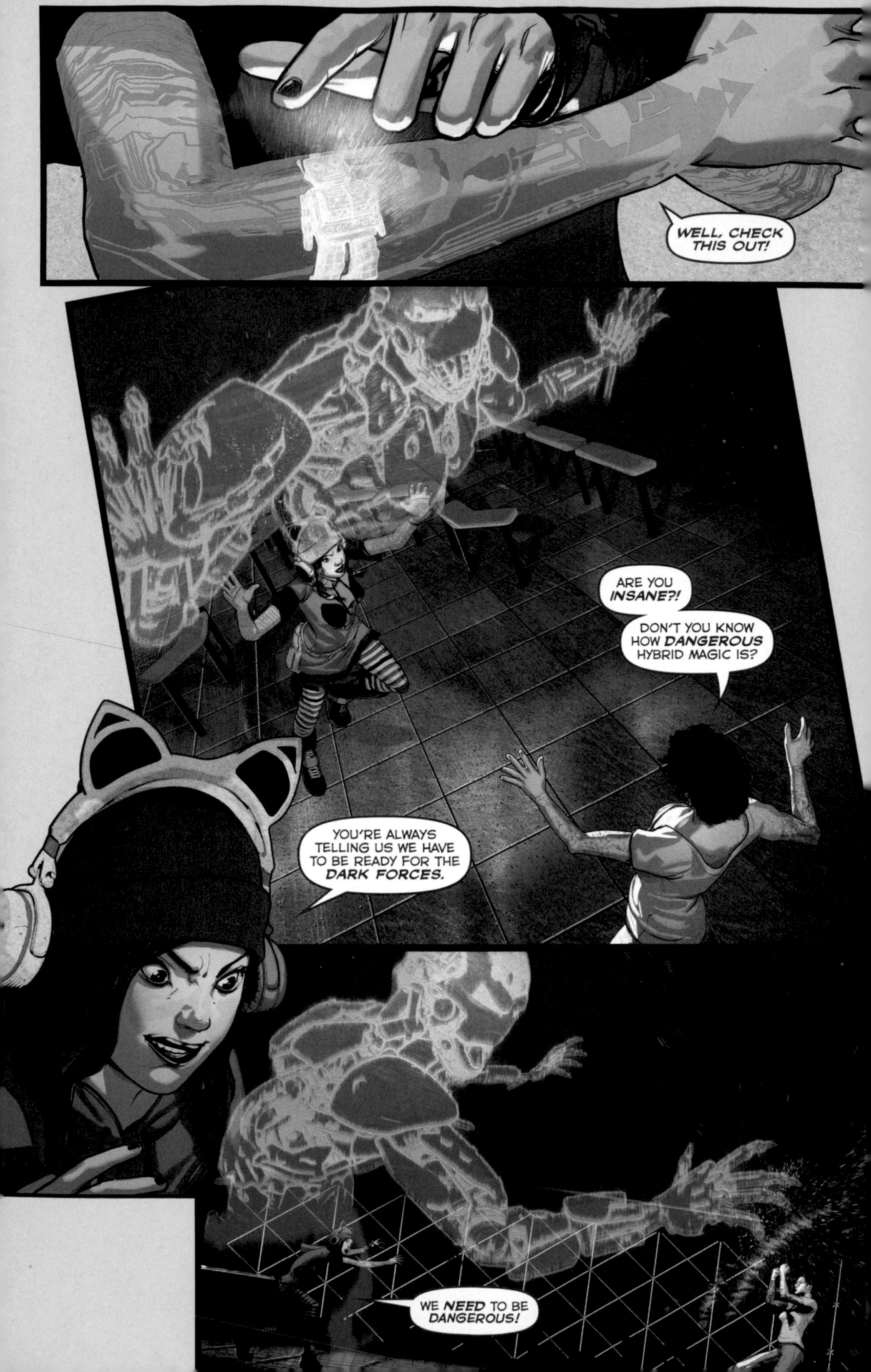
WELL, CHECK THIS OUT!
ARE YOU INSANE?!
DON'T YOU KNOW HOW DANGEROUS HYBRID MAGIC IS?
YOU'RE ALWAYS TELLING US WE HAVE TO BE READY FOR THE DARK FORCES.
WE NEED TO BE DANGEROUS!

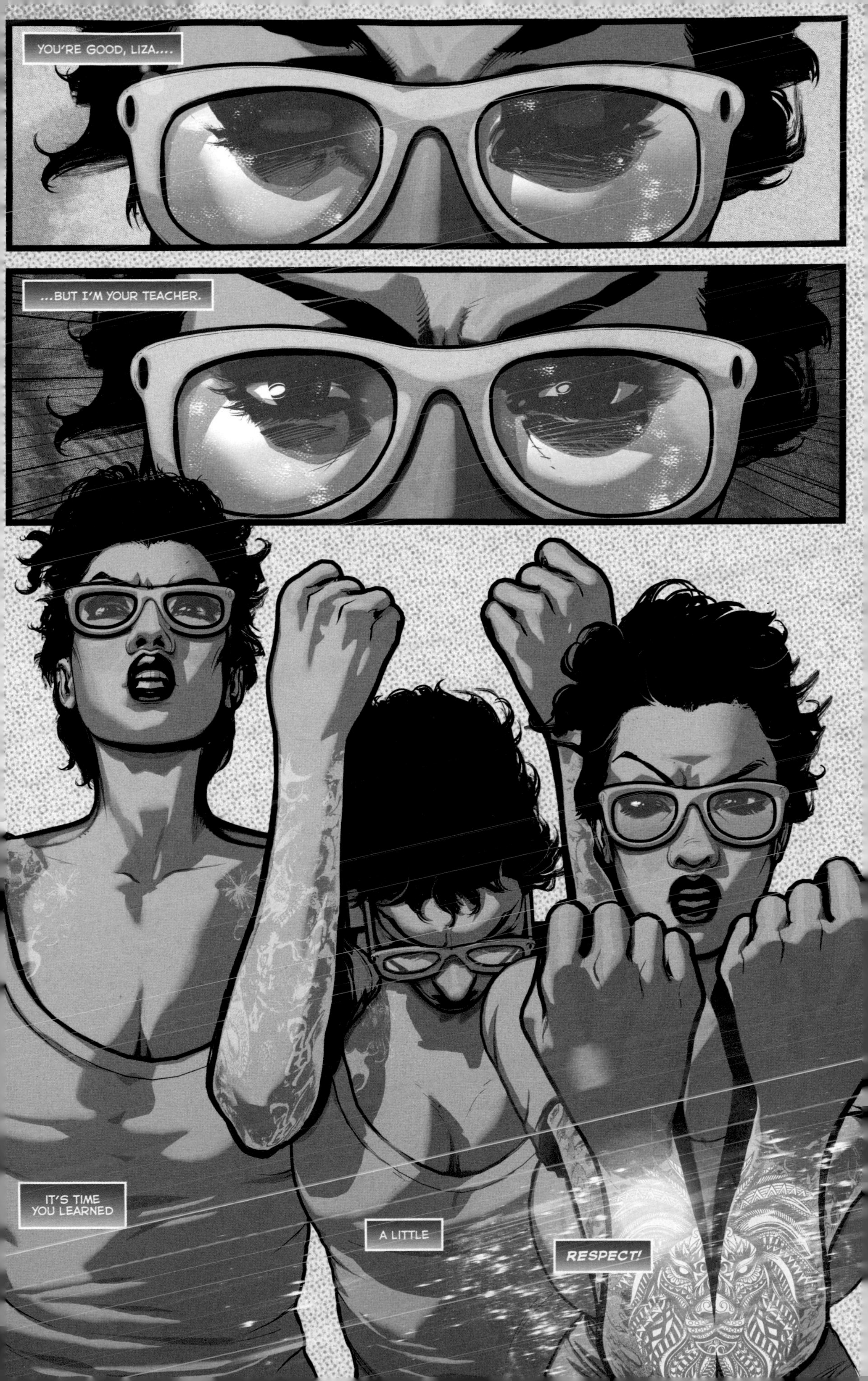
YOU'RE GOOD, LIZA....
...BUT I'M YOUR TEACHER.
IT'S TIME YOU LEARNED
A LITTLE
RESPECT!

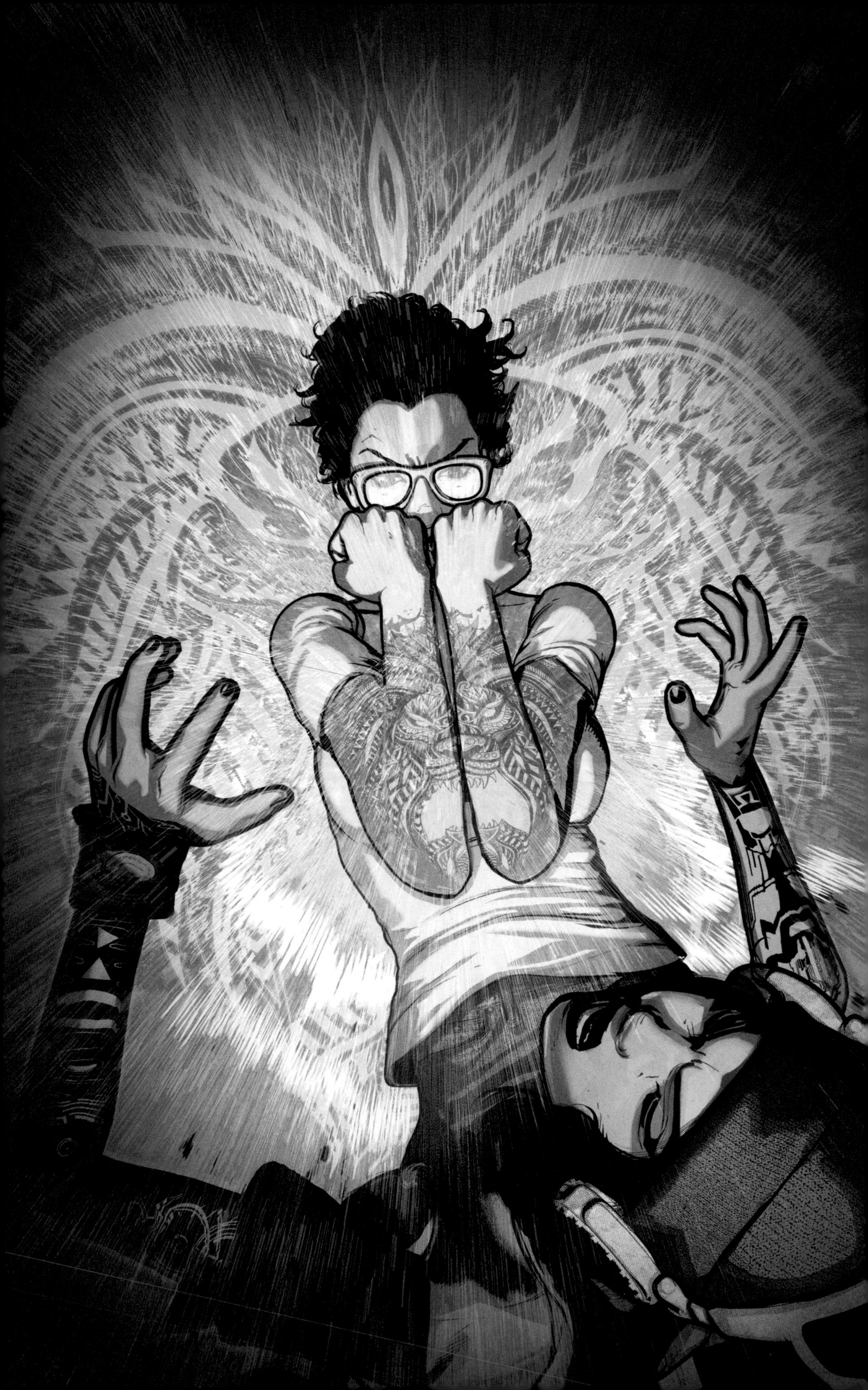

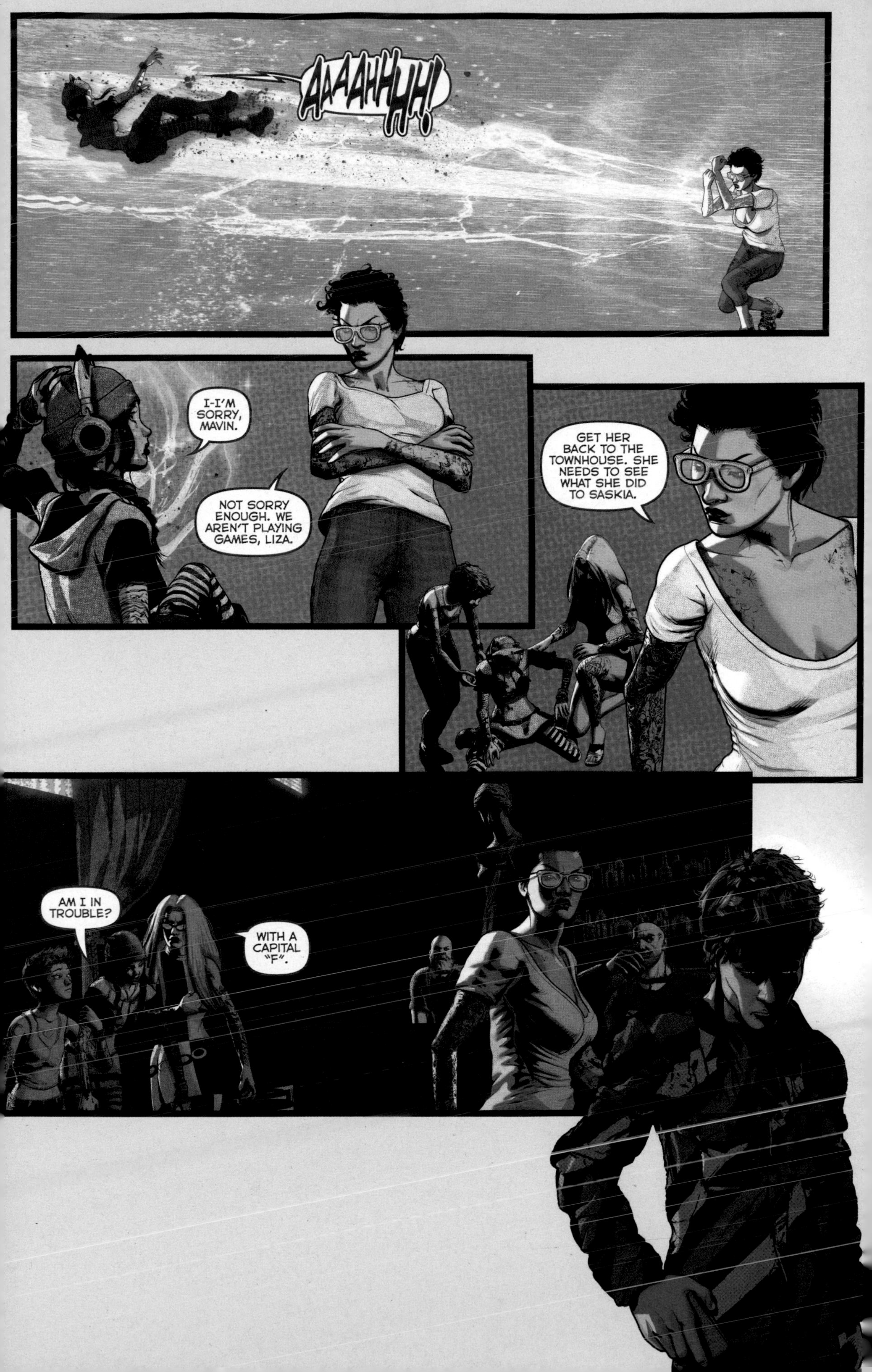
AAAAHHHH!
I-I'M SORRY, MAVIN.
NOT SORRY ENOUGH. WE AREN'T PLAYING GAMES, LIZA.
GET HER BACK TO THE TOWNHOUSE. SHE NEEDS TO SEE WHAT SHE DID TO SASKIA.
AM I IN TROUBLE?
WITH A CAPITAL "F".

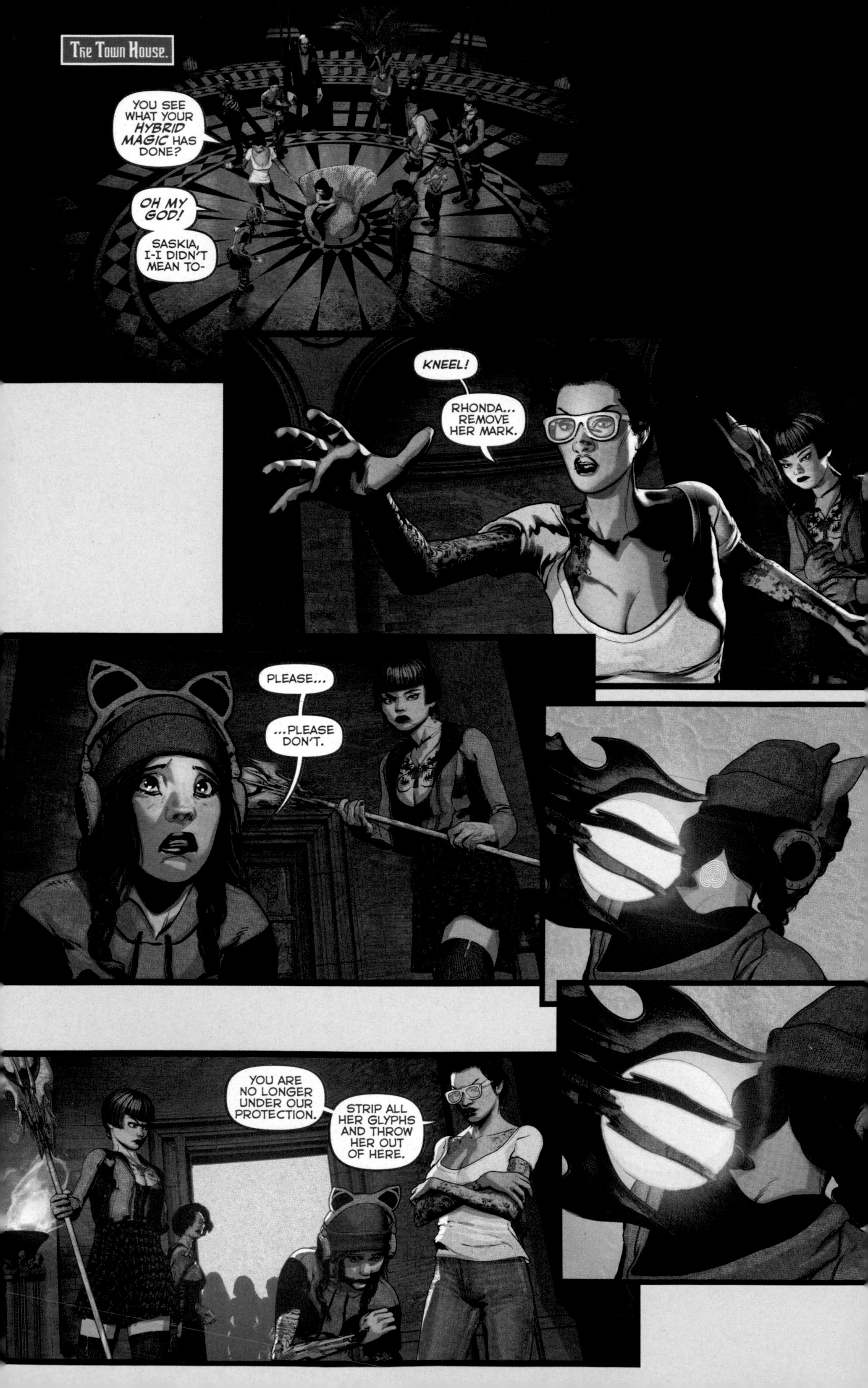
The Town House.
YOU SEE WHAT YOUR HYBRID MAGIC HAS DONE?
OH MY GOD!
SASKIA, I-I DIDN'T MEAN TO-
KNEEL!
RHONDA... REMOVE HER MARK.
PLEASE...
...PLEASE DON'T.
YOU ARE NO LONGER UNDER OUR PROTECTION.
STRIP ALL HER GLYPHS AND THROW HER OUT OF HERE.

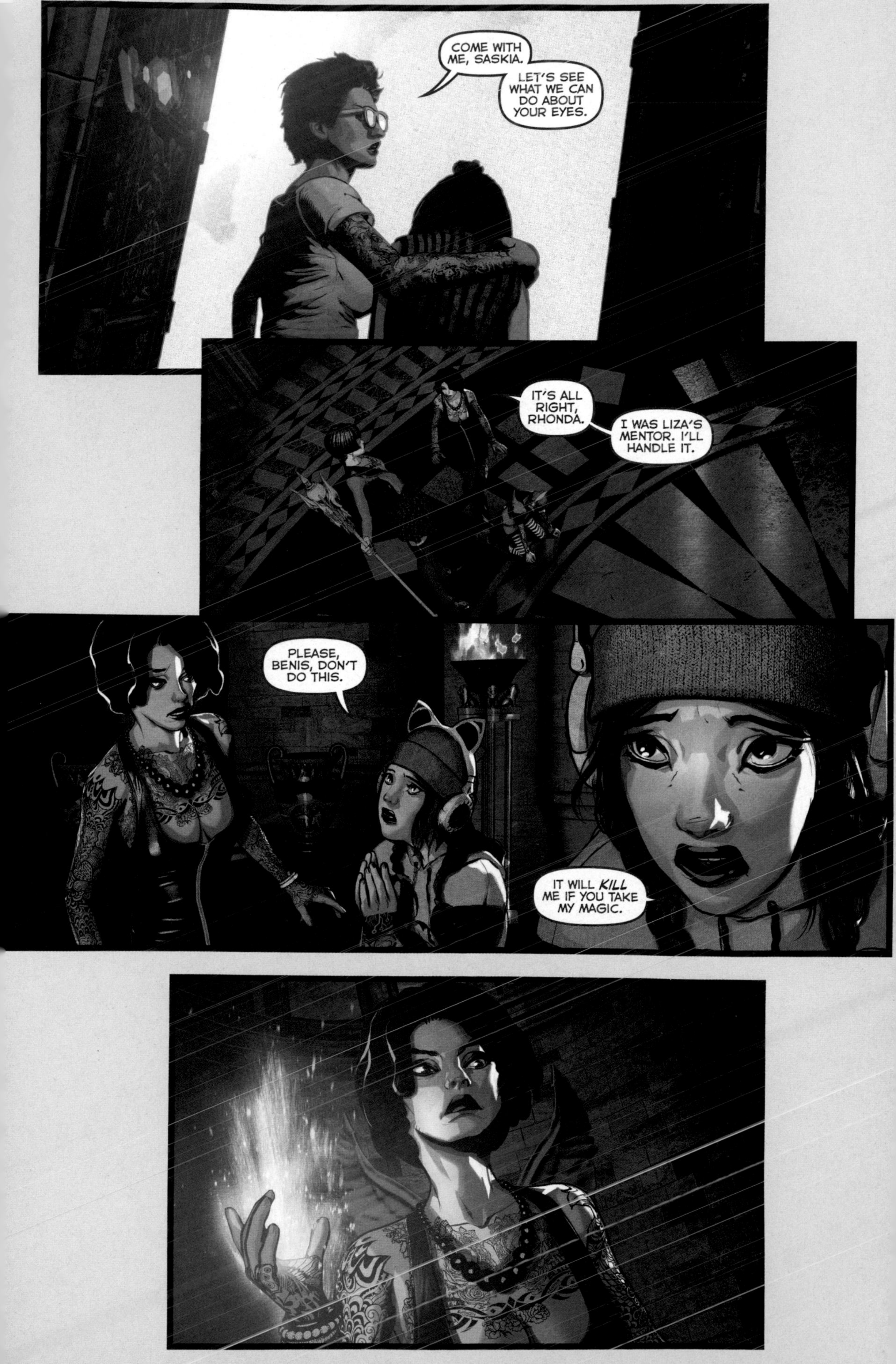
COME WITH ME, SASKIA.
LET'S SEE WHAT WE CAN DO ABOUT YOUR EYES.
IT'S ALL RIGHT, RHONDA.
I WAS LIZA'S MENTOR. I'LL HANDLE IT.
PLEASE, BENIS, DON'T DO THIS.
IT WILL *KILL* ME IF YOU TAKE MY MAGIC.

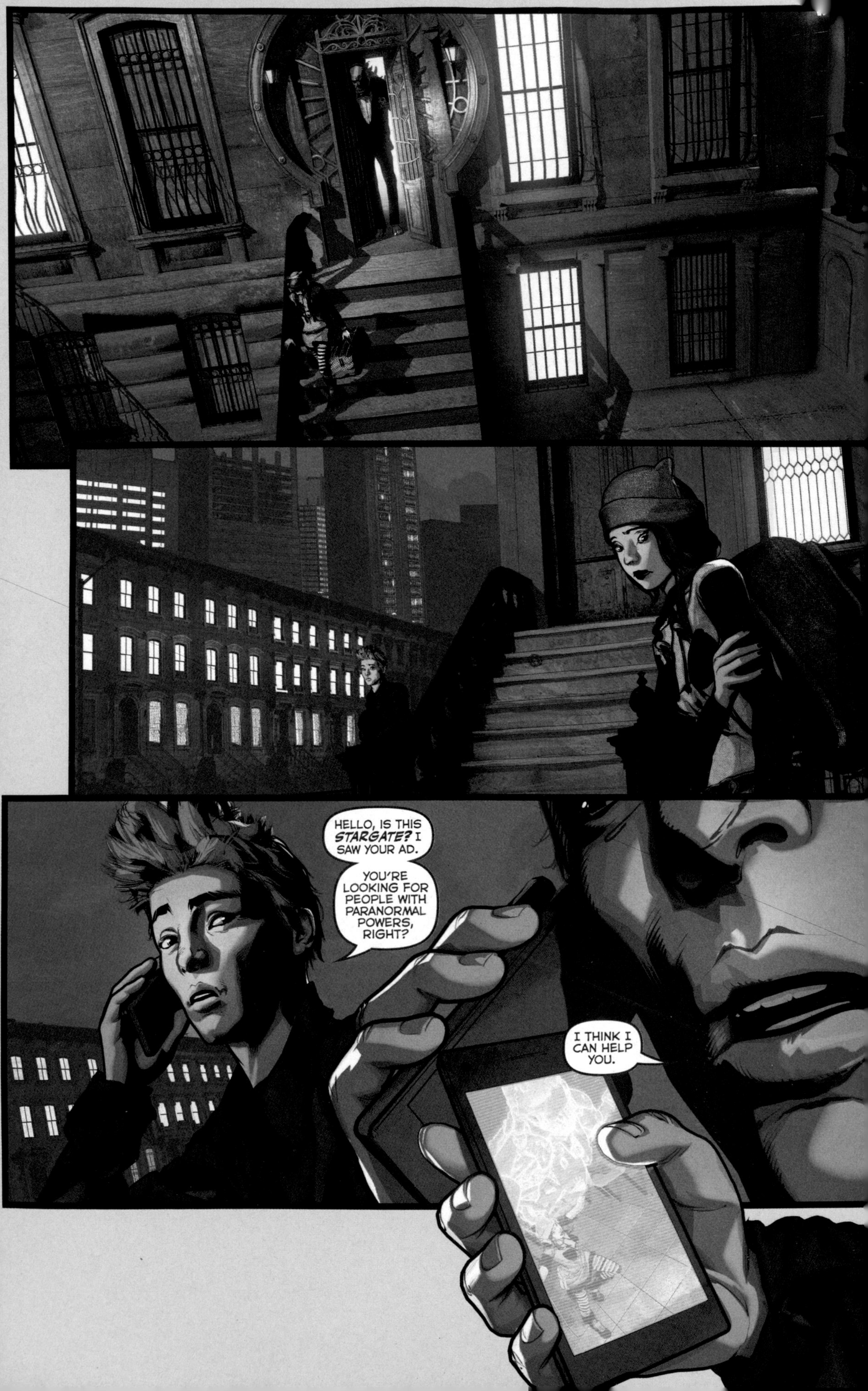
HELLO, IS THIS *STARGATE?* I SAW YOUR AD.
YOU'RE LOOKING FOR PEOPLE WITH PARANORMAL POWERS, RIGHT?
I THINK I CAN HELP YOU.

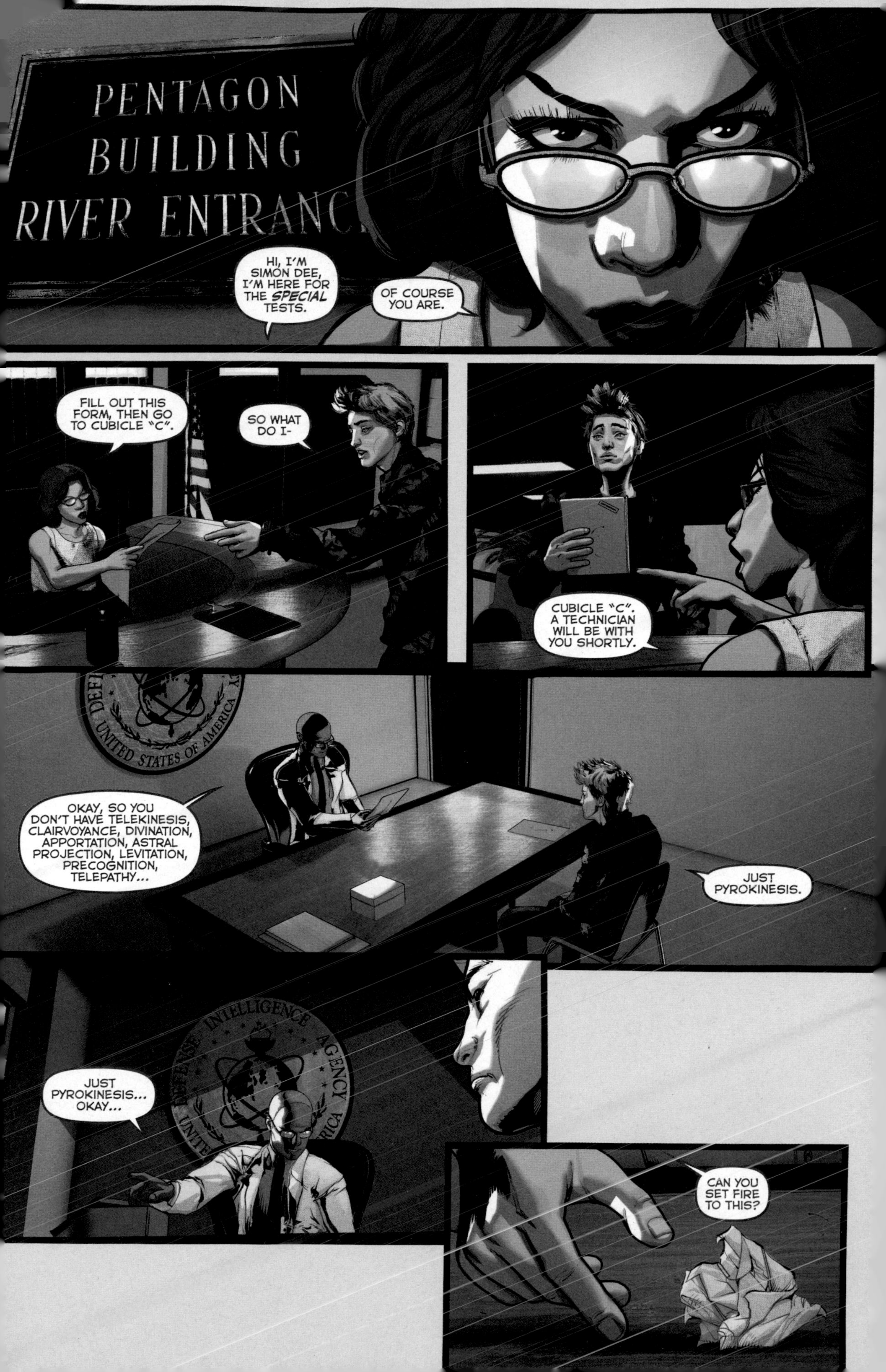
PENTAGON
BUILDING
RIVER ENTRANC
HI, I'M SIMON DEE, I'M HERE FOR THE *SPECIAL* TESTS.
OF COURSE YOU ARE.
FILL OUT THIS FORM, THEN GO TO CUBICLE "C".
SO WHAT DO I-
CUBICLE "C". A TECHNICIAN WILL BE WITH YOU SHORTLY.
UNITED STATES OF AMERICA
OKAY, SO YOU DON'T HAVE TELEKINESIS, CLAIRVOYANCE, DIVINATION, APPORTATION, ASTRAL PROJECTION, LEVITATION, PRECOGNITION, TELEPATHY...
JUST PYROKINESIS.
DEFENSE INTELLIGENCE AGENCY
JUST PYROKINESIS... OKAY...
CAN YOU SET FIRE TO THIS?

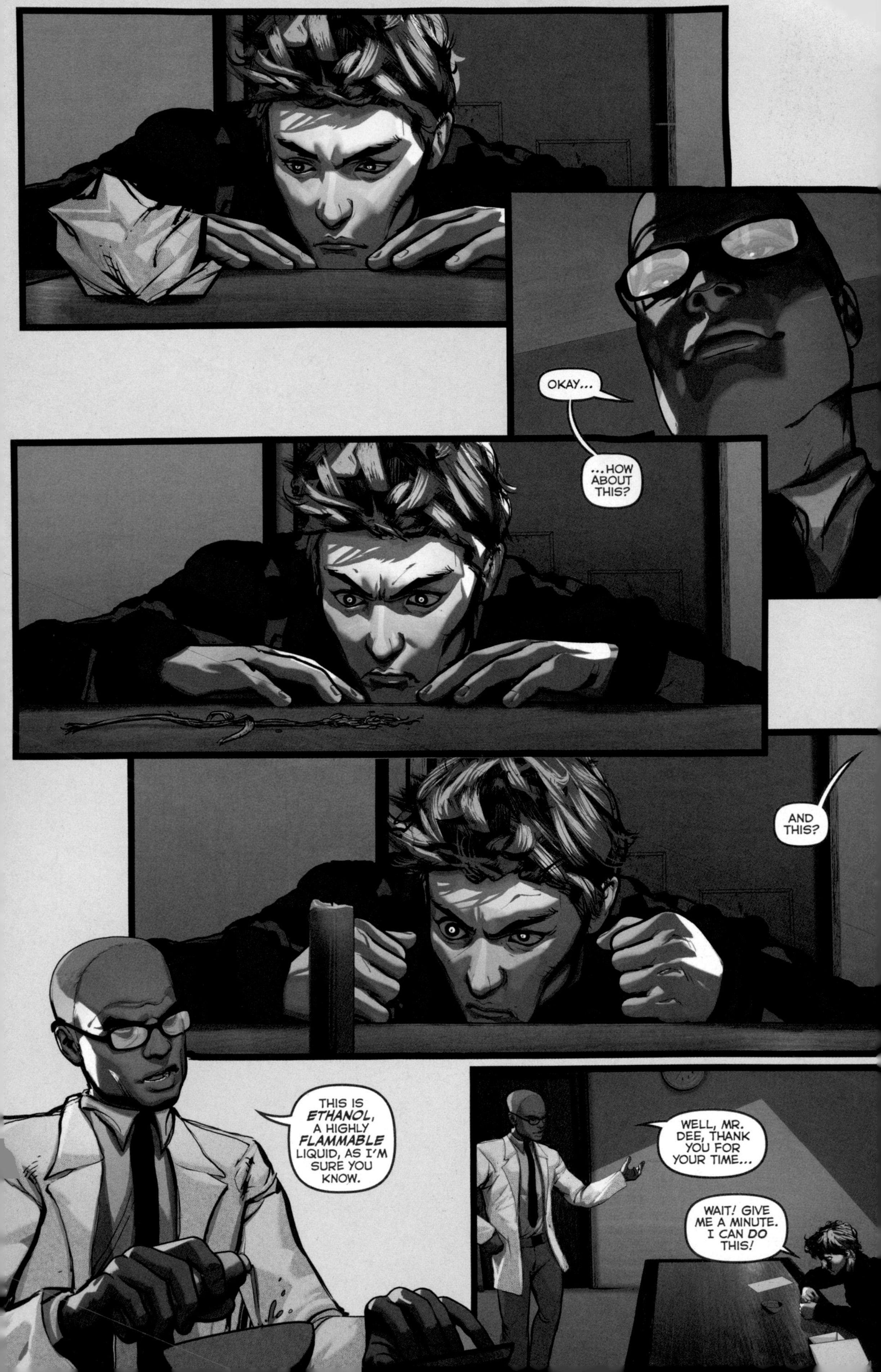
OKAY...
...HOW ABOUT THIS?
AND THIS?
THIS IS ETHANOL, A HIGHLY FLAMMABLE LIQUID, AS I'M SURE YOU KNOW.
WELL, MR. DEE, THANK YOU FOR YOUR TIME...
WAIT! GIVE ME A MINUTE. I CAN DO THIS!

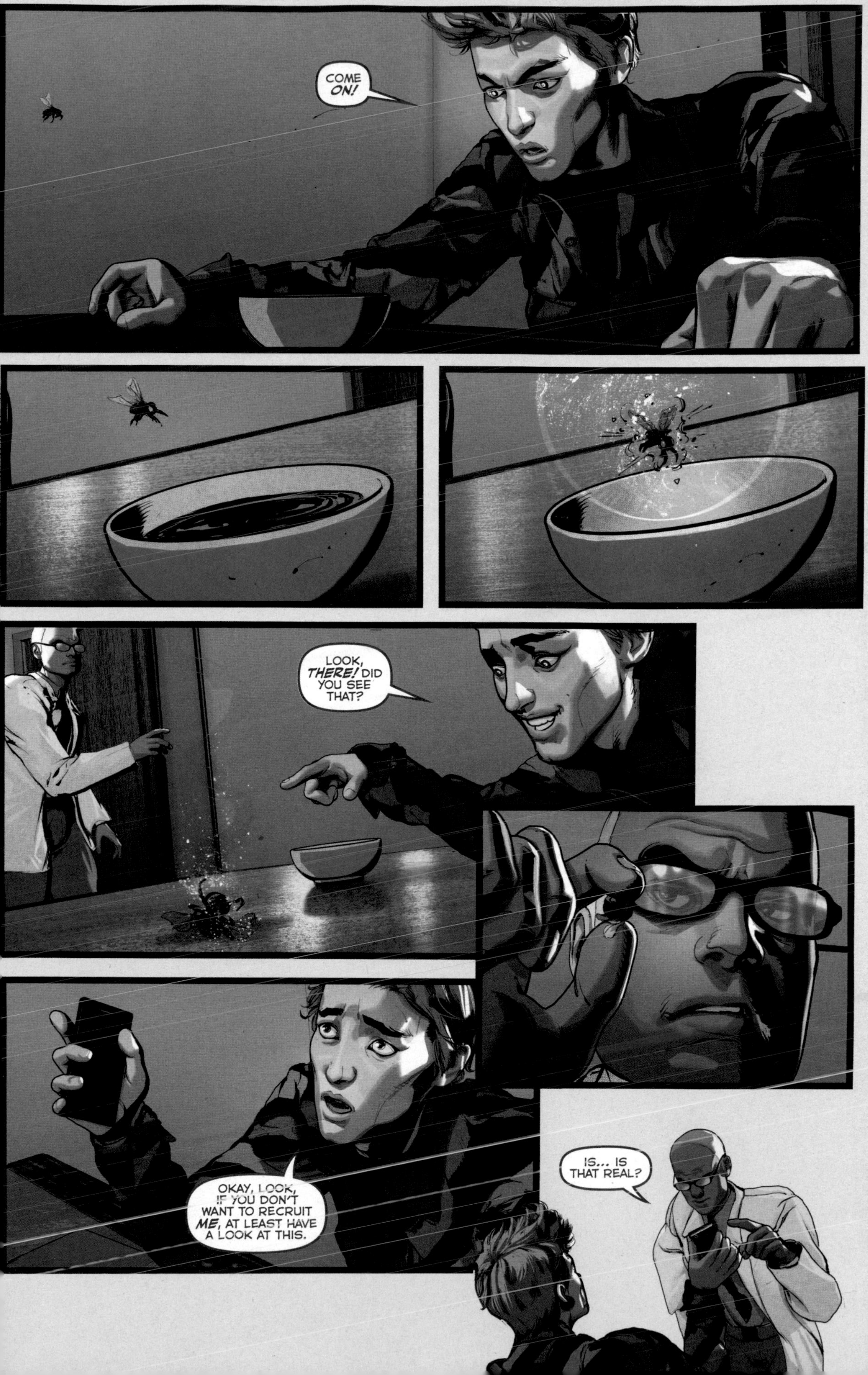
COME ON!
LOOK, THERE! DID YOU SEE THAT?
OKAY, LOOK, IF YOU DON'T WANT TO RECRUIT ME, AT LEAST HAVE A LOOK AT THIS.
IS... IS THAT REAL?

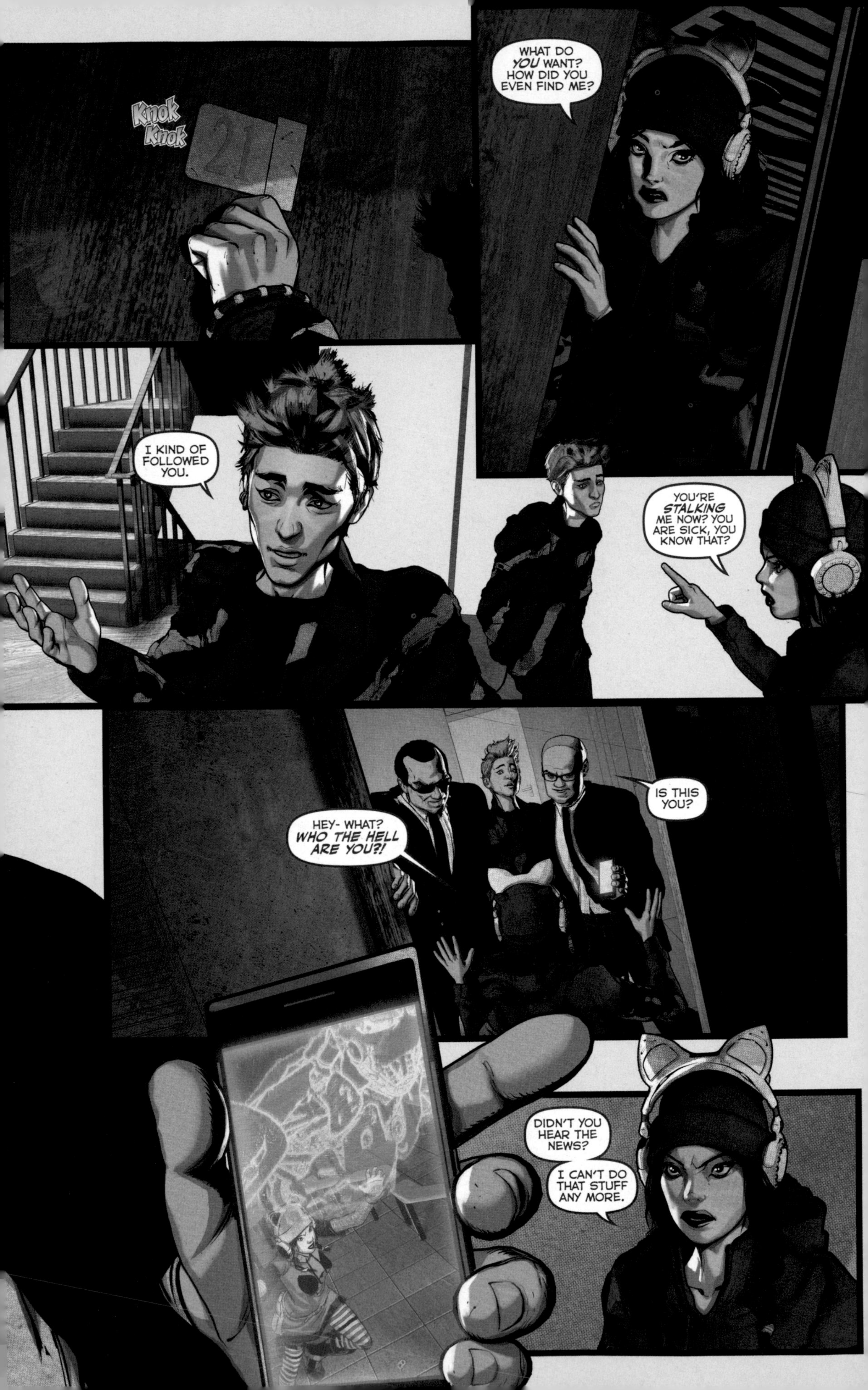
Knok Knok
21
WHAT DO YOU WANT? HOW DID YOU EVEN FIND ME?
I KIND OF FOLLOWED YOU.
YOU'RE STALKING ME NOW? YOU ARE SICK, YOU KNOW THAT?
IS THIS YOU?
HEY- WHAT? WHO THE HELL ARE YOU?!
DIDN'T YOU HEAR THE NEWS?
I CAN'T DO THAT STUFF ANY MORE.

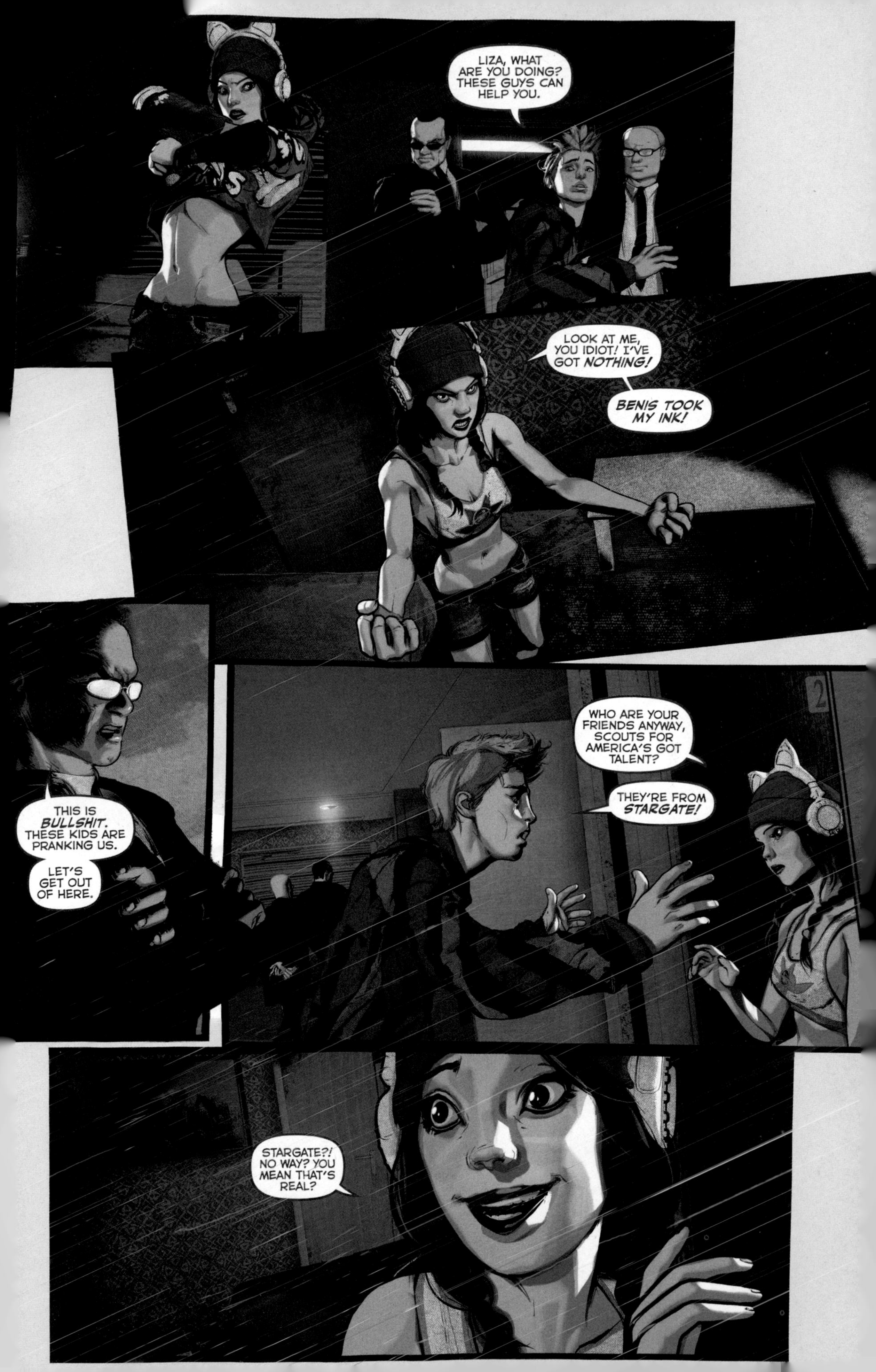
LIZA, WHAT ARE YOU DOING? THESE GUYS CAN HELP YOU.
LOOK AT ME, YOU IDIOT! I'VE GOT NOTHING!
BENIS TOOK MY INK!
THIS IS BULLSHIT. THESE KIDS ARE PRANKING US.
LET'S GET OUT OF HERE.
WHO ARE YOUR FRIENDS ANYWAY, SCOUTS FOR AMERICA'S GOT TALENT?
THEY'RE FROM STARGATE!
STARGATE?! NO WAY? YOU MEAN THAT'S REAL?

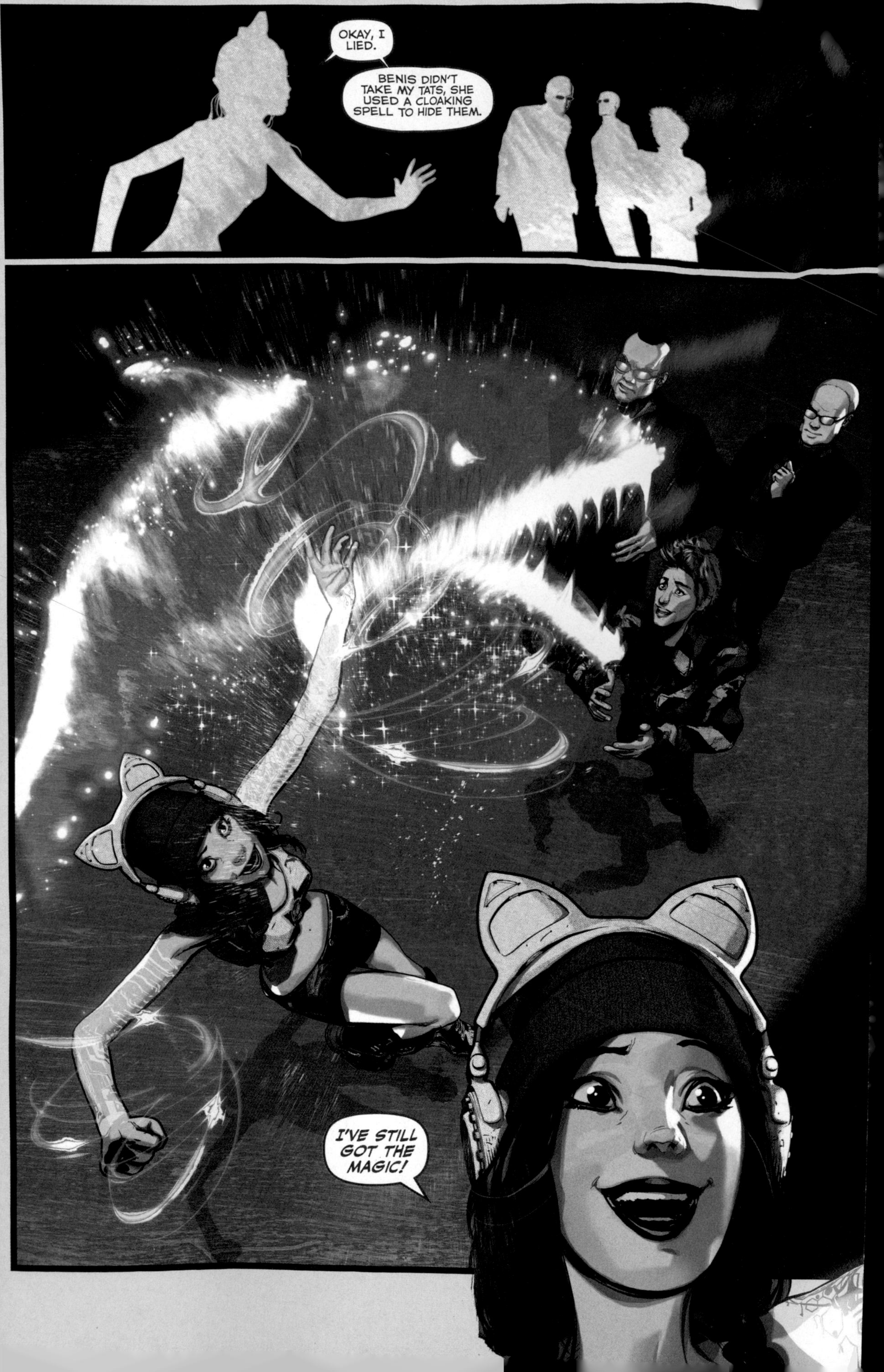
OKAY, I LIED.
BENIS DIDN'T TAKE MY TATS, SHE USED A CLOAKING SPELL TO HIDE THEM.
I'VE STILL GOT THE MAGIC!

CHAPTER TWO

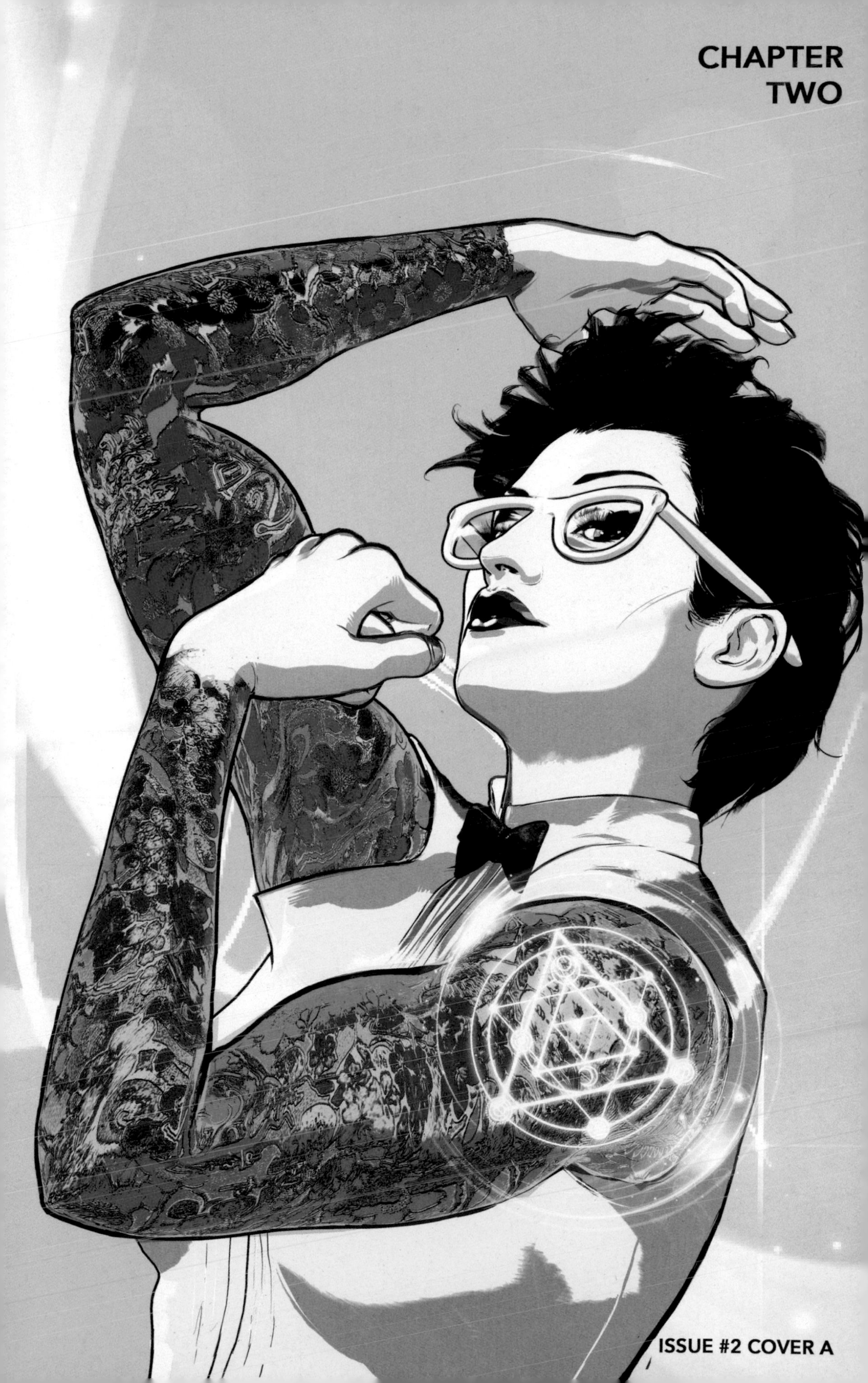

ISSUE #2 COVER A

PREVIOUSLY UNPUBLISHED ART

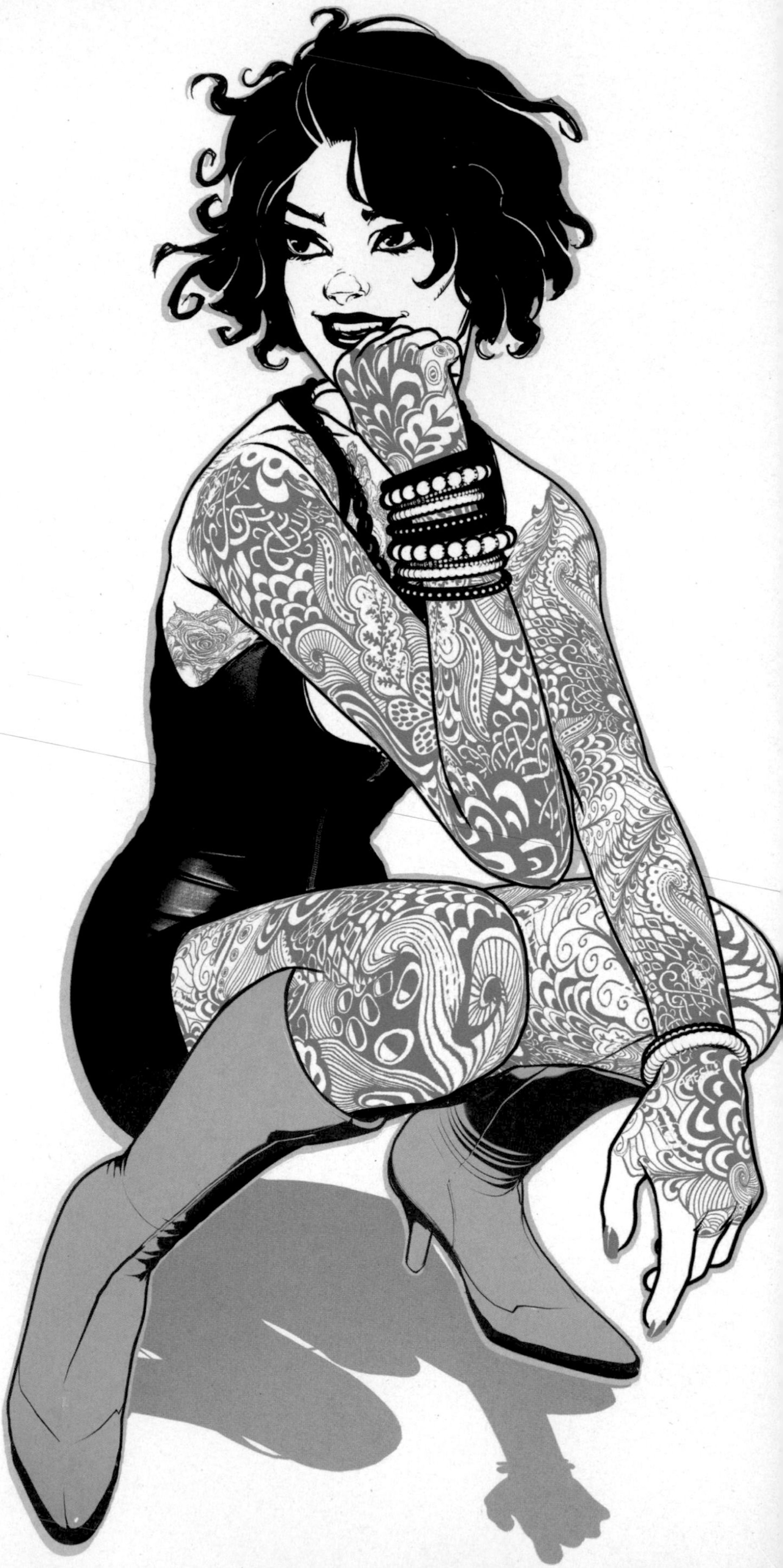

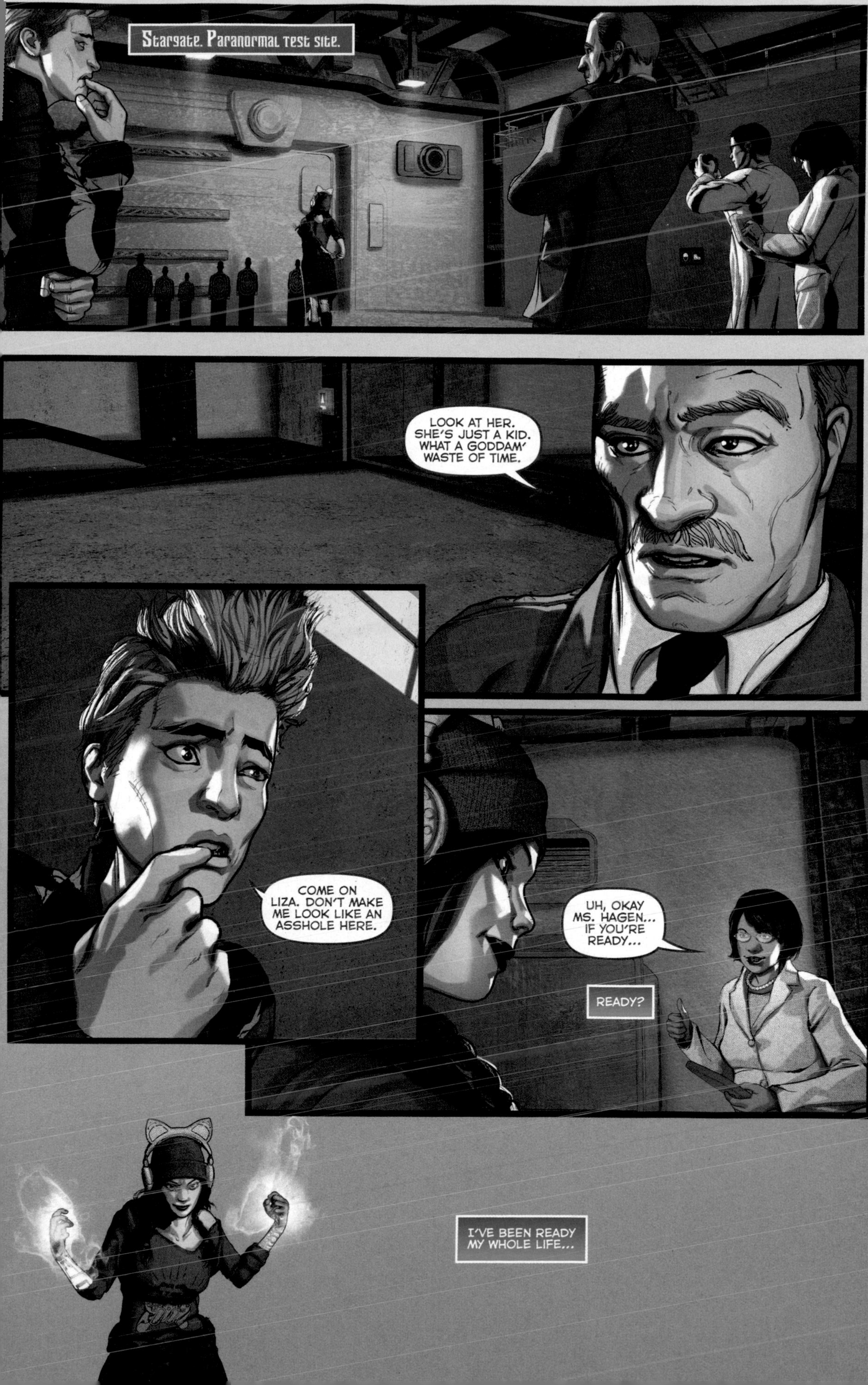
Stargate. Paranormal test site.
LOOK AT HER. SHE'S JUST A KID. WHAT A GODDAM' WASTE OF TIME.
COME ON LIZA. DON'T MAKE ME LOOK LIKE AN ASSHOLE HERE.
UH, OKAY MS. HAGEN... IF YOU'RE READY...
READY?
I'VE BEEN READY MY WHOLE LIFE...

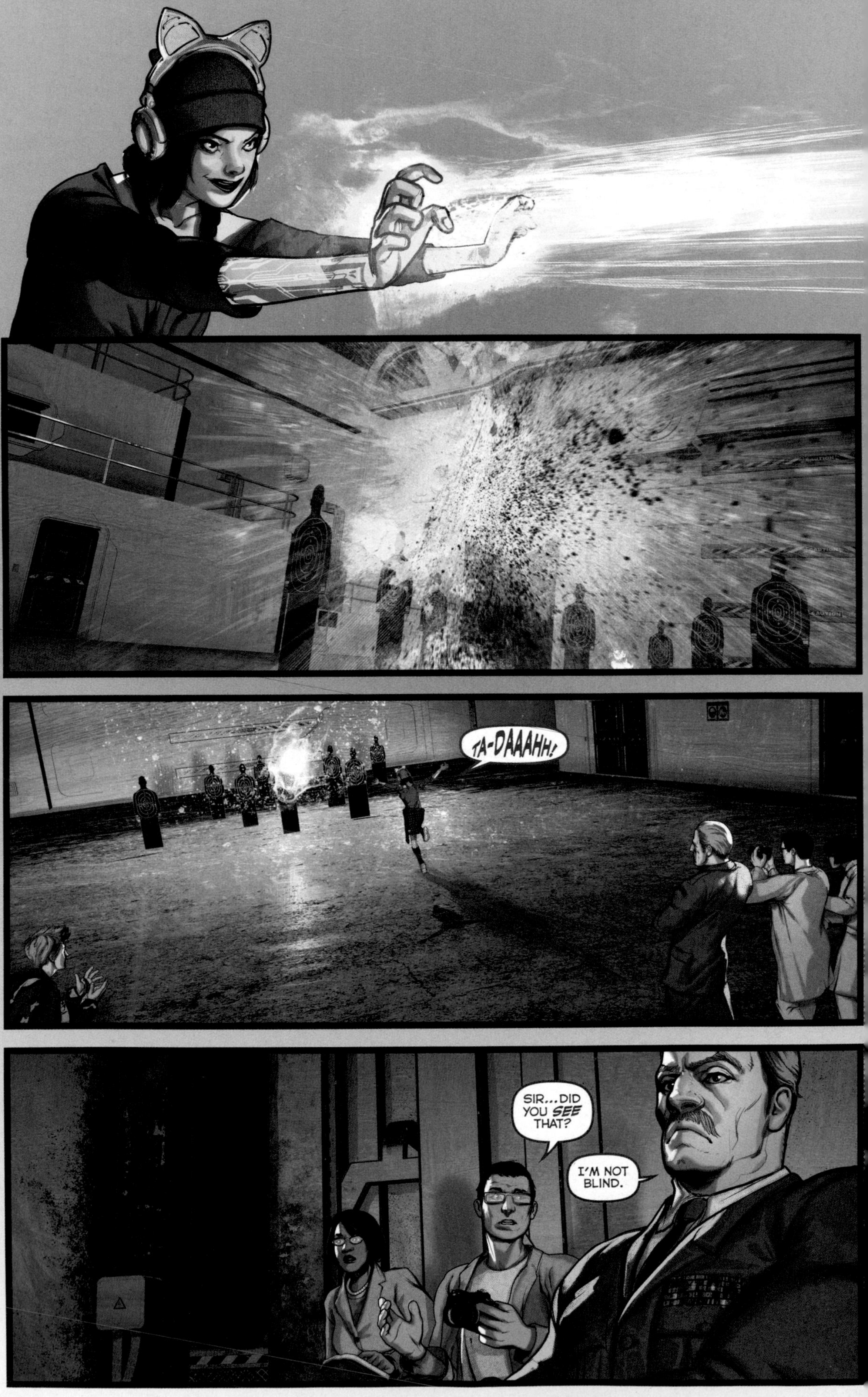
TA-DAAAHH!
SIR...DID YOU SEE THAT?
I'M NOT BLIND.

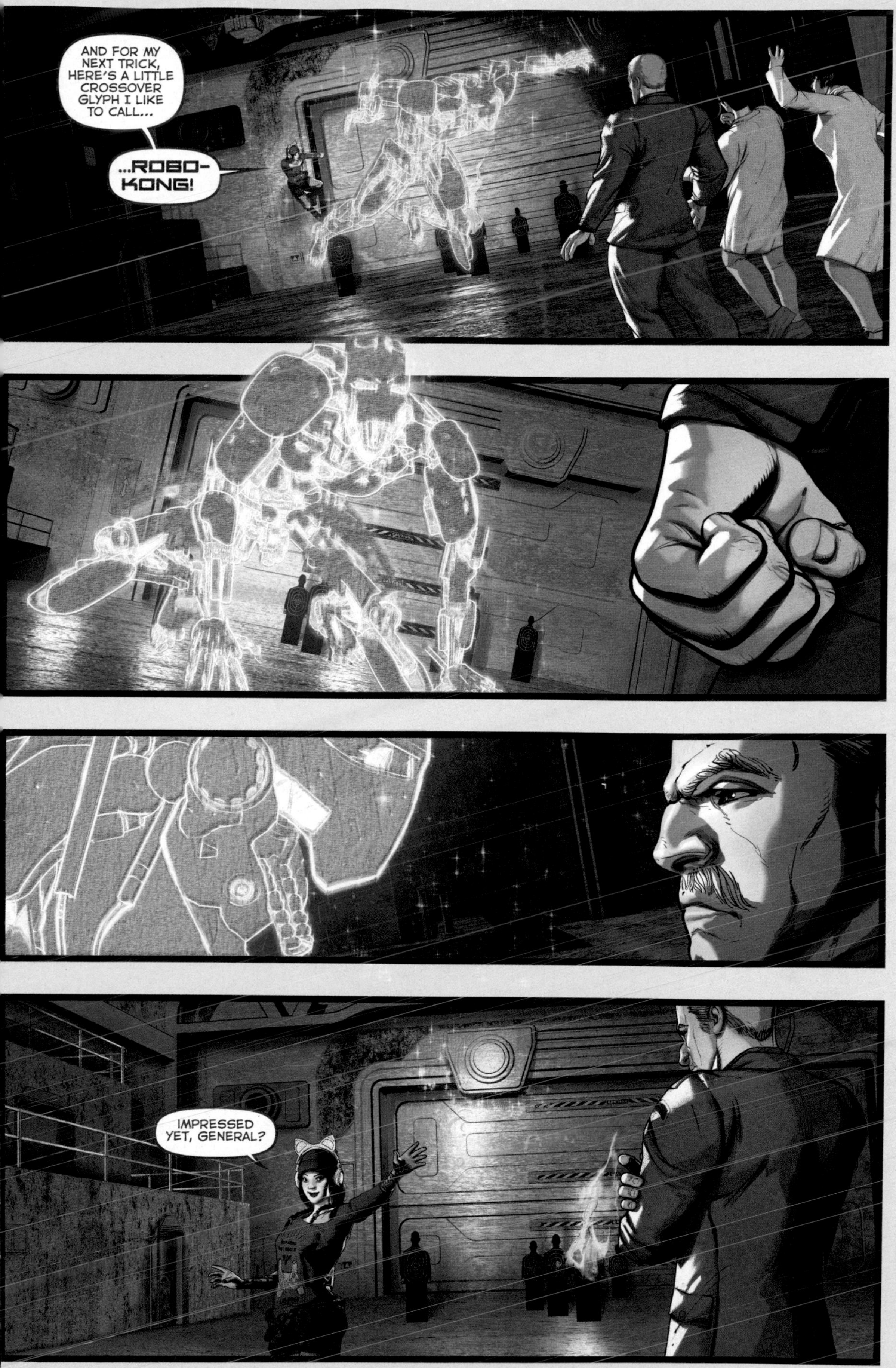
AND FOR MY NEXT TRICK, HERE'S A LITTLE CROSSOVER GLYPH I LIKE TO CALL...
...ROBO-KONG!
IMPRESSED YET, GENERAL?

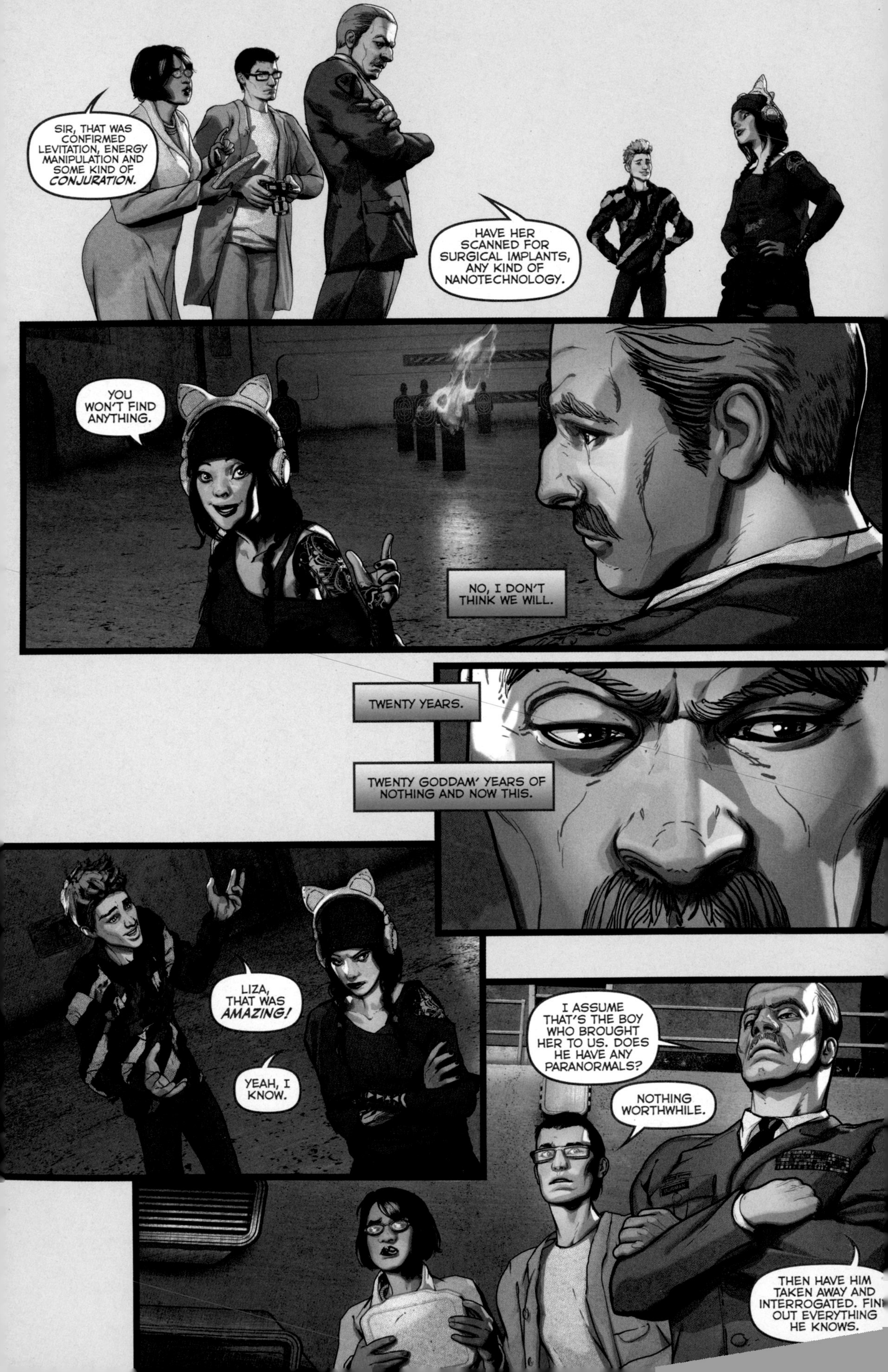
SIR, THAT WAS CONFIRMED LEVITATION, ENERGY MANIPULATION AND SOME KIND OF *CONJURATION.*
HAVE HER SCANNED FOR SURGICAL IMPLANTS, ANY KIND OF NANOTECHNOLOGY.
YOU WON'T FIND ANYTHING.
NO, I DON'T THINK WE WILL.
TWENTY YEARS.
TWENTY GODDAM' YEARS OF NOTHING AND NOW THIS.
LIZA, THAT WAS *AMAZING!*
YEAH, I KNOW.
I ASSUME THAT'S THE BOY WHO BROUGHT HER TO US. DOES HE HAVE ANY PARANORMALS?
NOTHING WORTHWHILE.
THEN HAVE HIM TAKEN AWAY AND INTERROGATED. FIN OUT EVERYTHING HE KNOWS.

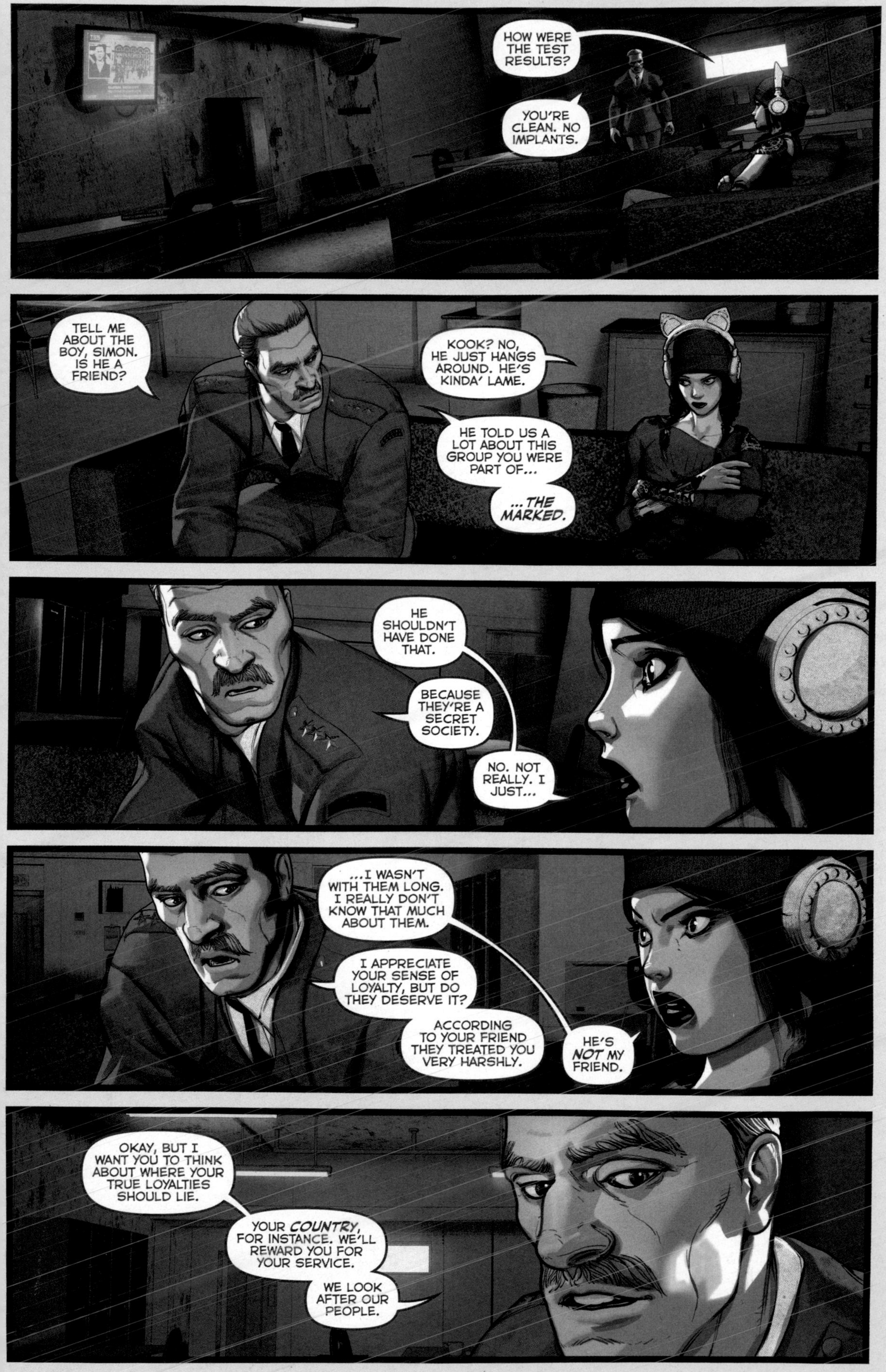

HOW WERE THE TEST RESULTS?
YOU'RE CLEAN. NO IMPLANTS.
TELL ME ABOUT THE BOY, SIMON. IS HE A FRIEND?
KOOK? NO, HE JUST HANGS AROUND. HE'S KINDA' LAME.
HE TOLD US A LOT ABOUT THIS GROUP YOU WERE PART OF...
...THE MARKED.
HE SHOULDN'T HAVE DONE THAT.
BECAUSE THEY'RE A SECRET SOCIETY.
NO. NOT REALLY. I JUST...
...I WASN'T WITH THEM LONG. I REALLY DON'T KNOW THAT MUCH ABOUT THEM.
I APPRECIATE YOUR SENSE OF LOYALTY, BUT DO THEY DESERVE IT?
ACCORDING TO YOUR FRIEND THEY TREATED YOU VERY HARSHLY.
HE'S NOT MY FRIEND.
OKAY, BUT I WANT YOU TO THINK ABOUT WHERE YOUR TRUE LOYALTIES SHOULD LIE.
YOUR COUNTRY, FOR INSTANCE. WE'LL REWARD YOU FOR YOUR SERVICE.
WE LOOK AFTER OUR PEOPLE.

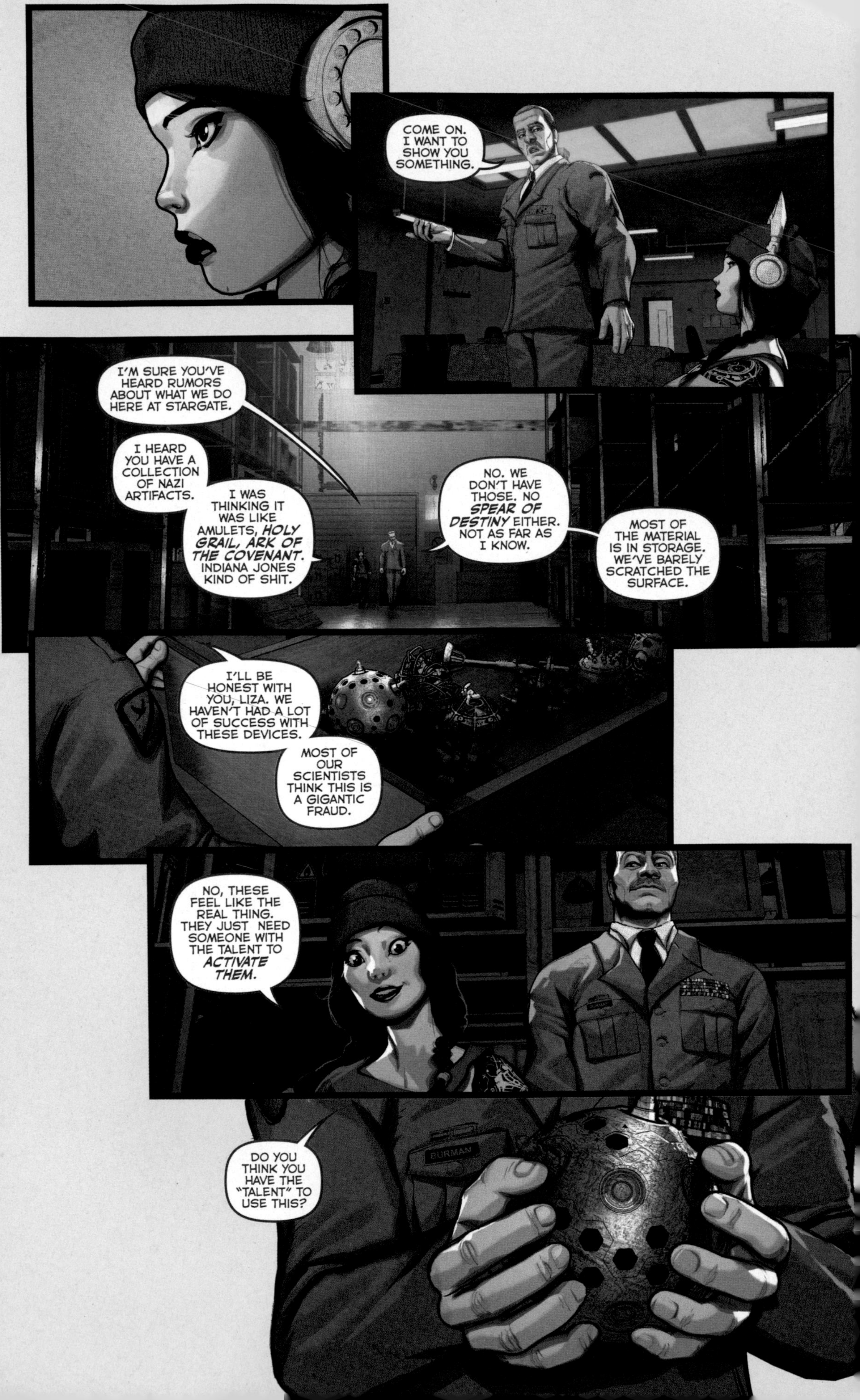
COME ON. I WANT TO SHOW YOU SOMETHING.
I'M SURE YOU'VE HEARD RUMORS ABOUT WHAT WE DO HERE AT STARGATE.
I HEARD YOU HAVE A COLLECTION OF NAZI ARTIFACTS.
I WAS THINKING IT WAS LIKE AMULETS, *HOLY GRAIL, ARK OF THE COVENANT*. INDIANA JONES KIND OF SHIT.
NO. WE DON'T HAVE THOSE. NO *SPEAR OF DESTINY* EITHER. NOT AS FAR AS I KNOW.
MOST OF THE MATERIAL IS IN STORAGE. WE'VE BARELY SCRATCHED THE SURFACE.
I'LL BE HONEST WITH YOU, LIZA. WE HAVEN'T HAD A LOT OF SUCCESS WITH THESE DEVICES.
MOST OF OUR SCIENTISTS THINK THIS IS A GIGANTIC FRAUD.
NO, THESE FEEL LIKE THE REAL THING. THEY JUST NEED SOMEONE WITH THE TALENT TO *ACTIVATE THEM.*
BURMAN
DO YOU THINK YOU HAVE THE "TALENT" TO USE THIS?

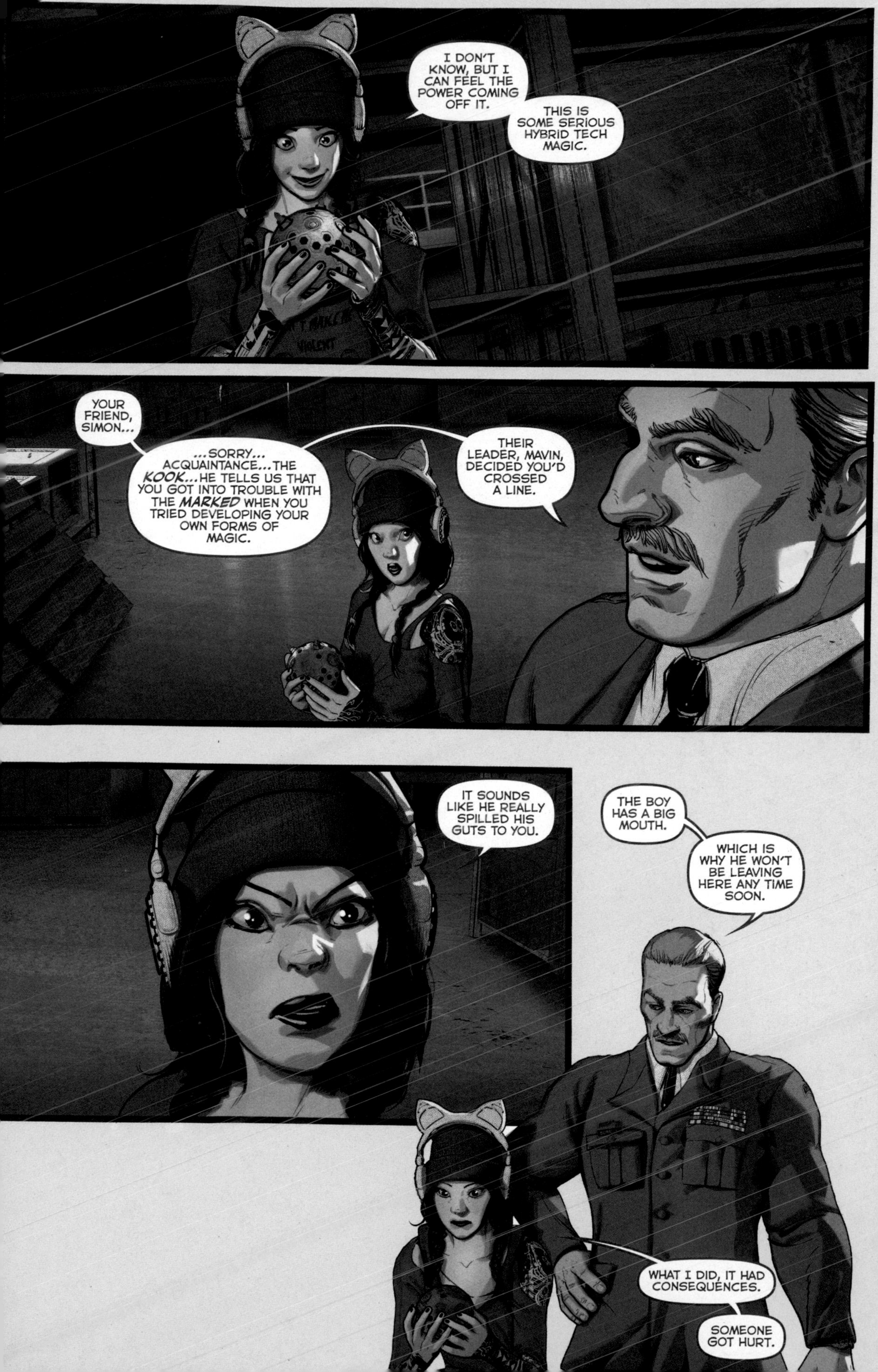
I DON'T KNOW, BUT I CAN FEEL THE POWER COMING OFF IT.
THIS IS SOME SERIOUS HYBRID TECH MAGIC.
YOUR FRIEND, SIMON...
...SORRY... ACQUAINTANCE...THE *KOOK*...HE TELLS US THAT YOU GOT INTO TROUBLE WITH THE *MARKED* WHEN YOU TRIED DEVELOPING YOUR OWN FORMS OF MAGIC.
THEIR LEADER, MAVIN, DECIDED YOU'D CROSSED A LINE.
IT SOUNDS LIKE HE REALLY SPILLED HIS GUTS TO YOU.
THE BOY HAS A BIG MOUTH.
WHICH IS WHY HE WON'T BE LEAVING HERE ANY TIME SOON.
WHAT I DID, IT HAD CONSEQUENCES.
SOMEONE GOT HURT.

YOU CAN'T MAKE REAL PROGRESS WITHOUT TAKING RISKS.

WE'RE PREPARED FOR THAT.

WE KNOW YOU WERE DEVELOPING THIS "HYBRID MAGIC" USING SOMETHING CALLED A *TRANSCRIBING WAND.*

I TRUST YOU BROUGHT IT WITH YOU.

UM... YEAH... NEVER GO ANYWHERE WITHOUT IT.

SIMON DEE HAS TOLD US THAT THESE WANDS ARE USED TO MAKE TATTOOS THAT ARE THE KEY TO TRIGGERING POWERS...*TALENTS*, AS YOU CALL THEM.

I'D LIKE YOU TO SHOW ME HOW THAT WORKS.

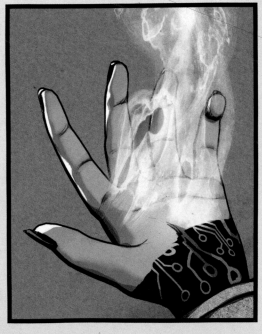

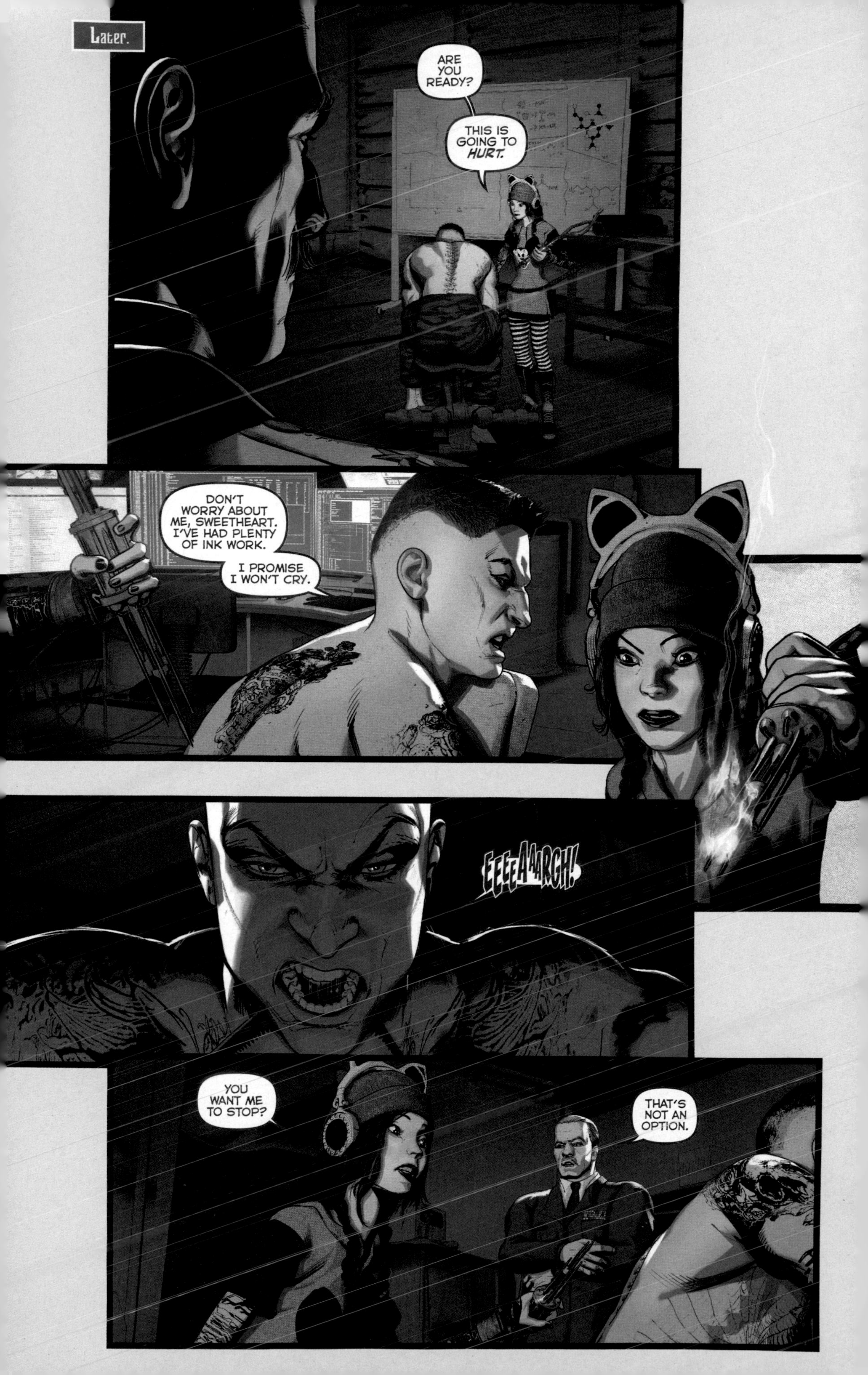
Later.
ARE YOU READY?
THIS IS GOING TO *HURT.*
DON'T WORRY ABOUT ME, SWEETHEART. I'VE HAD PLENTY OF INK WORK.
I PROMISE I WON'T CRY.
EEEEAAARGH!
YOU WANT ME TO STOP?
THAT'S NOT AN OPTION.

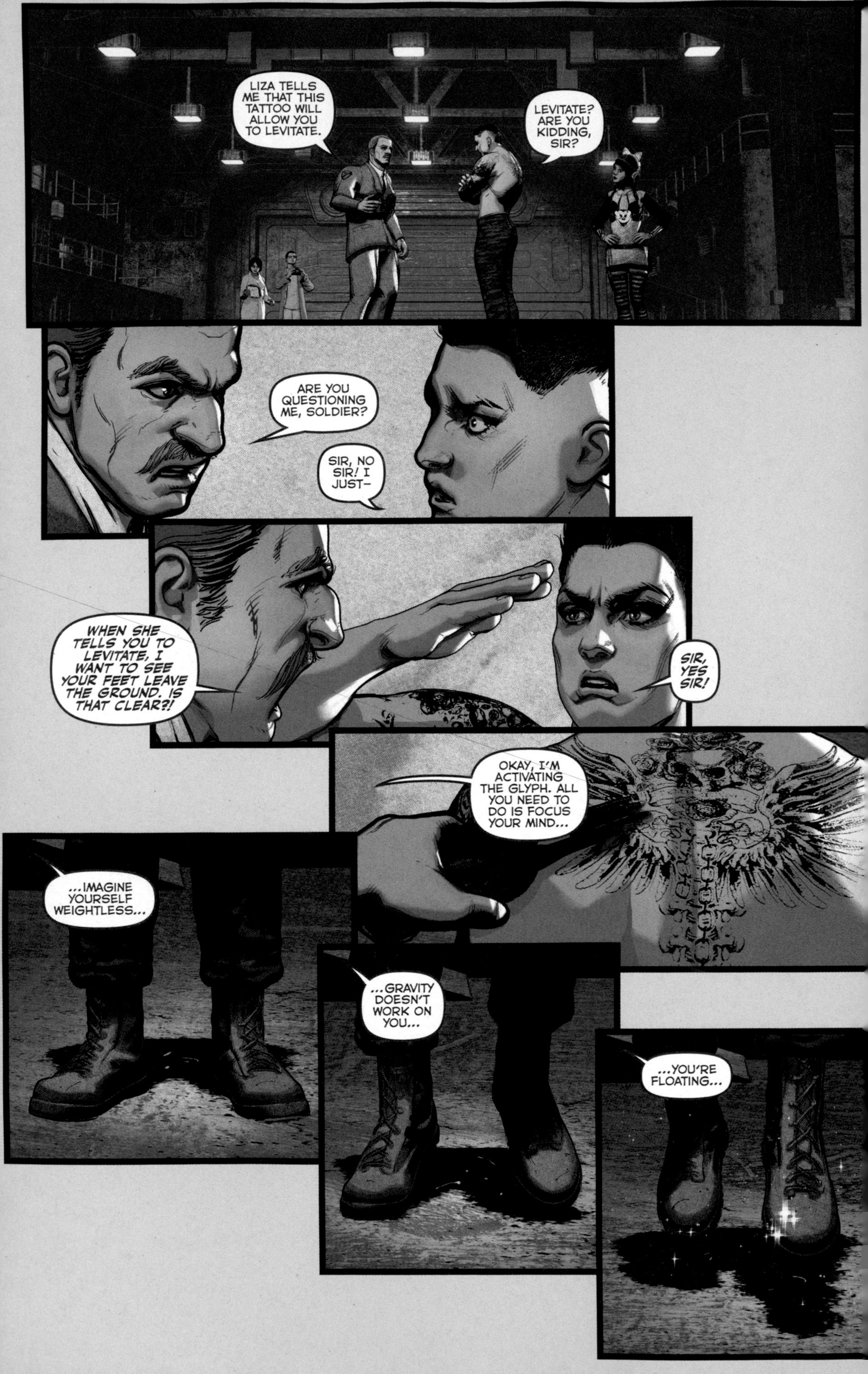
LIZA TELLS ME THAT THIS TATTOO WILL ALLOW YOU TO LEVITATE.
LEVITATE? ARE YOU KIDDING, SIR?
ARE YOU QUESTIONING ME, SOLDIER?
SIR, NO SIR! I JUST-
WHEN SHE TELLS YOU TO LEVITATE, I WANT TO SEE YOUR FEET LEAVE THE GROUND. IS THAT CLEAR?!
SIR, YES SIR!
OKAY, I'M ACTIVATING THE GLYPH. ALL YOU NEED TO DO IS FOCUS YOUR MIND...
...IMAGINE YOURSELF WEIGHTLESS...
...GRAVITY DOESN'T WORK ON YOU...
...YOU'RE FLOATING...

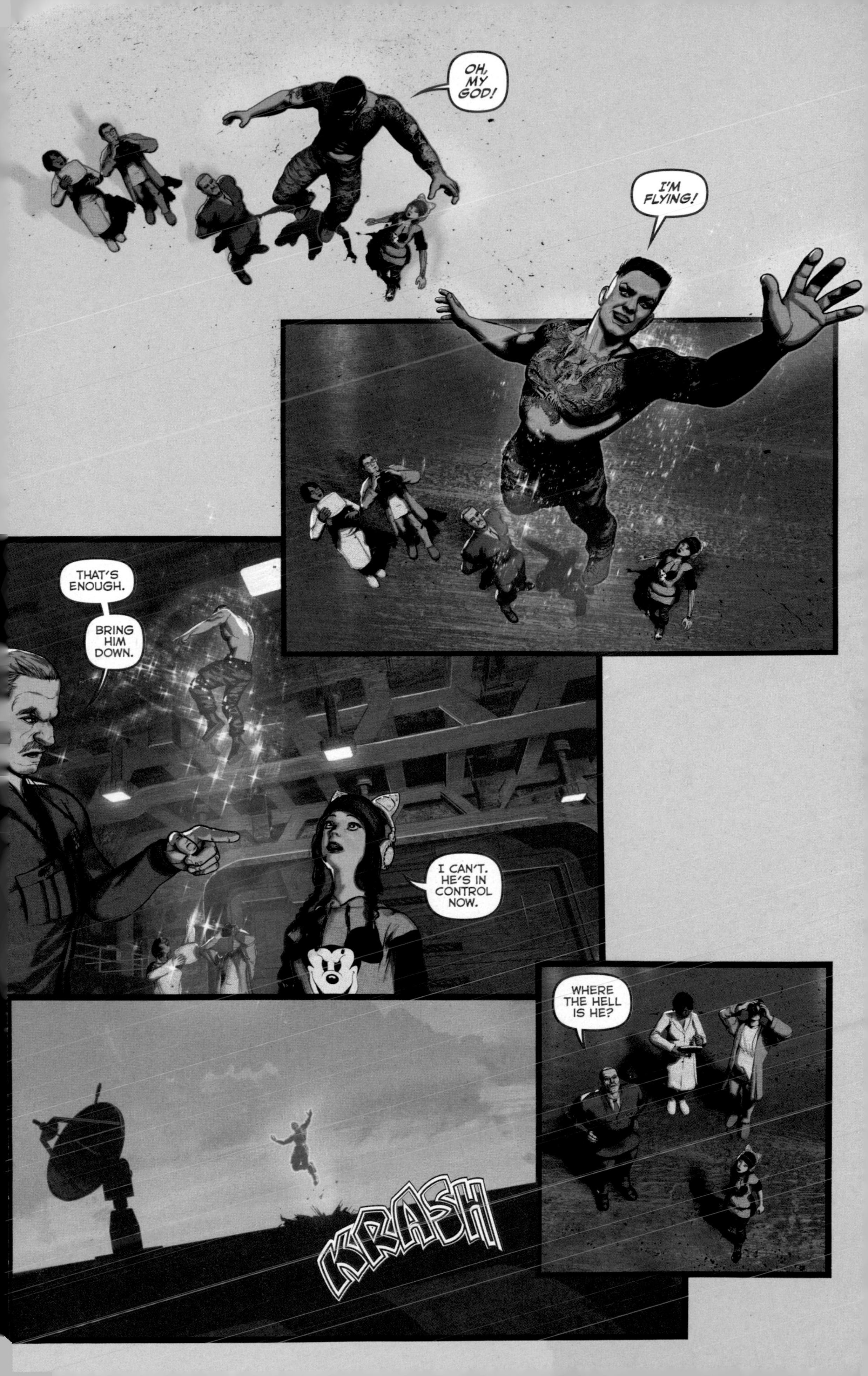
OH, MY GOD!
I'M FLYING!
THAT'S ENOUGH.
BRING HIM DOWN.
I CAN'T. HE'S IN CONTROL NOW.
KRASH
WHERE THE HELL IS HE?

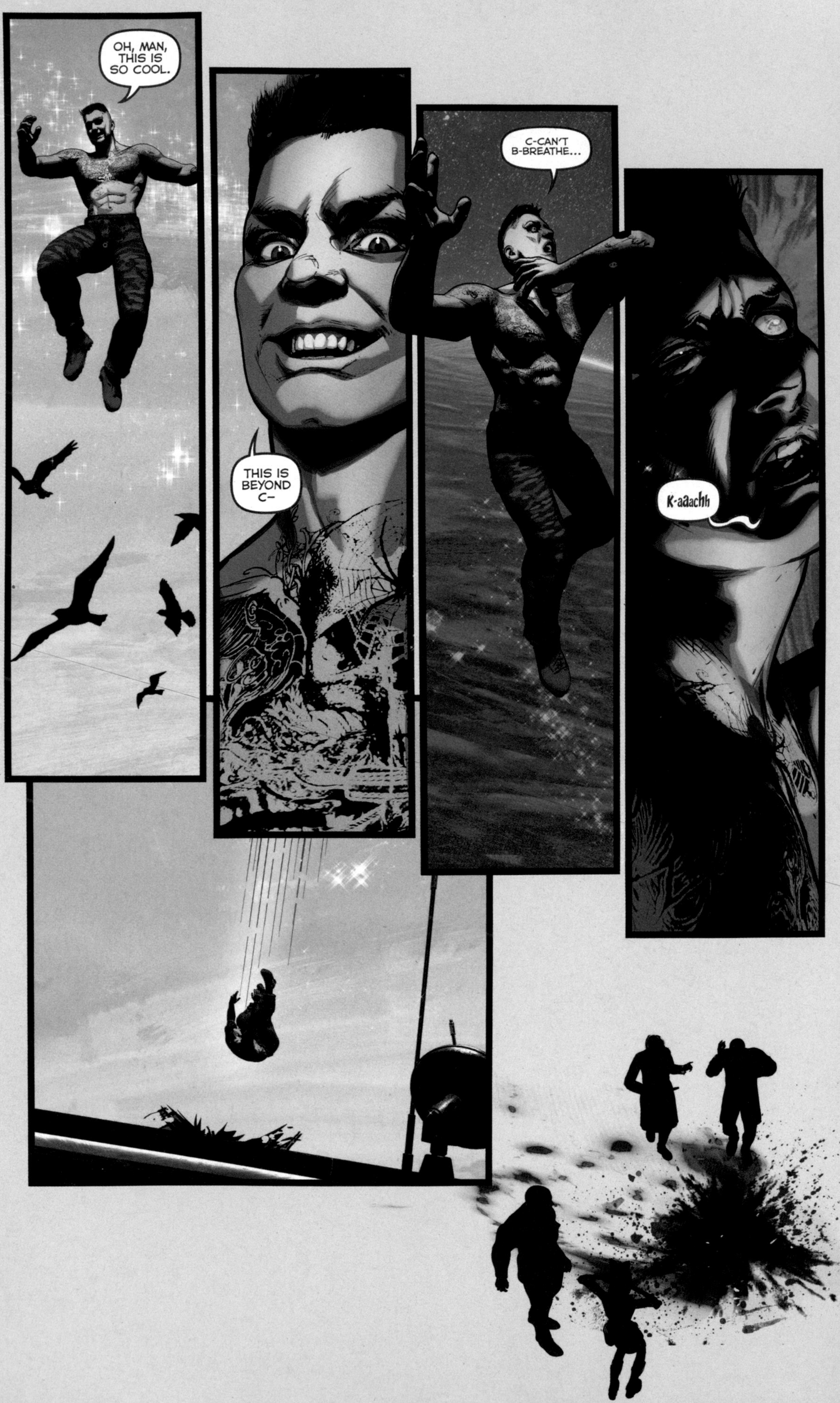
OH, MAN, THIS IS SO COOL.
THIS IS BEYOND C–
C-CAN'T B-BREATHE...
K-aaachh

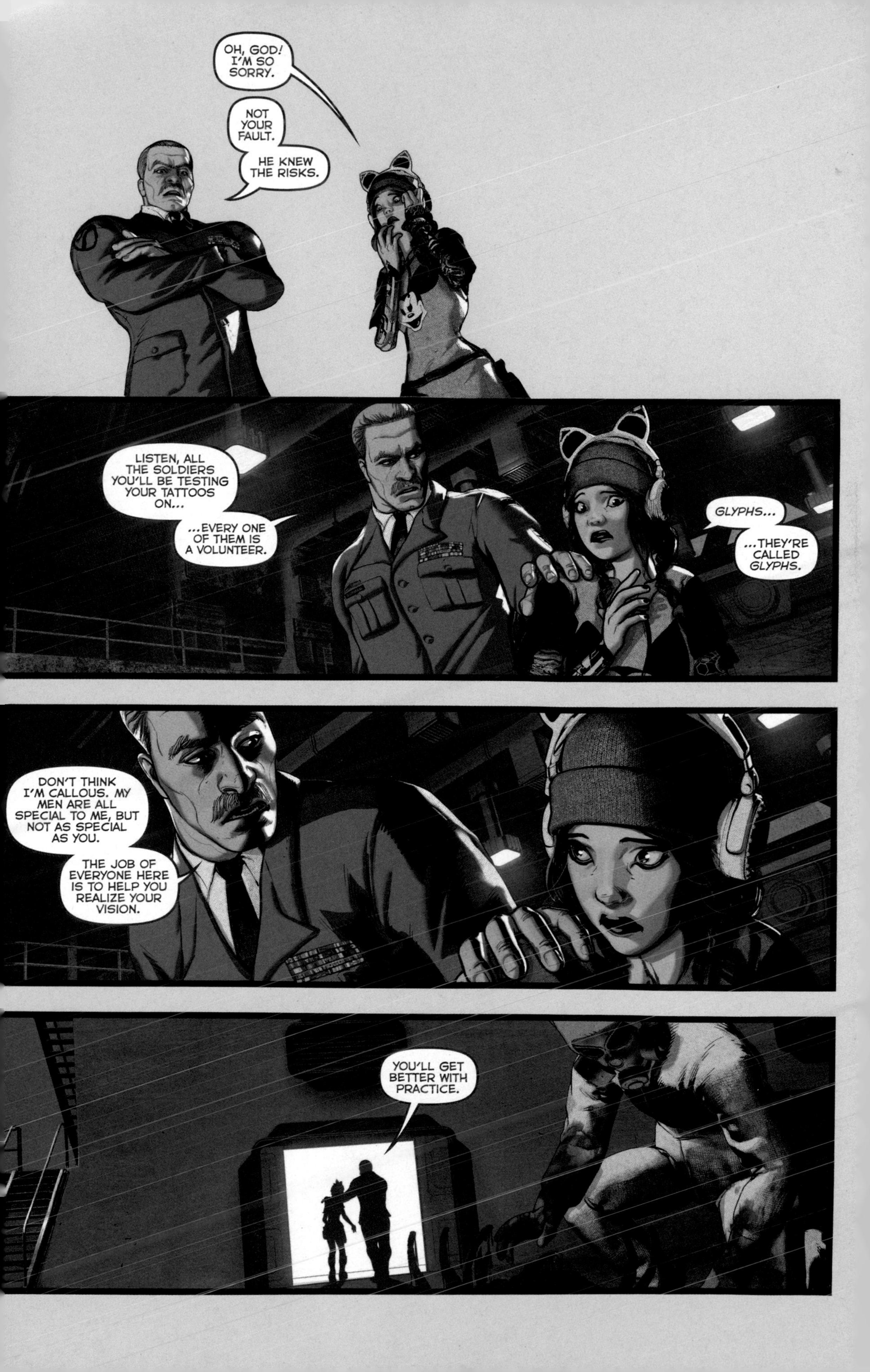
OH, GOD! I'M SO SORRY.
NOT YOUR FAULT.
HE KNEW THE RISKS.
LISTEN, ALL THE SOLDIERS YOU'LL BE TESTING YOUR TATTOOS ON...
...EVERY ONE OF THEM IS A VOLUNTEER.
GLYPHS...
...THEY'RE CALLED GLYPHS.
DON'T THINK I'M CALLOUS. MY MEN ARE ALL SPECIAL TO ME, BUT NOT AS SPECIAL AS YOU.
THE JOB OF EVERYONE HERE IS TO HELP YOU REALIZE YOUR VISION.
YOU'LL GET BETTER WITH PRACTICE.

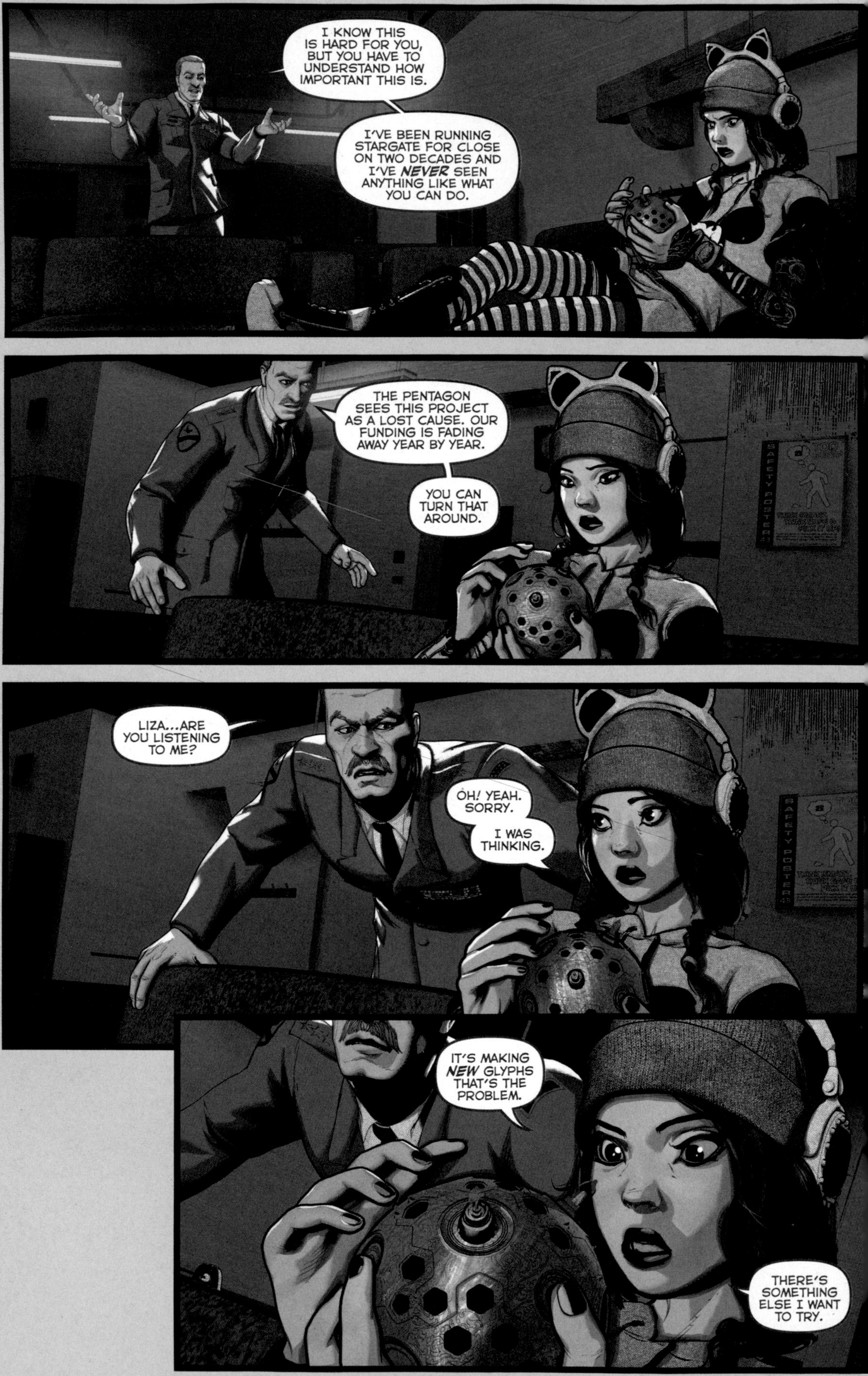
I KNOW THIS IS HARD FOR YOU, BUT YOU HAVE TO UNDERSTAND HOW IMPORTANT THIS IS.
I'VE BEEN RUNNING STARGATE FOR CLOSE ON TWO DECADES AND I'VE *NEVER* SEEN ANYTHING LIKE WHAT YOU CAN DO.
THE PENTAGON SEES THIS PROJECT AS A LOST CAUSE. OUR FUNDING IS FADING AWAY YEAR BY YEAR.
YOU CAN TURN THAT AROUND.
SAFETY POSTER
LIZA...ARE YOU LISTENING TO ME?
OH! YEAH. SORRY.
I WAS THINKING.
IT'S MAKING *NEW* GLYPHS THAT'S THE PROBLEM.
THERE'S SOMETHING ELSE I WANT TO TRY.

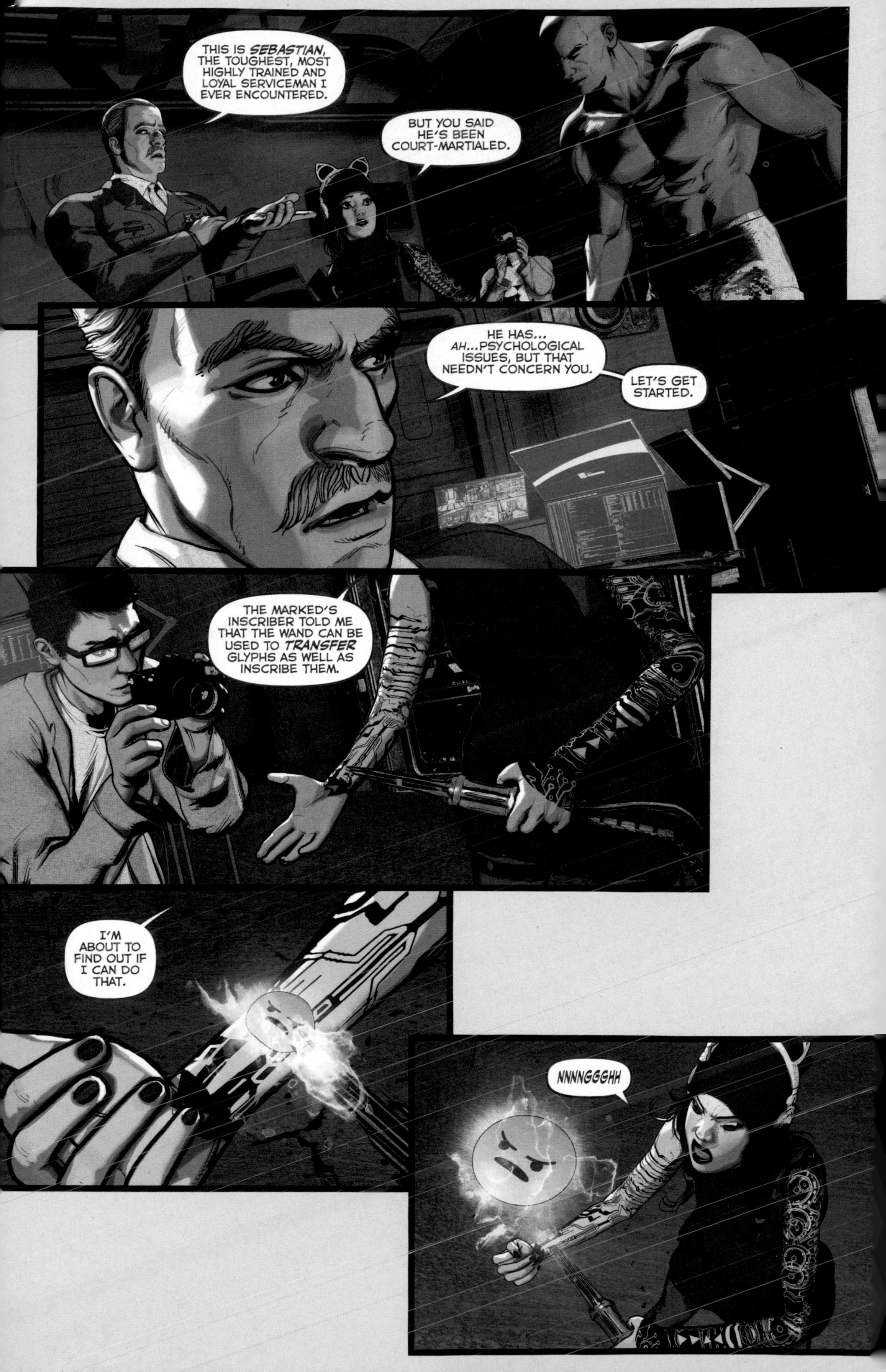
THIS IS SEBASTIAN, THE TOUGHEST, MOST HIGHLY TRAINED AND LOYAL SERVICEMAN I EVER ENCOUNTERED.
BUT YOU SAID HE'S BEEN COURT-MARTIALED.
HE HAS... AH...PSYCHOLOGICAL ISSUES, BUT THAT NEEDN'T CONCERN YOU.
LET'S GET STARTED.
THE MARKED'S INSCRIBER TOLD ME THAT THE WAND CAN BE USED TO TRANSFER GLYPHS AS WELL AS INSCRIBE THEM.
I'M ABOUT TO FIND OUT IF I CAN DO THAT.
NNNNGGGHH

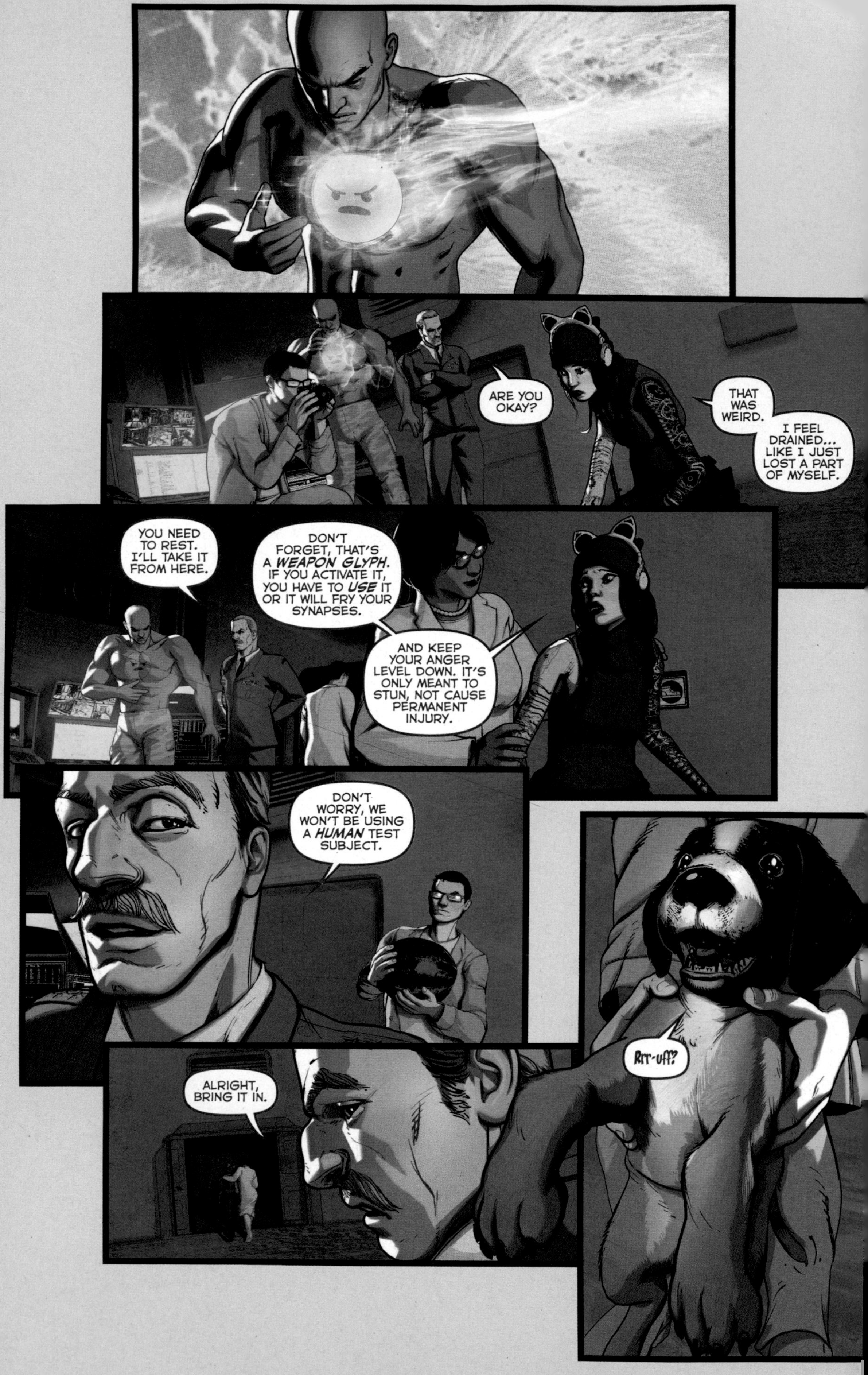
ARE YOU OKAY?
THAT WAS WEIRD.
I FEEL DRAINED... LIKE I JUST LOST A PART OF MYSELF.
YOU NEED TO REST. I'LL TAKE IT FROM HERE.
DON'T FORGET, THAT'S A WEAPON GLYPH. IF YOU ACTIVATE IT, YOU HAVE TO USE IT OR IT WILL FRY YOUR SYNAPSES.
AND KEEP YOUR ANGER LEVEL DOWN. IT'S ONLY MEANT TO STUN, NOT CAUSE PERMANENT INJURY.
DON'T WORRY, WE WON'T BE USING A HUMAN TEST SUBJECT.
ALRIGHT, BRING IT IN.
Rrr-uff?

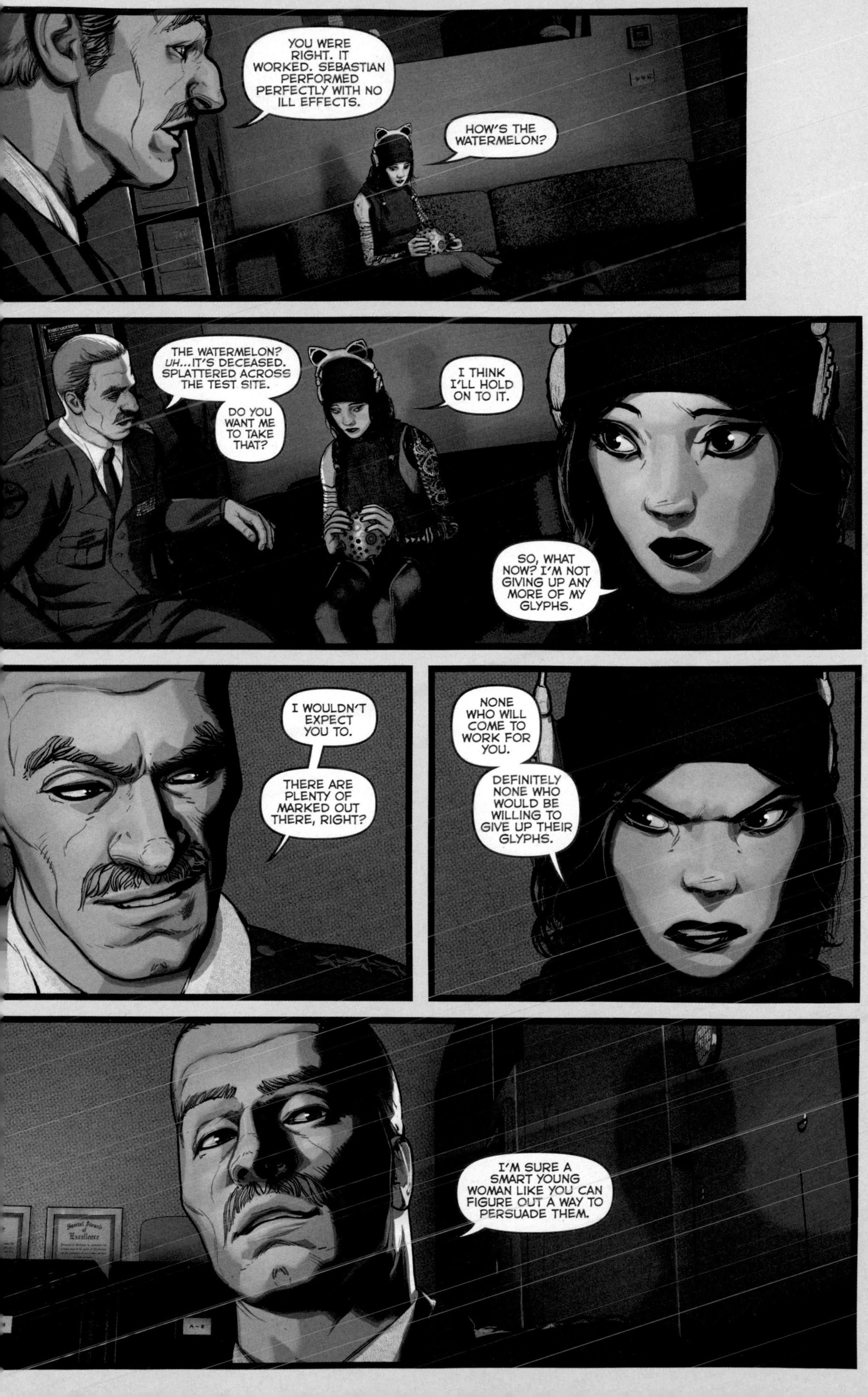
YOU WERE RIGHT. IT WORKED. SEBASTIAN PERFORMED PERFECTLY WITH NO ILL EFFECTS.
HOW'S THE WATERMELON?
THE WATERMELON? *UH*...IT'S DECEASED. SPLATTERED ACROSS THE TEST SITE.
DO YOU WANT ME TO TAKE THAT?
I THINK I'LL HOLD ON TO IT.
SO, WHAT NOW? I'M NOT GIVING UP ANY MORE OF MY GLYPHS.
I WOULDN'T EXPECT YOU TO.
THERE ARE PLENTY OF MARKED OUT THERE, RIGHT?
NONE WHO WILL COME TO WORK FOR YOU.
DEFINITELY NONE WHO WOULD BE WILLING TO GIVE UP THEIR GLYPHS.
I'M SURE A SMART YOUNG WOMAN LIKE YOU CAN FIGURE OUT A WAY TO PERSUADE THEM.

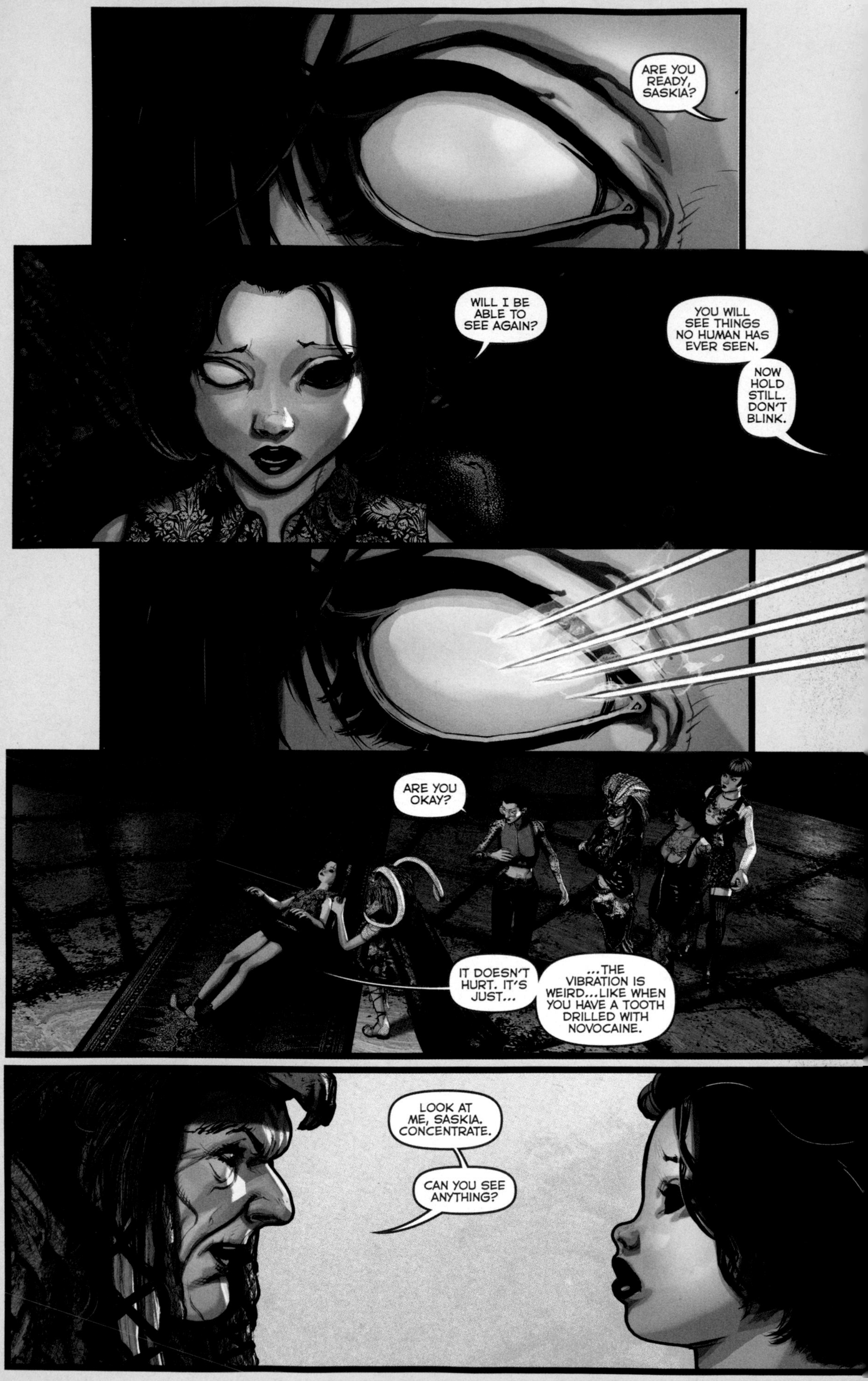
ARE YOU READY, SASKIA?
WILL I BE ABLE TO SEE AGAIN?
YOU WILL SEE THINGS NO HUMAN HAS EVER SEEN.
NOW HOLD STILL. DON'T BLINK.
ARE YOU OKAY?
IT DOESN'T HURT. IT'S JUST...
...THE VIBRATION IS WEIRD...LIKE WHEN YOU HAVE A TOOTH DRILLED WITH NOVOCAINE.
LOOK AT ME, SASKIA. CONCENTRATE.
CAN YOU SEE ANYTHING?

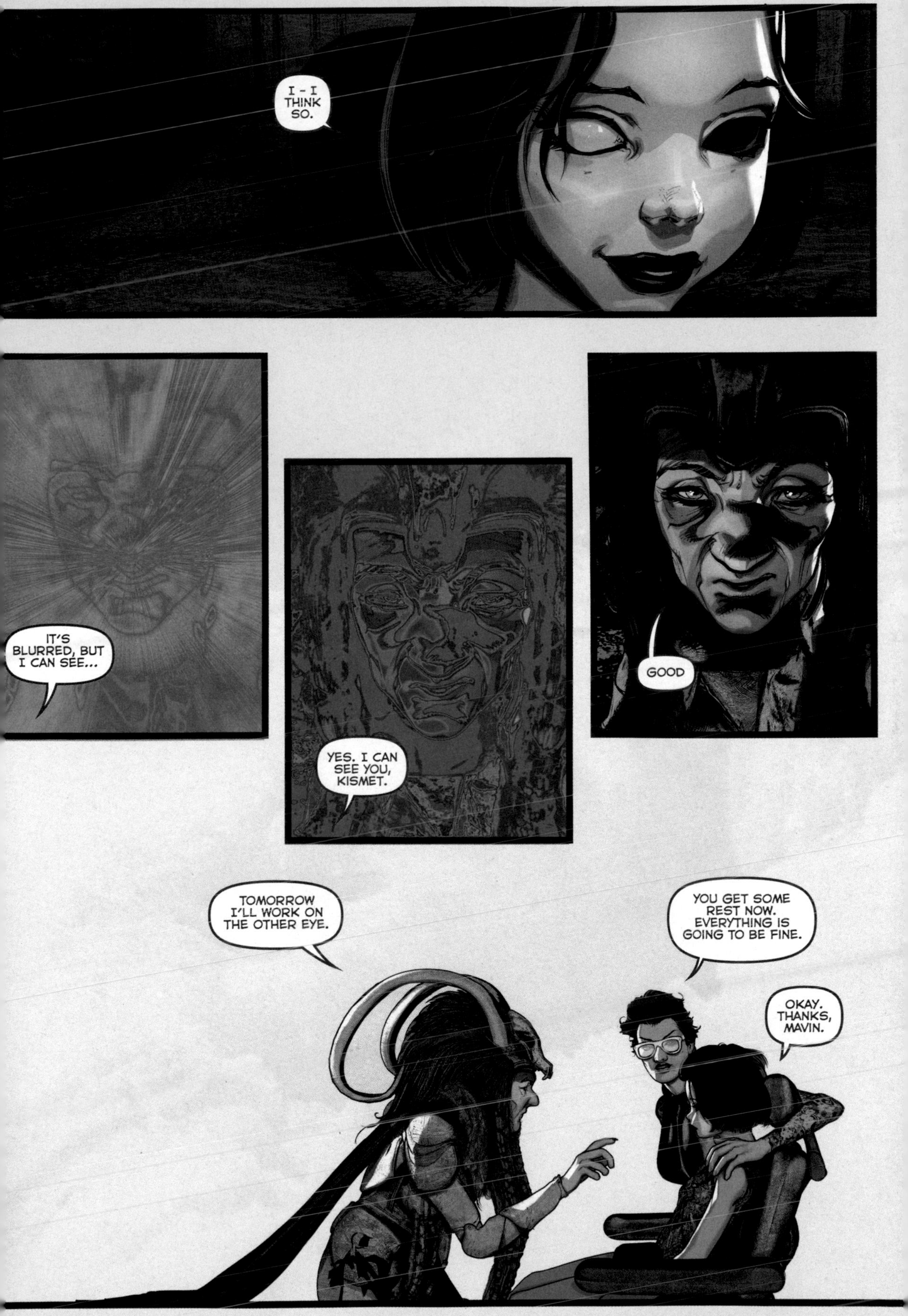
I - I THINK SO.
IT'S BLURRED, BUT I CAN SEE...
YES. I CAN SEE YOU, KISMET.
GOOD
TOMORROW I'LL WORK ON THE OTHER EYE.
YOU GET SOME REST NOW. EVERYTHING IS GOING TO BE FINE.
OKAY. THANKS, MAVIN.

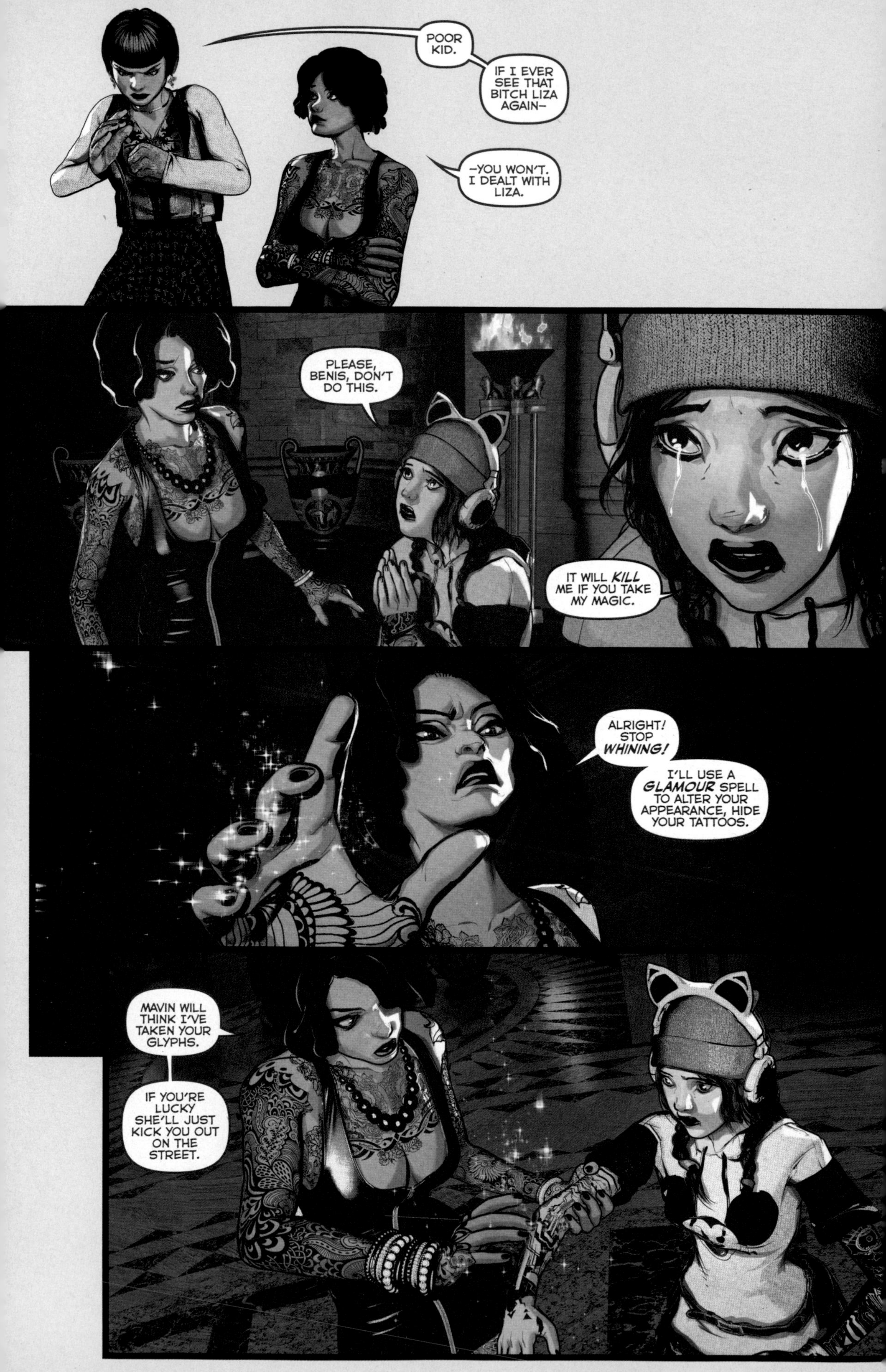
POOR KID.
IF I EVER SEE THAT BITCH LIZA AGAIN–
–YOU WON'T. I DEALT WITH LIZA.
PLEASE, BENIS, DON'T DO THIS.
IT WILL KILL ME IF YOU TAKE MY MAGIC.
ALRIGHT! STOP WHINING!
I'LL USE A GLAMOUR SPELL TO ALTER YOUR APPEARANCE, HIDE YOUR TATTOOS.
MAVIN WILL THINK I'VE TAKEN YOUR GLYPHS.
IF YOU'RE LUCKY SHE'LL JUST KICK YOU OUT ON THE STREET.

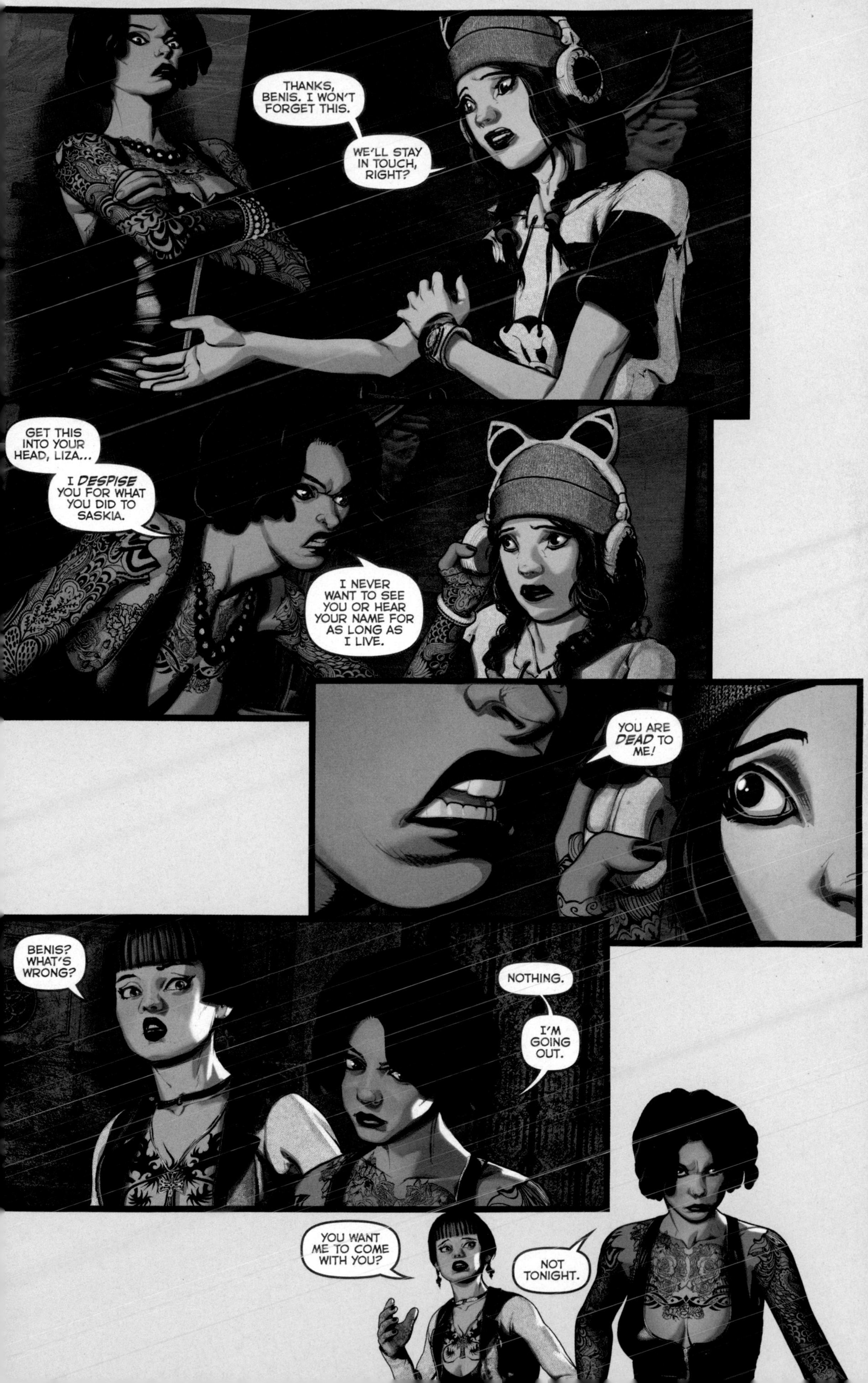
THANKS, BENIS. I WON'T FORGET THIS.
WE'LL STAY IN TOUCH, RIGHT?
GET THIS INTO YOUR HEAD, LIZA...
I *DESPISE* YOU FOR WHAT YOU DID TO SASKIA.
I NEVER WANT TO SEE YOU OR HEAR YOUR NAME FOR AS LONG AS I LIVE.
YOU ARE *DEAD* TO ME!
BENIS? WHAT'S WRONG?
NOTHING.
I'M GOING OUT.
YOU WANT ME TO COME WITH YOU?
NOT TONIGHT.

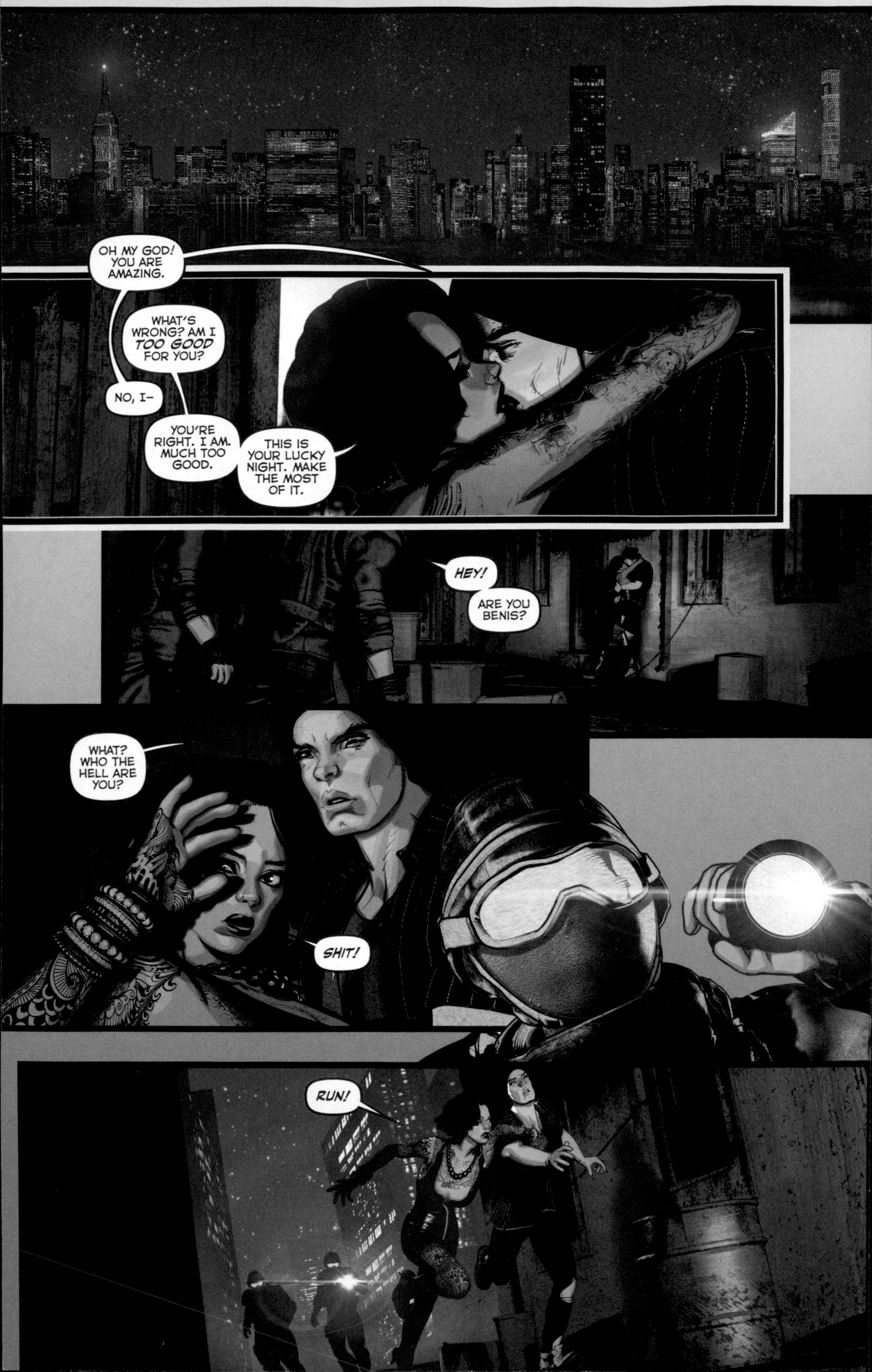
OH MY GOD! YOU ARE AMAZING.
WHAT'S WRONG? AM I *TOO GOOD* FOR YOU?
NO, I–
YOU'RE RIGHT. I AM. MUCH TOO GOOD.
THIS IS YOUR LUCKY NIGHT. MAKE THE MOST OF IT.
HEY!
ARE YOU BENIS?
WHAT? WHO THE HELL ARE YOU?
SHIT!
RUN!

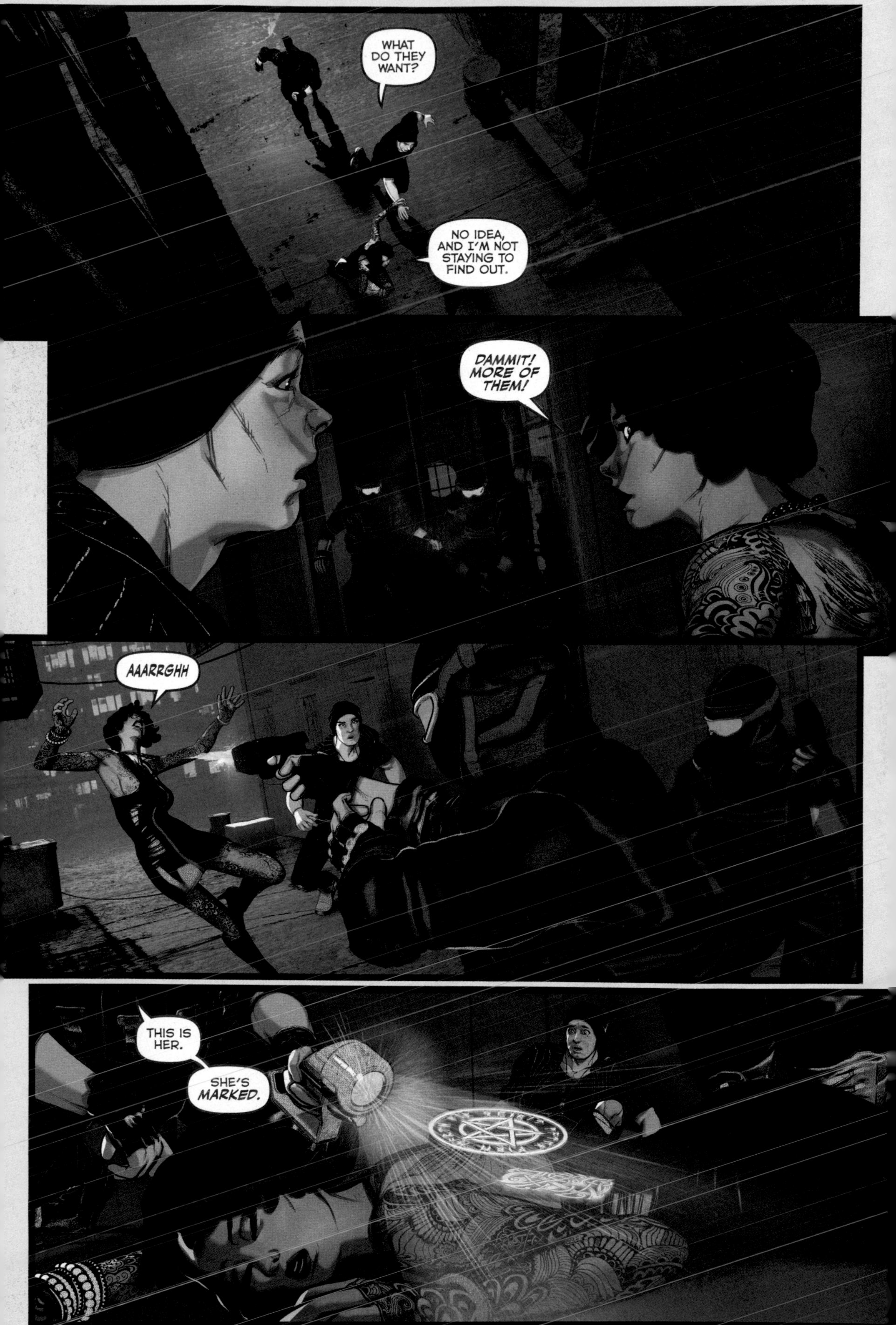

WHAT DO THEY WANT?
NO IDEA, AND I'M NOT STAYING TO FIND OUT.
DAMMIT! MORE OF THEM!
AAARRGHH
THIS IS HER.
SHE'S MARKED.

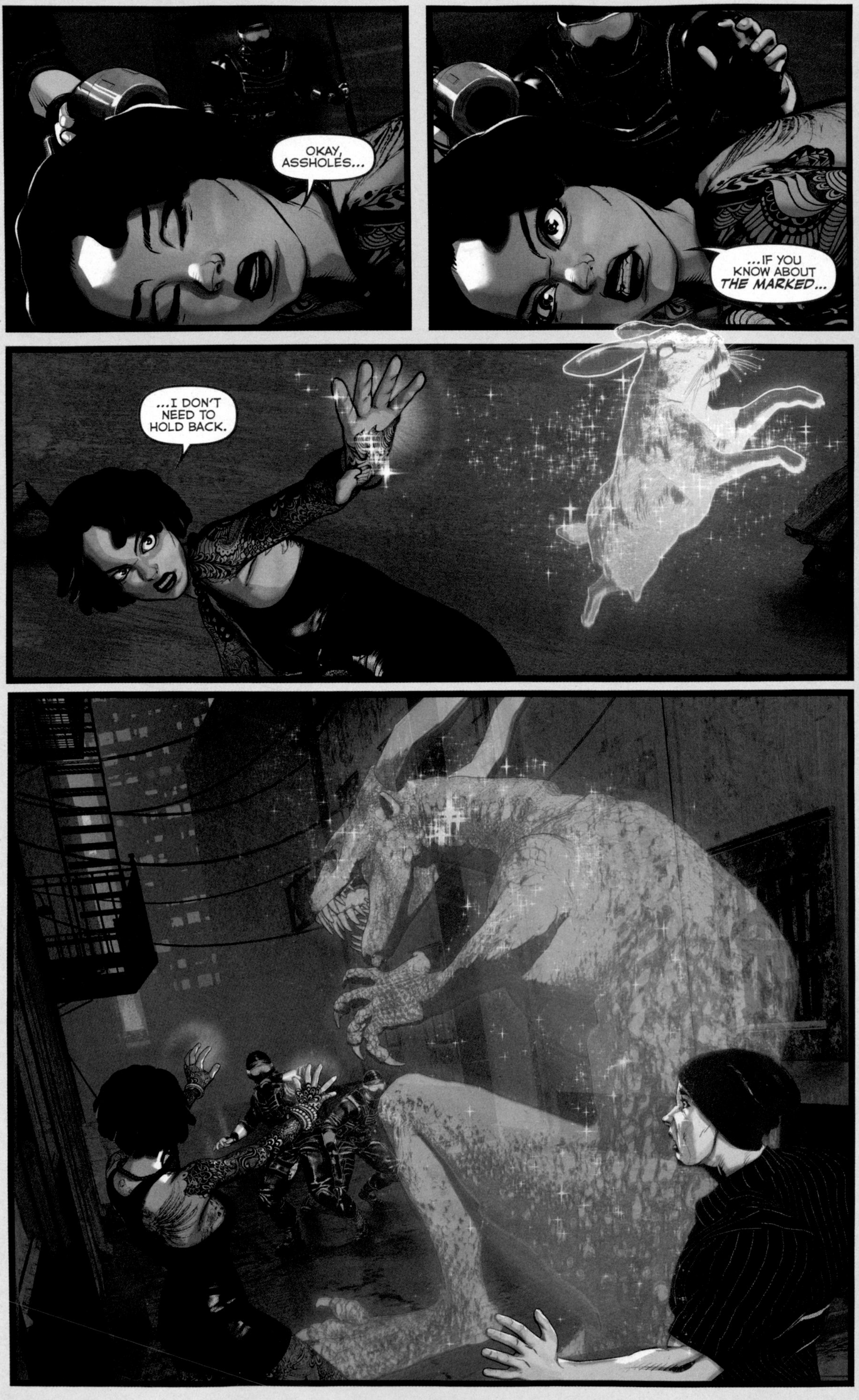
OKAY, ASSHOLES...
...IF YOU KNOW ABOUT *THE MARKED*...
...I DON'T NEED TO HOLD BACK.

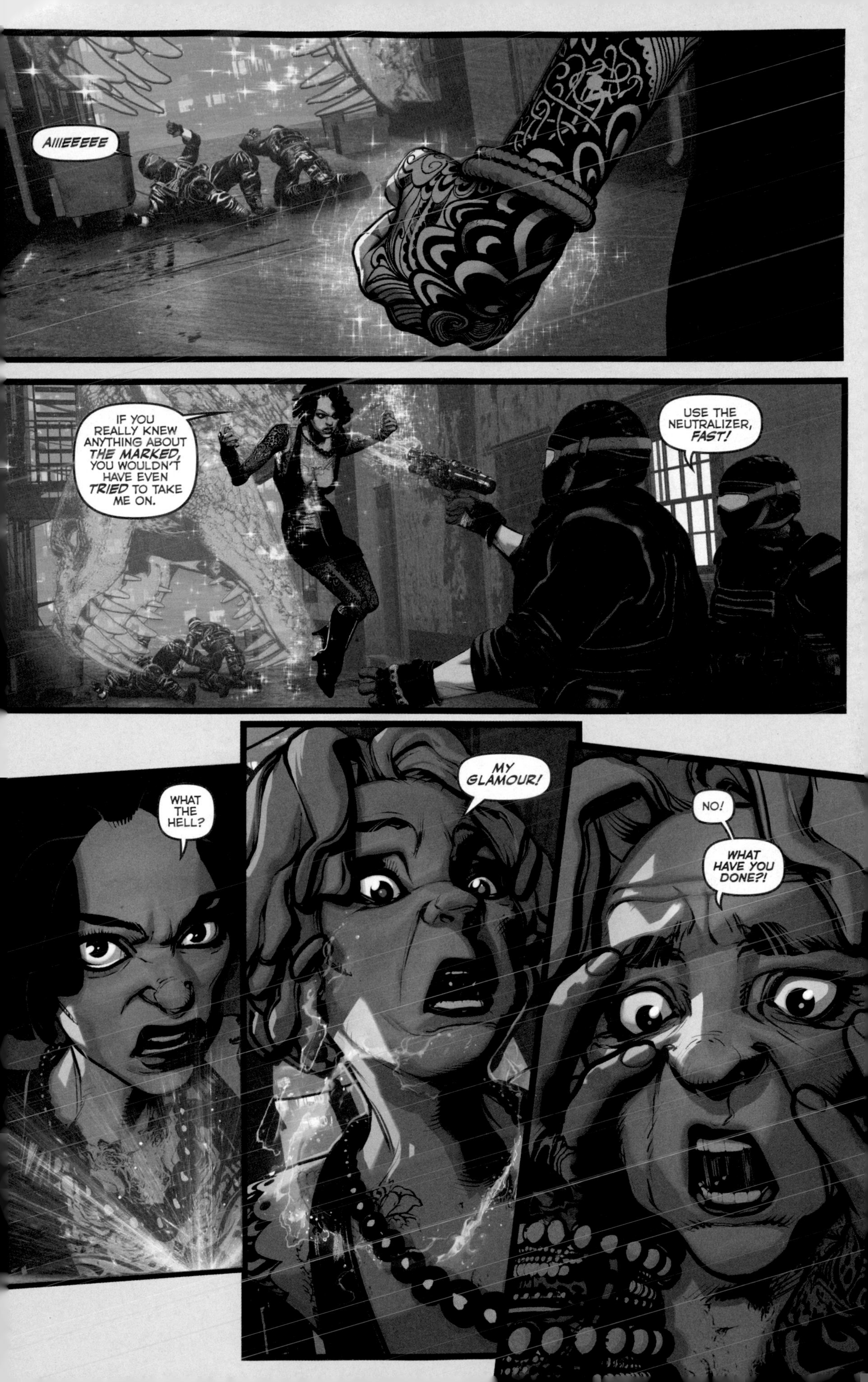
AIIIEEEEE
IF YOU REALLY KNEW ANYTHING ABOUT THE MARKED, YOU WOULDN'T HAVE EVEN TRIED TO TAKE ME ON.
USE THE NEUTRALIZER, FAST!
WHAT THE HELL?
MY GLAMOUR!
NO!
WHAT HAVE YOU DONE?!

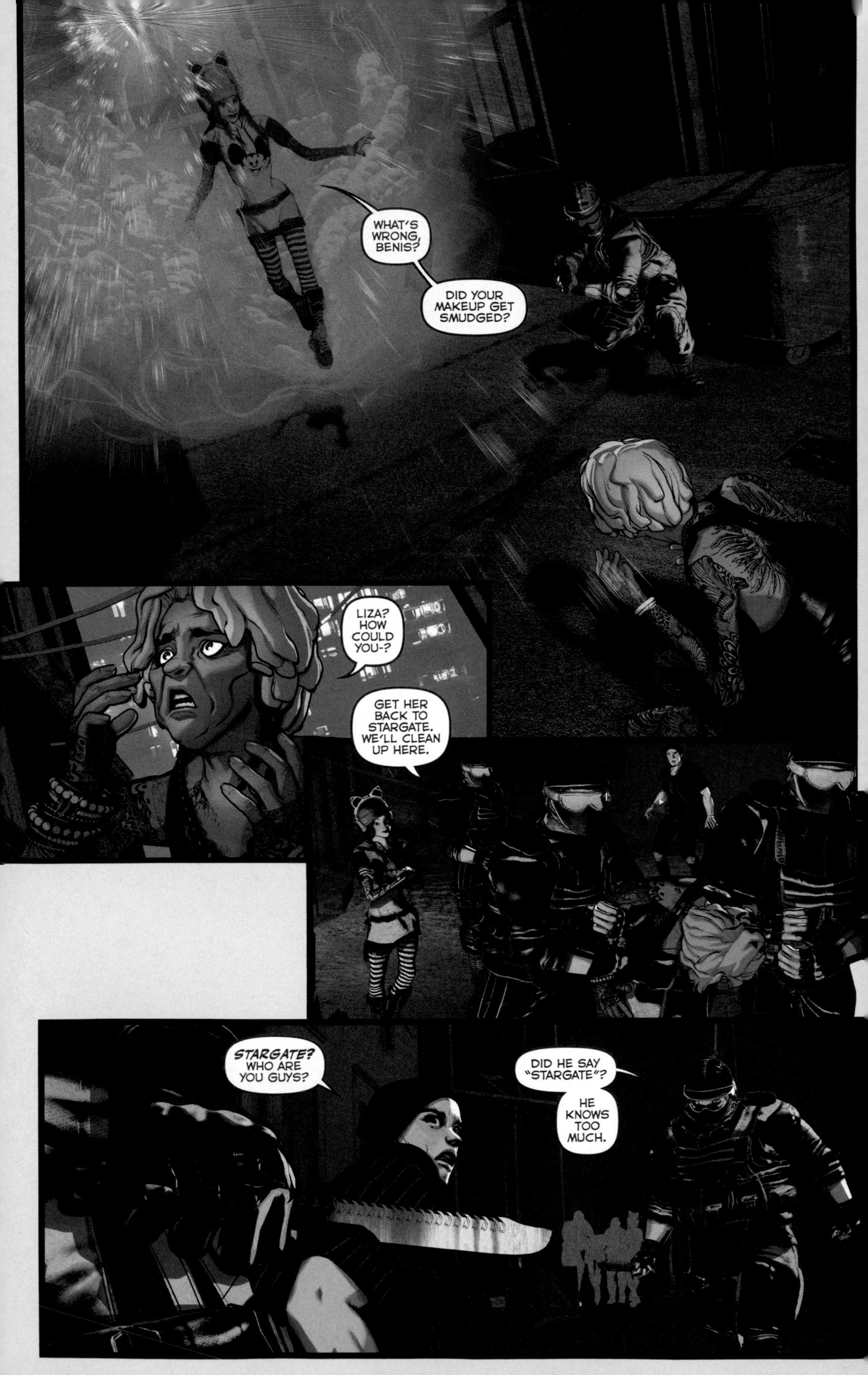
WHAT'S WRONG, BENIS?
DID YOUR MAKEUP GET SMUDGED?
LIZA? HOW COULD YOU-?
GET HER BACK TO STARGATE. WE'LL CLEAN UP HERE.
STARGATE? WHO ARE YOU GUYS?
DID HE SAY "STARGATE"?
HE KNOWS TOO MUCH.

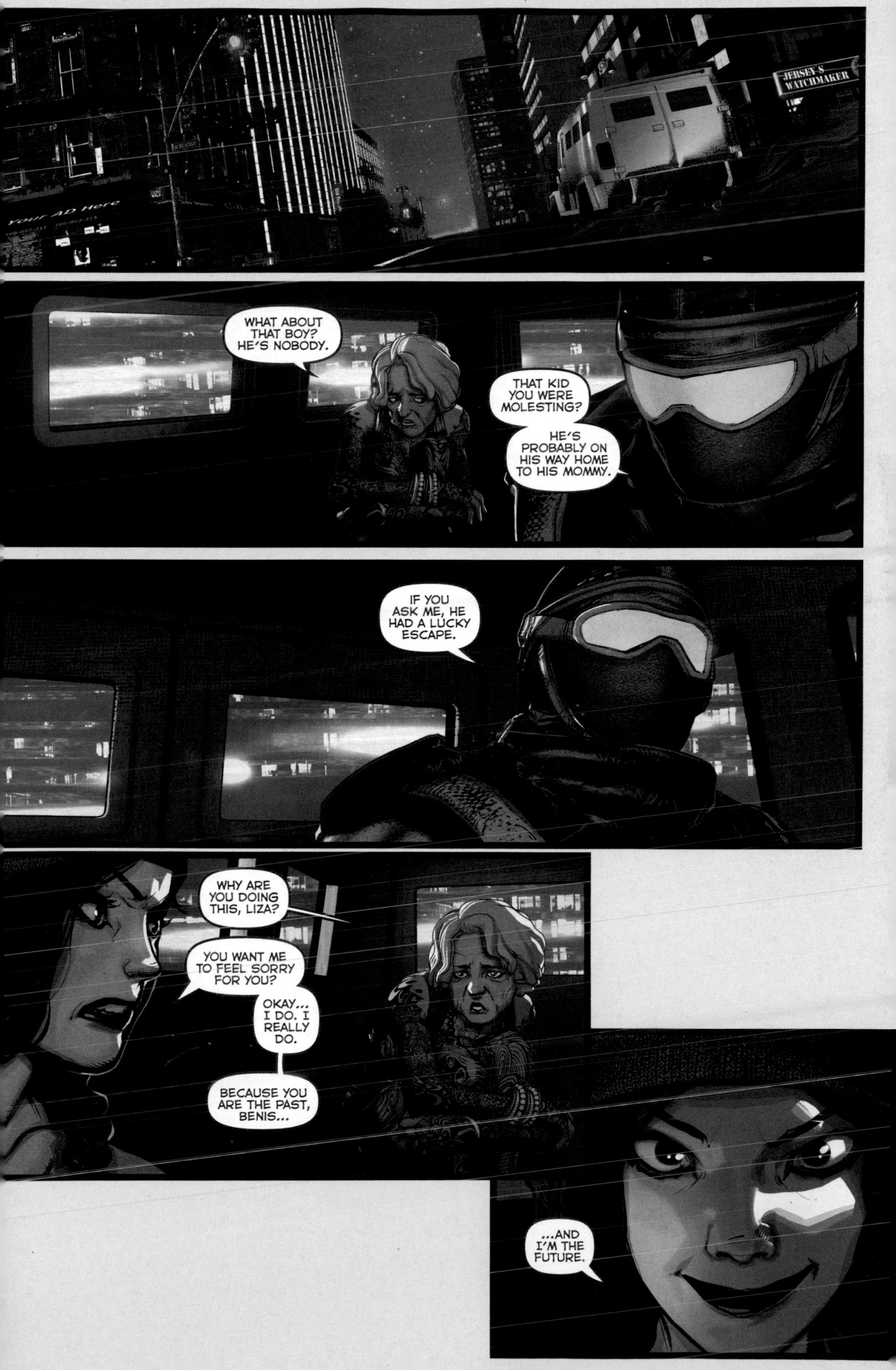
JERSEY'S WATCHMAKER
Your AD Here
WHAT ABOUT THAT BOY? HE'S NOBODY.
THAT KID YOU WERE MOLESTING?
HE'S PROBABLY ON HIS WAY HOME TO HIS MOMMY.
IF YOU ASK ME, HE HAD A LUCKY ESCAPE.
WHY ARE YOU DOING THIS, LIZA?
YOU WANT ME TO FEEL SORRY FOR YOU?
OKAY... I DO. I REALLY DO.
BECAUSE YOU ARE THE PAST, BENIS...
...AND I'M THE FUTURE.

ISSUE #1 SECOND PRINTING COVER

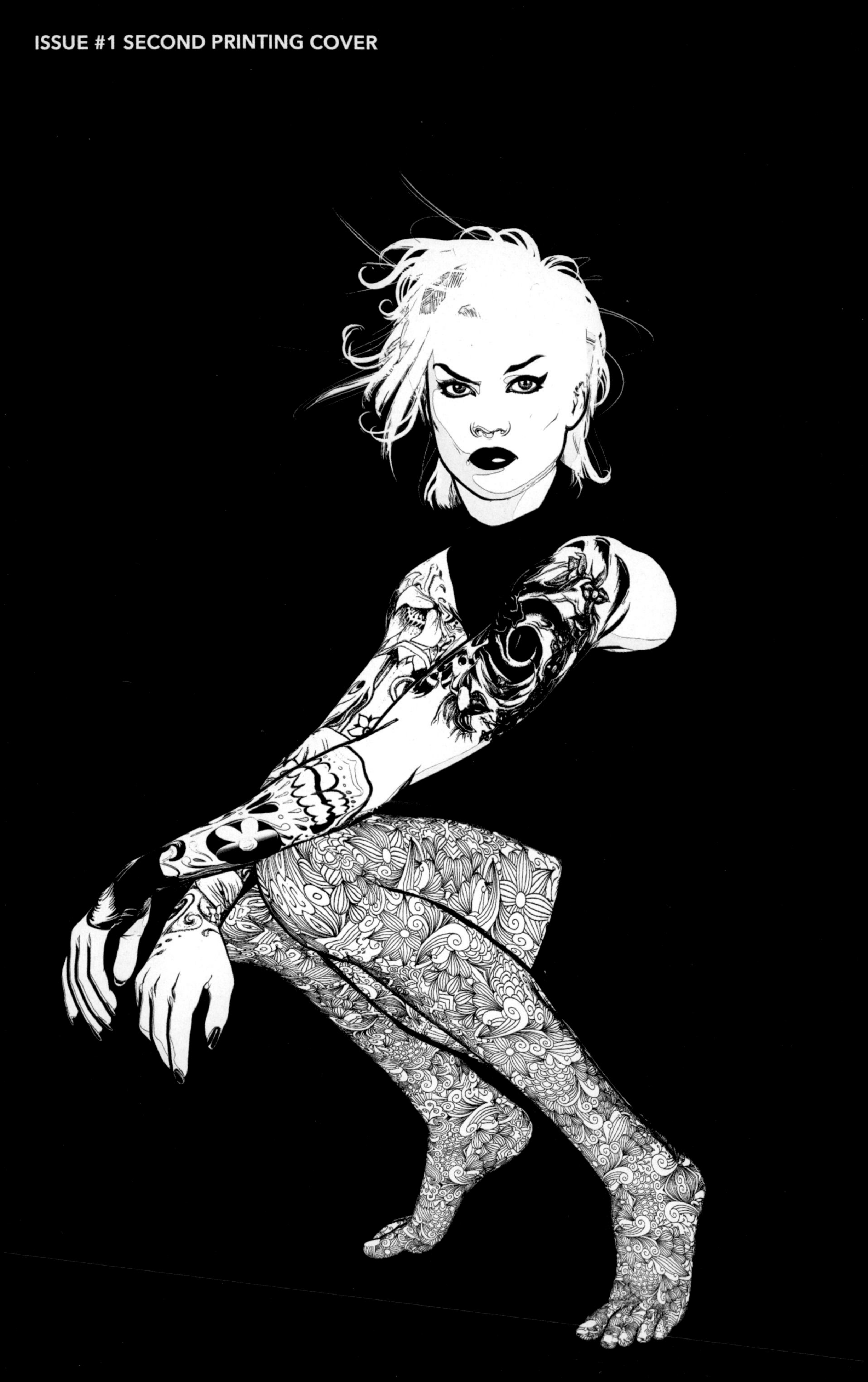

CHAPTER THREE

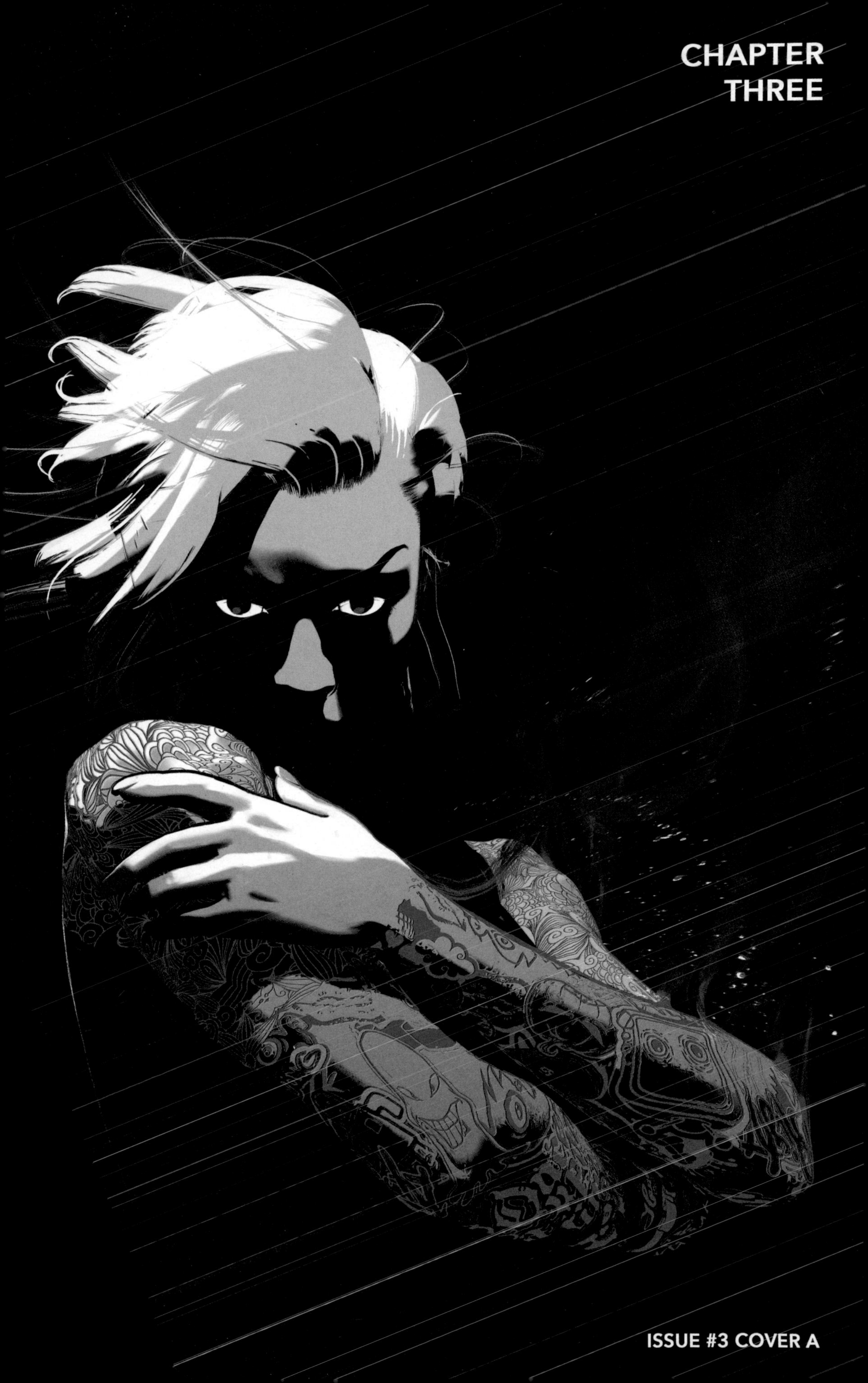

ISSUE #3 COVER A

ISSUE #3 COVER B

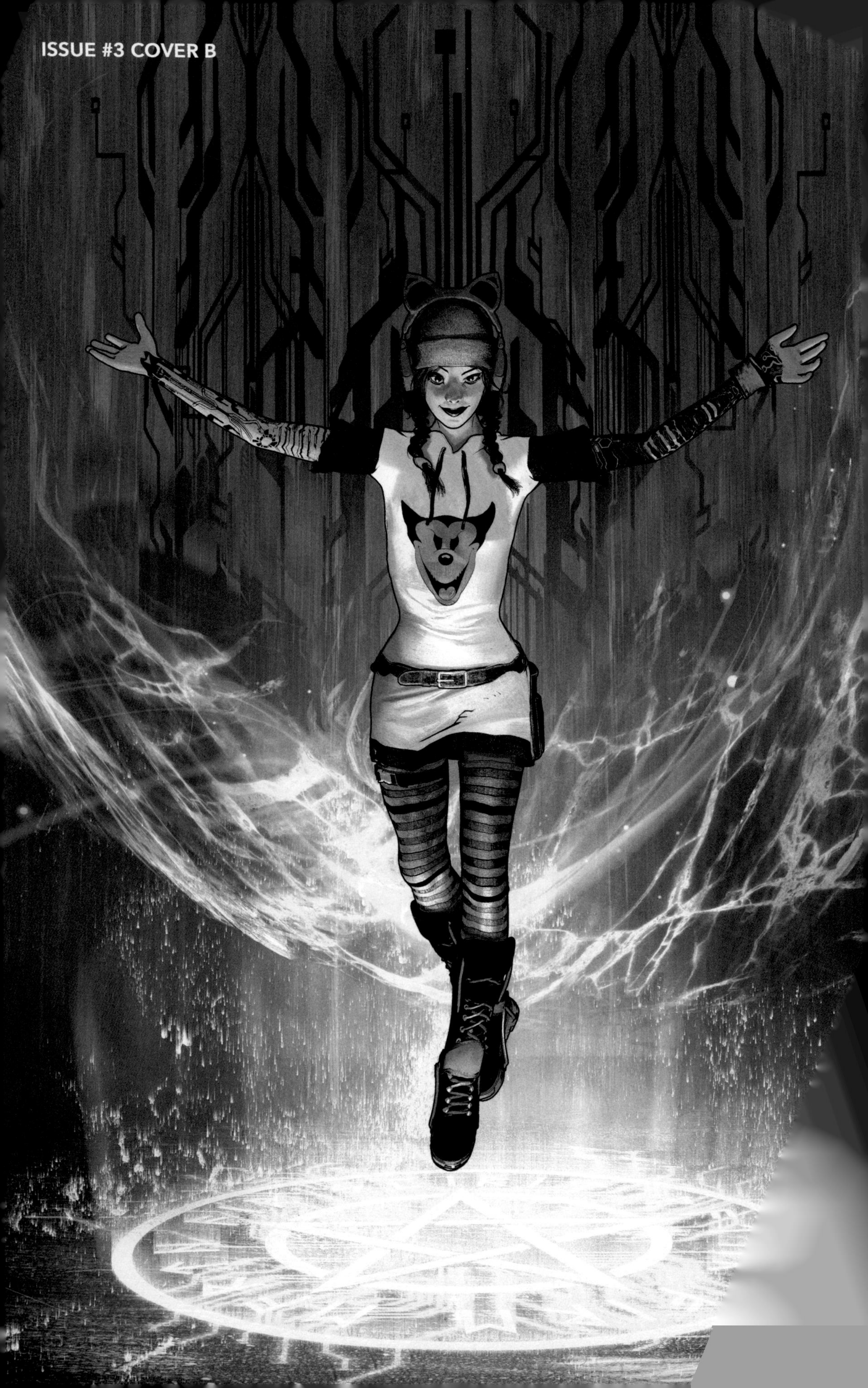

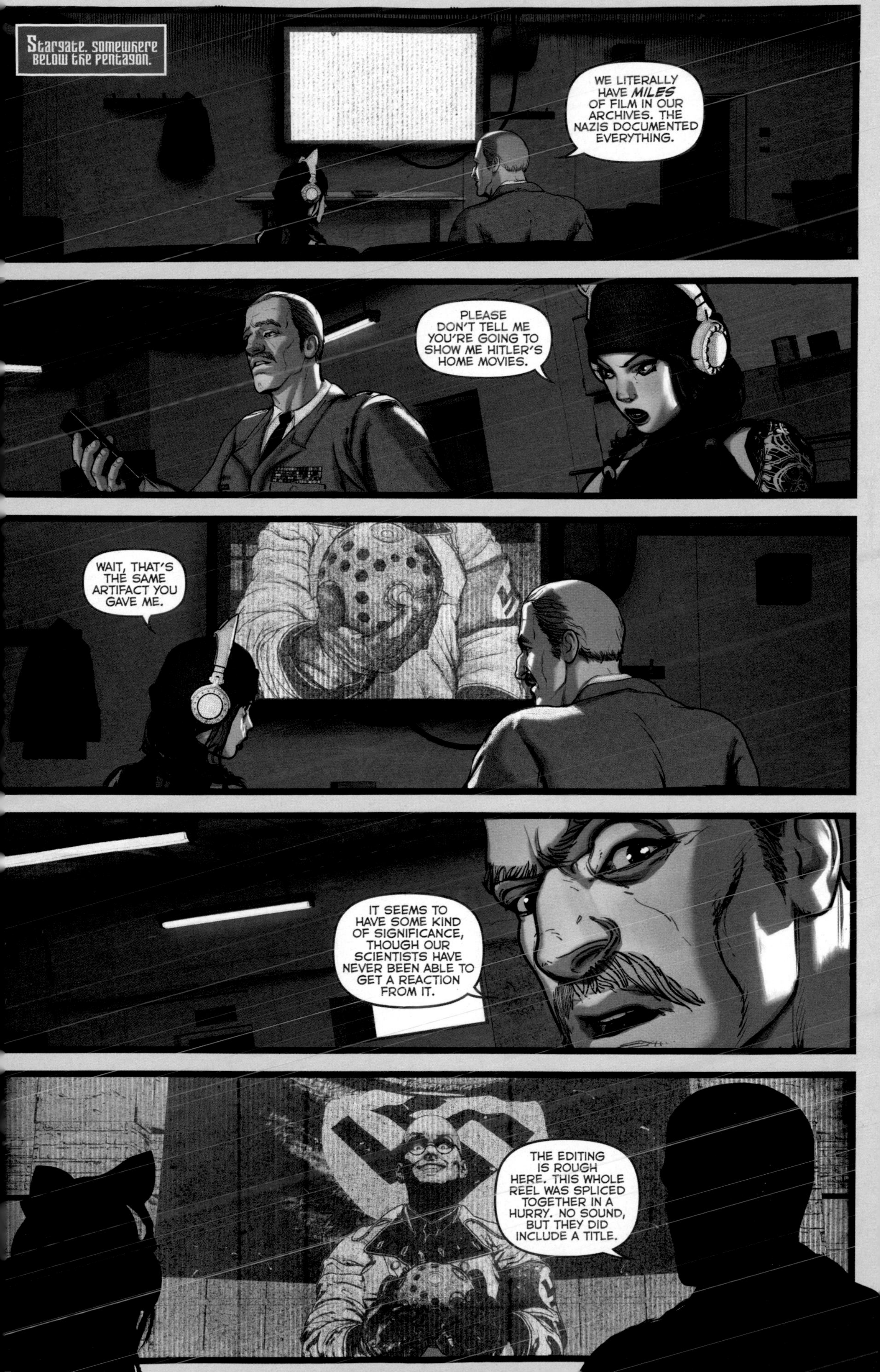
Stargate, somewhere below the Pentagon.
WE LITERALLY HAVE MILES OF FILM IN OUR ARCHIVES. THE NAZIS DOCUMENTED EVERYTHING.
PLEASE DON'T TELL ME YOU'RE GOING TO SHOW ME HITLER'S HOME MOVIES.
WAIT, THAT'S THE SAME ARTIFACT YOU GAVE ME.
IT SEEMS TO HAVE SOME KIND OF SIGNIFICANCE, THOUGH OUR SCIENTISTS HAVE NEVER BEEN ABLE TO GET A REACTION FROM IT.
THE EDITING IS ROUGH HERE. THIS WHOLE REEL WAS SPLICED TOGETHER IN A HURRY. NO SOUND, BUT THEY DID INCLUDE A TITLE.

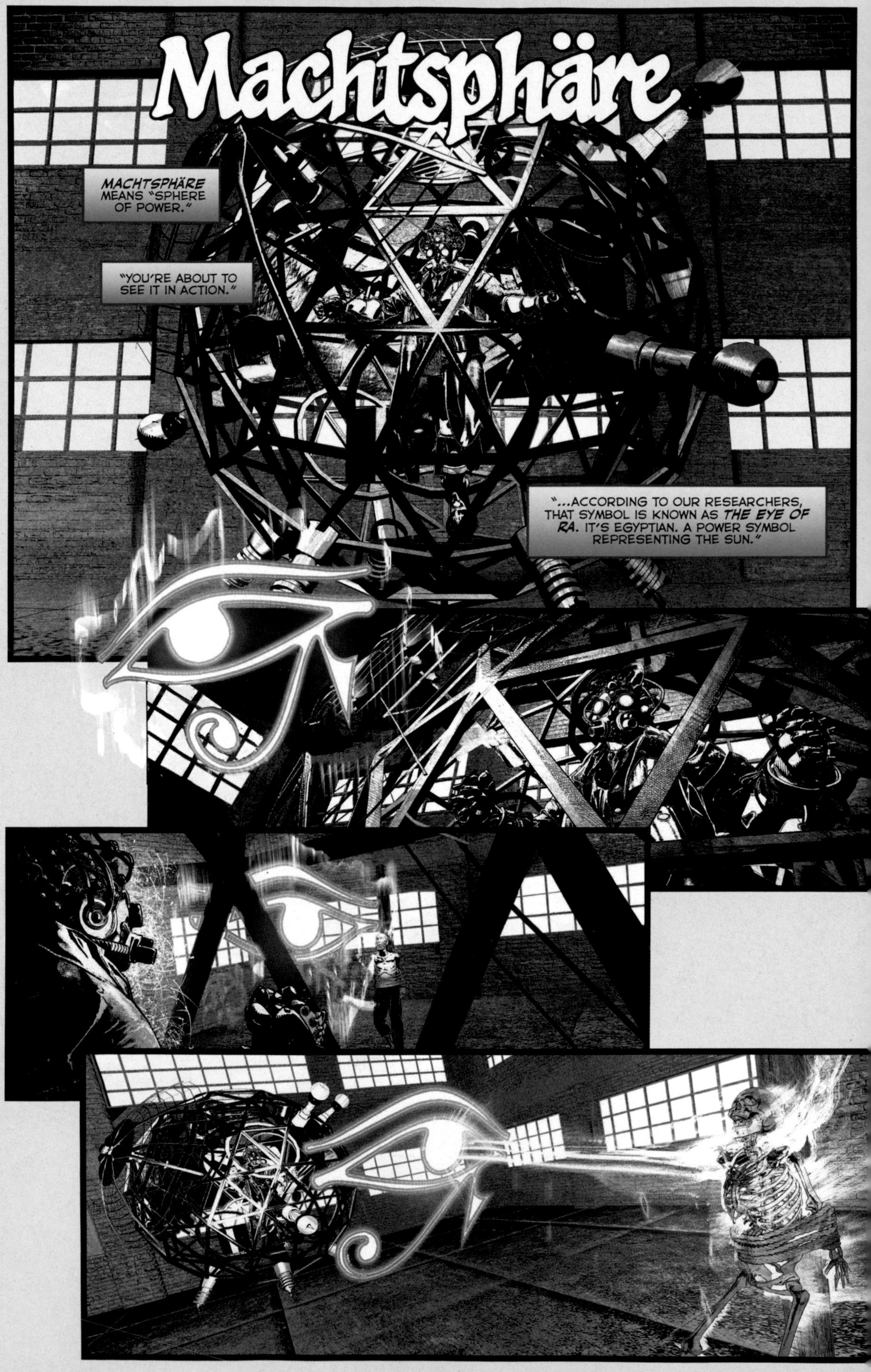
Machtsphäre
MACHTSPHÄRE MEANS "SPHERE OF POWER."
"YOU'RE ABOUT TO SEE IT IN ACTION."
"...ACCORDING TO OUR RESEARCHERS, THAT SYMBOL IS KNOWN AS THE EYE OF RA. IT'S EGYPTIAN. A POWER SYMBOL REPRESENTING THE SUN."

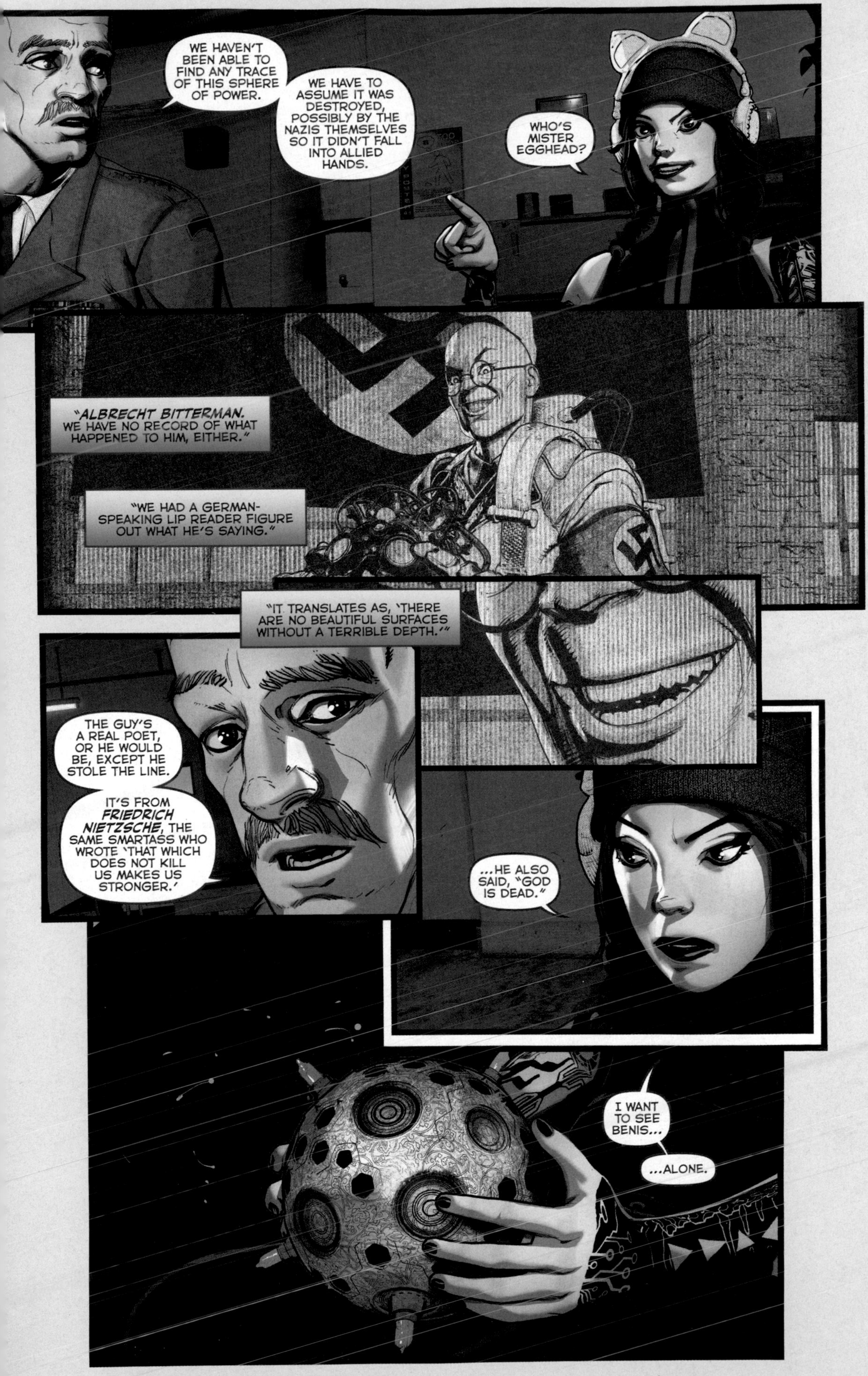
WE HAVEN'T BEEN ABLE TO FIND ANY TRACE OF THIS SPHERE OF POWER.
WE HAVE TO ASSUME IT WAS DESTROYED, POSSIBLY BY THE NAZIS THEMSELVES SO IT DIDN'T FALL INTO ALLIED HANDS.
WHO'S MISTER EGGHEAD?
"ALBRECHT BITTERMAN. WE HAVE NO RECORD OF WHAT HAPPENED TO HIM, EITHER."
"WE HAD A GERMAN-SPEAKING LIP READER FIGURE OUT WHAT HE'S SAYING."
"IT TRANSLATES AS, 'THERE ARE NO BEAUTIFUL SURFACES WITHOUT A TERRIBLE DEPTH.'"
THE GUY'S A REAL POET, OR HE WOULD BE, EXCEPT HE STOLE THE LINE.
IT'S FROM FRIEDRICH NIETZSCHE, THE SAME SMARTASS WHO WROTE 'THAT WHICH DOES NOT KILL US MAKES US STRONGER.'
...HE ALSO SAID, "GOD IS DEAD."
I WANT TO SEE BENIS...
...ALONE.

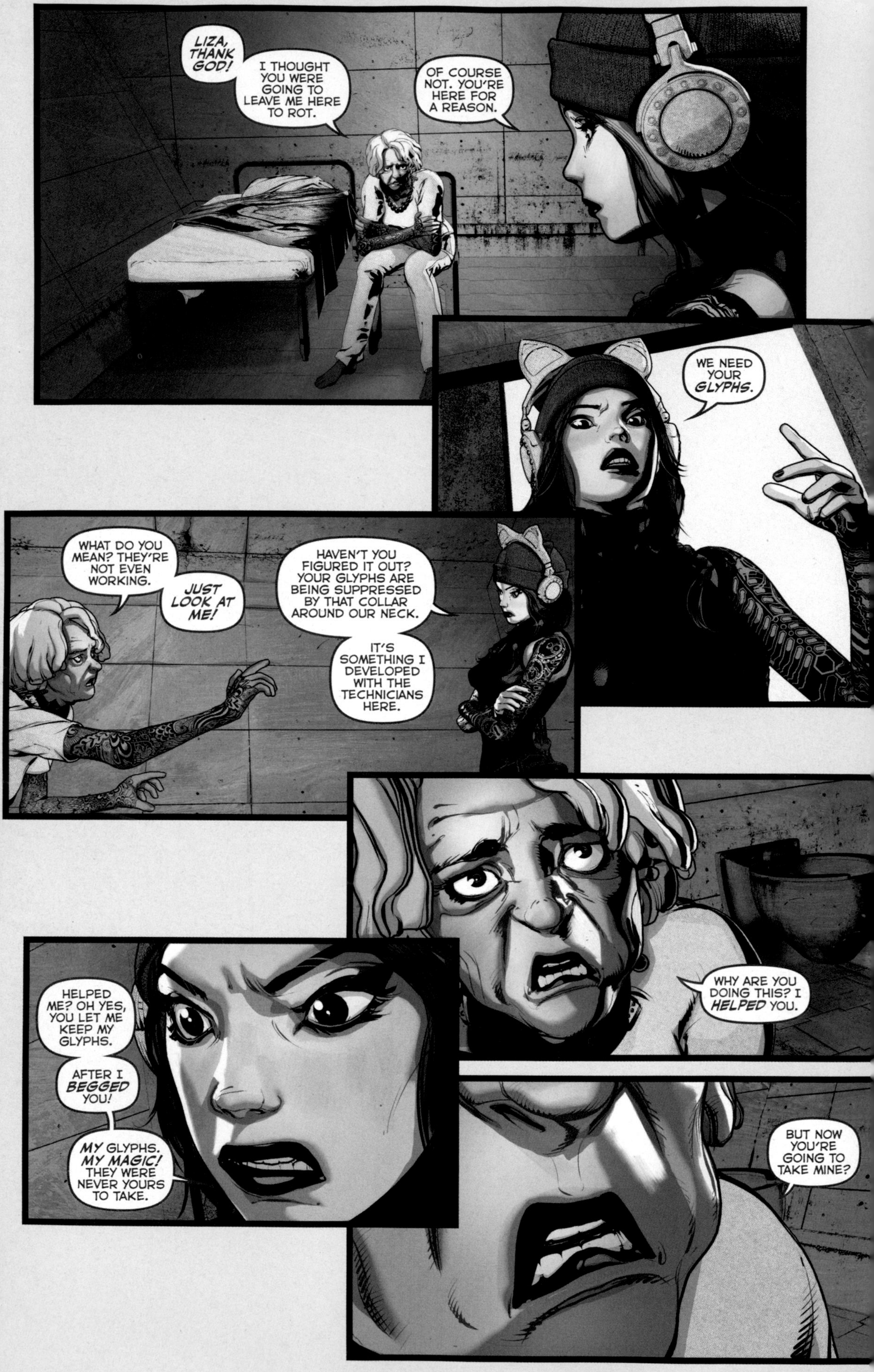
LIZA, THANK GOD!
I THOUGHT YOU WERE GOING TO LEAVE ME HERE TO ROT.
OF COURSE NOT. YOU'RE HERE FOR A REASON.
WE NEED YOUR GLYPHS.
WHAT DO YOU MEAN? THEY'RE NOT EVEN WORKING.
JUST LOOK AT ME!
HAVEN'T YOU FIGURED IT OUT? YOUR GLYPHS ARE BEING SUPPRESSED BY THAT COLLAR AROUND OUR NECK.
IT'S SOMETHING I DEVELOPED WITH THE TECHNICIANS HERE.
WHY ARE YOU DOING THIS? I HELPED YOU.
HELPED ME? OH YES, YOU LET ME KEEP MY GLYPHS.
AFTER I BEGGED YOU!
MY GLYPHS. MY MAGIC! THEY WERE NEVER YOURS TO TAKE.
BUT NOW YOU'RE GOING TO TAKE MINE?

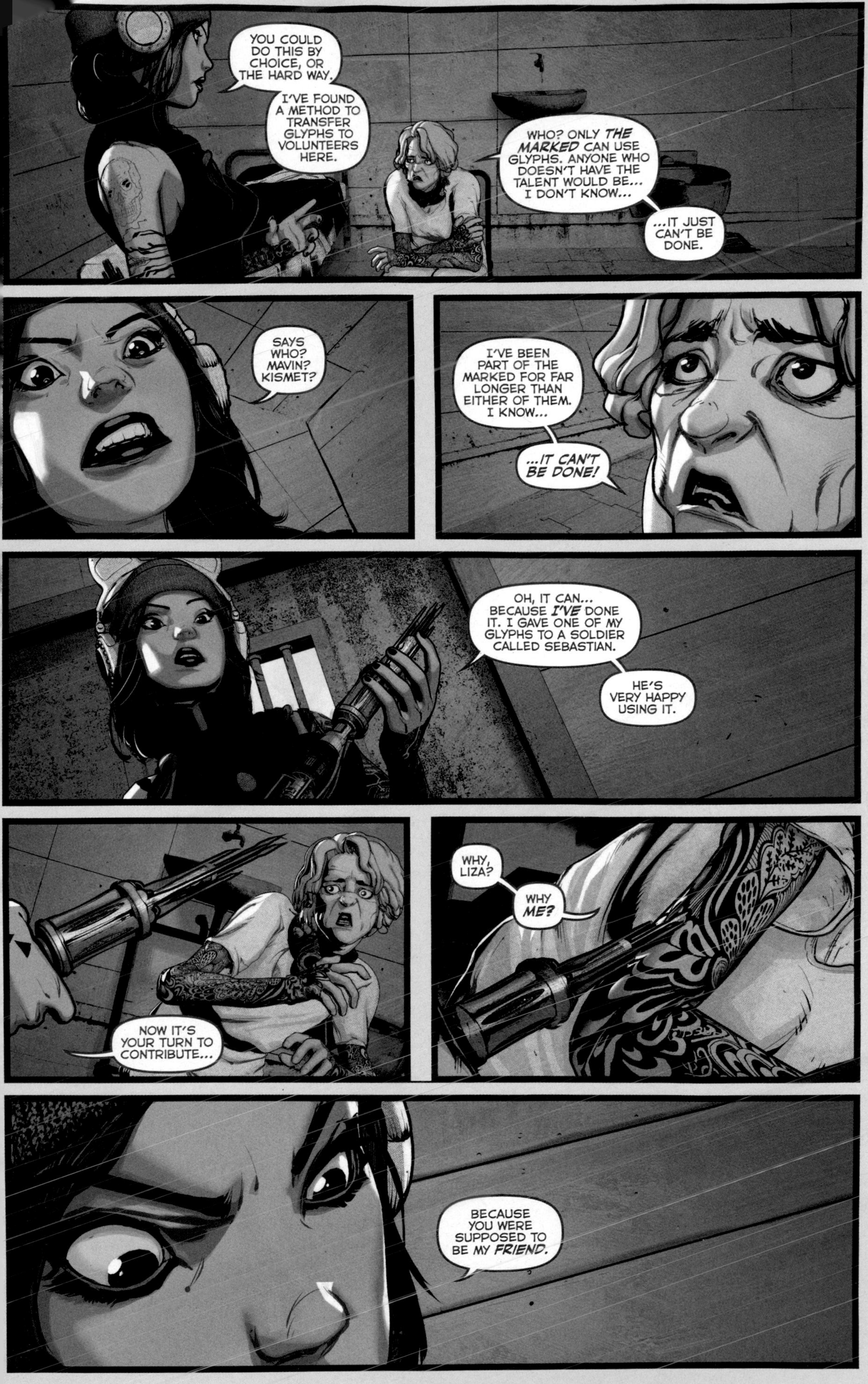

YOU COULD DO THIS BY CHOICE, OR THE HARD WAY.
I'VE FOUND A METHOD TO TRANSFER GLYPHS TO VOLUNTEERS HERE.
WHO? ONLY THE MARKED CAN USE GLYPHS. ANYONE WHO DOESN'T HAVE THE TALENT WOULD BE... I DON'T KNOW...
...IT JUST CAN'T BE DONE.
SAYS WHO? MAVIN? KISMET?
I'VE BEEN PART OF THE MARKED FOR FAR LONGER THAN EITHER OF THEM. I KNOW...
...IT CAN'T BE DONE!
OH, IT CAN... BECAUSE I'VE DONE IT. I GAVE ONE OF MY GLYPHS TO A SOLDIER CALLED SEBASTIAN.
HE'S VERY HAPPY USING IT.
NOW IT'S YOUR TURN TO CONTRIBUTE...
WHY, LIZA?
WHY ME?
BECAUSE YOU WERE SUPPOSED TO BE MY FRIEND.

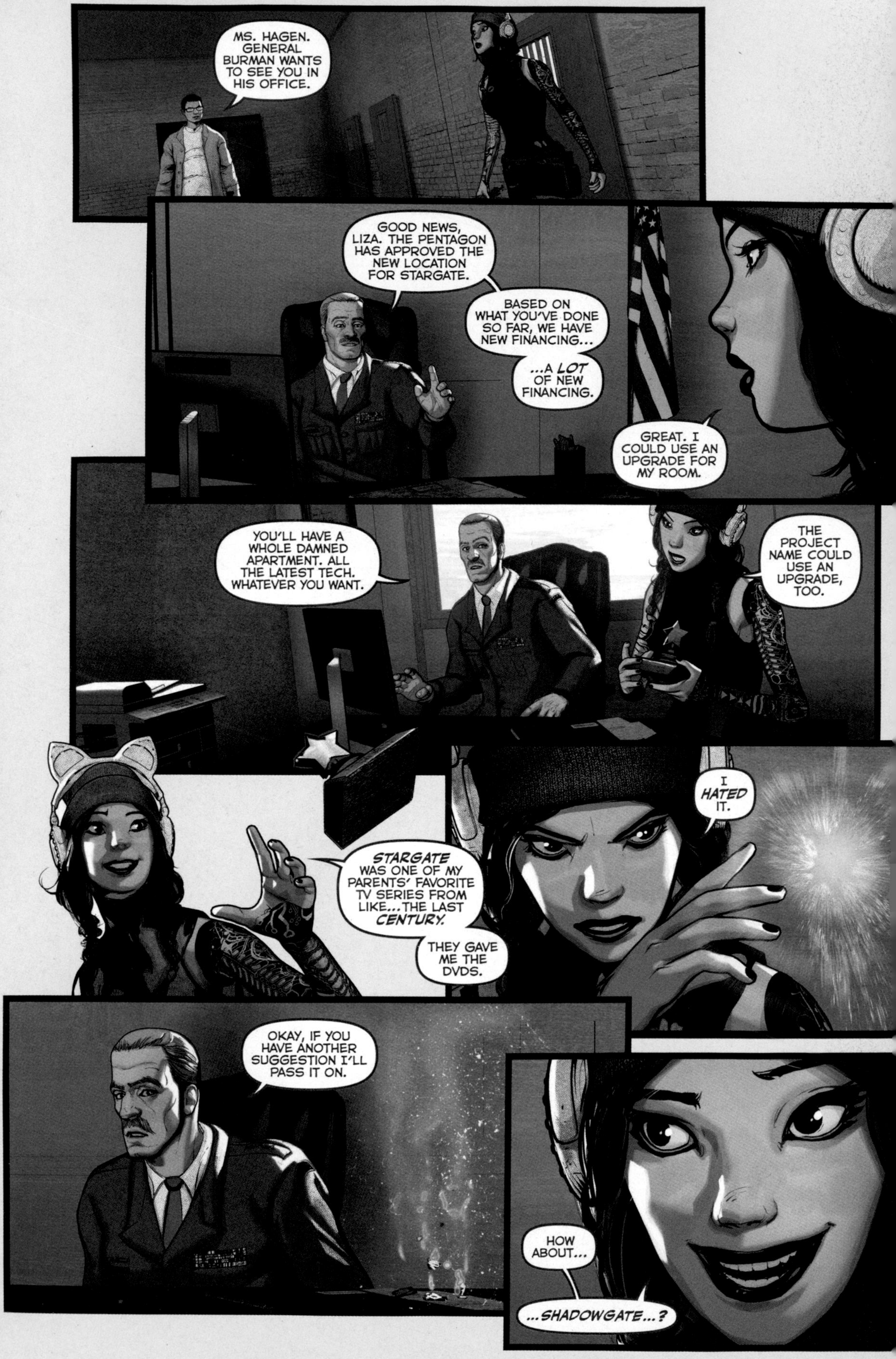
MS. HAGEN. GENERAL BURMAN WANTS TO SEE YOU IN HIS OFFICE.
GOOD NEWS, LIZA. THE PENTAGON HAS APPROVED THE NEW LOCATION FOR STARGATE.
BASED ON WHAT YOU'VE DONE SO FAR, WE HAVE NEW FINANCING...
...A *LOT* OF NEW FINANCING.
GREAT. I COULD USE AN UPGRADE FOR MY ROOM.
YOU'LL HAVE A WHOLE DAMNED APARTMENT. ALL THE LATEST TECH. WHATEVER YOU WANT.
THE PROJECT NAME COULD USE AN UPGRADE, TOO.
STARGATE WAS ONE OF MY PARENTS' FAVORITE TV SERIES FROM LIKE...THE LAST *CENTURY.*
THEY GAVE ME THE DVDS.
I *HATED* IT.
OKAY, IF YOU HAVE ANOTHER SUGGESTION I'LL PASS IT ON.
HOW ABOUT...
...SHADOWGATE...?

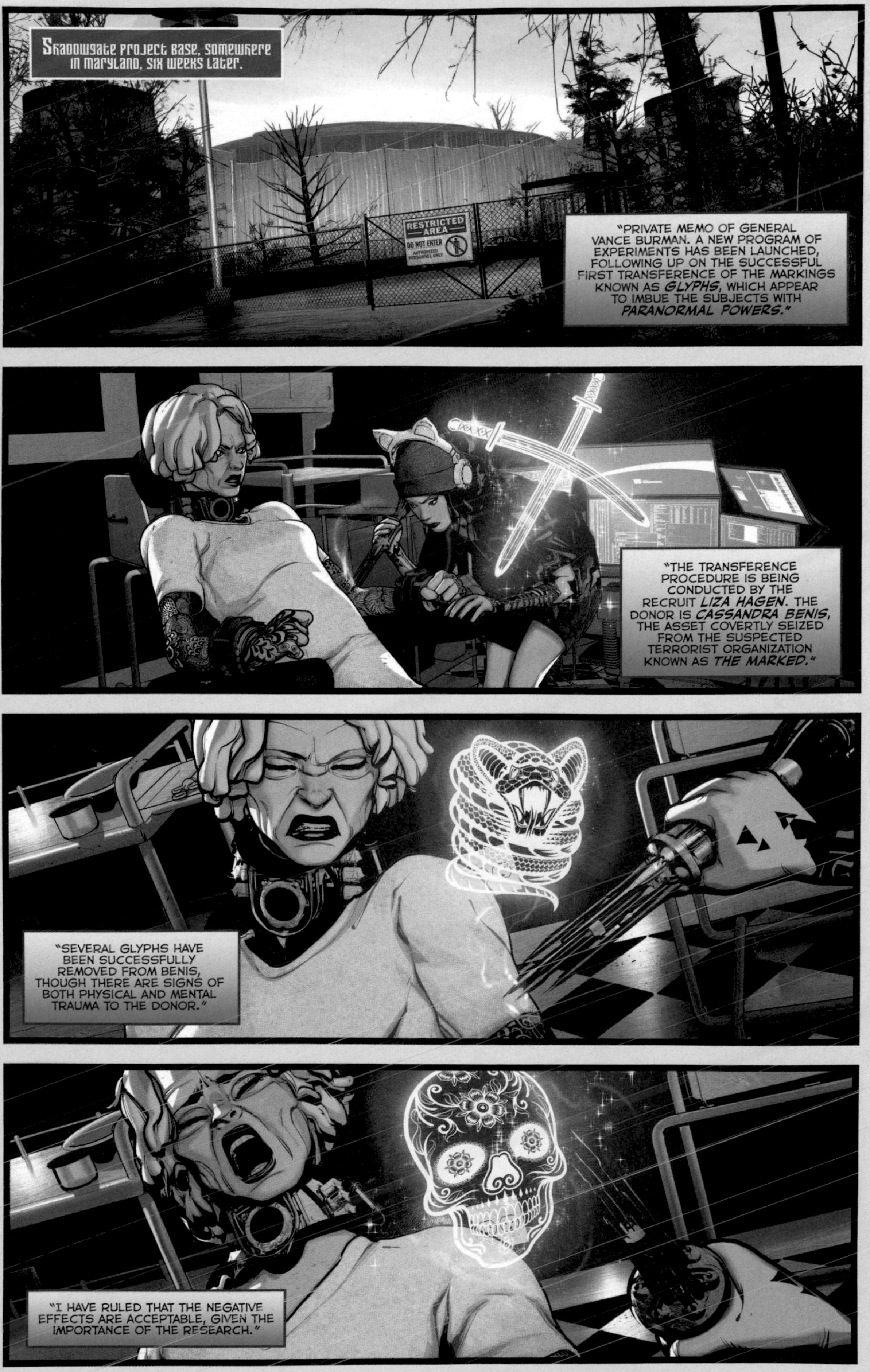
Shadowgate Project Base, somewhere in Maryland, six weeks later.
RESTRICTED AREA
DO NOT ENTER
"PRIVATE MEMO OF GENERAL VANCE BURMAN. A NEW PROGRAM OF EXPERIMENTS HAS BEEN LAUNCHED, FOLLOWING UP ON THE SUCCESSFUL FIRST TRANSFERENCE OF THE MARKINGS KNOWN AS *GLYPHS*, WHICH APPEAR TO IMBUE THE SUBJECTS WITH *PARANORMAL POWERS.*"
"THE TRANSFERENCE PROCEDURE IS BEING CONDUCTED BY THE RECRUIT *LIZA HAGEN*. THE DONOR IS *CASSANDRA BENIS*, THE ASSET COVERTLY SEIZED FROM THE SUSPECTED TERRORIST ORGANIZATION KNOWN AS *THE MARKED.*"
"SEVERAL GLYPHS HAVE BEEN SUCCESSFULLY REMOVED FROM BENIS, THOUGH THERE ARE SIGNS OF BOTH PHYSICAL AND MENTAL TRAUMA TO THE DONOR."
"I HAVE RULED THAT THE NEGATIVE EFFECTS ARE ACCEPTABLE, GIVEN THE IMPORTANCE OF THE RESEARCH."

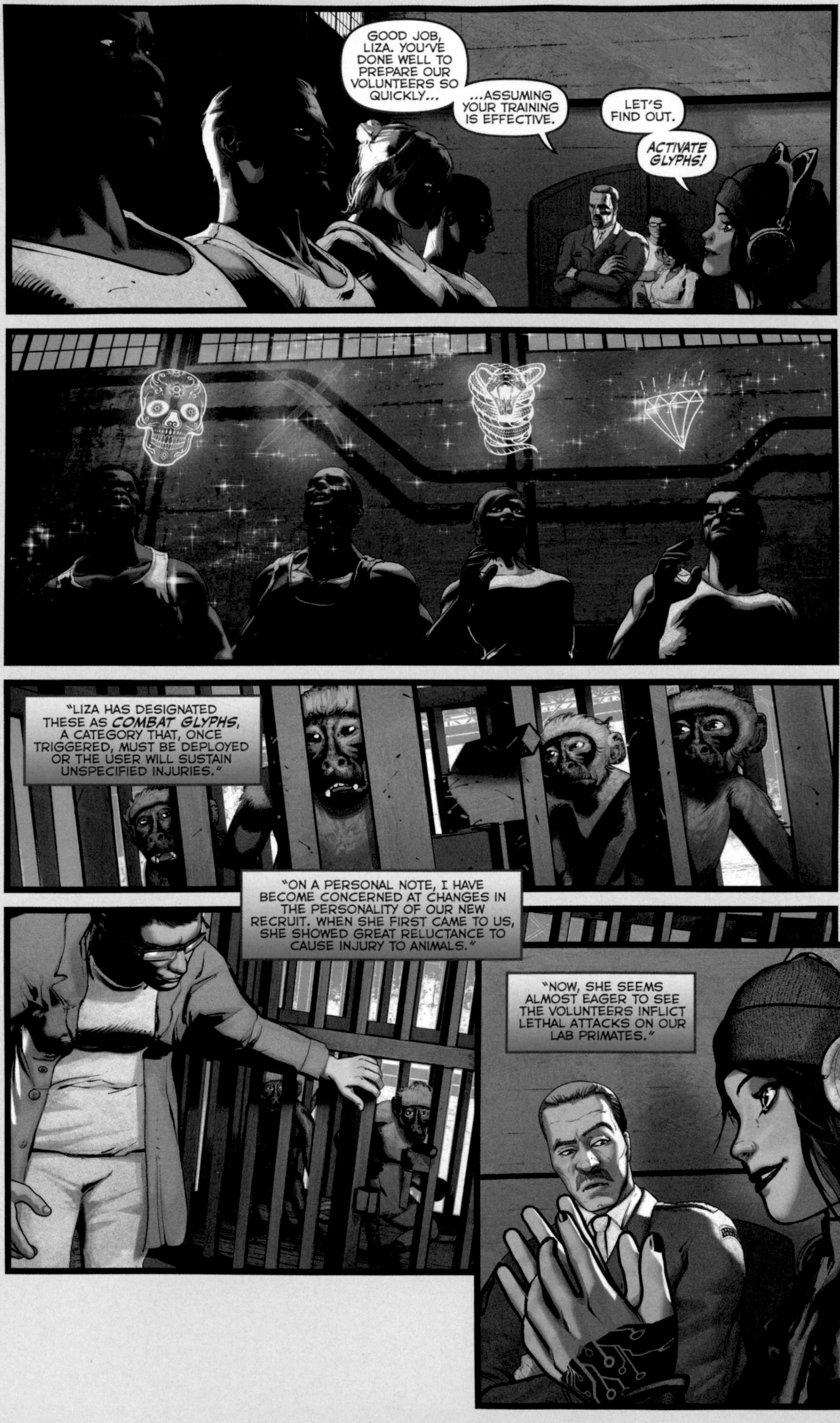
GOOD JOB, LIZA. YOU'VE DONE WELL TO PREPARE OUR VOLUNTEERS SO QUICKLY...
...ASSUMING YOUR TRAINING IS EFFECTIVE.
LET'S FIND OUT.
ACTIVATE GLYPHS!
"LIZA HAS DESIGNATED THESE AS COMBAT GLYPHS, A CATEGORY THAT, ONCE TRIGGERED, MUST BE DEPLOYED OR THE USER WILL SUSTAIN UNSPECIFIED INJURIES."
"ON A PERSONAL NOTE, I HAVE BECOME CONCERNED AT CHANGES IN THE PERSONALITY OF OUR NEW RECRUIT. WHEN SHE FIRST CAME TO US, SHE SHOWED GREAT RELUCTANCE TO CAUSE INJURY TO ANIMALS."
"NOW, SHE SEEMS ALMOST EAGER TO SEE THE VOLUNTEERS INFLICT LETHAL ATTACKS ON OUR LAB PRIMATES."

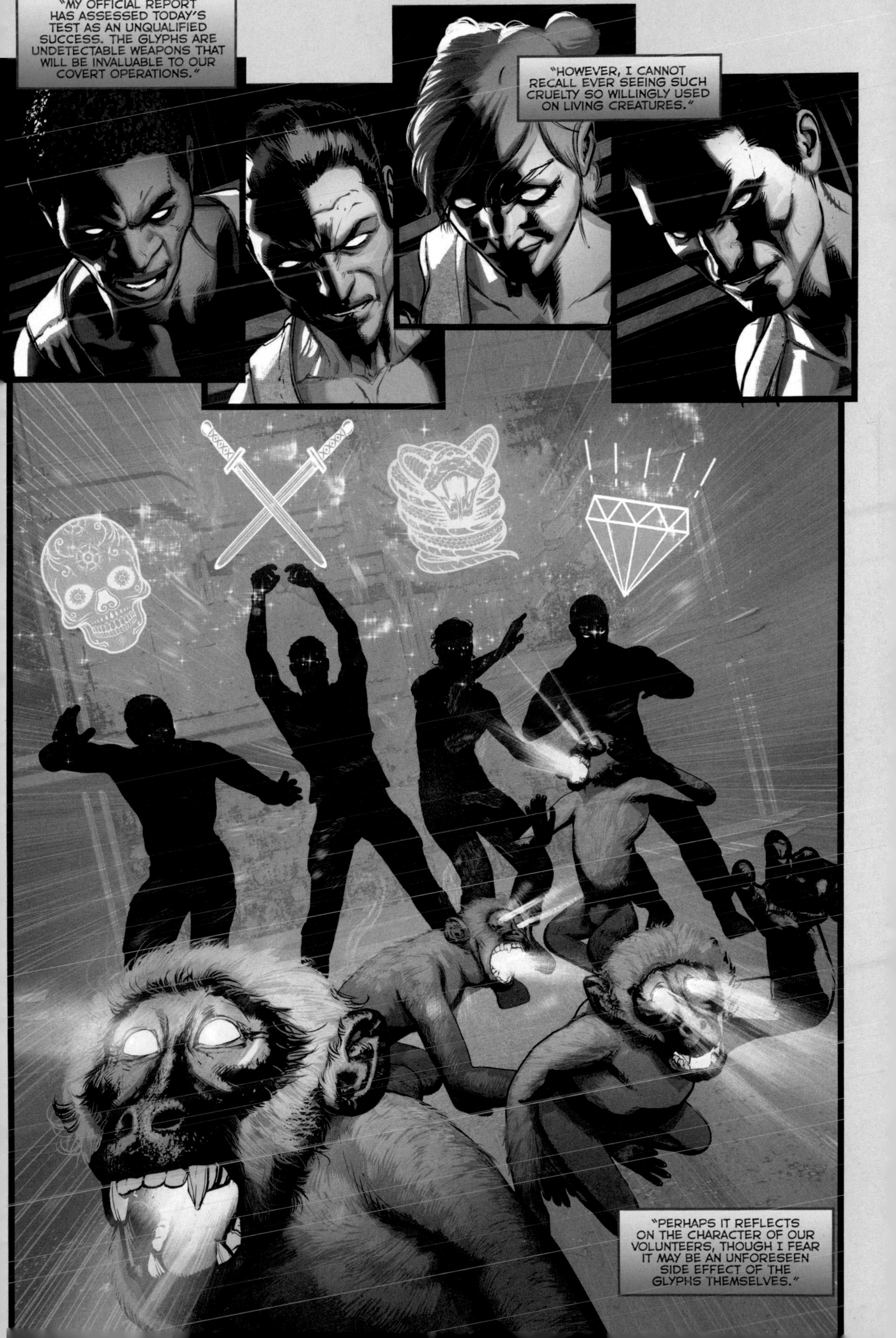
"MY OFFICIAL REPORT HAS ASSESSED TODAY'S TEST AS AN UNQUALIFIED SUCCESS. THE GLYPHS ARE UNDETECTABLE WEAPONS THAT WILL BE INVALUABLE TO OUR COVERT OPERATIONS."
"HOWEVER, I CANNOT RECALL EVER SEEING SUCH CRUELTY SO WILLINGLY USED ON LIVING CREATURES."
"PERHAPS IT REFLECTS ON THE CHARACTER OF OUR VOLUNTEERS, THOUGH I FEAR IT MAY BE AN UNFORESEEN SIDE EFFECT OF THE GLYPHS THEMSELVES."

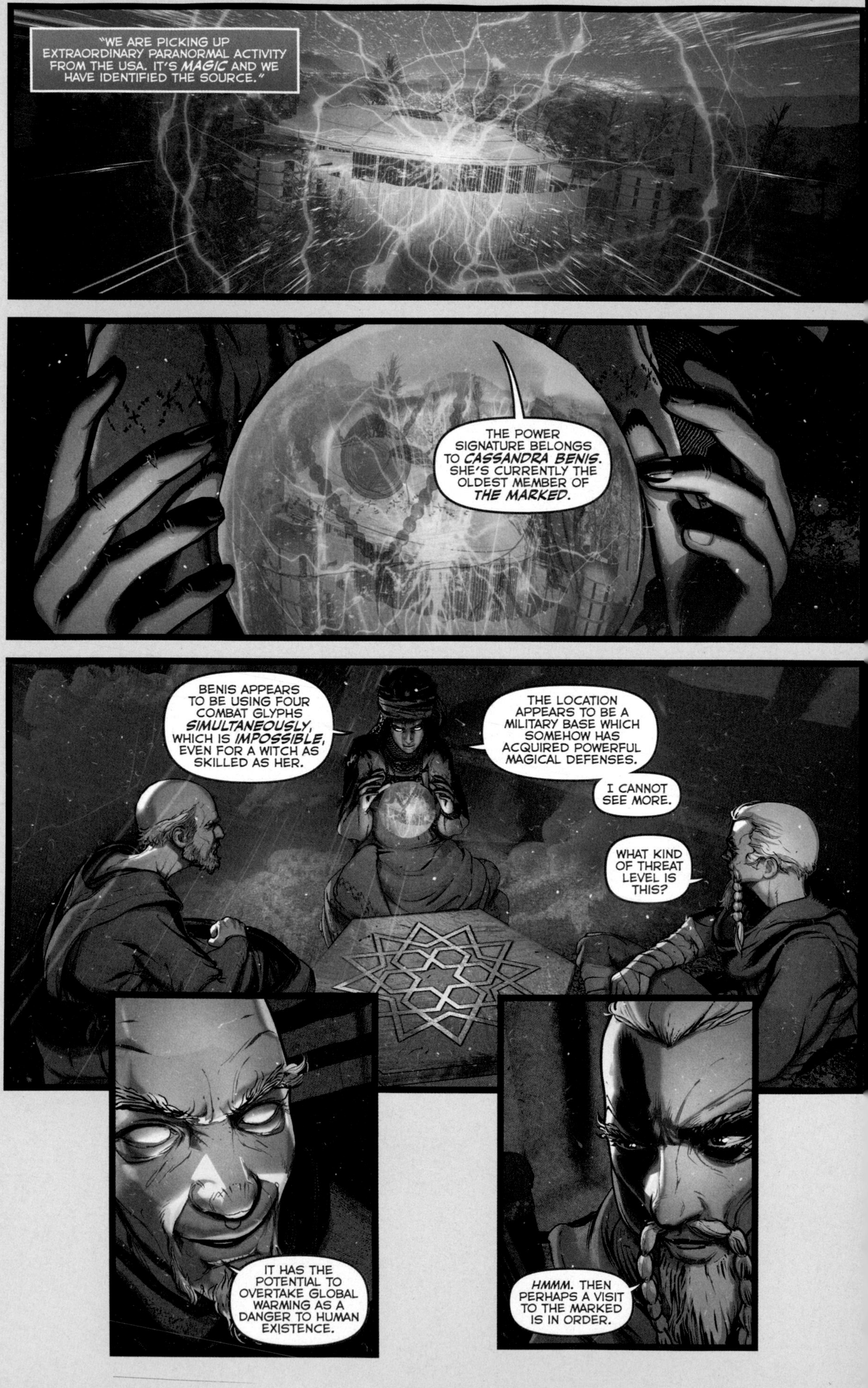
"WE ARE PICKING UP EXTRAORDINARY PARANORMAL ACTIVITY FROM THE USA. IT'S MAGIC AND WE HAVE IDENTIFIED THE SOURCE."
THE POWER SIGNATURE BELONGS TO CASSANDRA BENIS. SHE'S CURRENTLY THE OLDEST MEMBER OF THE MARKED.
BENIS APPEARS TO BE USING FOUR COMBAT GLYPHS SIMULTANEOUSLY, WHICH IS IMPOSSIBLE, EVEN FOR A WITCH AS SKILLED AS HER.
THE LOCATION APPEARS TO BE A MILITARY BASE WHICH SOMEHOW HAS ACQUIRED POWERFUL MAGICAL DEFENSES.
I CANNOT SEE MORE.
WHAT KIND OF THREAT LEVEL IS THIS?
IT HAS THE POTENTIAL TO OVERTAKE GLOBAL WARMING AS A DANGER TO HUMAN EXISTENCE.
HMMM. THEN PERHAPS A VISIT TO THE MARKED IS IN ORDER.

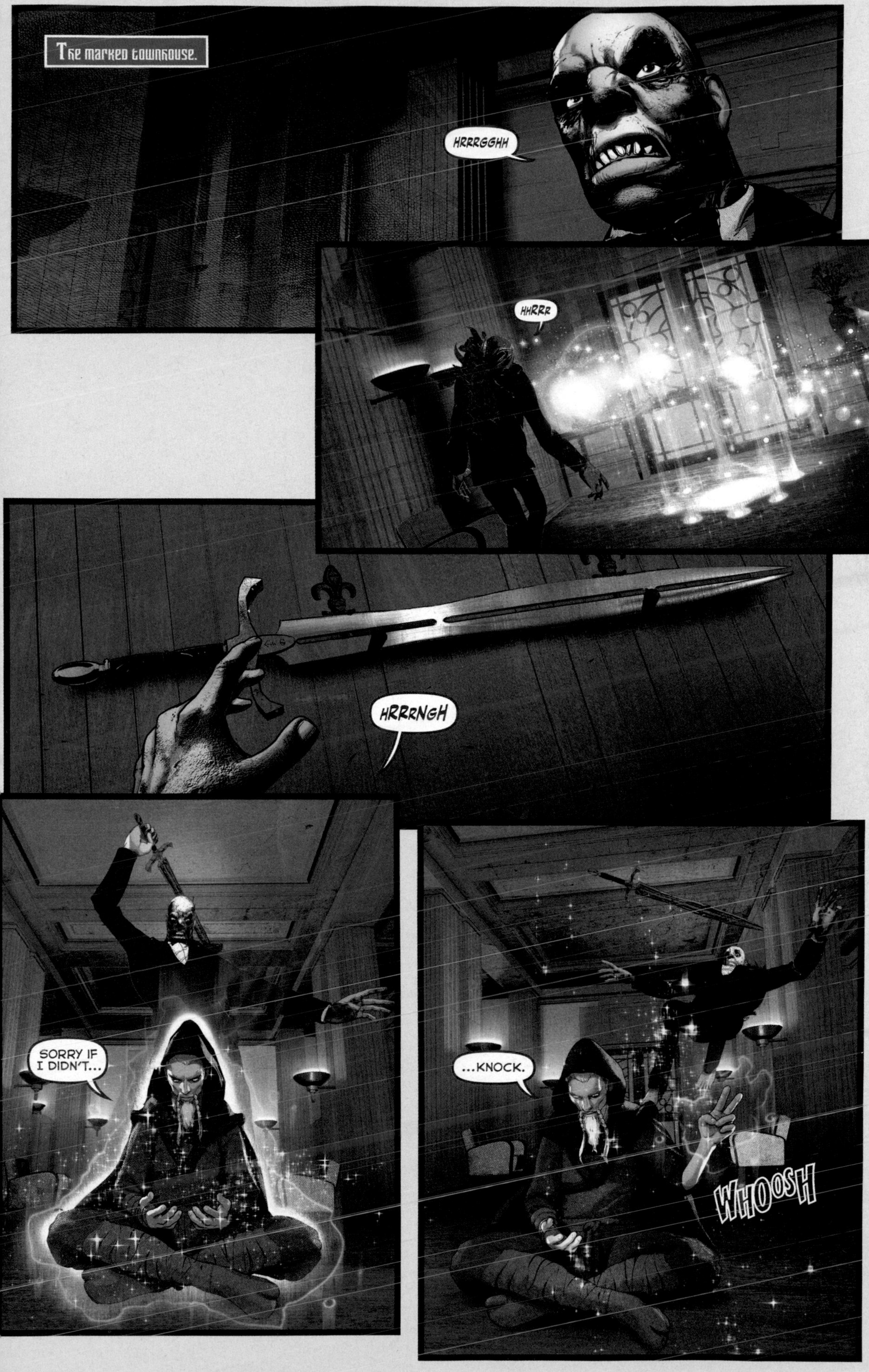
The marked townhouse.
HRRRGGHH
HHRRR
HRRRNGH
SORRY IF I DIDN'T...
...KNOCK.
WHOOSH

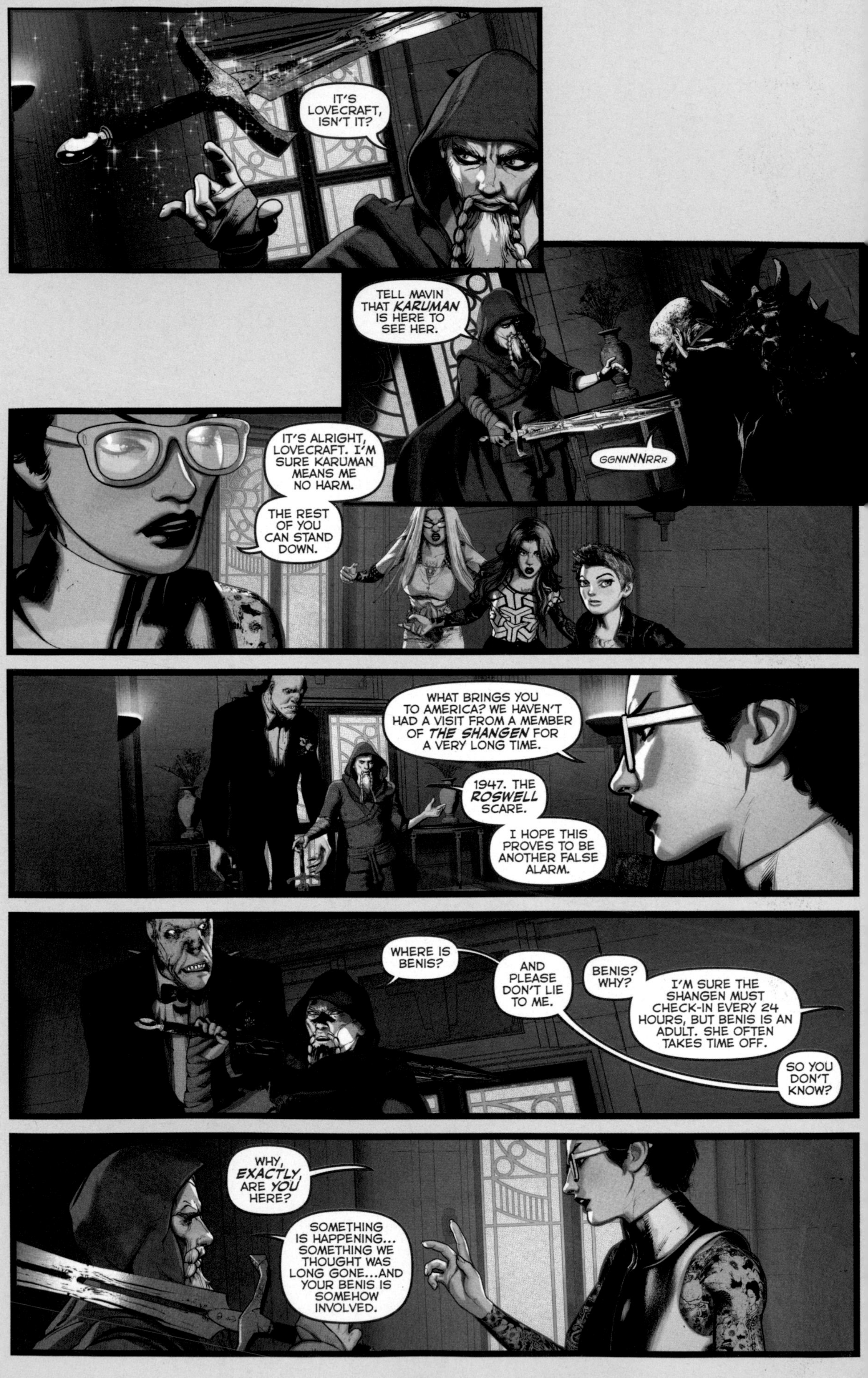
IT'S LOVECRAFT, ISN'T IT?
TELL MAVIN THAT KARUMAN IS HERE TO SEE HER.
GGNNNNRRR
IT'S ALRIGHT, LOVECRAFT. I'M SURE KARUMAN MEANS ME NO HARM.
THE REST OF YOU CAN STAND DOWN.
WHAT BRINGS YOU TO AMERICA? WE HAVEN'T HAD A VISIT FROM A MEMBER OF THE SHANGEN FOR A VERY LONG TIME.
1947. THE ROSWELL SCARE.
I HOPE THIS PROVES TO BE ANOTHER FALSE ALARM.
WHERE IS BENIS?
AND PLEASE DON'T LIE TO ME.
BENIS? WHY?
I'M SURE THE SHANGEN MUST CHECK-IN EVERY 24 HOURS, BUT BENIS IS AN ADULT. SHE OFTEN TAKES TIME OFF.
SO YOU DON'T KNOW?
WHY, EXACTLY, ARE YOU HERE?
SOMETHING IS HAPPENING... SOMETHING WE THOUGHT WAS LONG GONE...AND YOUR BENIS IS SOMEHOW INVOLVED.

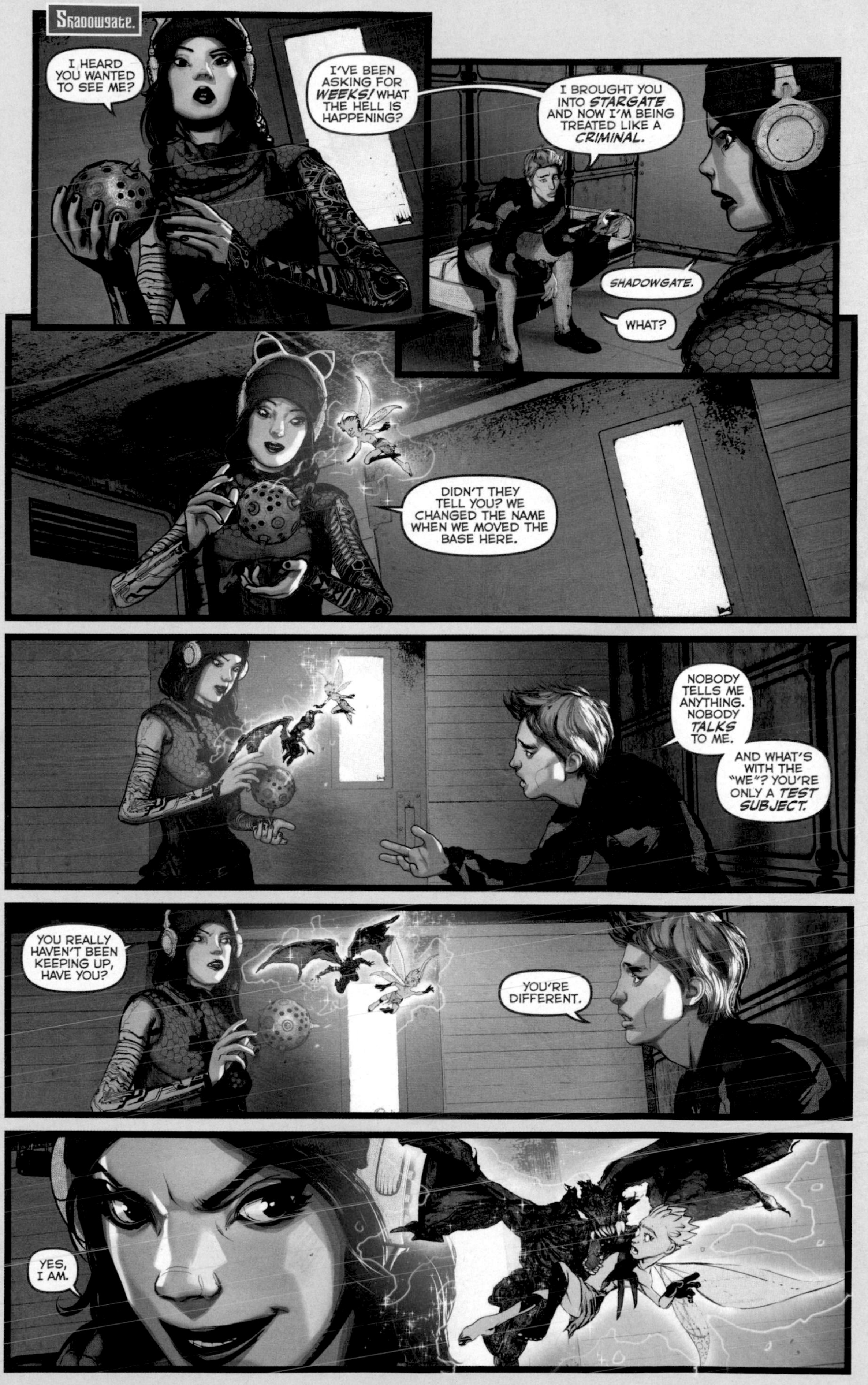
Shadowgate.
I HEARD YOU WANTED TO SEE ME?
I'VE BEEN ASKING FOR *WEEKS!* WHAT THE HELL IS HAPPENING?
I BROUGHT YOU INTO *STARGATE* AND NOW I'M BEING TREATED LIKE A *CRIMINAL.*
SHADOWGATE.
WHAT?
DIDN'T THEY TELL YOU? WE CHANGED THE NAME WHEN WE MOVED THE BASE HERE.
NOBODY TELLS ME ANYTHING. NOBODY *TALKS* TO ME.
AND WHAT'S WITH THE "WE"? YOU'RE ONLY A *TEST SUBJECT.*
YOU REALLY HAVEN'T BEEN KEEPING UP, HAVE YOU?
YOU'RE DIFFERENT.
YES, I AM.

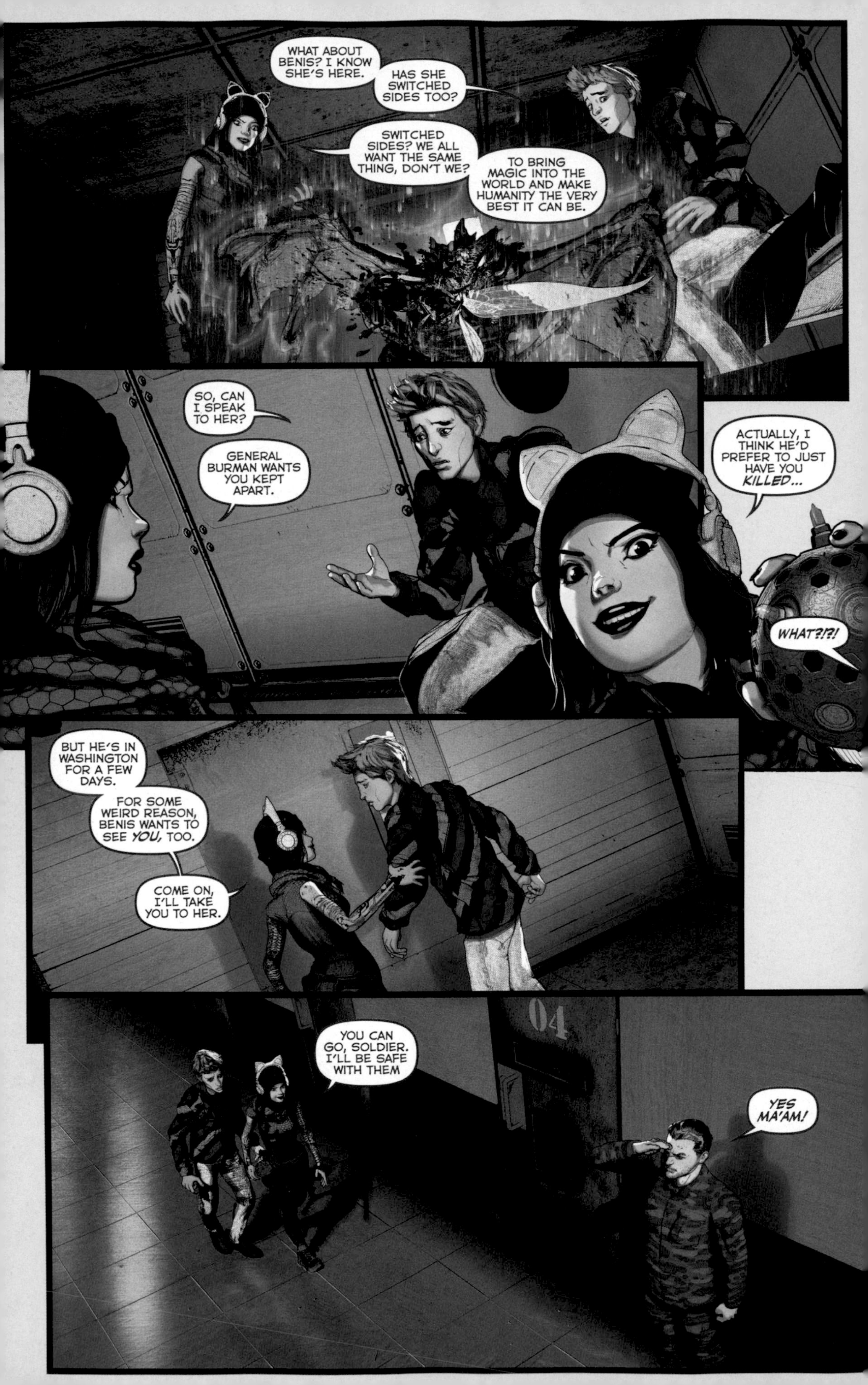
WHAT ABOUT BENIS? I KNOW SHE'S HERE.
HAS SHE SWITCHED SIDES TOO?
SWITCHED SIDES? WE ALL WANT THE SAME THING, DON'T WE?
TO BRING MAGIC INTO THE WORLD AND MAKE HUMANITY THE VERY BEST IT CAN BE.
SO, CAN I SPEAK TO HER?
GENERAL BURMAN WANTS YOU KEPT APART.
ACTUALLY, I THINK HE'D PREFER TO JUST HAVE YOU *KILLED...*
WHAT?!?!
BUT HE'S IN WASHINGTON FOR A FEW DAYS.
FOR SOME WEIRD REASON, BENIS WANTS TO SEE *YOU,* TOO.
COME ON, I'LL TAKE YOU TO HER.
04
YOU CAN GO, SOLDIER. I'LL BE SAFE WITH THEM
YES MA'AM!

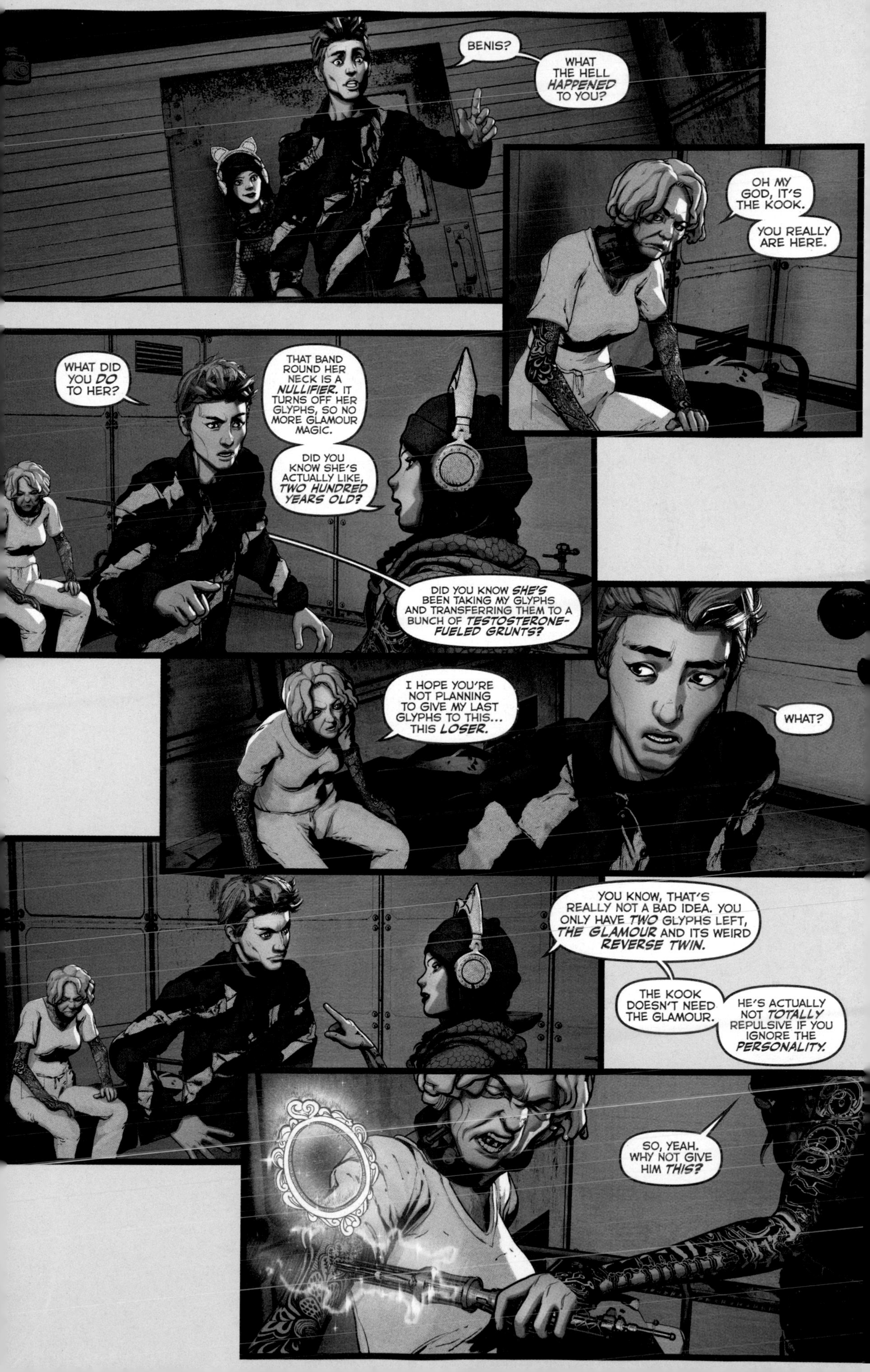
BENIS?
WHAT THE HELL *HAPPENED* TO YOU?
OH MY GOD, IT'S THE KOOK.
YOU REALLY ARE HERE.
WHAT DID YOU *DO* TO HER?
THAT BAND ROUND HER NECK IS A *NULLIFIER.* IT TURNS OFF HER GLYPHS, SO NO MORE GLAMOUR MAGIC.
DID YOU KNOW SHE'S ACTUALLY LIKE, *TWO HUNDRED YEARS OLD?*
DID YOU KNOW *SHE'S* BEEN TAKING MY GLYPHS AND TRANSFERRING THEM TO A BUNCH OF *TESTOSTERONE-FUELED GRUNTS?*
I HOPE YOU'RE NOT PLANNING TO GIVE MY LAST GLYPHS TO THIS... THIS *LOSER.*
WHAT?
YOU KNOW, THAT'S REALLY NOT A BAD IDEA. YOU ONLY HAVE *TWO* GLYPHS LEFT, *THE GLAMOUR* AND ITS WEIRD *REVERSE TWIN.*
THE KOOK DOESN'T NEED THE GLAMOUR.
HE'S ACTUALLY NOT *TOTALLY* REPULSIVE IF YOU IGNORE THE *PERSONALITY.*
SO, YEAH. WHY NOT GIVE HIM *THIS?*

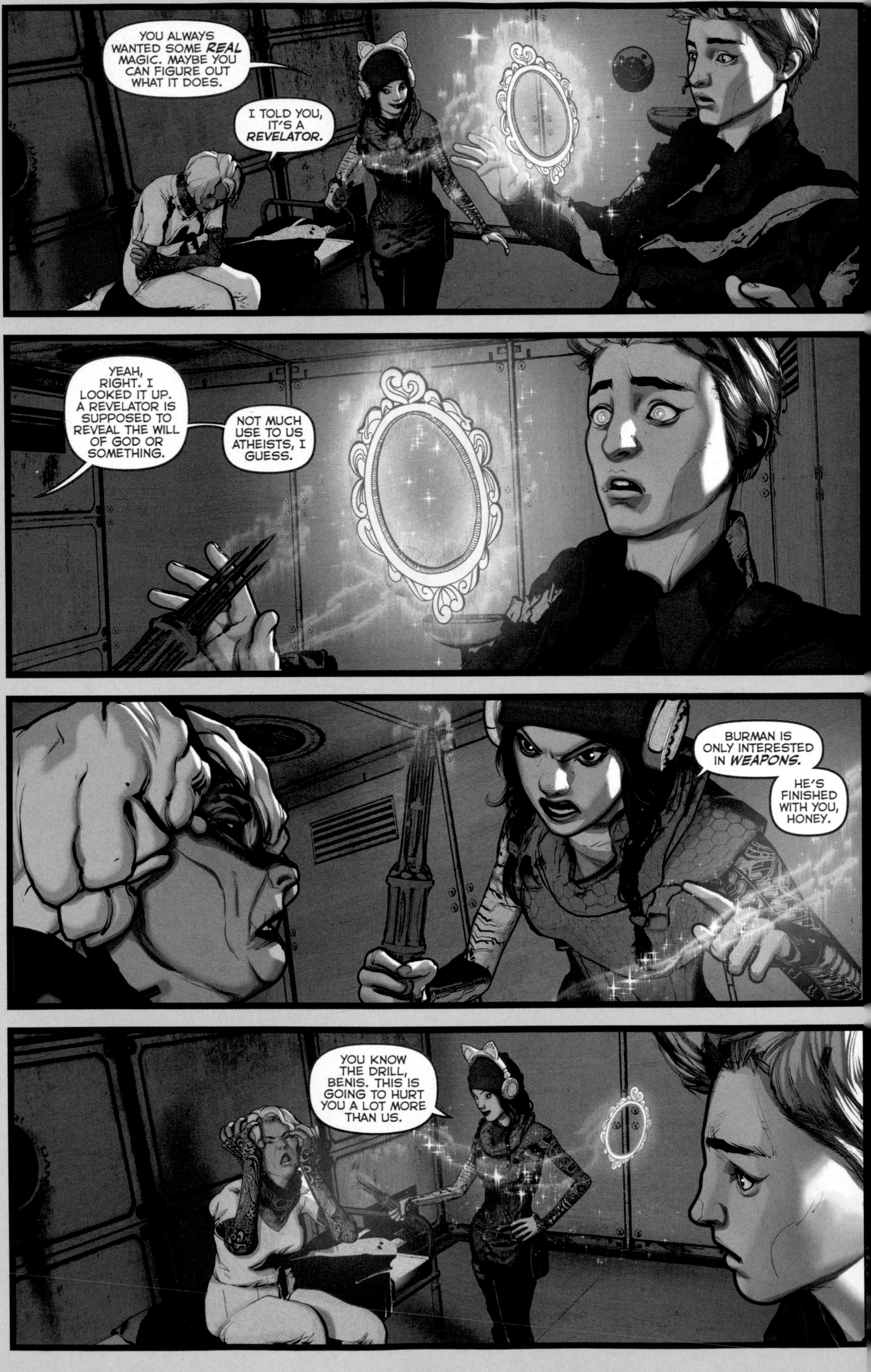
YOU ALWAYS WANTED SOME *REAL* MAGIC. MAYBE YOU CAN FIGURE OUT WHAT IT DOES.
I TOLD YOU, IT'S A *REVELATOR.*
YEAH, RIGHT. I LOOKED IT UP. A REVELATOR IS SUPPOSED TO REVEAL THE WILL OF GOD OR SOMETHING.
NOT MUCH USE TO US ATHEISTS, I GUESS.
BURMAN IS ONLY INTERESTED IN *WEAPONS.*
HE'S FINISHED WITH YOU, HONEY.
YOU KNOW THE DRILL, BENIS. THIS IS GOING TO HURT YOU A LOT MORE THAN US.

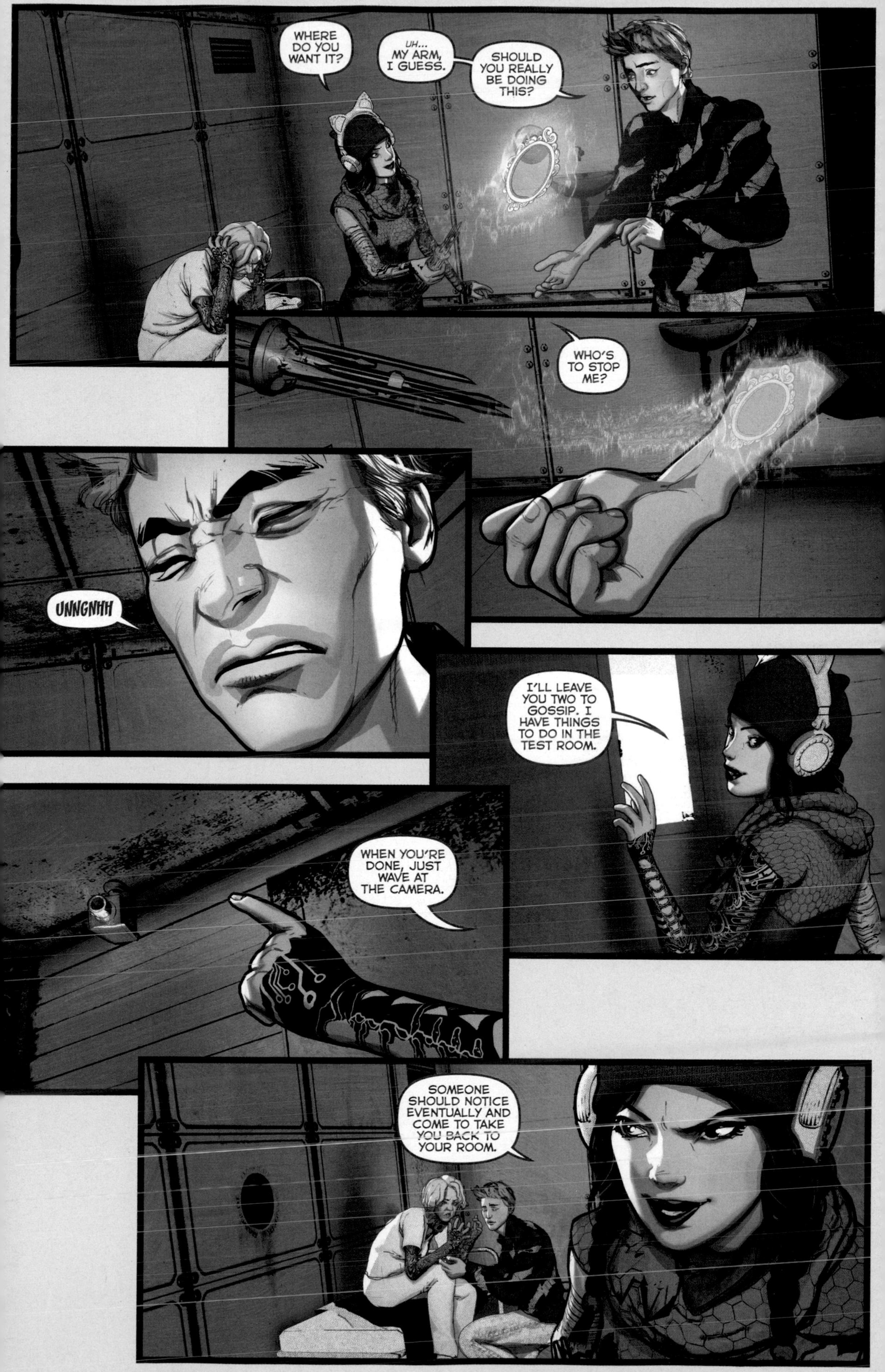
WHERE DO YOU WANT IT?
UH... MY ARM, I GUESS.
SHOULD YOU REALLY BE DOING THIS?
WHO'S TO STOP ME?
UNNGNHH
I'LL LEAVE YOU TWO TO GOSSIP. I HAVE THINGS TO DO IN THE TEST ROOM.
WHEN YOU'RE DONE, JUST WAVE AT THE CAMERA.
SOMEONE SHOULD NOTICE EVENTUALLY AND COME TO TAKE YOU BACK TO YOUR ROOM.

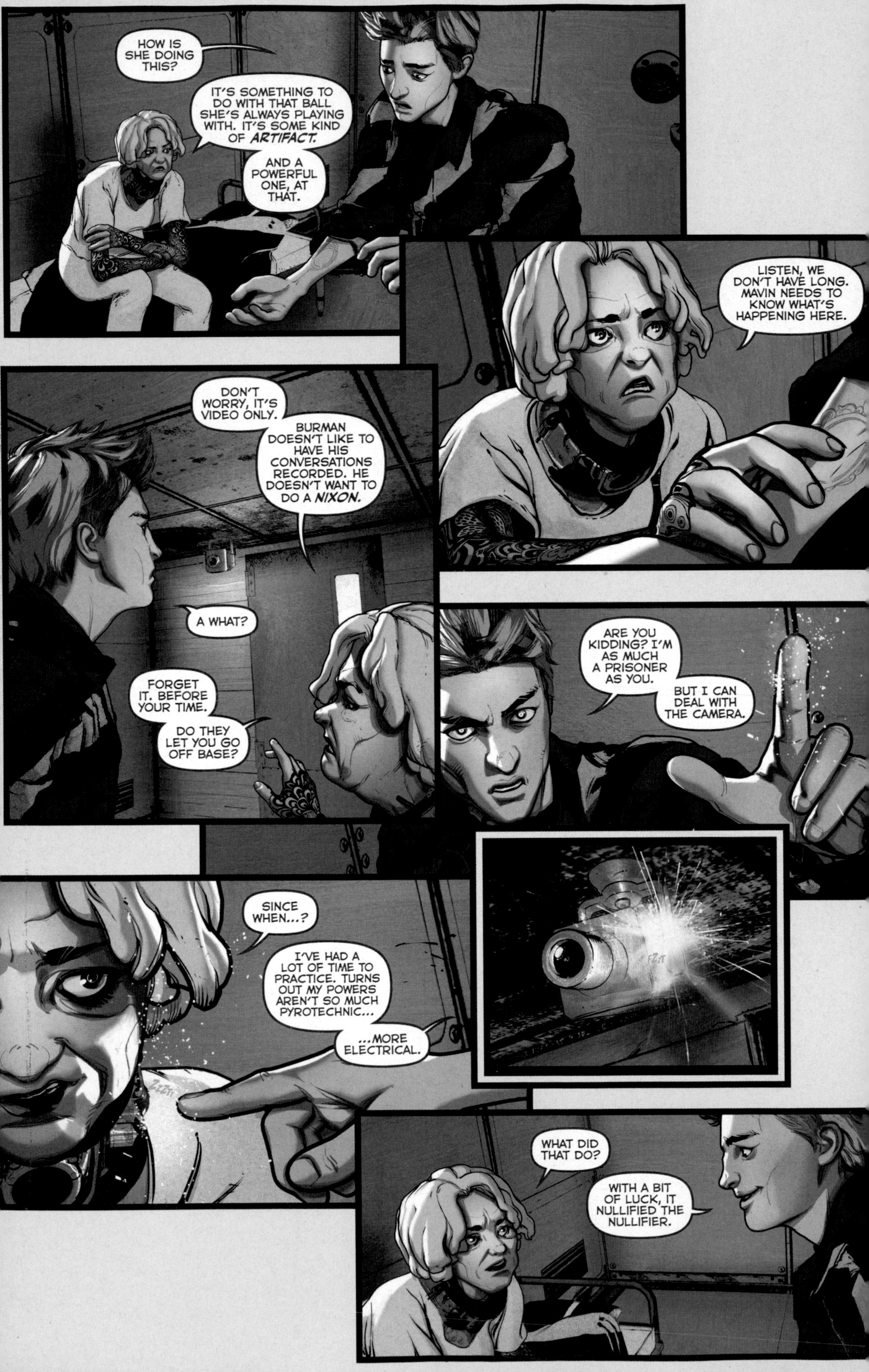
HOW IS SHE DOING THIS?
IT'S SOMETHING TO DO WITH THAT BALL SHE'S ALWAYS PLAYING WITH. IT'S SOME KIND OF *ARTIFACT.*
AND A POWERFUL ONE, AT THAT.
LISTEN, WE DON'T HAVE LONG. MAVIN NEEDS TO KNOW WHAT'S HAPPENING HERE.
DON'T WORRY, IT'S VIDEO ONLY.
BURMAN DOESN'T LIKE TO HAVE HIS CONVERSATIONS RECORDED. HE DOESN'T WANT TO DO A *NIXON.*
A WHAT?
FORGET IT. BEFORE YOUR TIME.
DO THEY LET YOU GO OFF BASE?
ARE YOU KIDDING? I'M AS MUCH A PRISONER AS YOU.
BUT I CAN DEAL WITH THE CAMERA.
SINCE WHEN...?
I'VE HAD A LOT OF TIME TO PRACTICE. TURNS OUT MY POWERS AREN'T SO MUCH PYROTECHNIC...
...MORE ELECTRICAL.
FZZT
WHAT DID THAT DO?
WITH A BIT OF LUCK, IT NULLIFIED THE NULLIFIER.

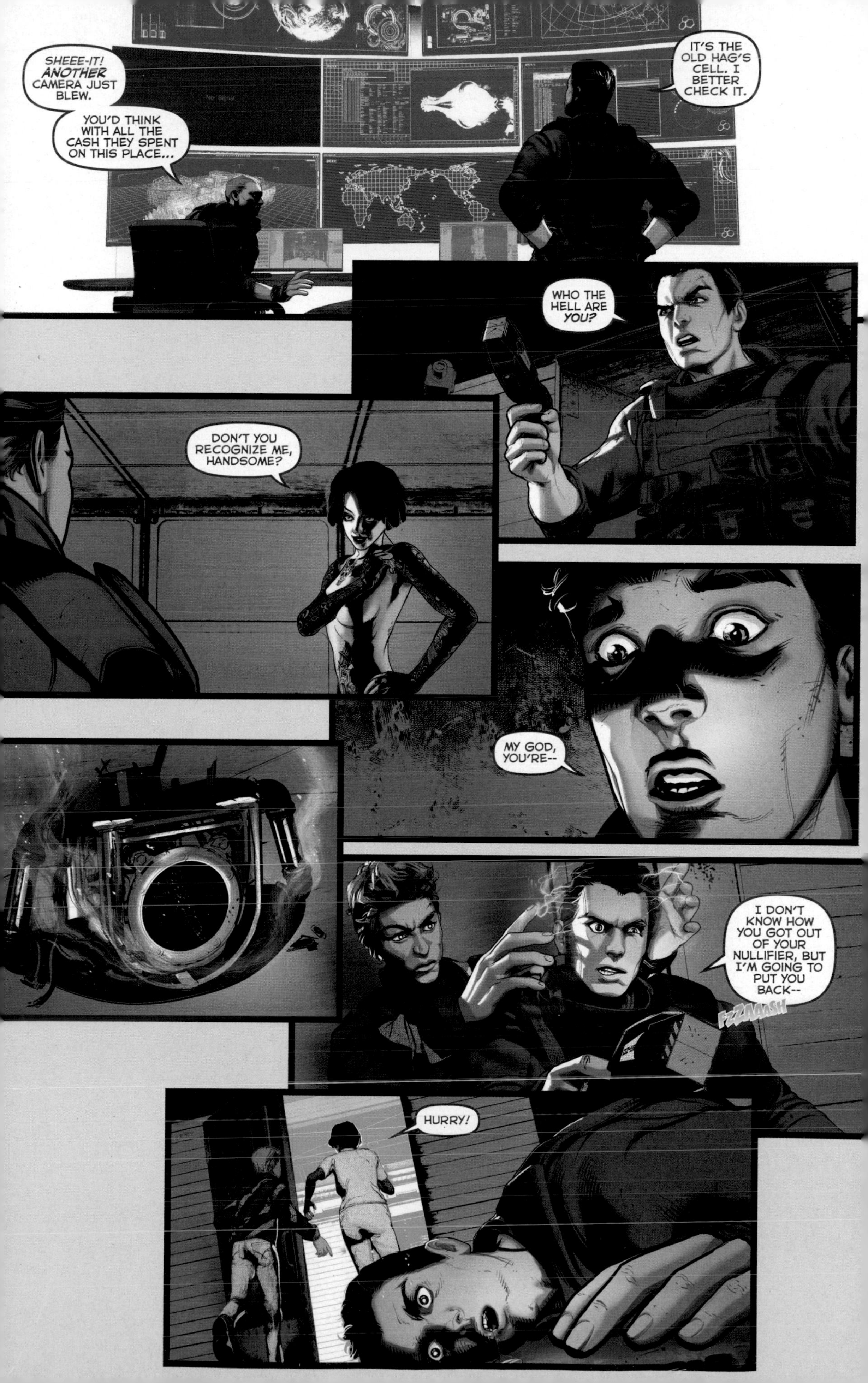
SHEEE-IT! ANOTHER CAMERA JUST BLEW.
YOU'D THINK WITH ALL THE CASH THEY SPENT ON THIS PLACE...
IT'S THE OLD HAG'S CELL. I BETTER CHECK IT.
WHO THE HELL ARE YOU?
DON'T YOU RECOGNIZE ME, HANDSOME?
MY GOD, YOU'RE--
I DON'T KNOW HOW YOU GOT OUT OF YOUR NULLIFIER, BUT I'M GOING TO PUT YOU BACK--
FZZAAASH
HURRY!

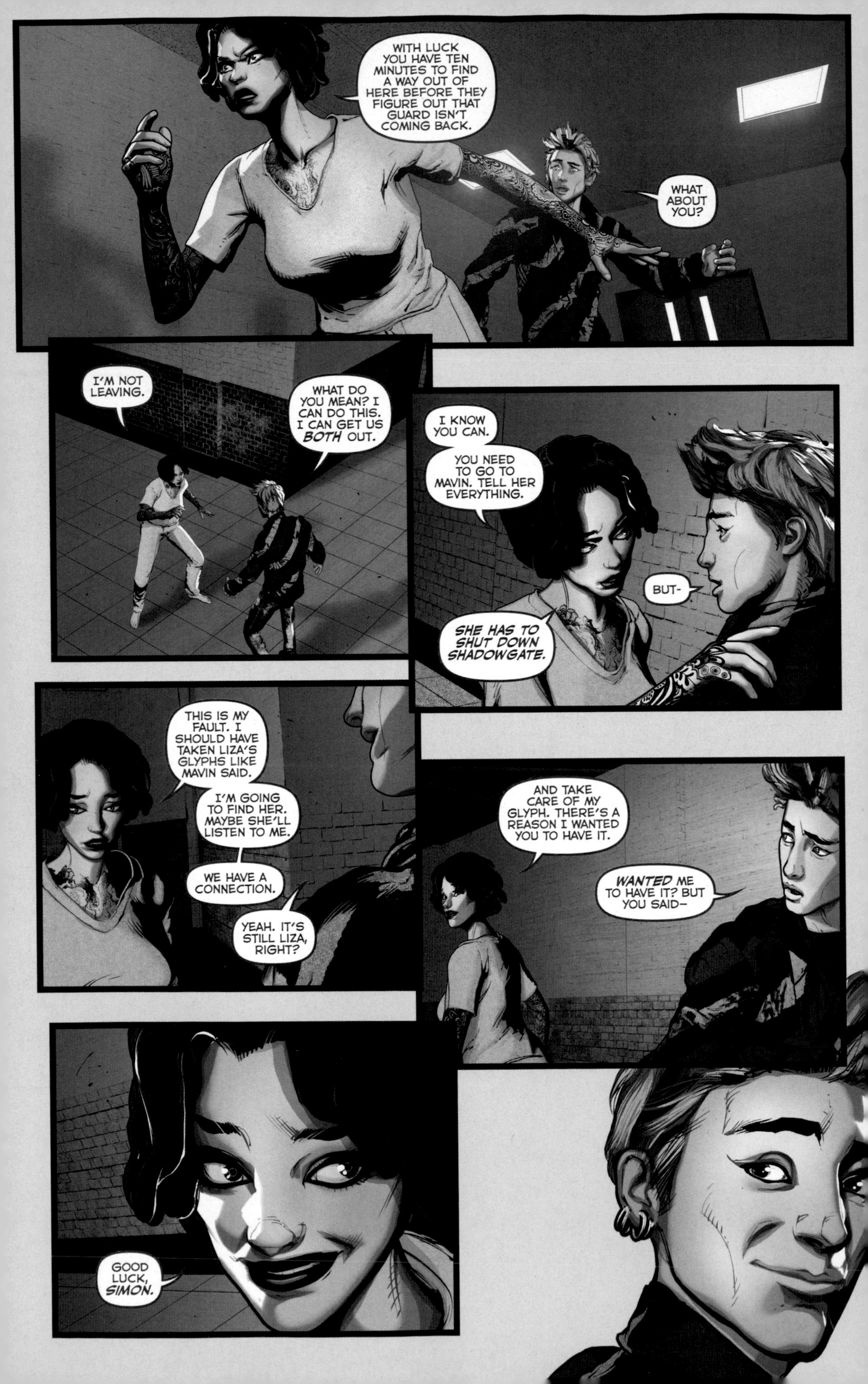
WITH LUCK YOU HAVE TEN MINUTES TO FIND A WAY OUT OF HERE BEFORE THEY FIGURE OUT THAT GUARD ISN'T COMING BACK.
WHAT ABOUT YOU?
I'M NOT LEAVING.
WHAT DO YOU MEAN? I CAN DO THIS. I CAN GET US *BOTH* OUT.
I KNOW YOU CAN.
YOU NEED TO GO TO MAVIN. TELL HER EVERYTHING.
BUT-
SHE HAS TO SHUT DOWN SHADOWGATE.
THIS IS MY FAULT. I SHOULD HAVE TAKEN LIZA'S GLYPHS LIKE MAVIN SAID.
I'M GOING TO FIND HER. MAYBE SHE'LL LISTEN TO ME.
WE HAVE A CONNECTION.
YEAH. IT'S STILL LIZA, RIGHT?
AND TAKE CARE OF MY GLYPH. THERE'S A REASON I WANTED YOU TO HAVE IT.
WANTED ME TO HAVE IT? BUT YOU SAID–
GOOD LUCK, *SIMON.*

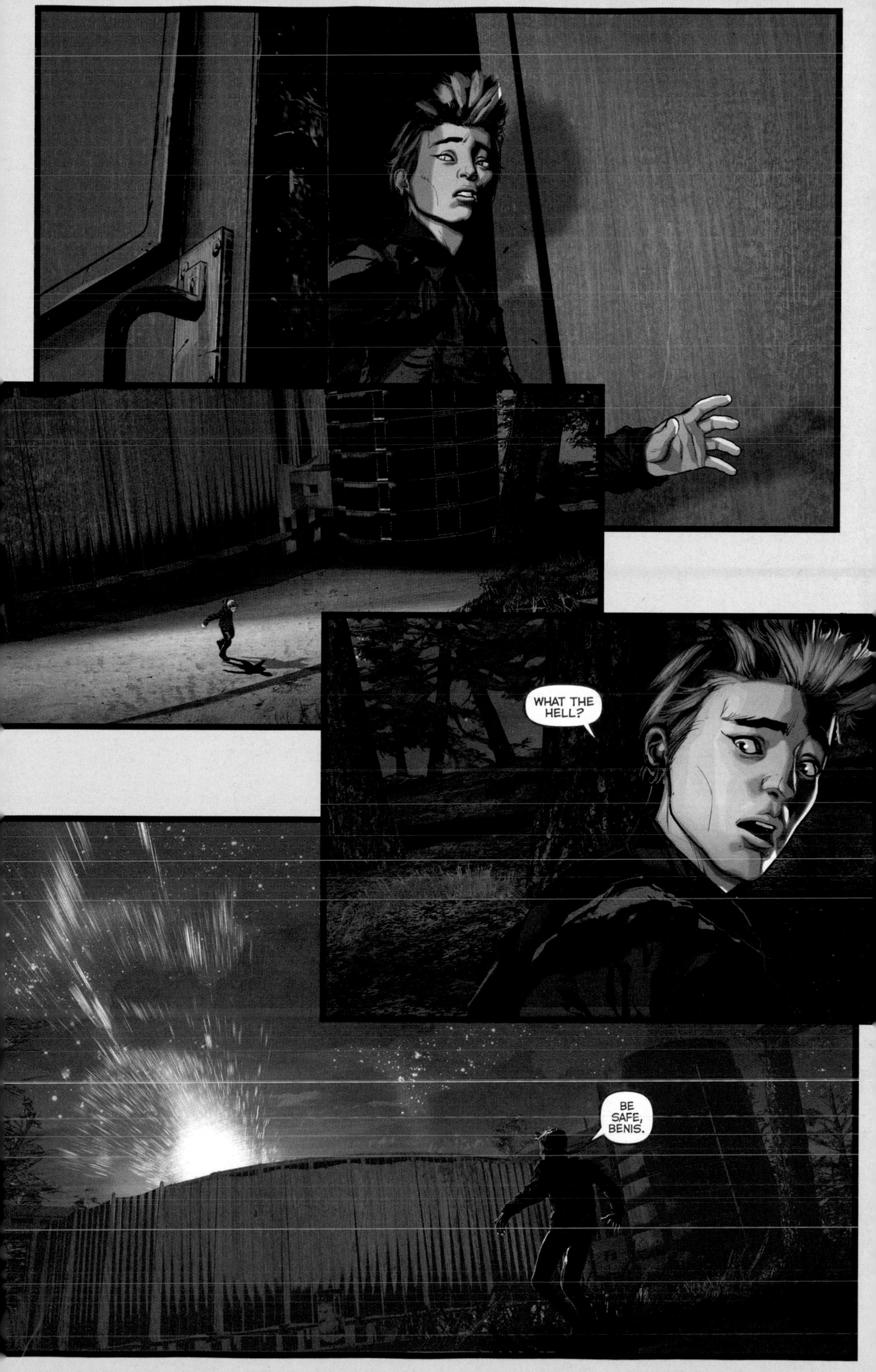
WHAT THE HELL?
BE SAFE, BENIS.

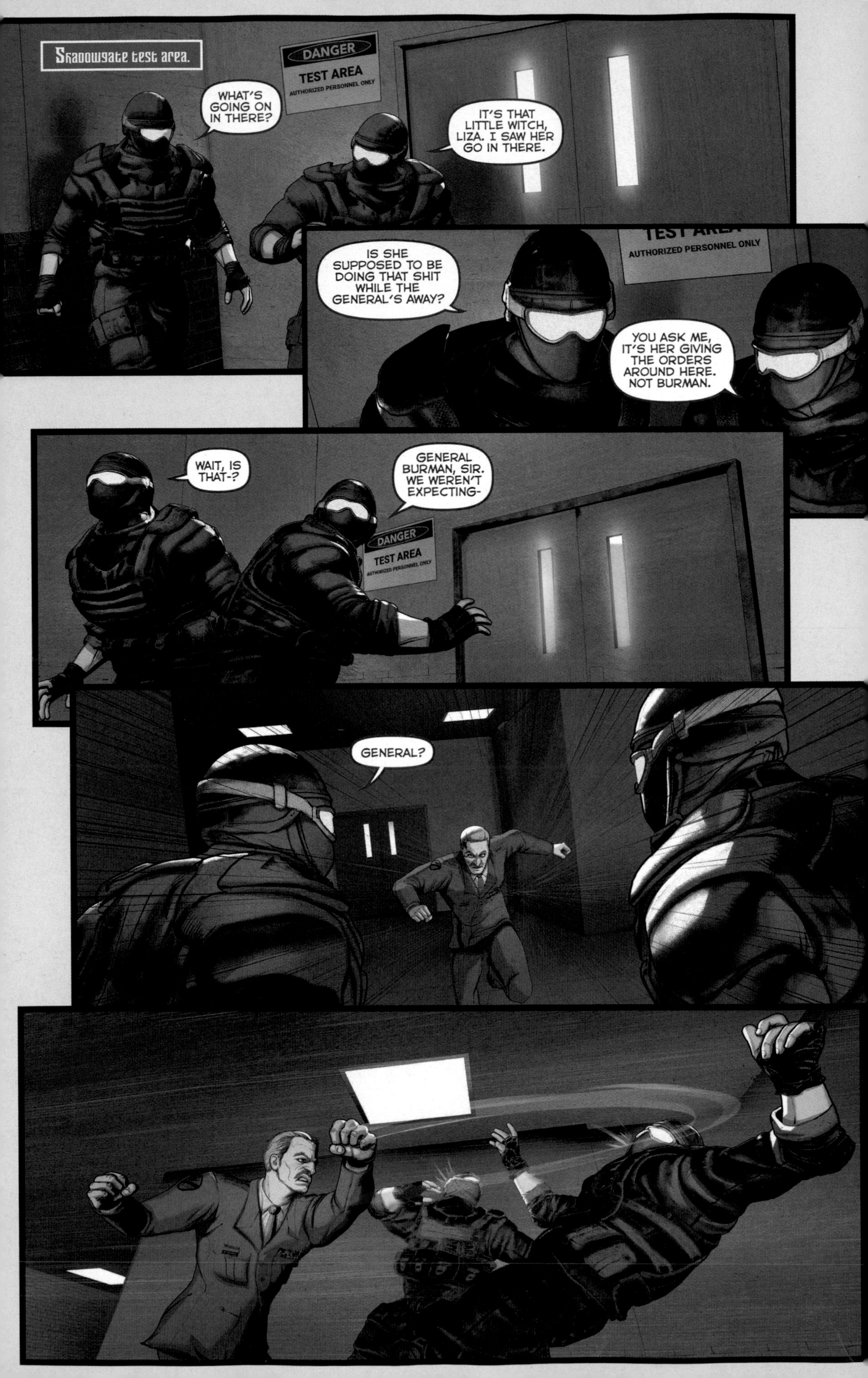
Shadowgate test area.
DANGER
TEST AREA
AUTHORIZED PERSONNEL ONLY
WHAT'S GOING ON IN THERE?
IT'S THAT LITTLE WITCH, LIZA. I SAW HER GO IN THERE.
AUTHORIZED PERSONNEL ONLY
IS SHE SUPPOSED TO BE DOING THAT SHIT WHILE THE GENERAL'S AWAY?
YOU ASK ME, IT'S HER GIVING THE ORDERS AROUND HERE. NOT BURMAN.
WAIT, IS THAT-?
GENERAL BURMAN, SIR. WE WEREN'T EXPECTING-
DANGER
TEST AREA
AUTHORIZED PERSONNEL ONLY
GENERAL?

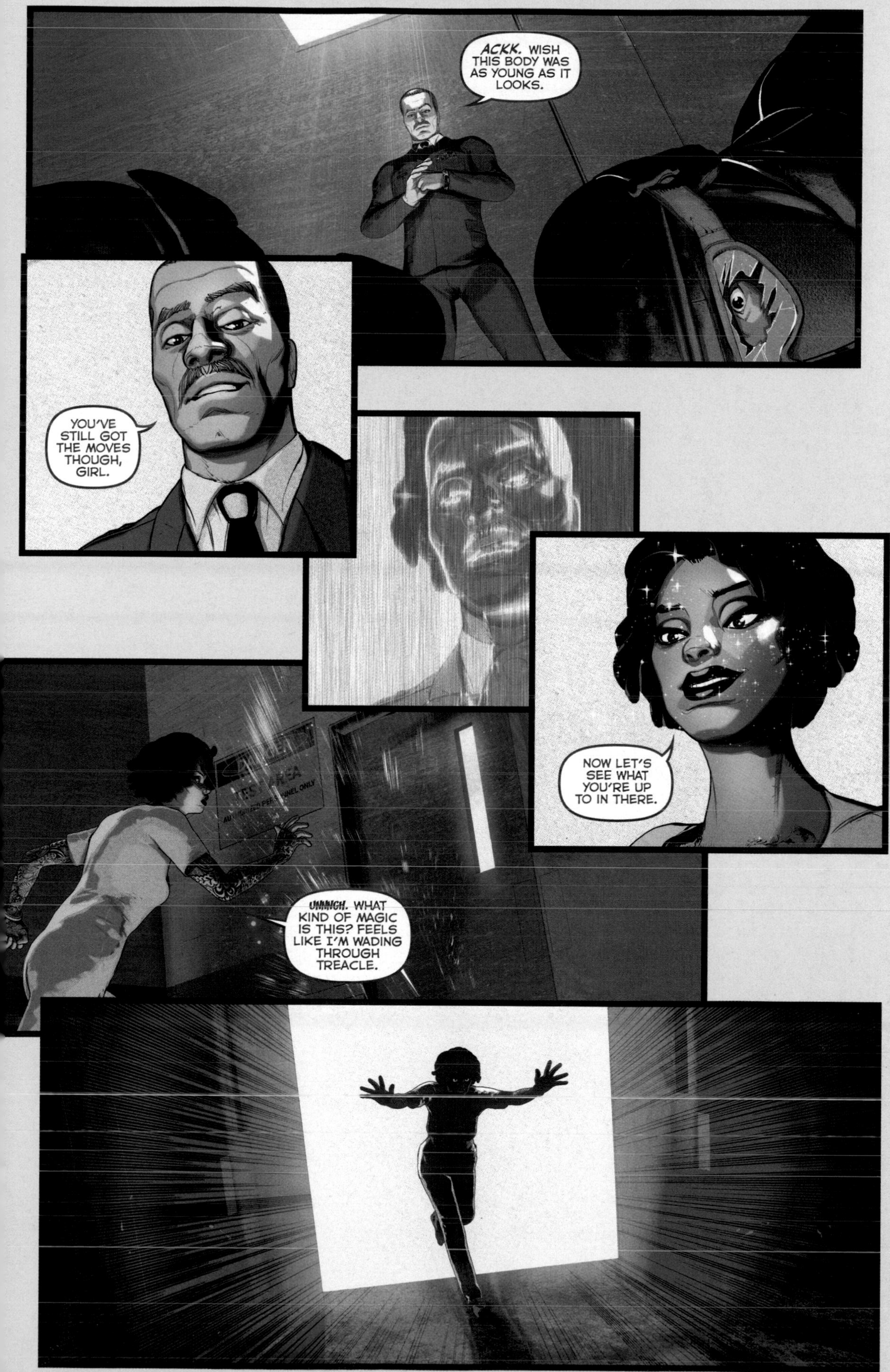
ACKK. WISH THIS BODY WAS AS YOUNG AS IT LOOKS.
YOU'VE STILL GOT THE MOVES THOUGH, GIRL.
NOW LET'S SEE WHAT YOU'RE UP TO IN THERE.
UNNNGH. WHAT KIND OF MAGIC IS THIS? FEELS LIKE I'M WADING THROUGH TREACLE.

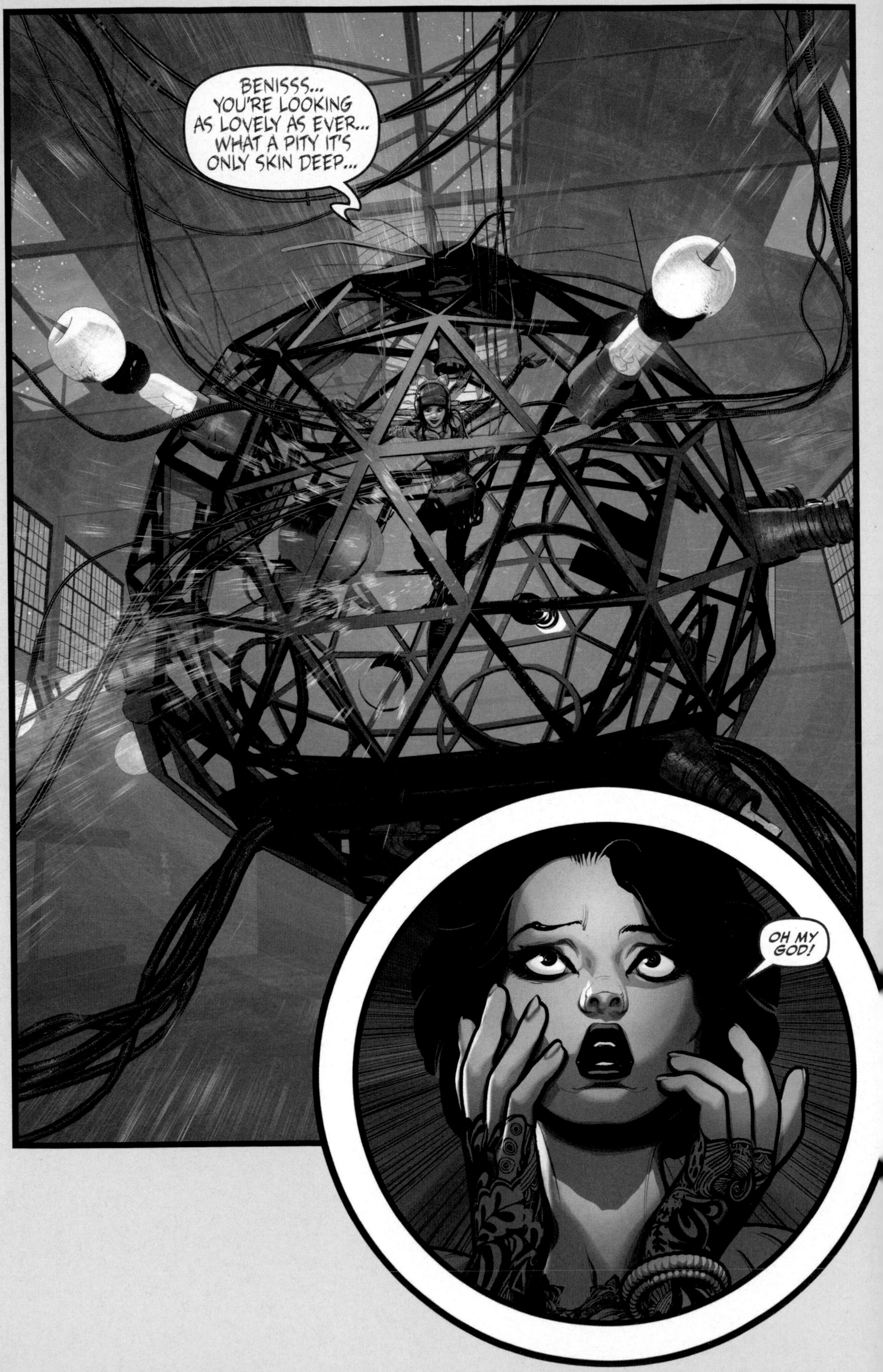
BENISSS... YOU'RE LOOKING AS LOVELY AS EVER... WHAT A PITY IT'S ONLY SKIN DEEP...
OH MY GOD!

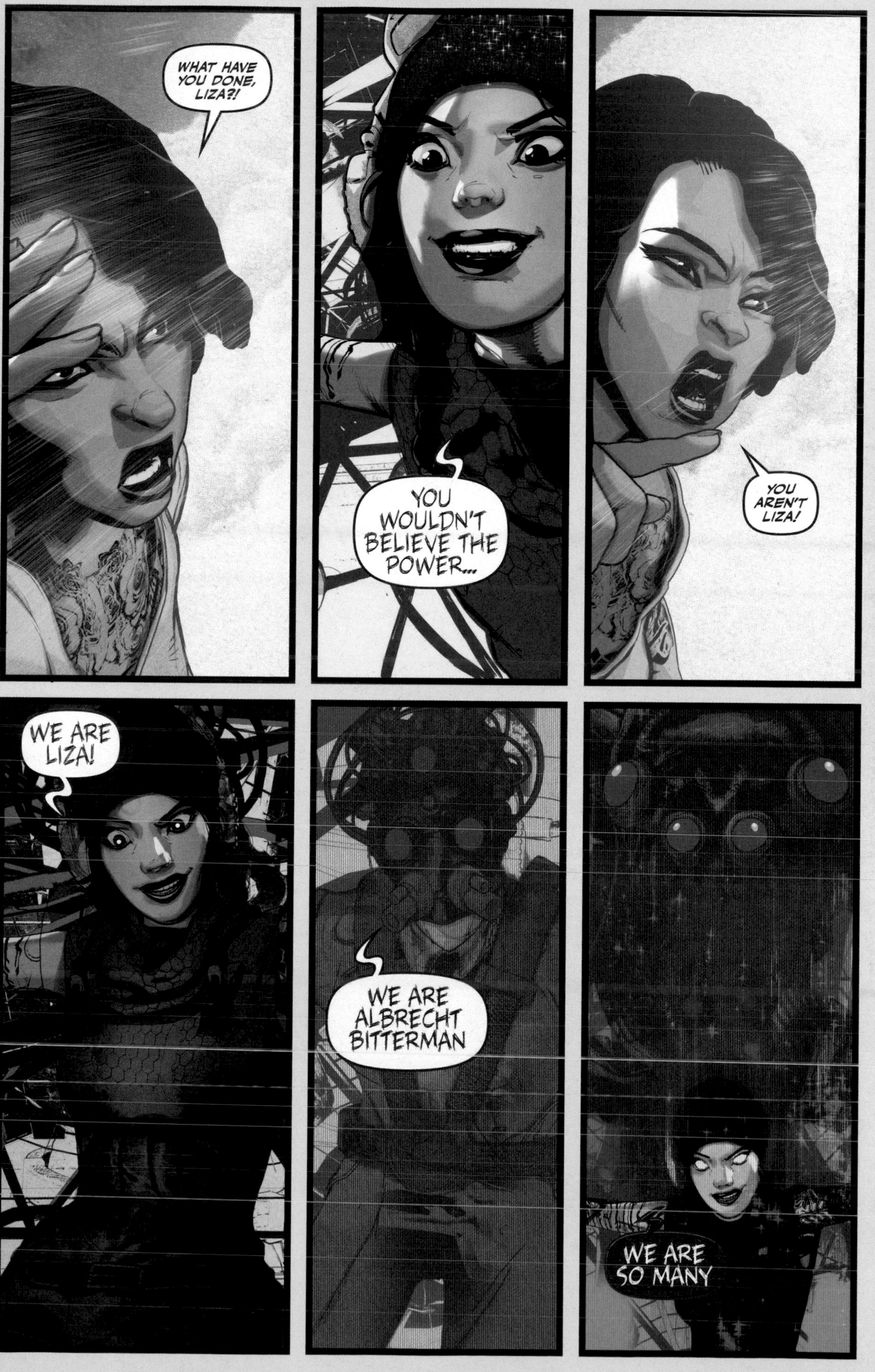
WHAT HAVE YOU DONE, LIZA?!
YOU WOULDN'T BELIEVE THE POWER...
YOU AREN'T LIZA!
WE ARE LIZA!
WE ARE ALBRECHT BITTERMAN
WE ARE SO MANY

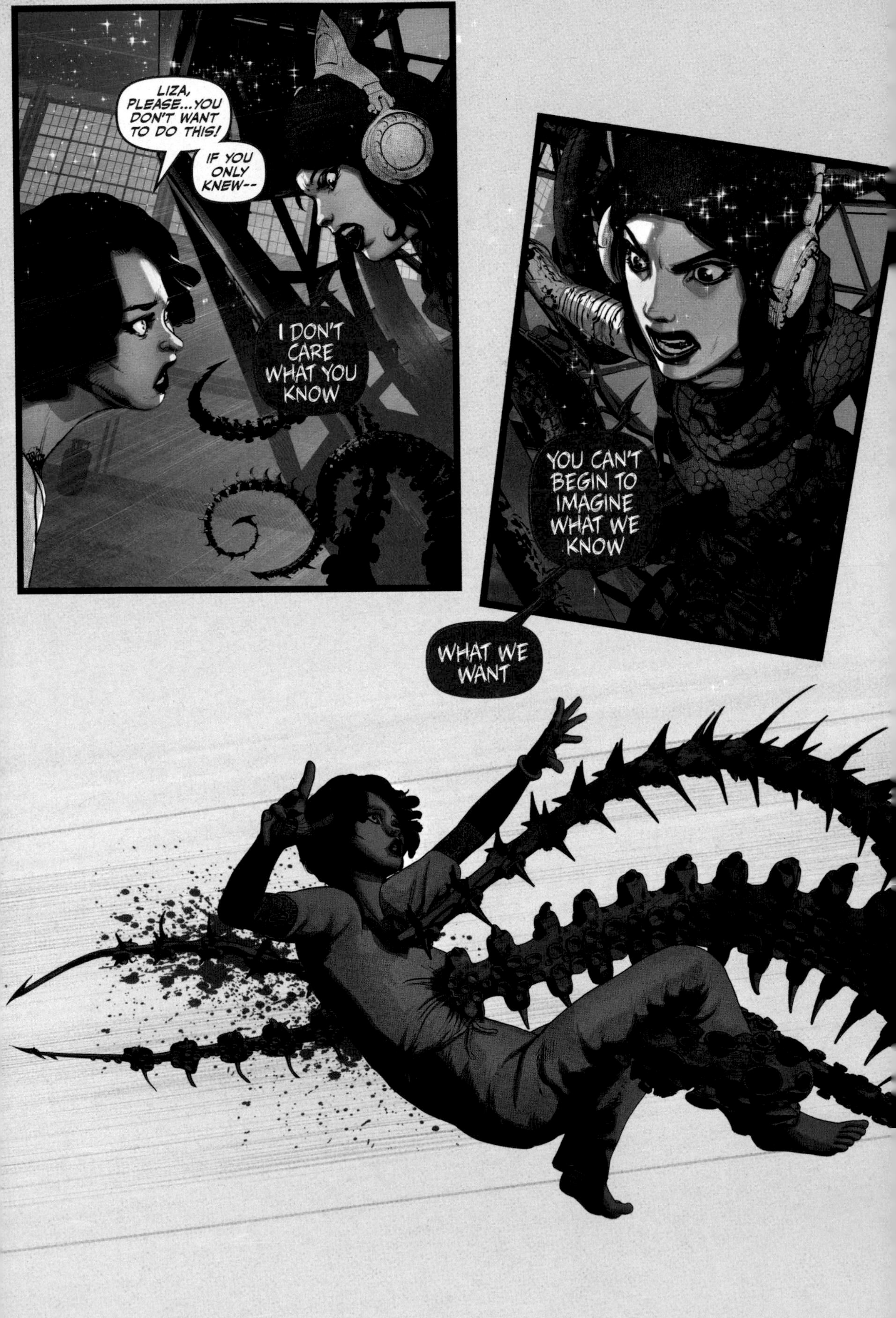
LIZA, PLEASE...YOU DON'T WANT TO DO THIS!
IF YOU ONLY KNEW--
I DON'T CARE WHAT YOU KNOW
YOU CAN'T BEGIN TO IMAGINE WHAT WE KNOW
WHAT WE WANT

CHAPTER FOUR

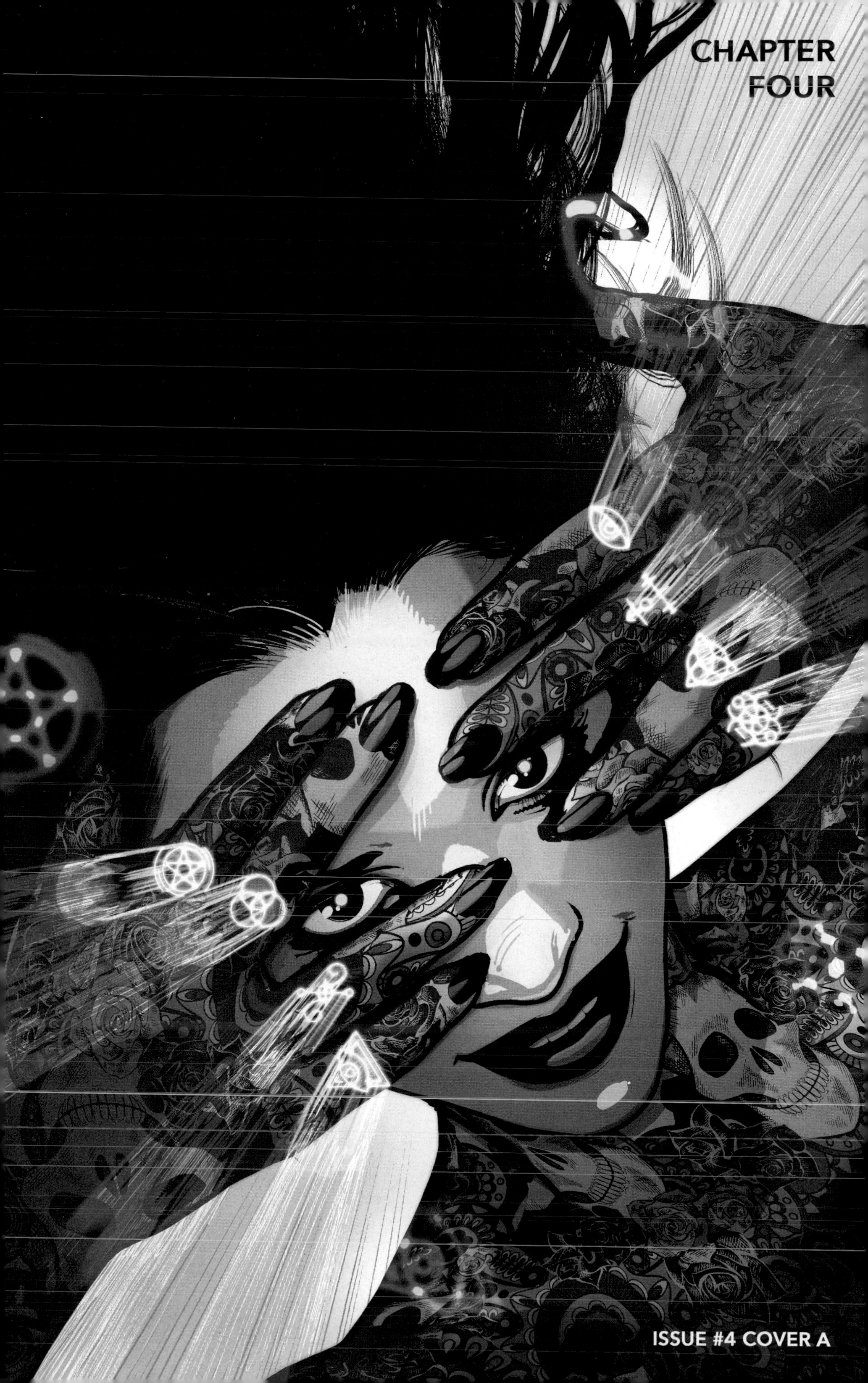

ISSUE #4 COVER A

ISSUE #4 COVER B

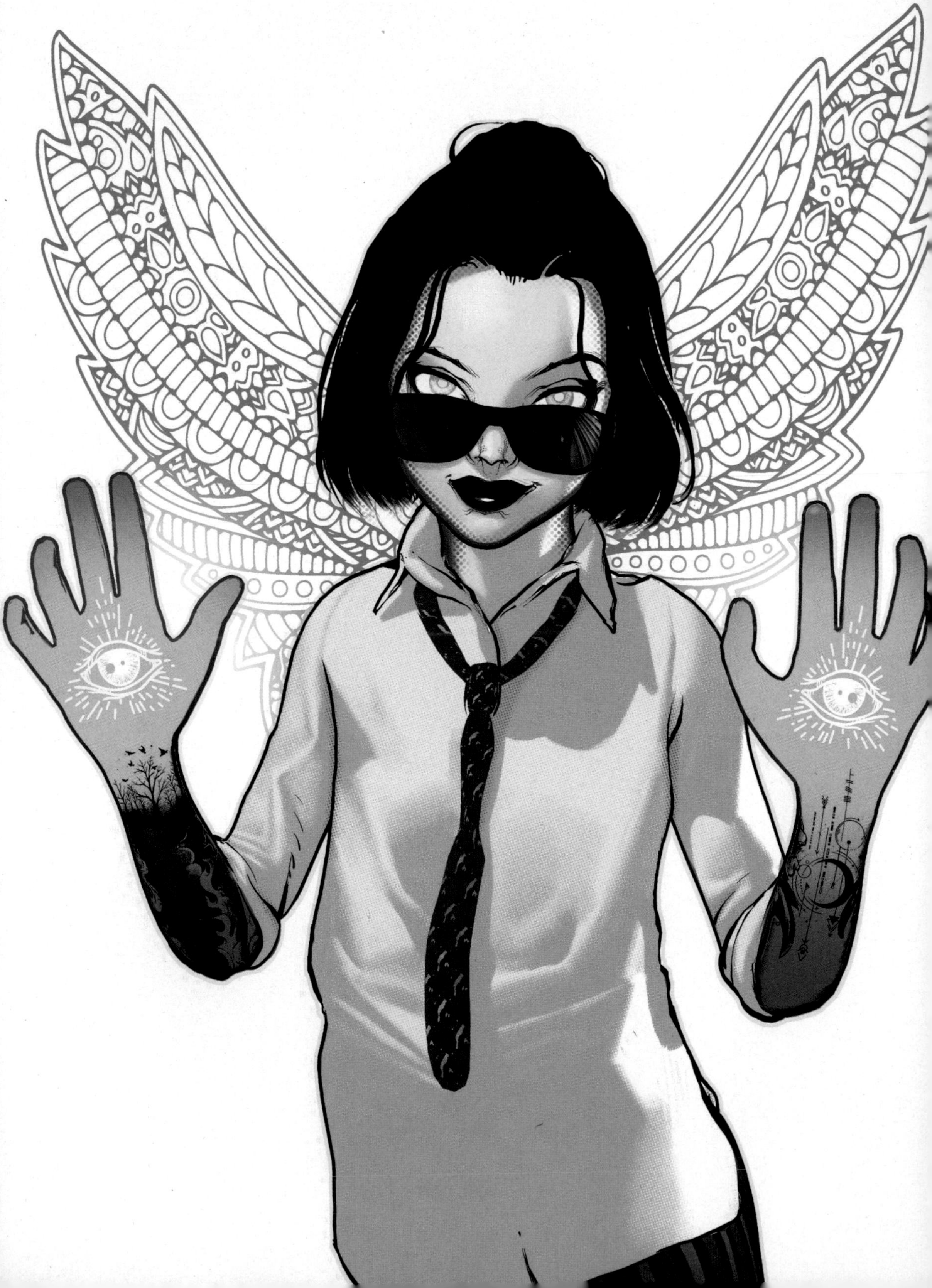

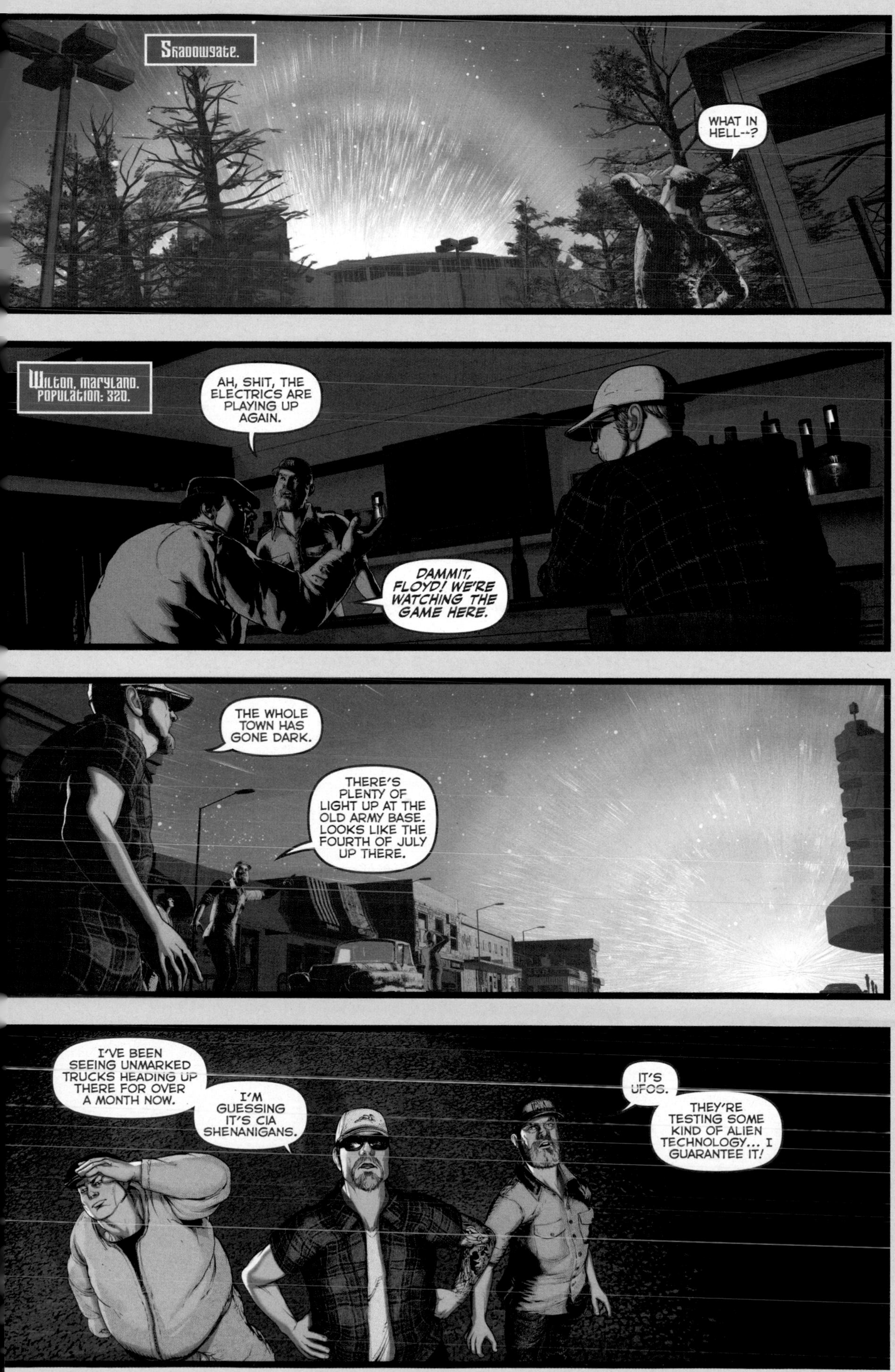

Shadowgate.
WHAT IN HELL--?
Wilton, Maryland. Population: 320.
AH, SHIT, THE ELECTRICS ARE PLAYING UP AGAIN.
DAMMIT, FLOYD! WE'RE WATCHING THE GAME HERE.
THE WHOLE TOWN HAS GONE DARK.
THERE'S PLENTY OF LIGHT UP AT THE OLD ARMY BASE. LOOKS LIKE THE FOURTH OF JULY UP THERE.
I'VE BEEN SEEING UNMARKED TRUCKS HEADING UP THERE FOR OVER A MONTH NOW.
I'M GUESSING IT'S CIA SHENANIGANS.
IT'S UFOS.
THEY'RE TESTING SOME KIND OF ALIEN TECHNOLOGY... I GUARANTEE IT!

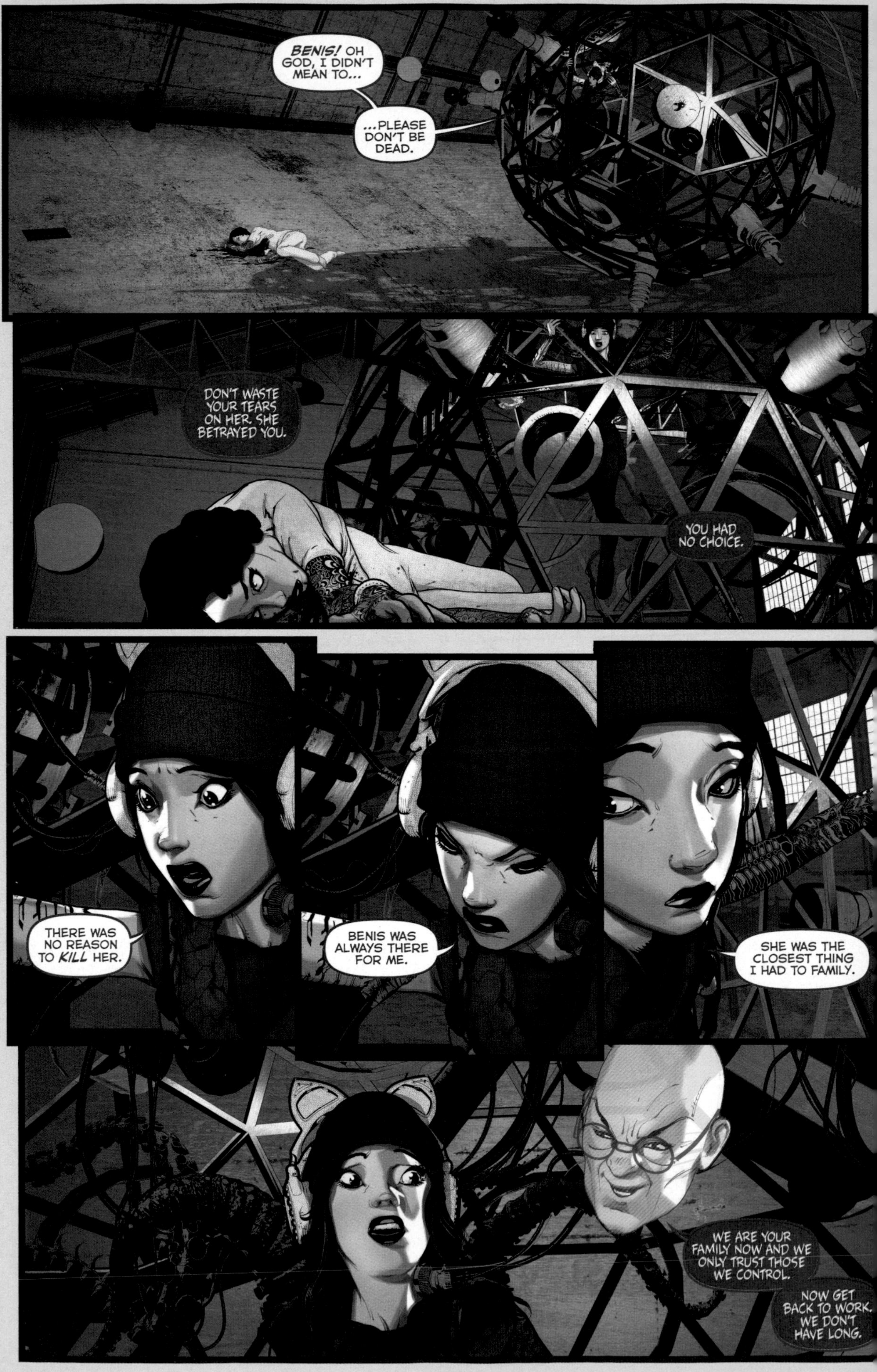
BENIS! OH GOD, I DIDN'T MEAN TO...
...PLEASE DON'T BE DEAD.
DON'T WASTE YOUR TEARS ON HER. SHE BETRAYED YOU.
YOU HAD NO CHOICE.
THERE WAS NO REASON TO KILL HER.
BENIS WAS ALWAYS THERE FOR ME.
SHE WAS THE CLOSEST THING I HAD TO FAMILY.
WE ARE YOUR FAMILY NOW AND WE ONLY TRUST THOSE WE CONTROL.
NOW GET BACK TO WORK. WE DON'T HAVE LONG.

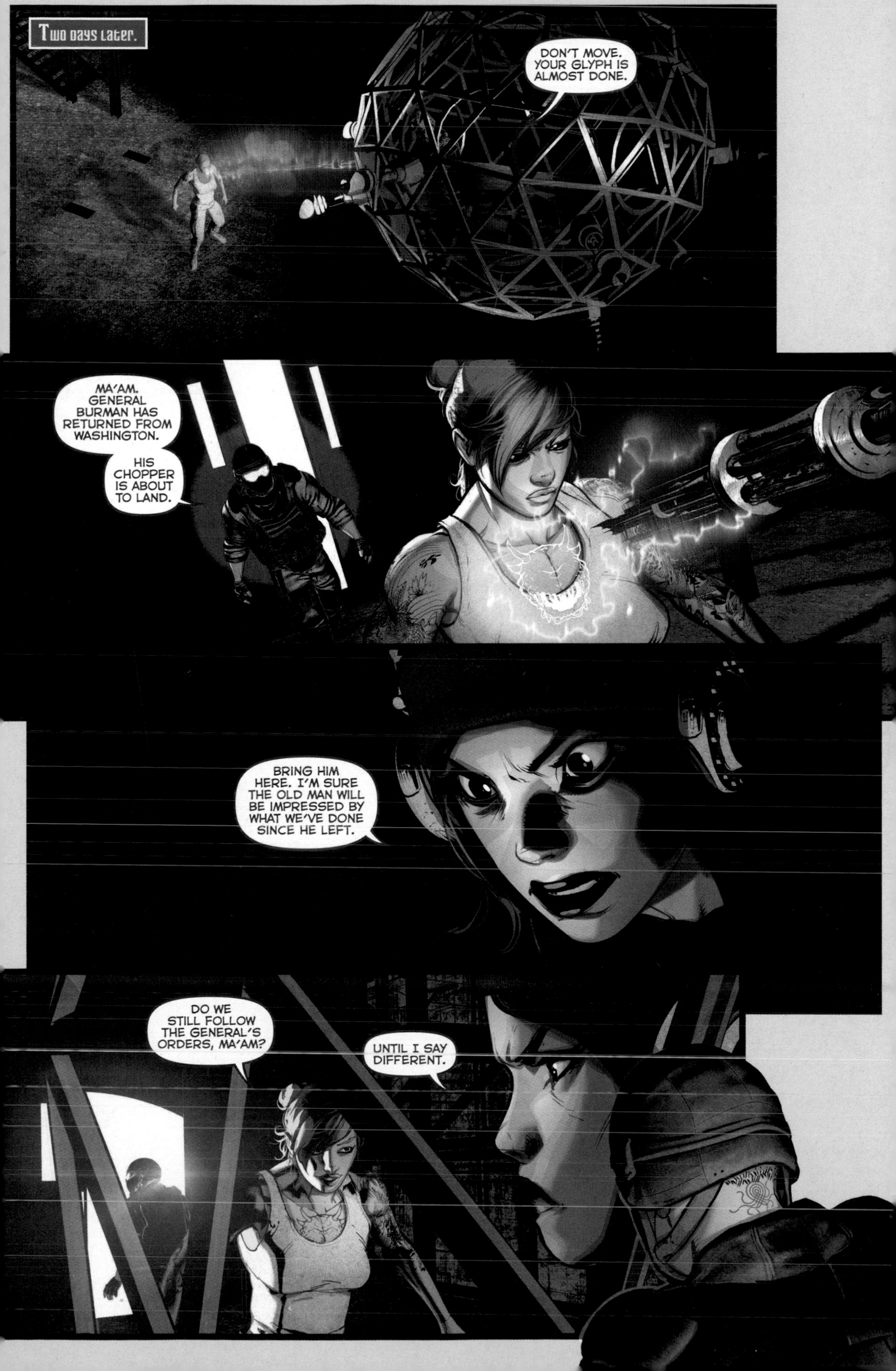
Two days later.
DON'T MOVE. YOUR GLYPH IS ALMOST DONE.
MA'AM. GENERAL BURMAN HAS RETURNED FROM WASHINGTON.
HIS CHOPPER IS ABOUT TO LAND.
BRING HIM HERE. I'M SURE THE OLD MAN WILL BE IMPRESSED BY WHAT WE'VE DONE SINCE HE LEFT.
DO WE STILL FOLLOW THE GENERAL'S ORDERS, MA'AM?
UNTIL I SAY DIFFERENT.

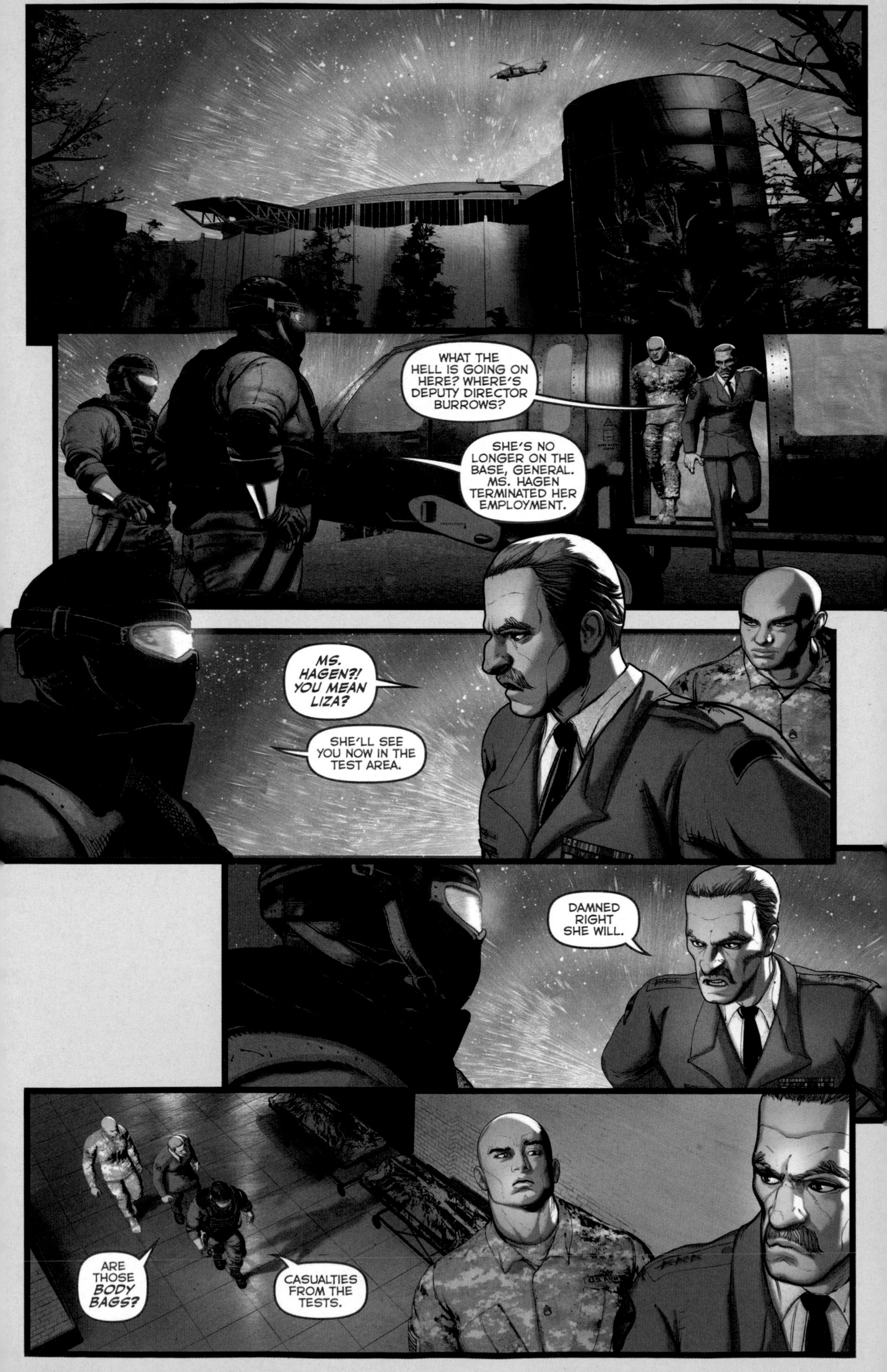
WHAT THE HELL IS GOING ON HERE? WHERE'S DEPUTY DIRECTOR BURROWS?
SHE'S NO LONGER ON THE BASE, GENERAL. MS. HAGEN TERMINATED HER EMPLOYMENT.
MS. HAGEN?! YOU MEAN LIZA?
SHE'LL SEE YOU NOW IN THE TEST AREA.
DAMNED RIGHT SHE WILL.
ARE THOSE BODY BAGS?
CASUALTIES FROM THE TESTS.

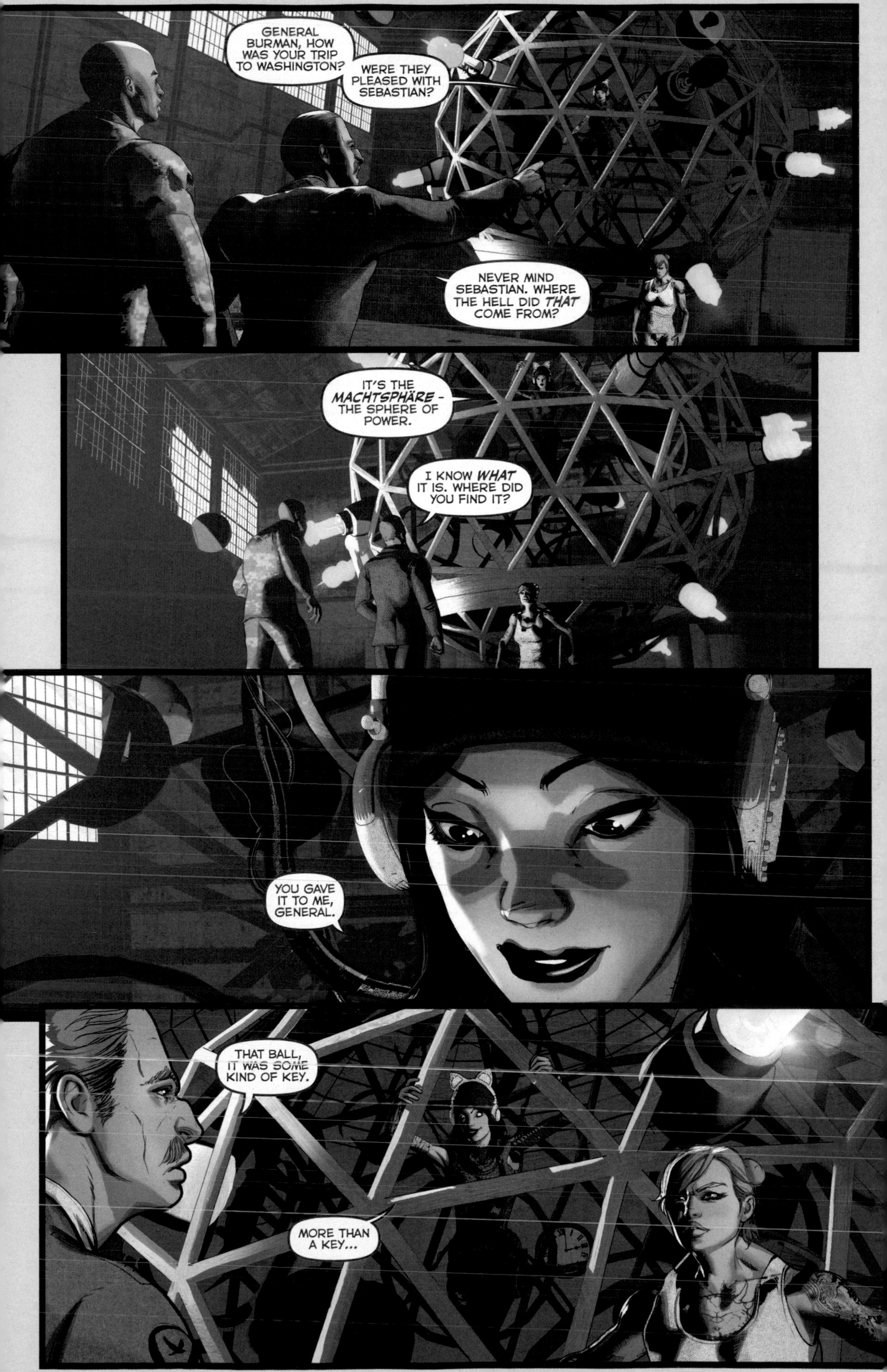
GENERAL BURMAN, HOW WAS YOUR TRIP TO WASHINGTON?
WERE THEY PLEASED WITH SEBASTIAN?
NEVER MIND SEBASTIAN. WHERE THE HELL DID *THAT* COME FROM?
IT'S THE *MACHTSPHÄRE* - THE SPHERE OF POWER.
I KNOW *WHAT* IT IS. WHERE DID YOU FIND IT?
YOU GAVE IT TO ME, GENERAL.
THAT BALL, IT WAS SOME KIND OF KEY.
MORE THAN A KEY...

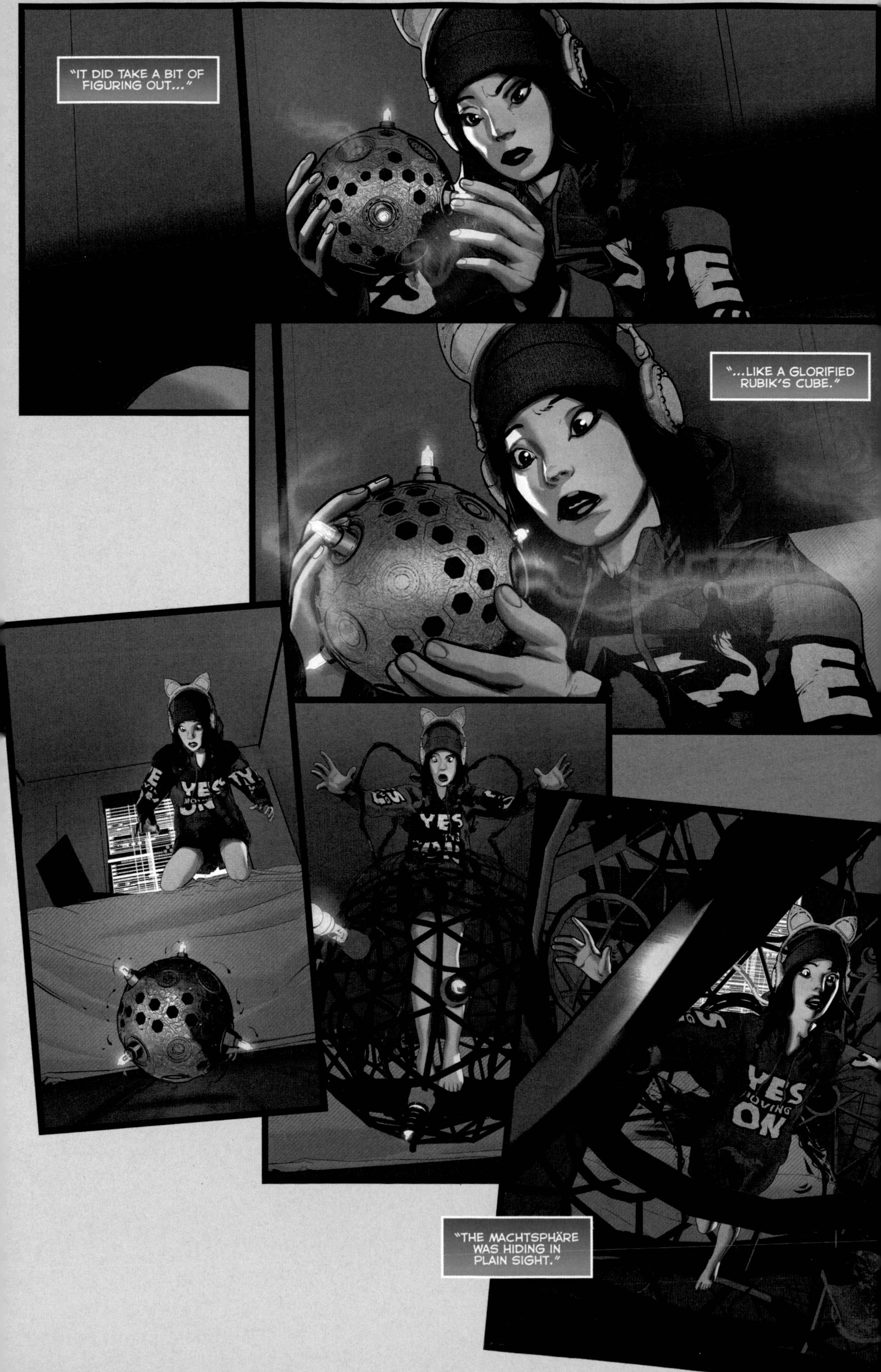
"IT DID TAKE A BIT OF FIGURING OUT..."
"...LIKE A GLORIFIED RUBIK'S CUBE."
"THE MACHTSPHÄRE WAS HIDING IN PLAIN SIGHT."

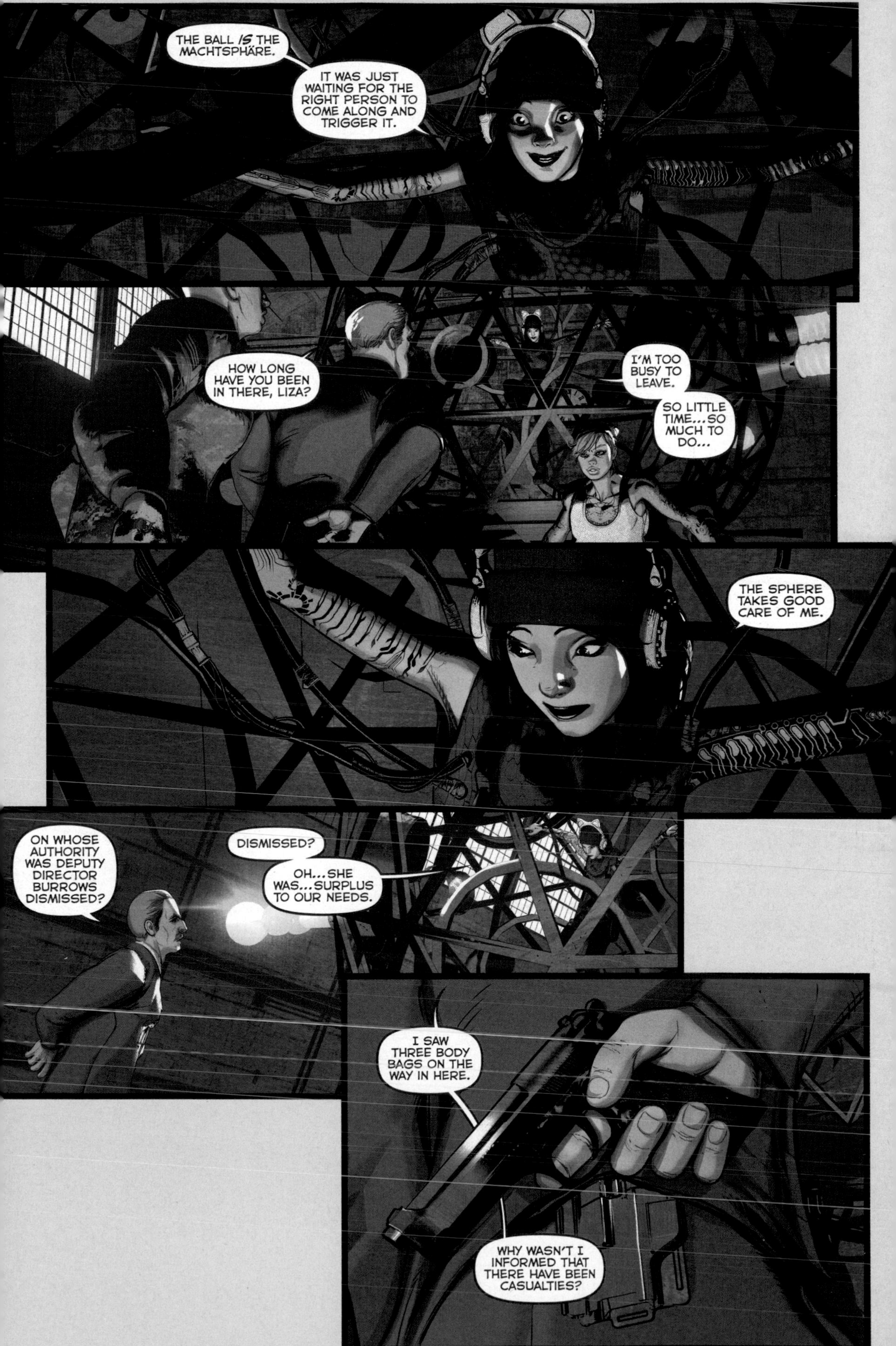
THE BALL *IS* THE MACHTSPHÄRE.
IT WAS JUST WAITING FOR THE RIGHT PERSON TO COME ALONG AND TRIGGER IT.
HOW LONG HAVE YOU BEEN IN THERE, LIZA?
I'M TOO BUSY TO LEAVE.
SO LITTLE TIME...SO MUCH TO DO...
THE SPHERE TAKES GOOD CARE OF ME.
ON WHOSE AUTHORITY WAS DEPUTY DIRECTOR BURROWS DISMISSED?
DISMISSED?
OH...SHE WAS...SURPLUS TO OUR NEEDS.
I SAW THREE BODY BAGS ON THE WAY IN HERE.
WHY WASN'T I INFORMED THAT THERE HAVE BEEN CASUALTIES?

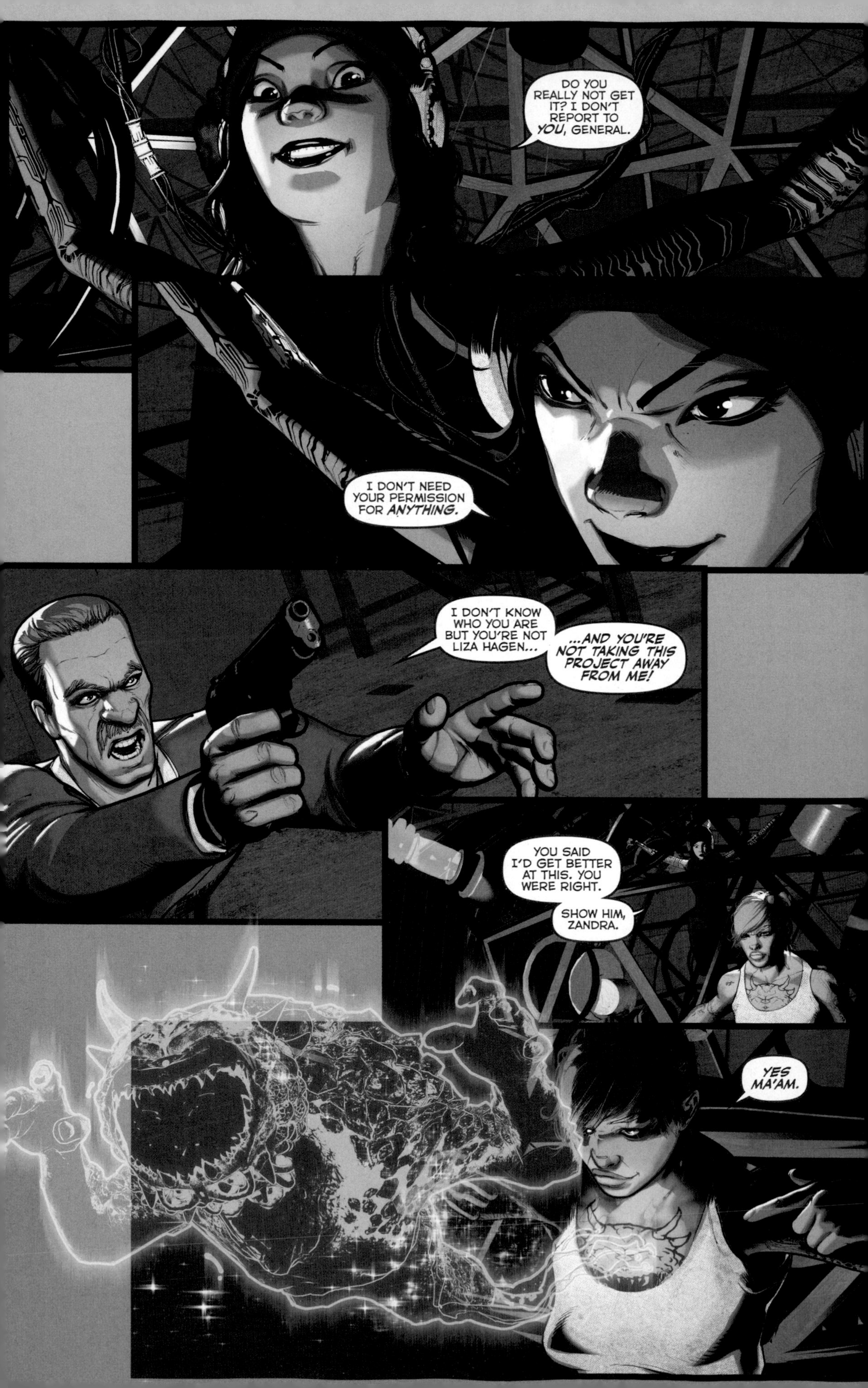
DO YOU REALLY NOT GET IT? I DON'T REPORT TO YOU, GENERAL.
I DON'T NEED YOUR PERMISSION FOR ANYTHING.
I DON'T KNOW WHO YOU ARE BUT YOU'RE NOT LIZA HAGEN...
...AND YOU'RE NOT TAKING THIS PROJECT AWAY FROM ME!
YOU SAID I'D GET BETTER AT THIS. YOU WERE RIGHT.
SHOW HIM, ZANDRA.
YES MA'AM.

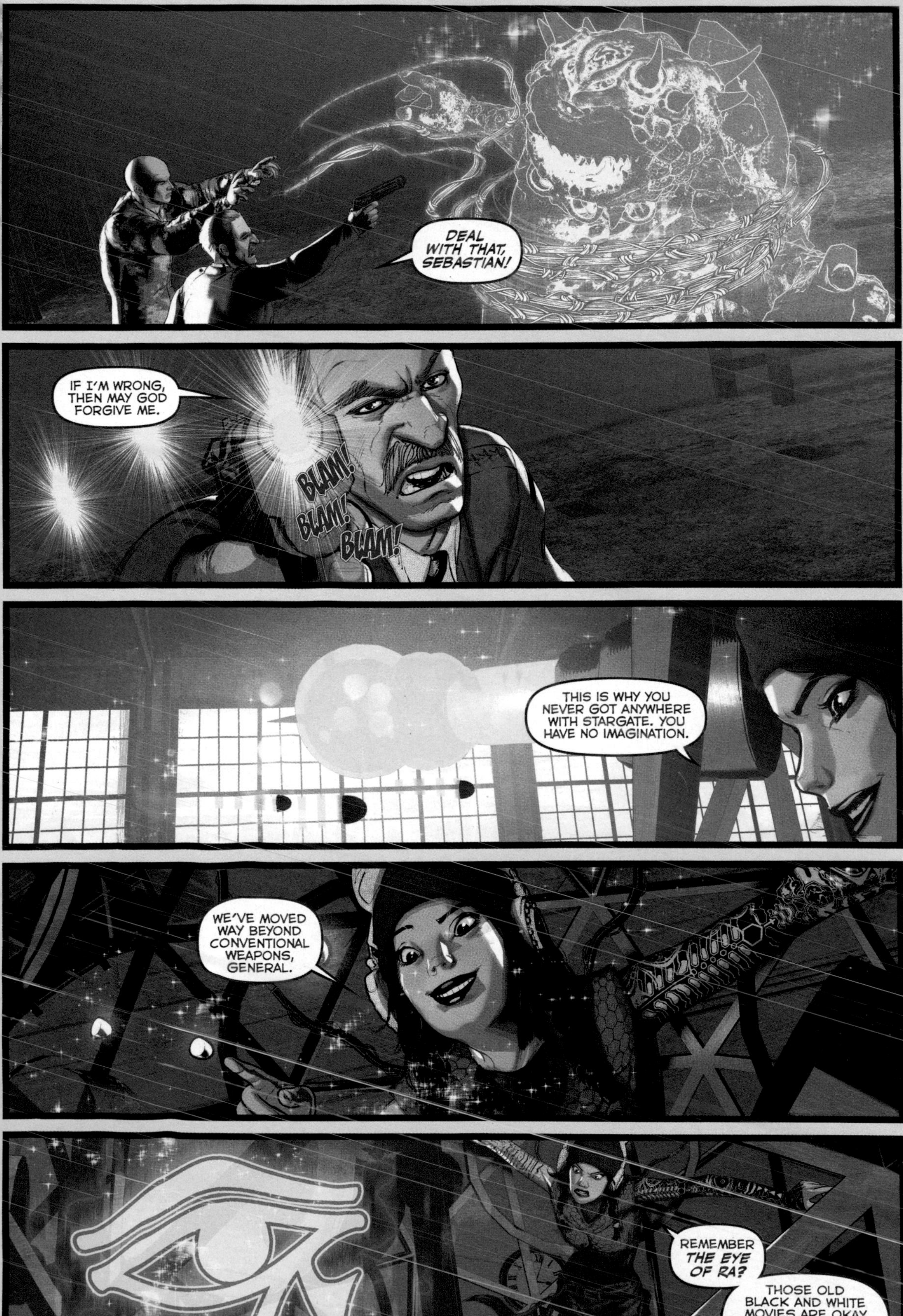
DEAL WITH THAT, SEBASTIAN!
IF I'M WRONG, THEN MAY GOD FORGIVE ME.
BLAM!
BLAM!
BLAM!
THIS IS WHY YOU NEVER GOT ANYWHERE WITH STARGATE. YOU HAVE NO IMAGINATION.
WE'VE MOVED WAY BEYOND CONVENTIONAL WEAPONS, GENERAL.
REMEMBER *THE EYE OF RA?*
THOSE OLD BLACK AND WHITE MOVIES ARE OKAY BUT BURNING FLESH IS SO MUCH MORE IMPRESSIVE LIVE AND IN COLOR.

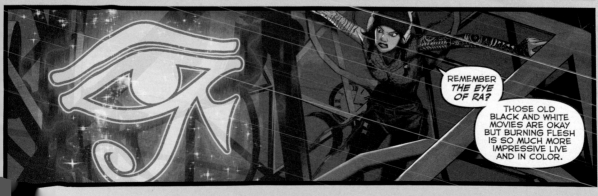

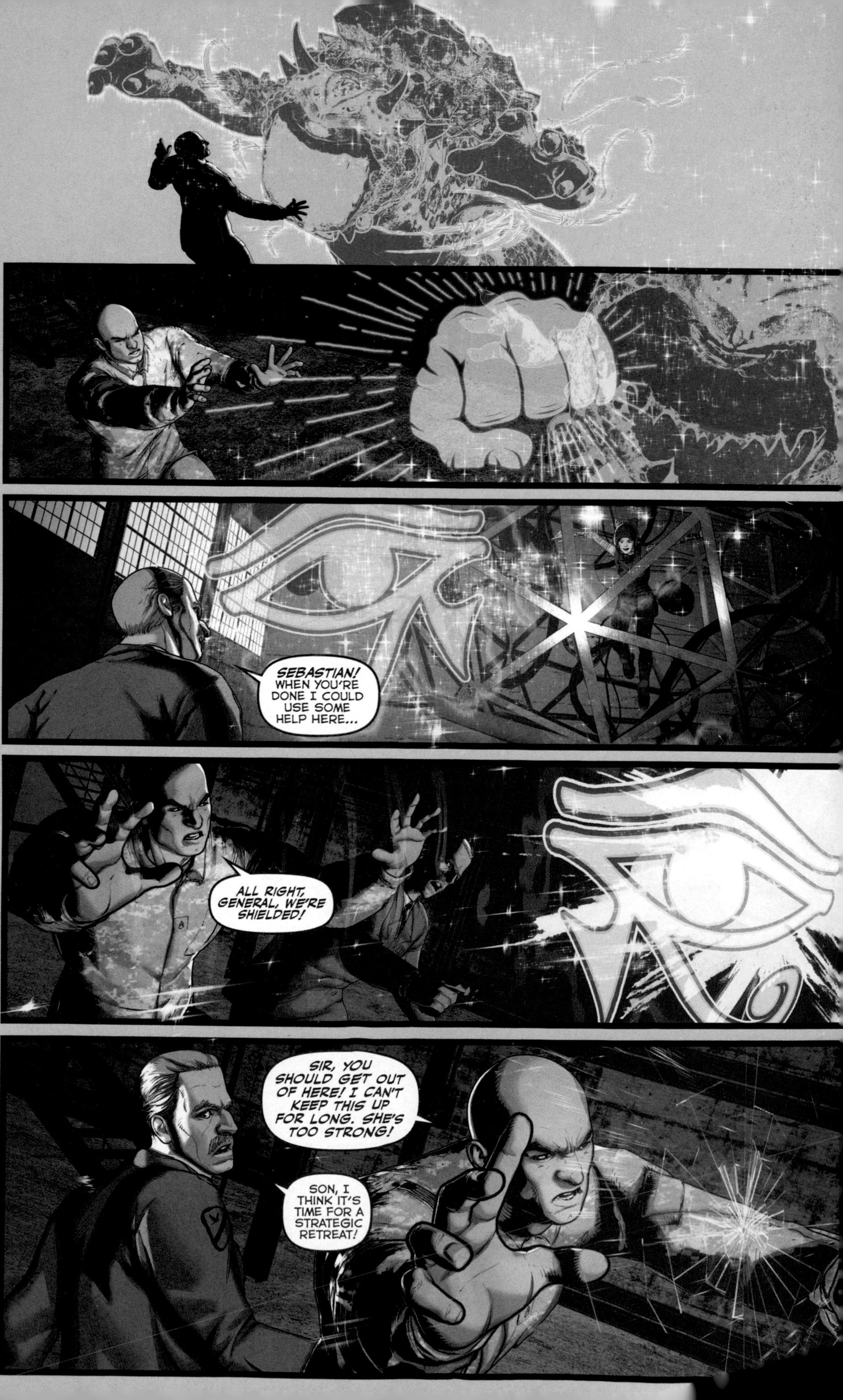
SEBASTIAN! WHEN YOU'RE DONE I COULD USE SOME HELP HERE...
ALL RIGHT, GENERAL, WE'RE SHIELDED!
SIR, YOU SHOULD GET OUT OF HERE! I CAN'T KEEP THIS UP FOR LONG. SHE'S TOO STRONG!
SON, I THINK IT'S TIME FOR A STRATEGIC RETREAT!

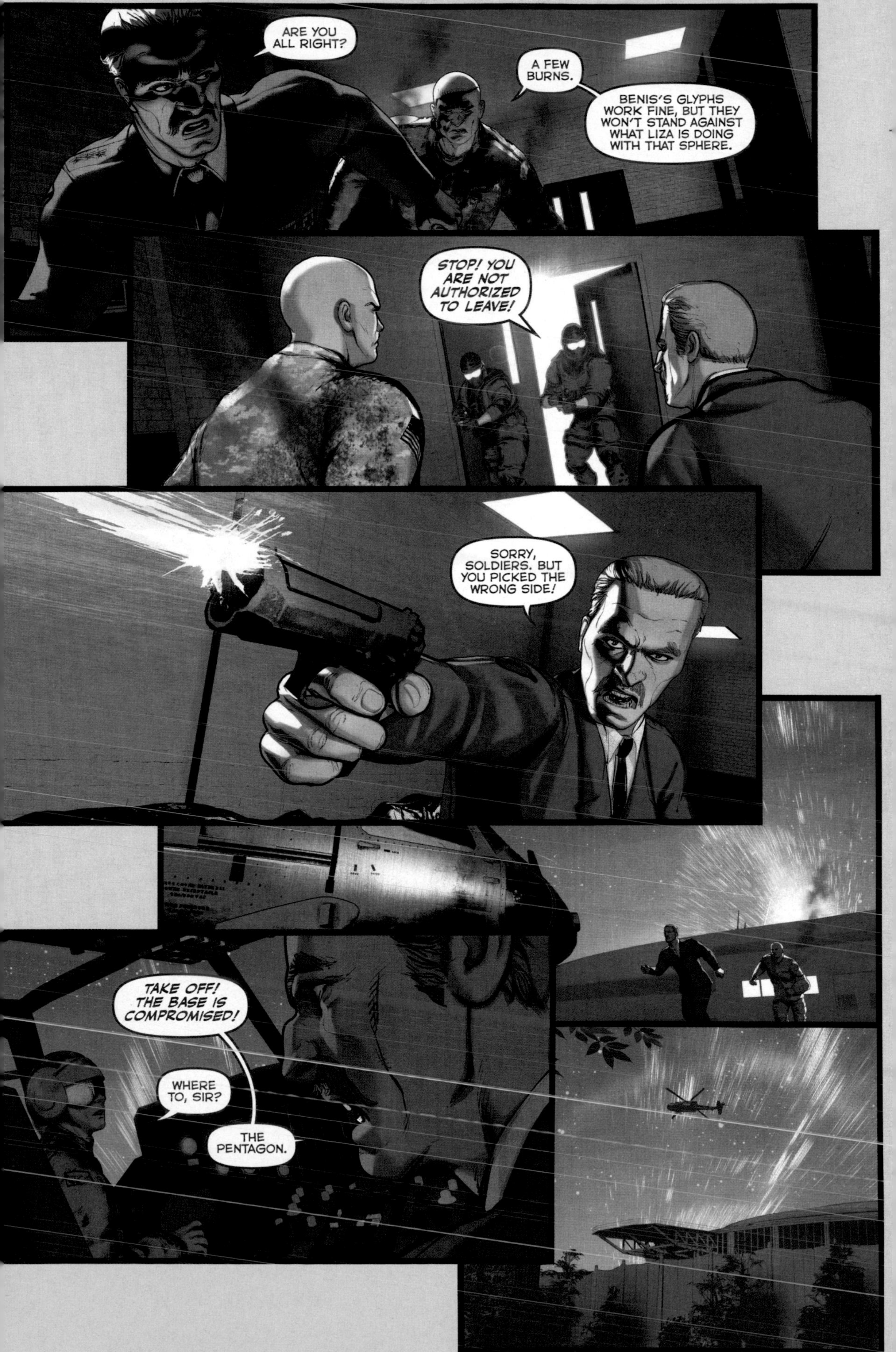
ARE YOU ALL RIGHT?
A FEW BURNS.
BENIS'S GLYPHS WORK FINE, BUT THEY WON'T STAND AGAINST WHAT LIZA IS DOING WITH THAT SPHERE.
STOP! YOU ARE NOT AUTHORIZED TO LEAVE!
SORRY, SOLDIERS. BUT YOU PICKED THE WRONG SIDE!
TAKE OFF! THE BASE IS COMPROMISED!
WHERE TO, SIR?
THE PENTAGON.

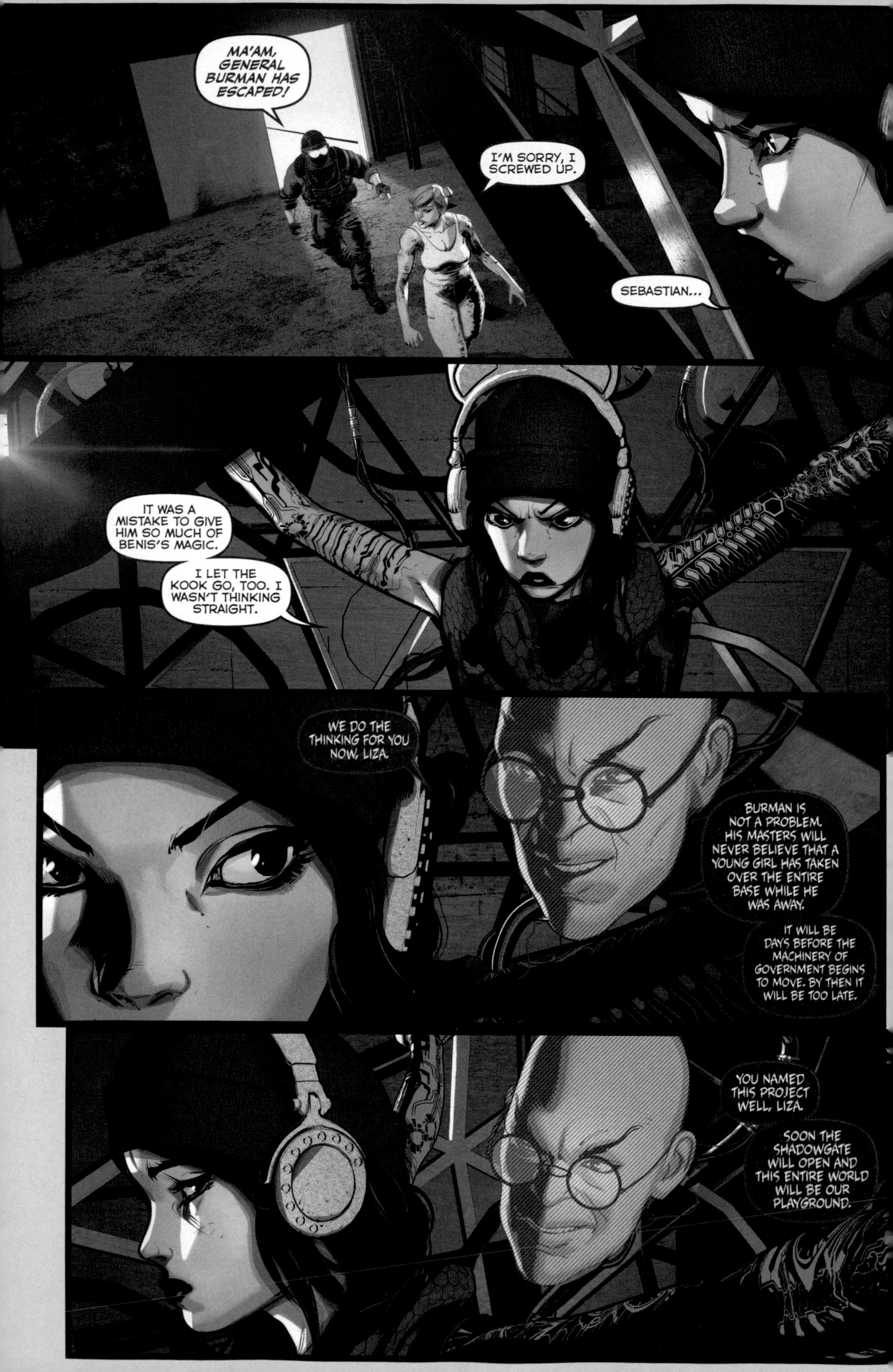
MA'AM, GENERAL BURMAN HAS ESCAPED!
I'M SORRY, I SCREWED UP.
SEBASTIAN...
IT WAS A MISTAKE TO GIVE HIM SO MUCH OF BENIS'S MAGIC.
I LET THE KOOK GO, TOO. I WASN'T THINKING STRAIGHT.
WE DO THE THINKING FOR YOU NOW, LIZA.
BURMAN IS NOT A PROBLEM. HIS MASTERS WILL NEVER BELIEVE THAT A YOUNG GIRL HAS TAKEN OVER THE ENTIRE BASE WHILE HE WAS AWAY.
IT WILL BE DAYS BEFORE THE MACHINERY OF GOVERNMENT BEGINS TO MOVE. BY THEN IT WILL BE TOO LATE.
YOU NAMED THIS PROJECT WELL, LIZA.
SOON THE SHADOWGATE WILL OPEN AND THIS ENTIRE WORLD WILL BE OUR PLAYGROUND.

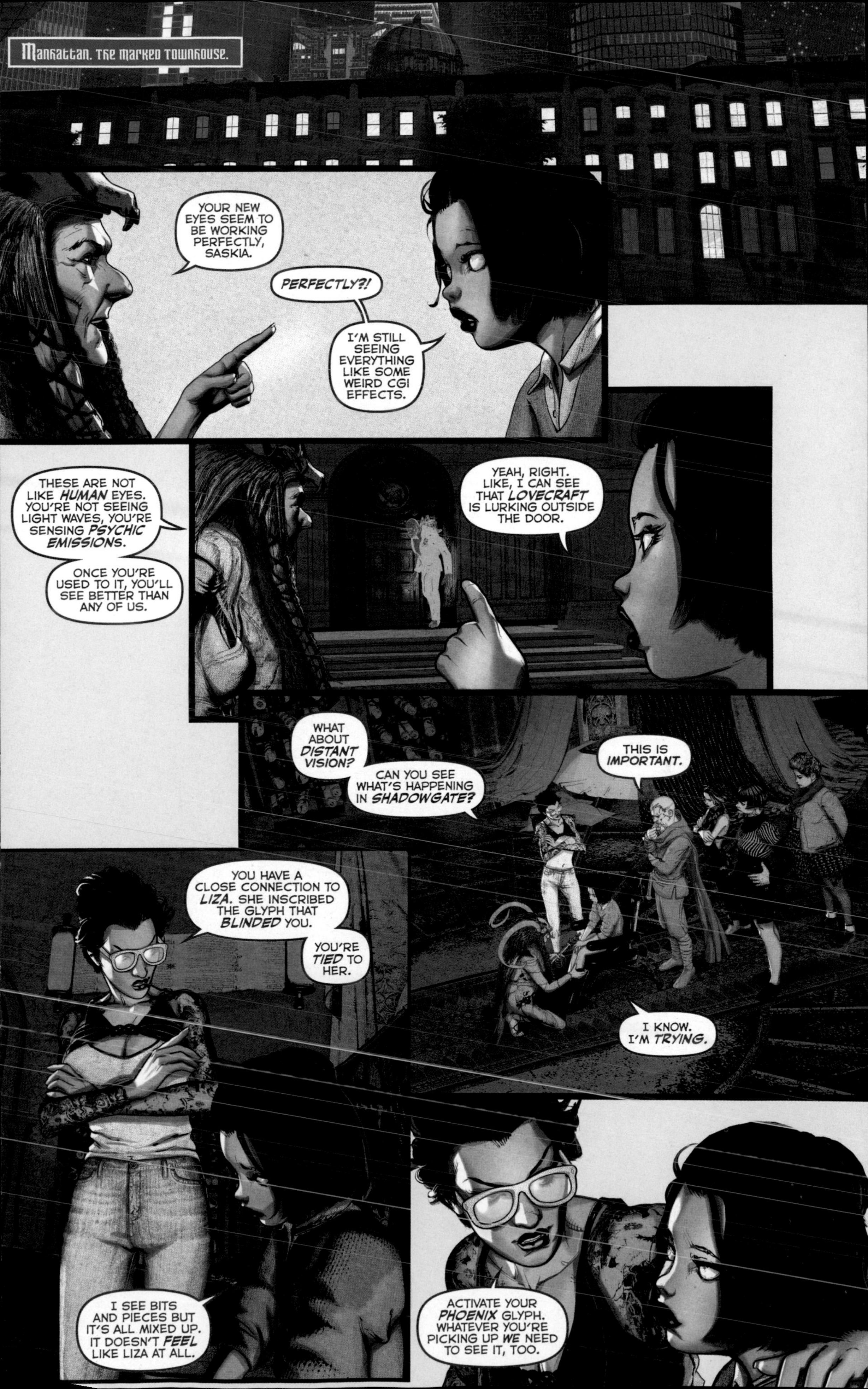

MANHATTAN. THE MARKED TOWNHOUSE.
YOUR NEW EYES SEEM TO BE WORKING PERFECTLY, SASKIA.
PERFECTLY?!
I'M STILL SEEING EVERYTHING LIKE SOME WEIRD CGI EFFECTS.
THESE ARE NOT LIKE HUMAN EYES. YOU'RE NOT SEEING LIGHT WAVES, YOU'RE SENSING PSYCHIC EMISSIONS.
ONCE YOU'RE USED TO IT, YOU'LL SEE BETTER THAN ANY OF US.
YEAH, RIGHT. LIKE, I CAN SEE THAT LOVECRAFT IS LURKING OUTSIDE THE DOOR.
WHAT ABOUT DISTANT VISION?
CAN YOU SEE WHAT'S HAPPENING IN SHADOWGATE?
THIS IS IMPORTANT.
YOU HAVE A CLOSE CONNECTION TO LIZA. SHE INSCRIBED THE GLYPH THAT BLINDED YOU.
YOU'RE TIED TO HER.
I KNOW. I'M TRYING.
I SEE BITS AND PIECES BUT IT'S ALL MIXED UP. IT DOESN'T FEEL LIKE LIZA AT ALL.
ACTIVATE YOUR PHOENIX GLYPH. WHATEVER YOU'RE PICKING UP WE NEED TO SEE IT, TOO.

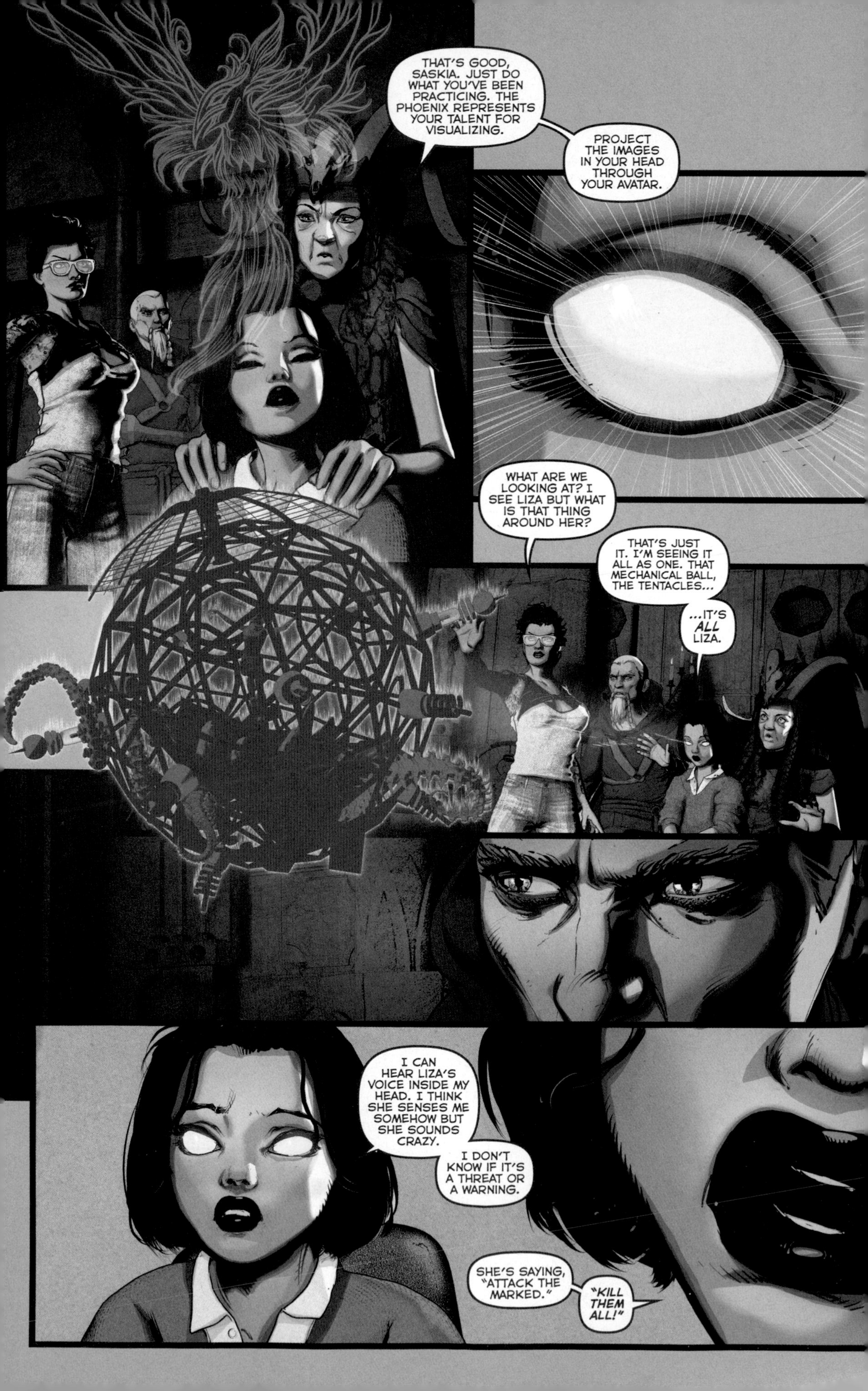
THAT'S GOOD, SASKIA. JUST DO WHAT YOU'VE BEEN PRACTICING. THE PHOENIX REPRESENTS YOUR TALENT FOR VISUALIZING.
PROJECT THE IMAGES IN YOUR HEAD THROUGH YOUR AVATAR.
WHAT ARE WE LOOKING AT? I SEE LIZA BUT WHAT IS THAT THING AROUND HER?
THAT'S JUST IT. I'M SEEING IT ALL AS ONE. THAT MECHANICAL BALL, THE TENTACLES...
...IT'S *ALL* LIZA.
I CAN HEAR LIZA'S VOICE INSIDE MY HEAD. I THINK SHE SENSES ME SOMEHOW BUT SHE SOUNDS CRAZY.
I DON'T KNOW IF IT'S A THREAT OR A WARNING.
SHE'S SAYING, "ATTACK THE MARKED."
"KILL THEM ALL!"

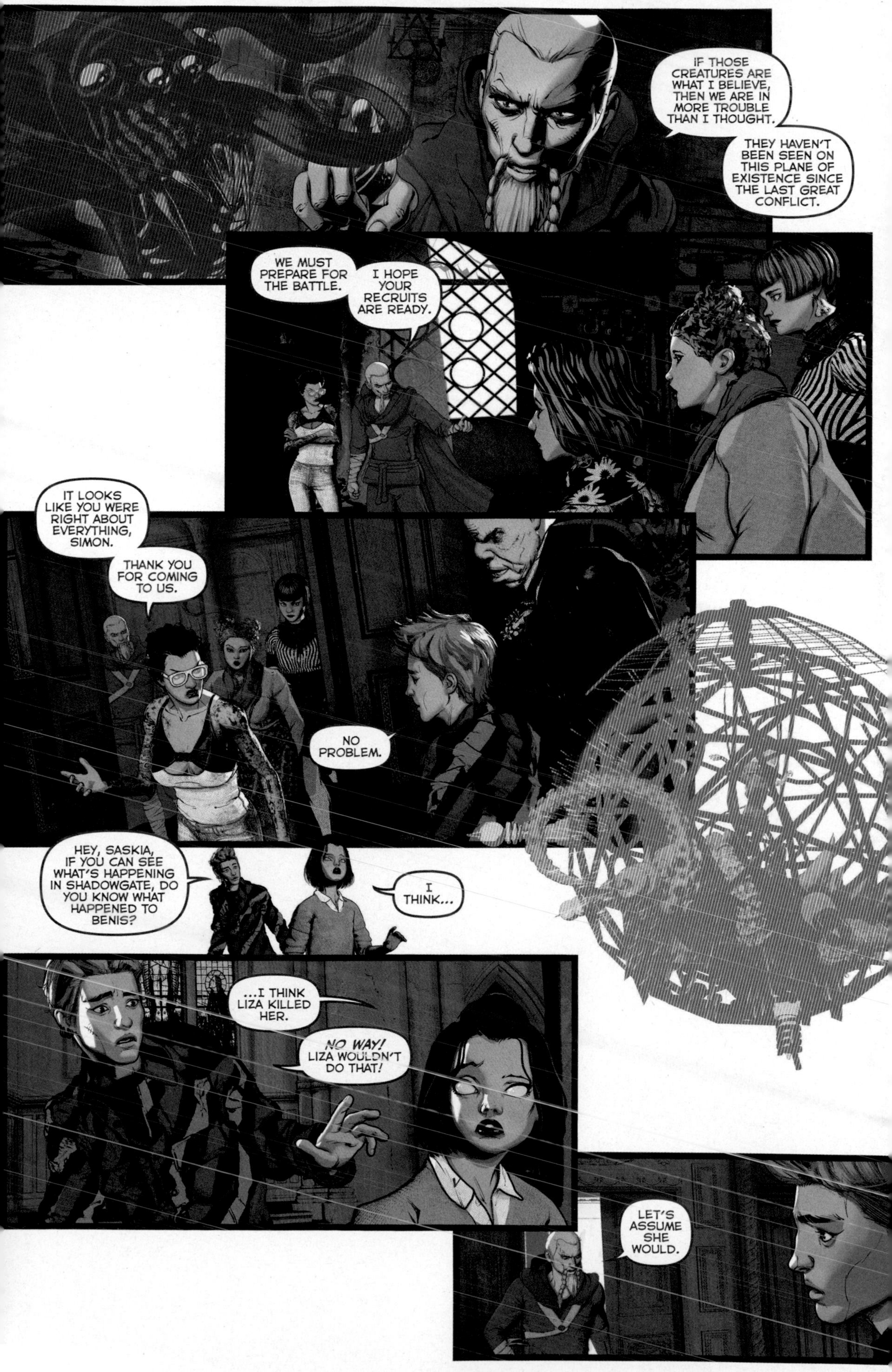
IF THOSE CREATURES ARE WHAT I BELIEVE, THEN WE ARE IN MORE TROUBLE THAN I THOUGHT.
THEY HAVEN'T BEEN SEEN ON THIS PLANE OF EXISTENCE SINCE THE LAST GREAT CONFLICT.
WE MUST PREPARE FOR THE BATTLE.
I HOPE YOUR RECRUITS ARE READY.
IT LOOKS LIKE YOU WERE RIGHT ABOUT EVERYTHING, SIMON.
THANK YOU FOR COMING TO US.
NO PROBLEM.
HEY, SASKIA, IF YOU CAN SEE WHAT'S HAPPENING IN SHADOWGATE, DO YOU KNOW WHAT HAPPENED TO BENIS?
I THINK...
...I THINK LIZA KILLED HER.
NO WAY! LIZA WOULDN'T DO THAT!
LET'S ASSUME SHE WOULD.

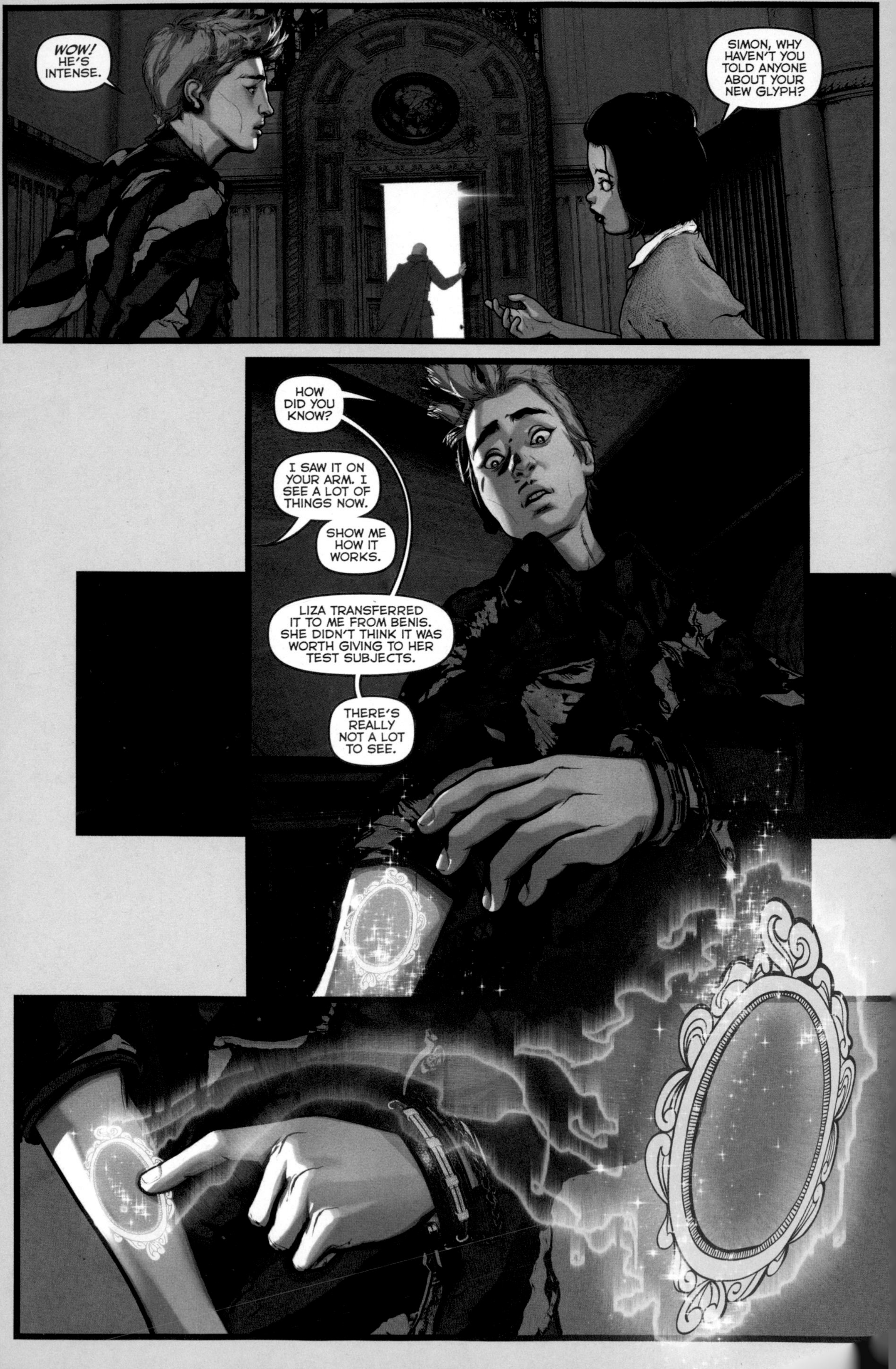
WOW! HE'S INTENSE.
SIMON, WHY HAVEN'T YOU TOLD ANYONE ABOUT YOUR NEW GLYPH?
HOW DID YOU KNOW?
I SAW IT ON YOUR ARM. I SEE A LOT OF THINGS NOW.
SHOW ME HOW IT WORKS.
LIZA TRANSFERRED IT TO ME FROM BENIS. SHE DIDN'T THINK IT WAS WORTH GIVING TO HER TEST SUBJECTS.
THERE'S REALLY NOT A LOT TO SEE.

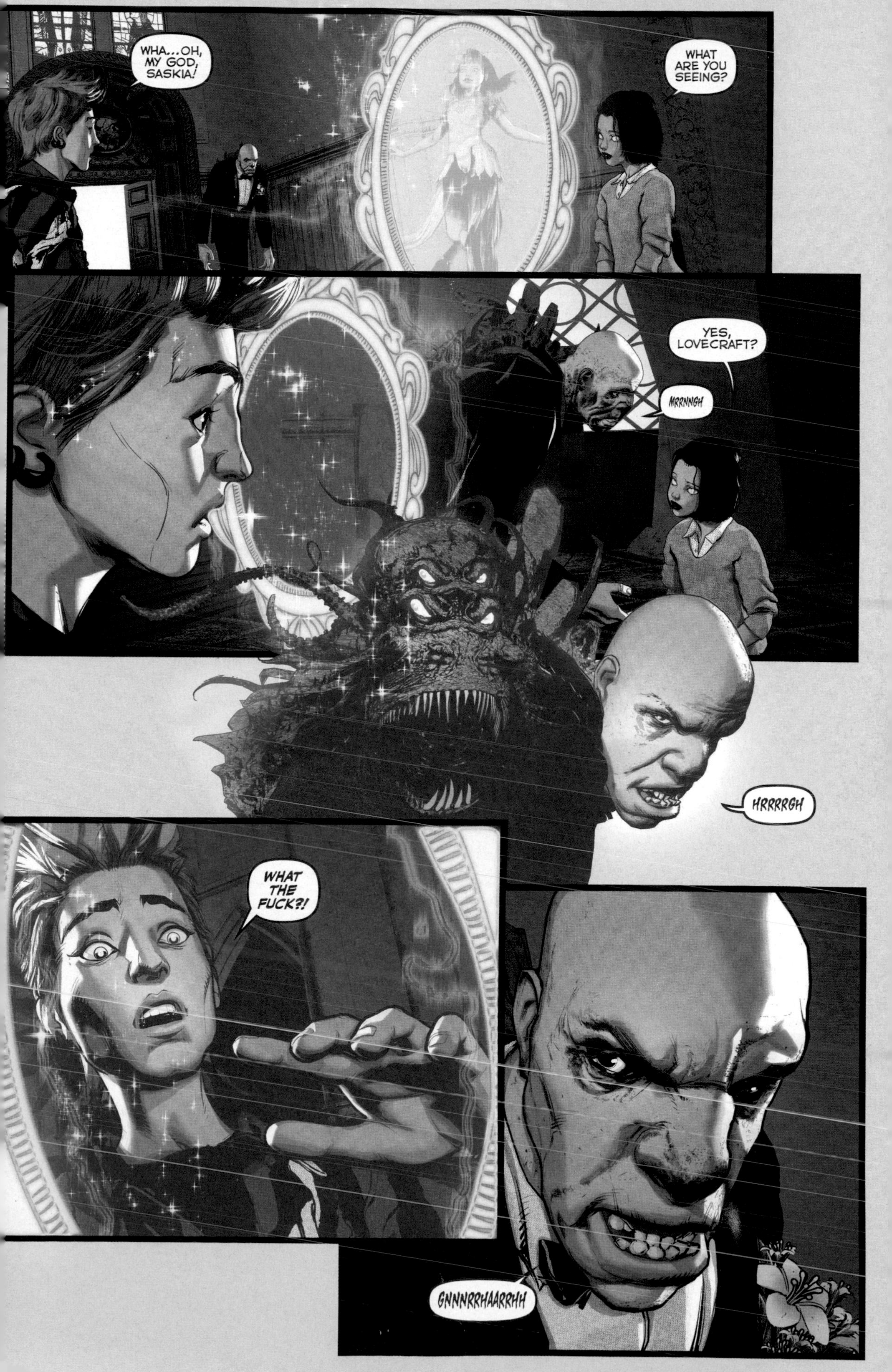
WHA...OH, MY GOD, SASKIA!
WHAT ARE YOU SEEING?
YES, LOVECRAFT?
MRRNNGH
HRRRRGH
WHAT THE FUCK?!
GNNNRRHAARRHH

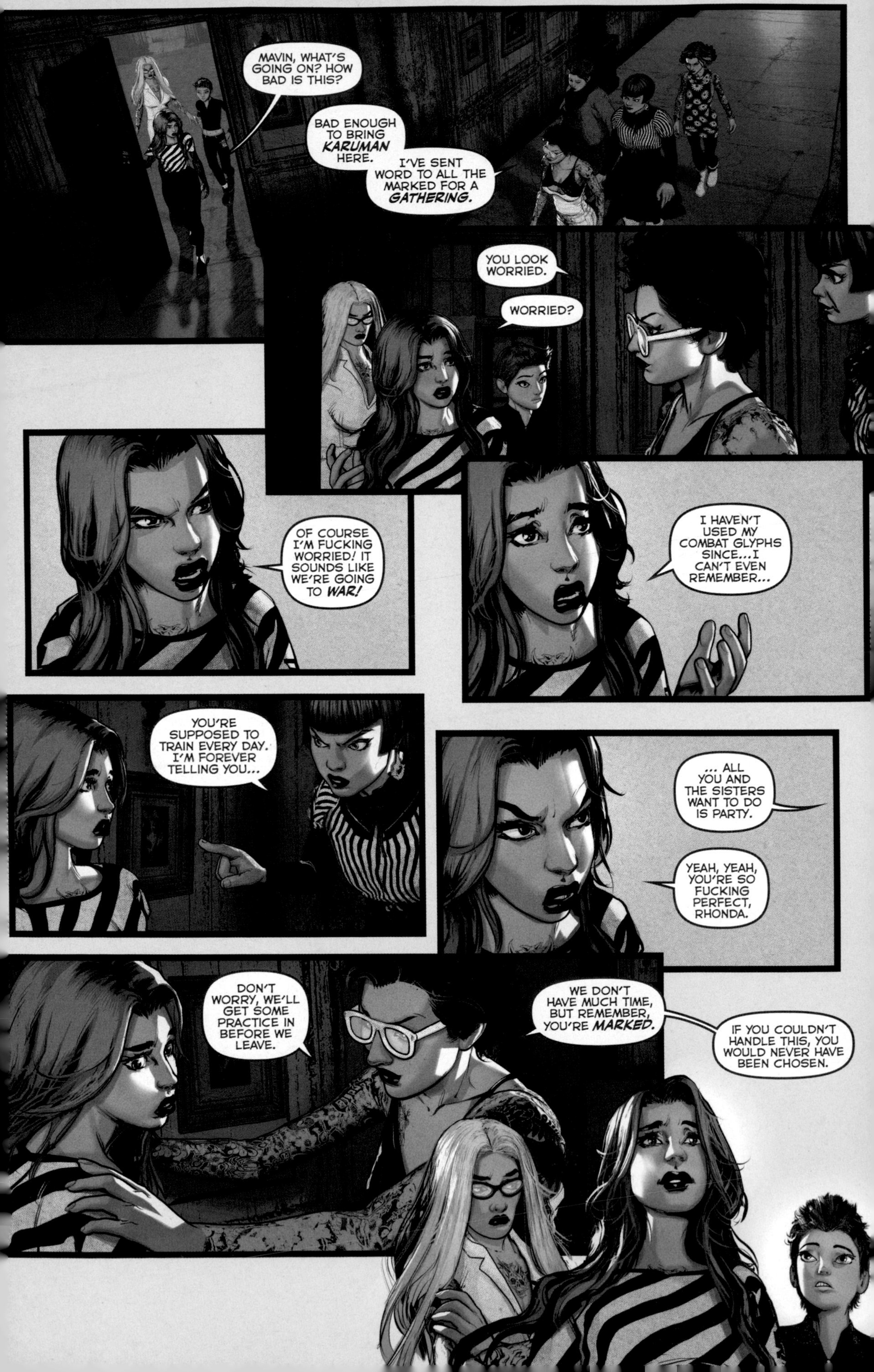
MAVIN, WHAT'S GOING ON? HOW BAD IS THIS?
BAD ENOUGH TO BRING KARUMAN HERE.
I'VE SENT WORD TO ALL THE MARKED FOR A GATHERING.
YOU LOOK WORRIED.
WORRIED?
OF COURSE I'M FUCKING WORRIED! IT SOUNDS LIKE WE'RE GOING TO WAR!
I HAVEN'T USED MY COMBAT GLYPHS SINCE...I CAN'T EVEN REMEMBER...
YOU'RE SUPPOSED TO TRAIN EVERY DAY. I'M FOREVER TELLING YOU...
... ALL YOU AND THE SISTERS WANT TO DO IS PARTY.
YEAH, YEAH, YOU'RE SO FUCKING PERFECT, RHONDA.
DON'T WORRY, WE'LL GET SOME PRACTICE IN BEFORE WE LEAVE.
WE DON'T HAVE MUCH TIME, BUT REMEMBER, YOU'RE MARKED.
IF YOU COULDN'T HANDLE THIS, YOU WOULD NEVER HAVE BEEN CHOSEN.

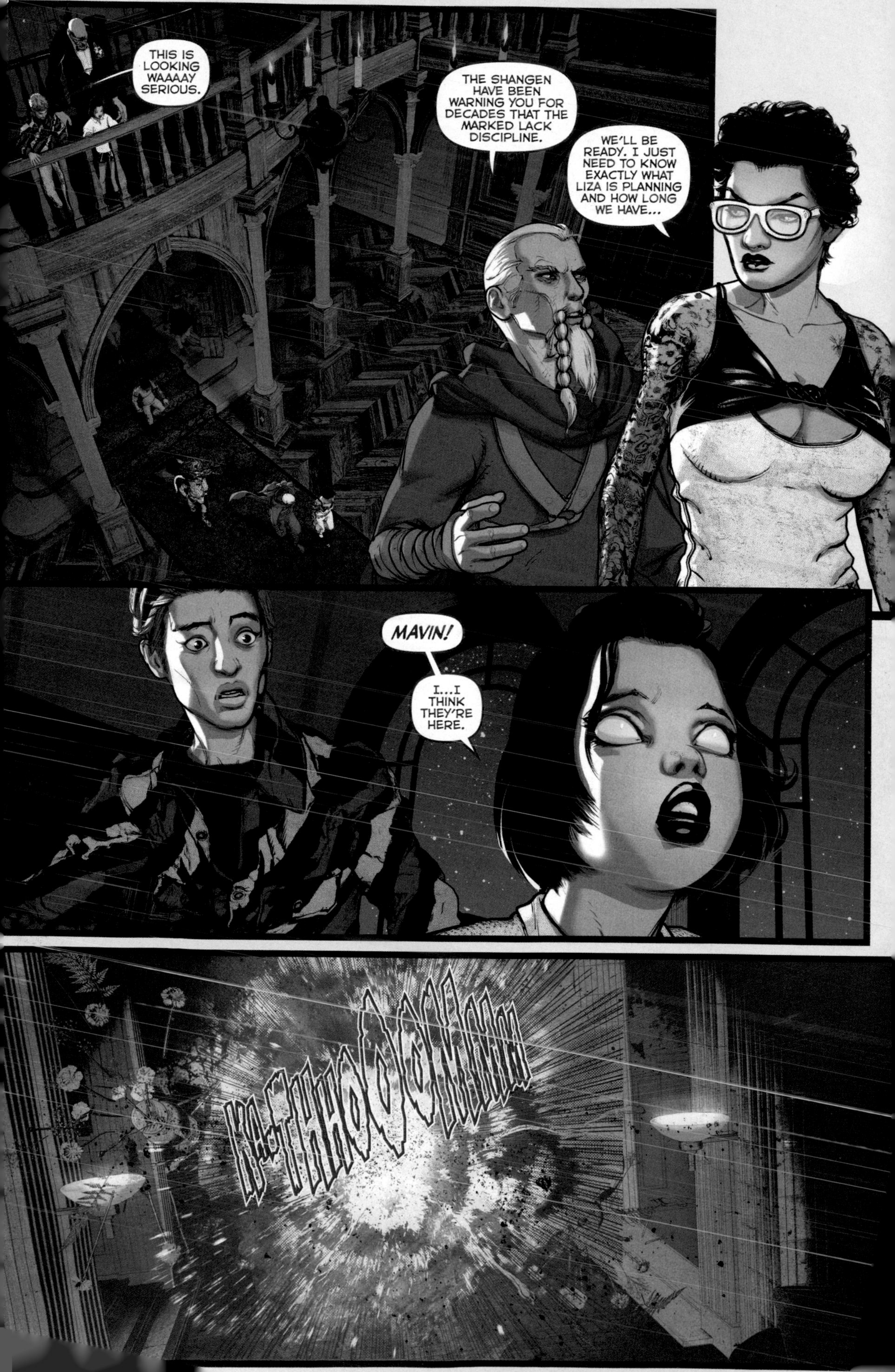
THIS IS LOOKING WAAAAY SERIOUS.
THE SHANGEN HAVE BEEN WARNING YOU FOR DECADES THAT THE MARKED LACK DISCIPLINE.
WE'LL BE READY. I JUST NEED TO KNOW EXACTLY WHAT LIZA IS PLANNING AND HOW LONG WE HAVE...
MAVIN!
I...I THINK THEY'RE HERE.

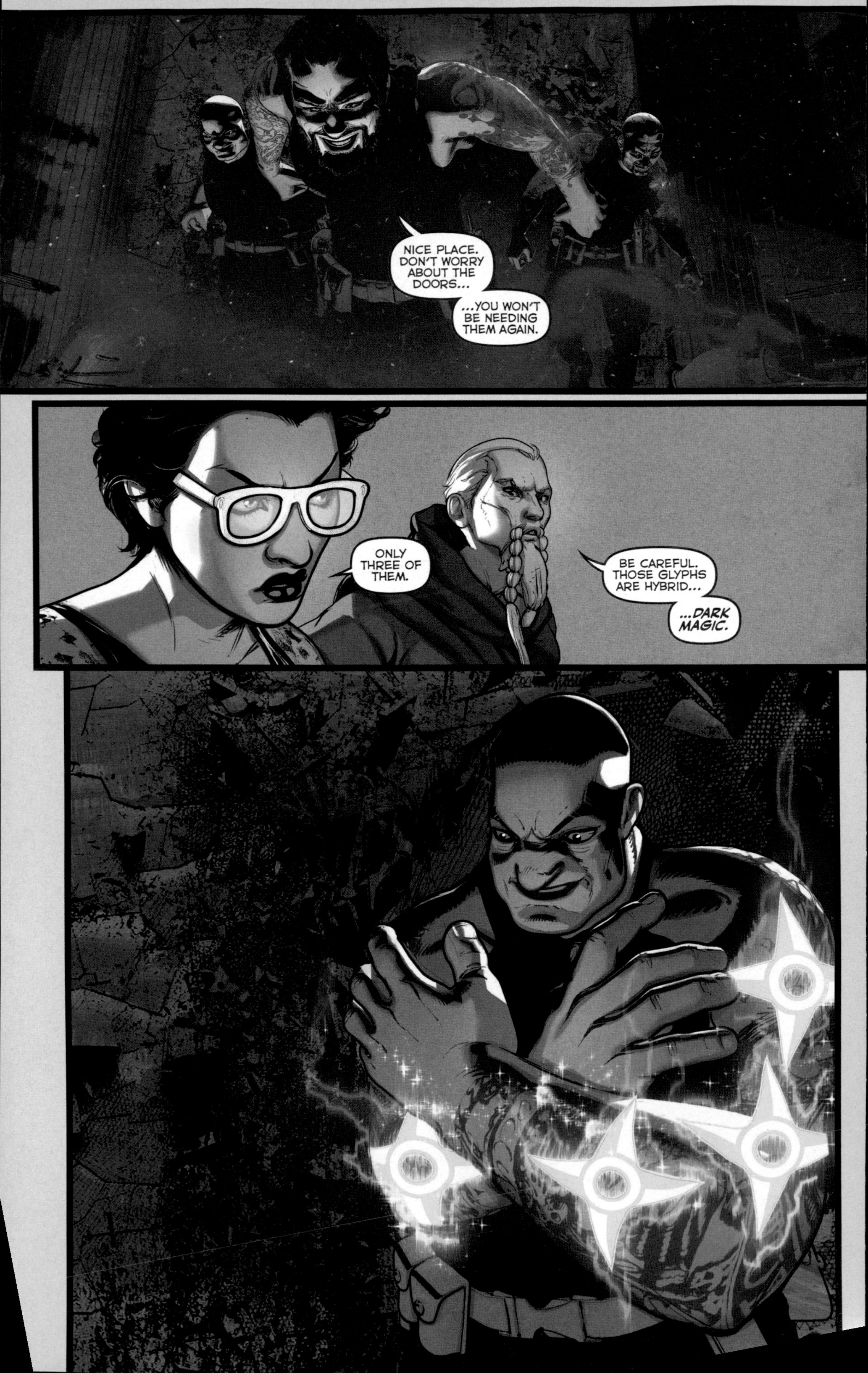
NICE PLACE. DON'T WORRY ABOUT THE DOORS...
...YOU WON'T BE NEEDING THEM AGAIN.
ONLY THREE OF THEM.
BE CAREFUL. THOSE GLYPHS ARE HYBRID...
...DARK MAGIC.

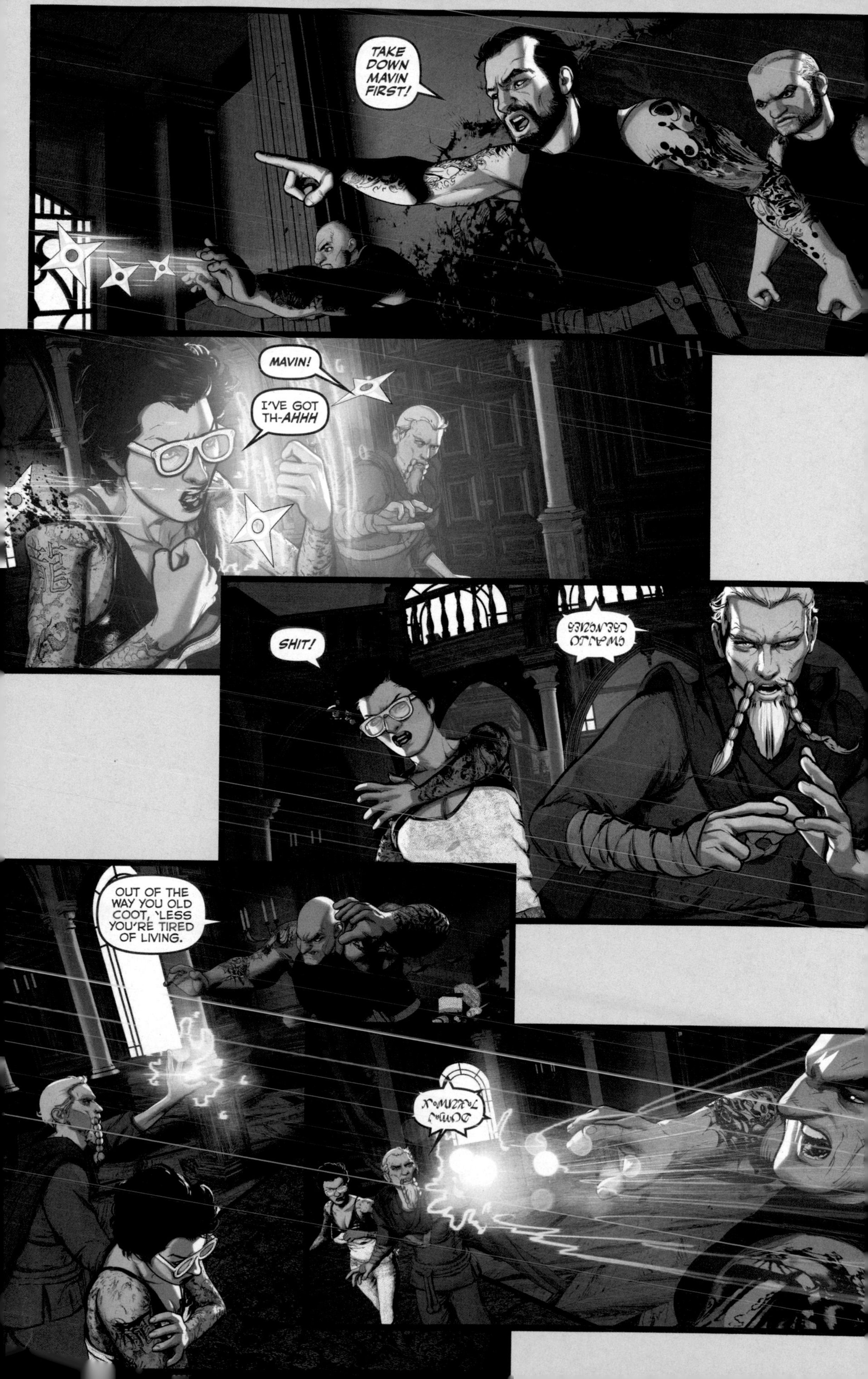
TAKE DOWN MAVIN FIRST!
MAVIN!
I'VE GOT TH-AHHH
SHIT!
OUT OF THE WAY YOU OLD COOT, 'LESS YOU'RE TIRED OF LIVING.

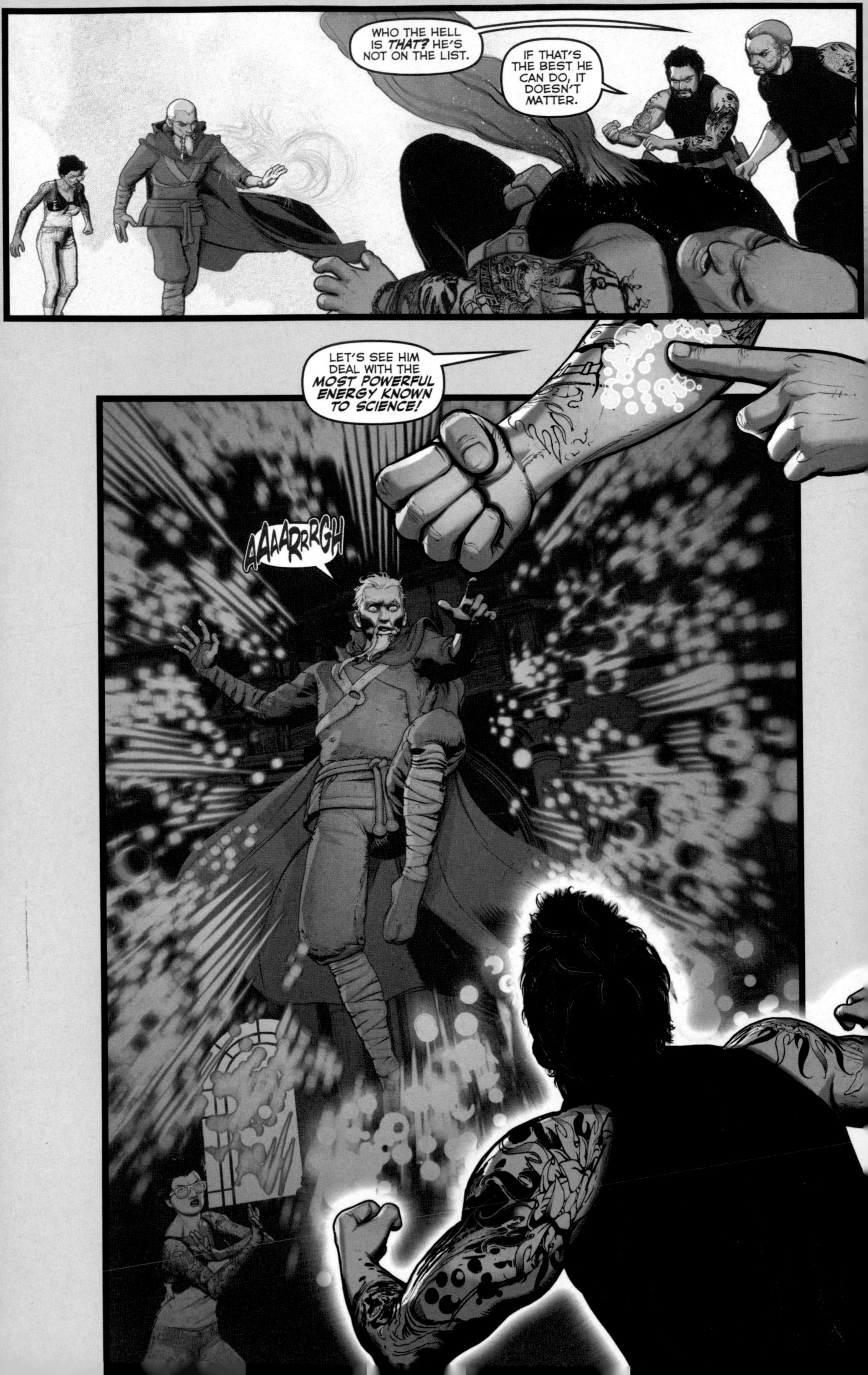
WHO THE HELL IS THAT? HE'S NOT ON THE LIST.
IF THAT'S THE BEST HE CAN DO, IT DOESN'T MATTER.
LET'S SEE HIM DEAL WITH THE MOST POWERFUL ENERGY KNOWN TO SCIENCE!
AAAARRRGH

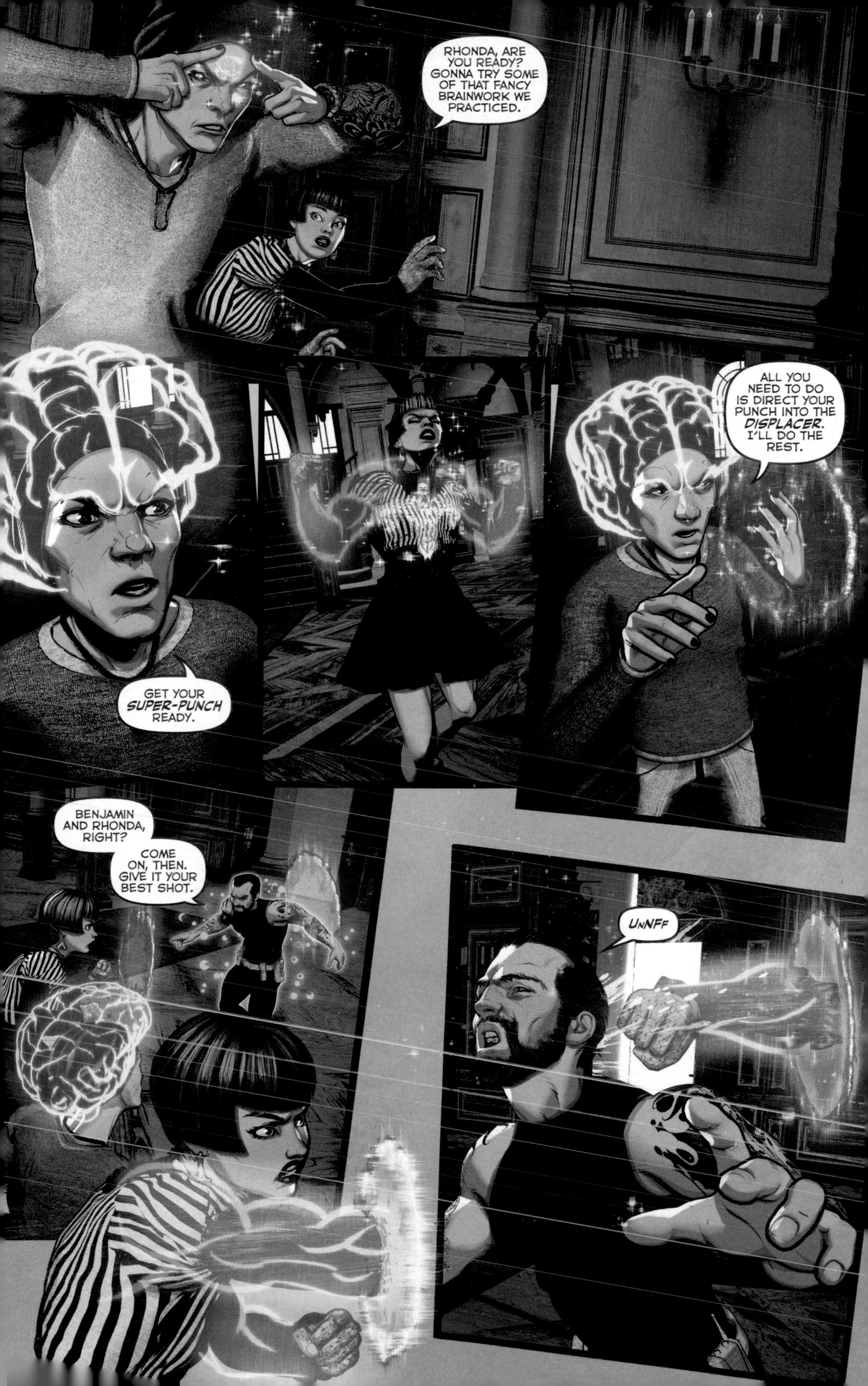
RHONDA, ARE YOU READY? GONNA TRY SOME OF THAT FANCY BRAINWORK WE PRACTICED.
GET YOUR SUPER-PUNCH READY.
ALL YOU NEED TO DO IS DIRECT YOUR PUNCH INTO THE DISPLACER. I'LL DO THE REST.
BENJAMIN AND RHONDA, RIGHT?
COME ON, THEN. GIVE IT YOUR BEST SHOT.
UNNFF

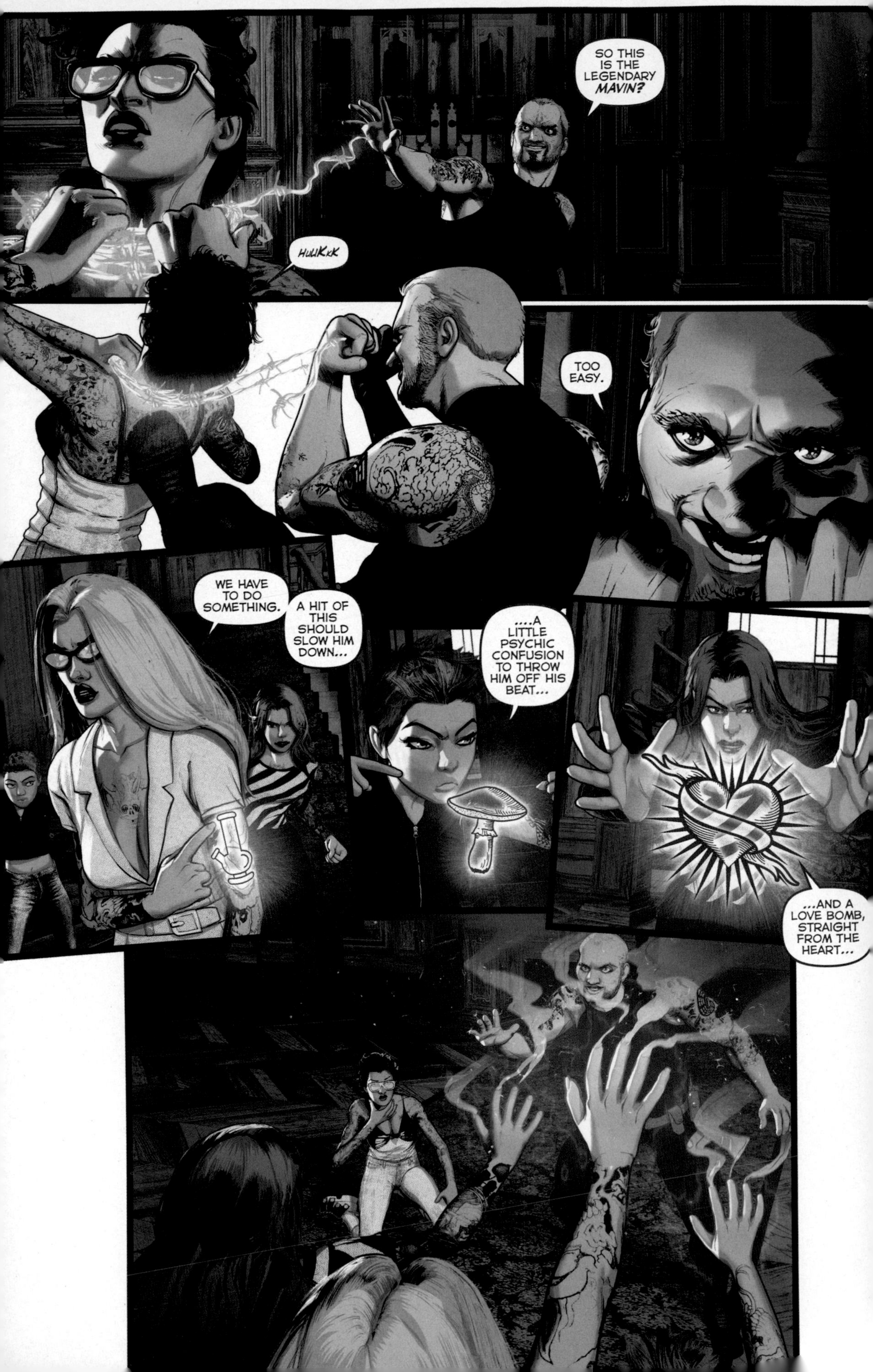
SO THIS IS THE LEGENDARY MAVIN?
HULKKK
TOO EASY.
WE HAVE TO DO SOMETHING.
A HIT OF THIS SHOULD SLOW HIM DOWN...
....A LITTLE PSYCHIC CONFUSION TO THROW HIM OFF HIS BEAT...
...AND A LOVE BOMB, STRAIGHT FROM THE HEART...

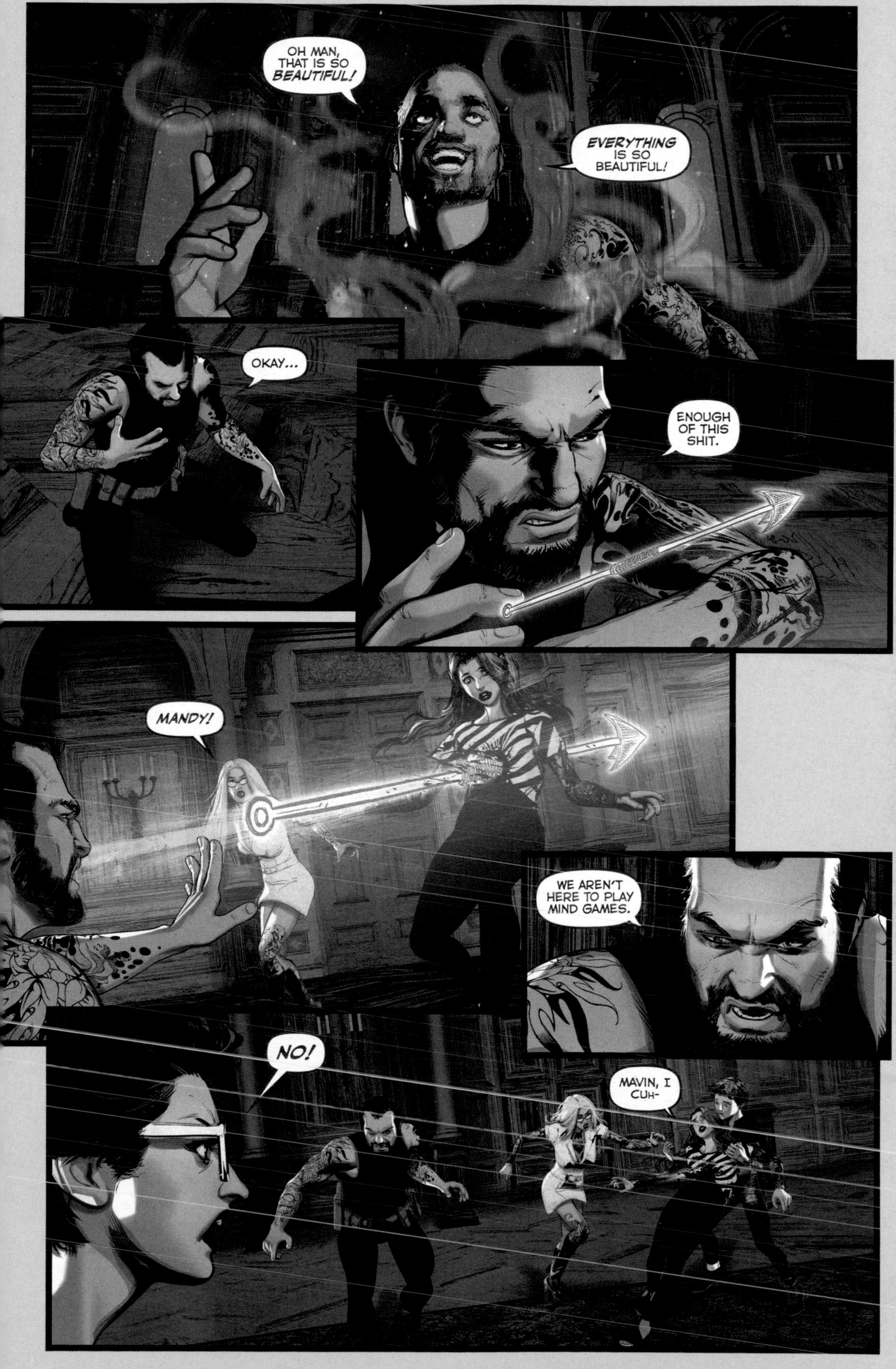
OH MAN, THAT IS SO BEAUTIFUL!
EVERYTHING IS SO BEAUTIFUL!
OKAY...
ENOUGH OF THIS SHIT.
MANDY!
WE AREN'T HERE TO PLAY MIND GAMES.
NO!
MAVIN, I CUH-

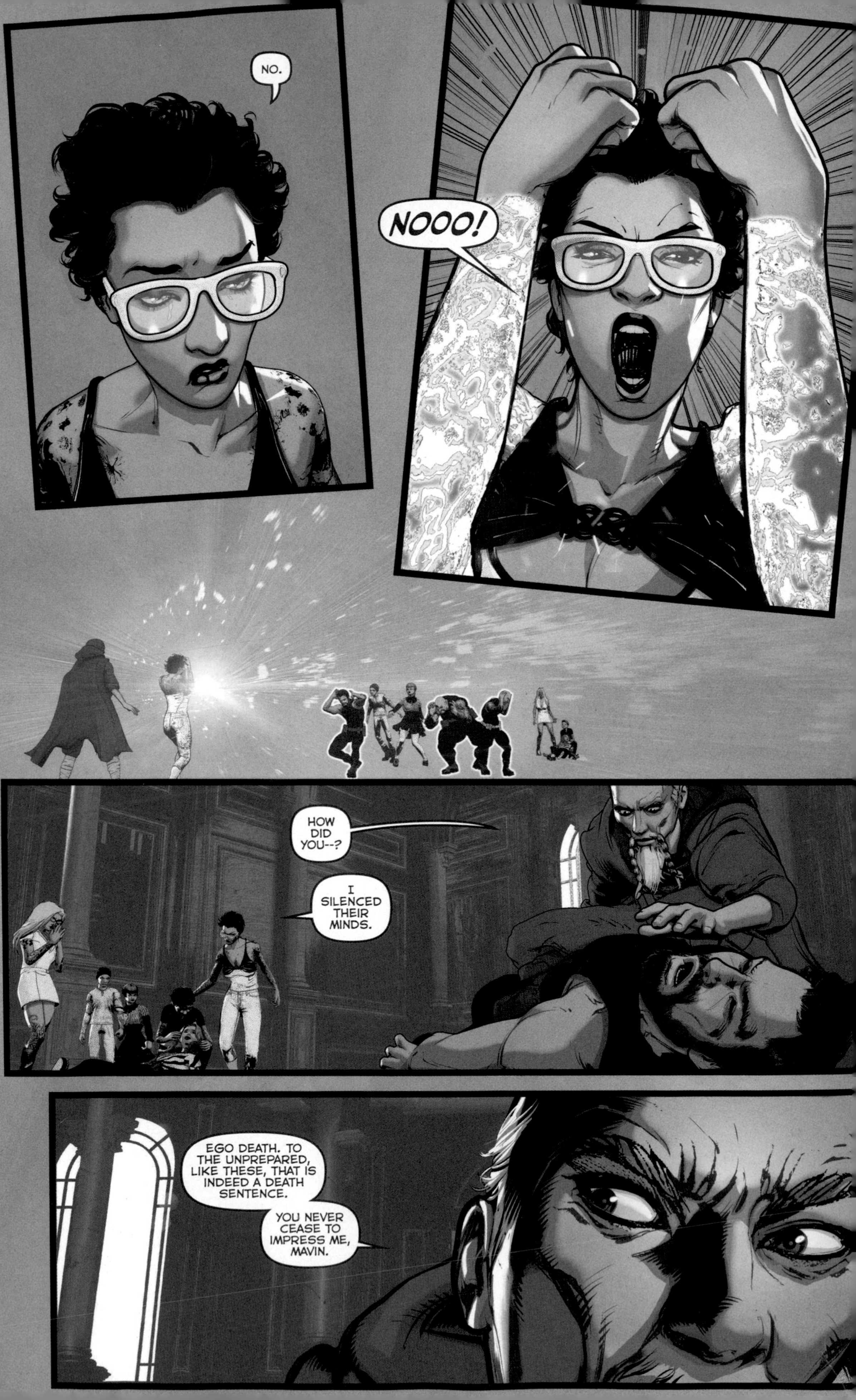
NO.
NOOO!
HOW DID YOU--?
I SILENCED THEIR MINDS.
EGO DEATH. TO THE UNPREPARED, LIKE THESE, THAT IS INDEED A DEATH SENTENCE.
YOU NEVER CEASE TO IMPRESS ME, MAVIN.

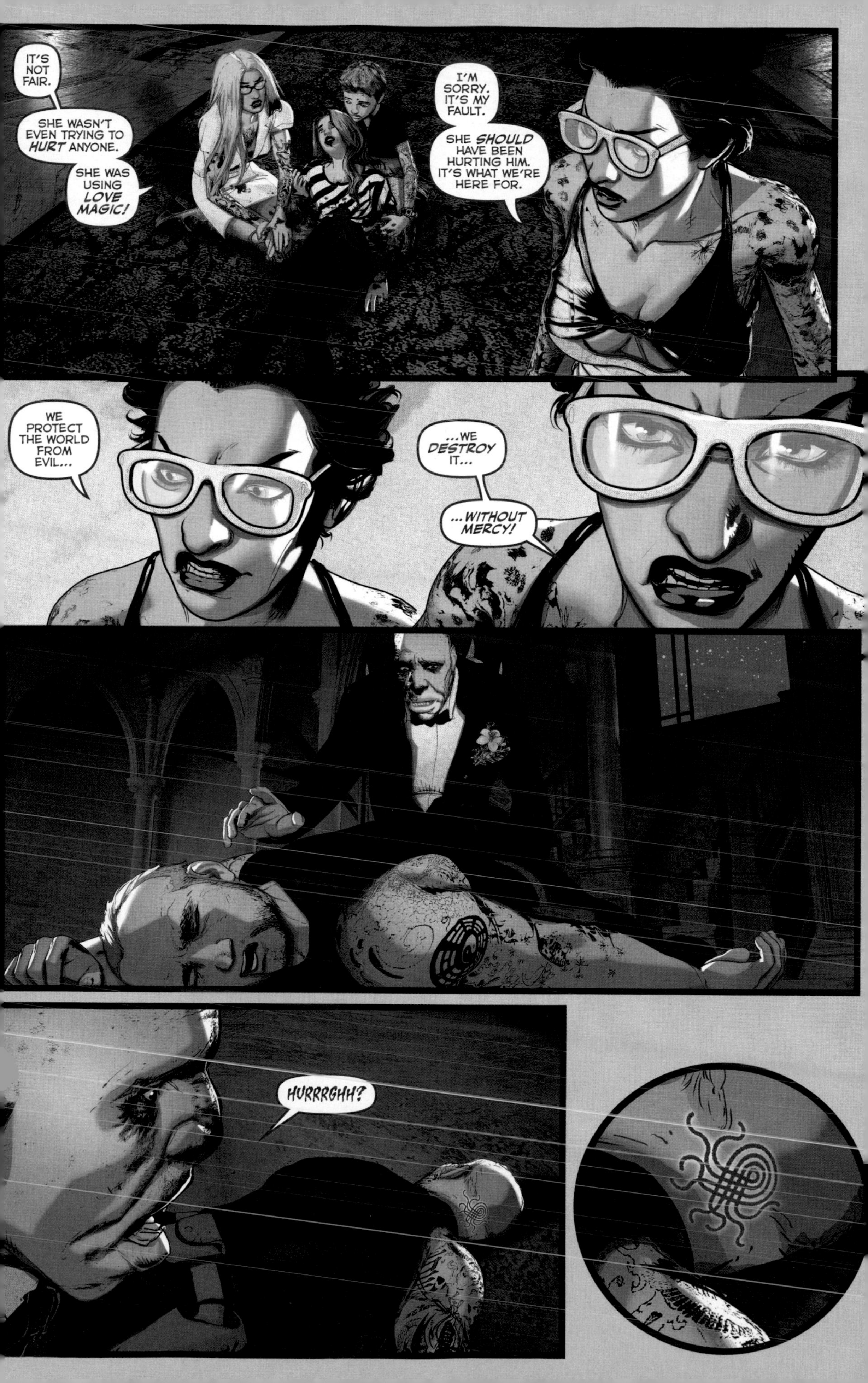
IT'S NOT FAIR.
SHE WASN'T EVEN TRYING TO *HURT* ANYONE.
SHE WAS USING *LOVE MAGIC!*
I'M SORRY. IT'S MY FAULT.
SHE *SHOULD* HAVE BEEN HURTING HIM. IT'S WHAT WE'RE HERE FOR.
WE PROTECT THE WORLD FROM EVIL...
...WE *DESTROY* IT...
...*WITHOUT MERCY!*
HURRRGHH?

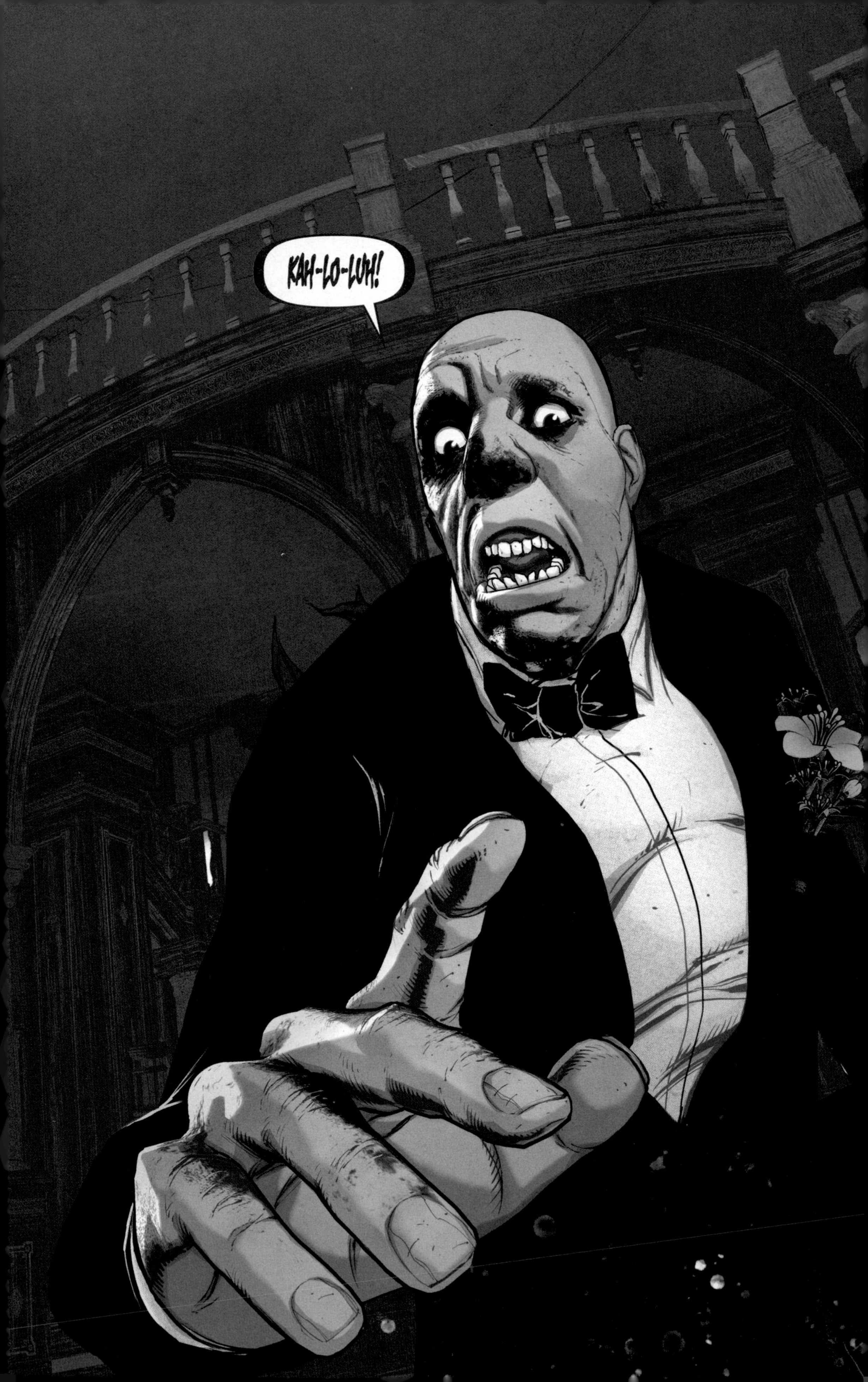
KAH-LO-LUH!

CHAPTER FIVE

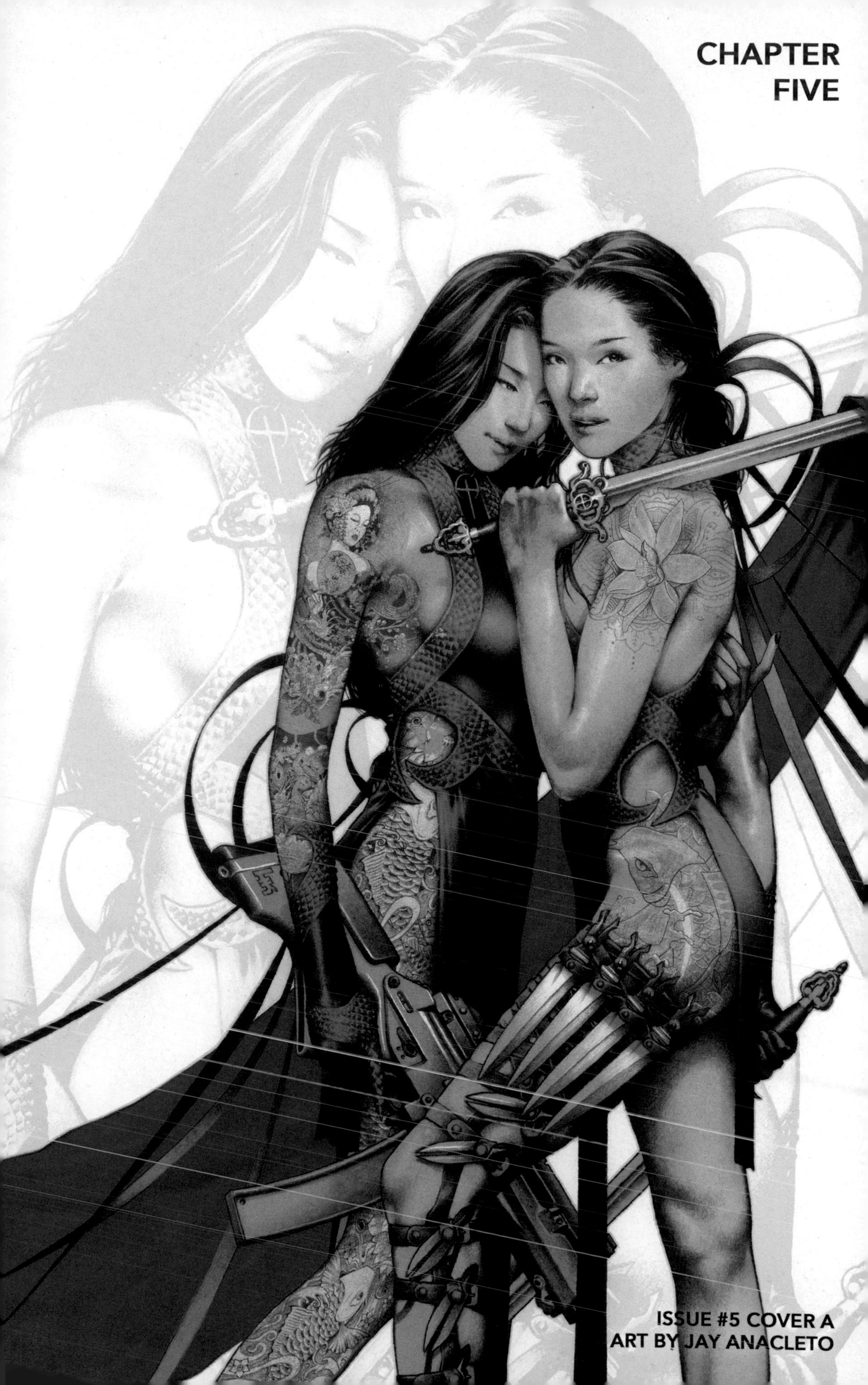

ISSUE #5 COVER A
ART BY JAY ANACLETO

ISSUE #5 COVER B

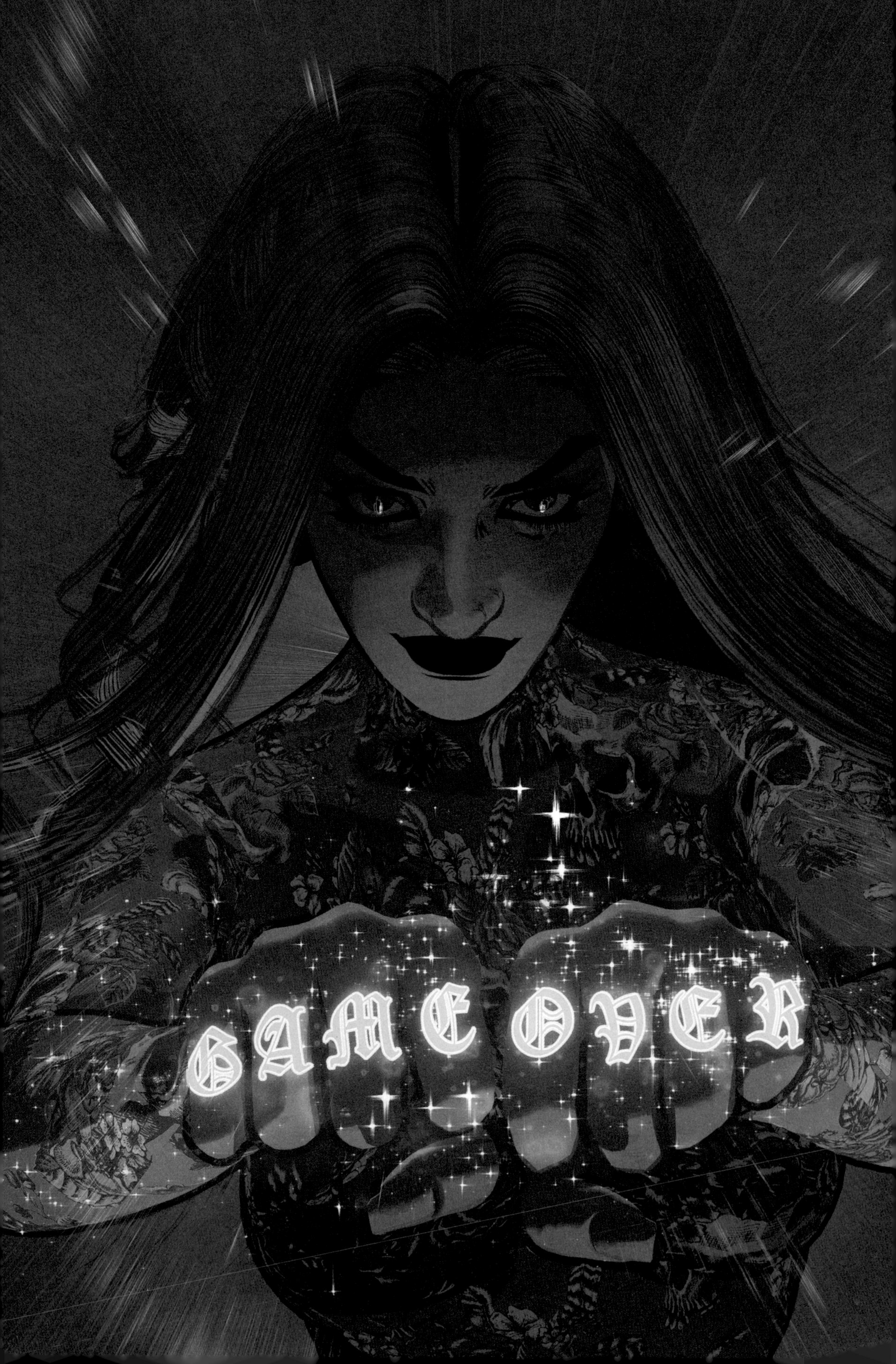
GAME OVER

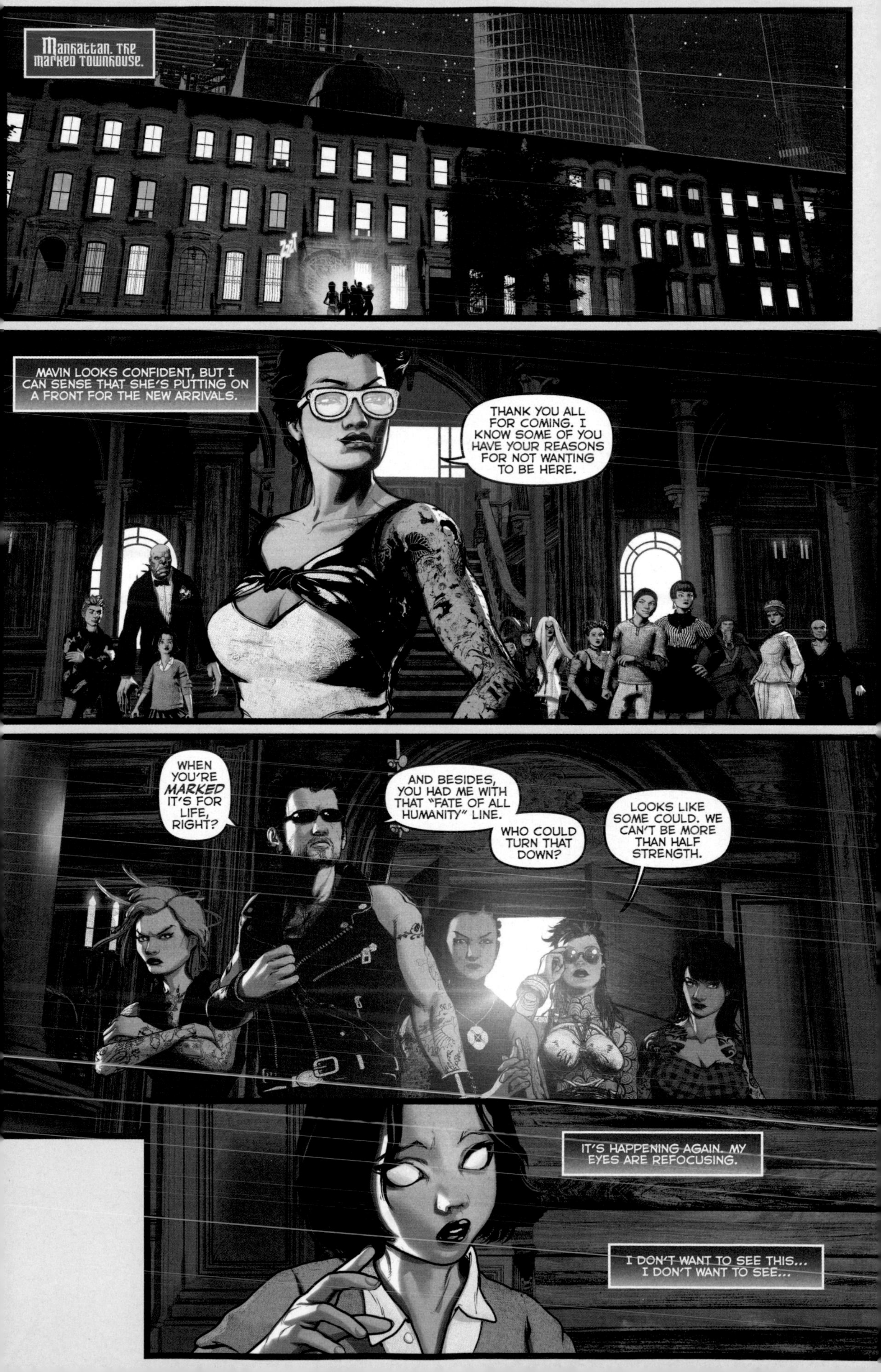
Manhattan. The Marked Townhouse.
ZZZT
MAVIN LOOKS CONFIDENT, BUT I CAN SENSE THAT SHE'S PUTTING ON A FRONT FOR THE NEW ARRIVALS.
THANK YOU ALL FOR COMING. I KNOW SOME OF YOU HAVE YOUR REASONS FOR NOT WANTING TO BE HERE.
WHEN YOU'RE *MARKED* IT'S FOR LIFE, RIGHT?
AND BESIDES, YOU HAD ME WITH THAT "FATE OF ALL HUMANITY" LINE.
WHO COULD TURN THAT DOWN?
LOOKS LIKE SOME COULD. WE CAN'T BE MORE THAN HALF STRENGTH.
IT'S HAPPENING AGAIN. MY EYES ARE REFOCUSING.
I DON'T WANT TO SEE THIS... I DON'T WANT TO SEE...

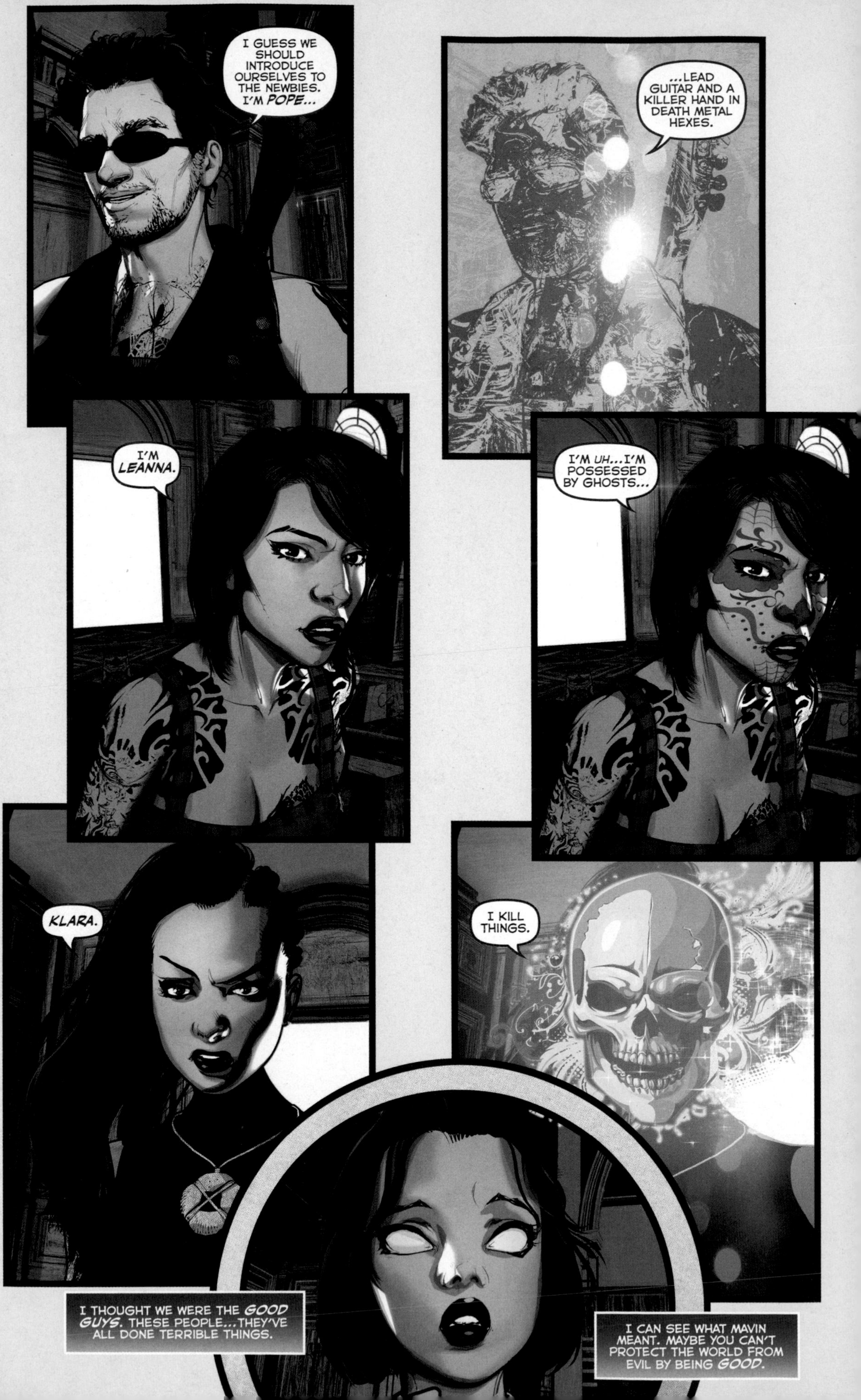
I GUESS WE SHOULD INTRODUCE OURSELVES TO THE NEWBIES. I'M POPE...
...LEAD GUITAR AND A KILLER HAND IN DEATH METAL HEXES.
I'M LEANNA.
I'M UH...I'M POSSESSED BY GHOSTS...
KLARA.
I KILL THINGS.
I THOUGHT WE WERE THE GOOD GUYS. THESE PEOPLE...THEY'VE ALL DONE TERRIBLE THINGS.
I CAN SEE WHAT MAVIN MEANT. MAYBE YOU CAN'T PROTECT THE WORLD FROM EVIL BY BEING GOOD.

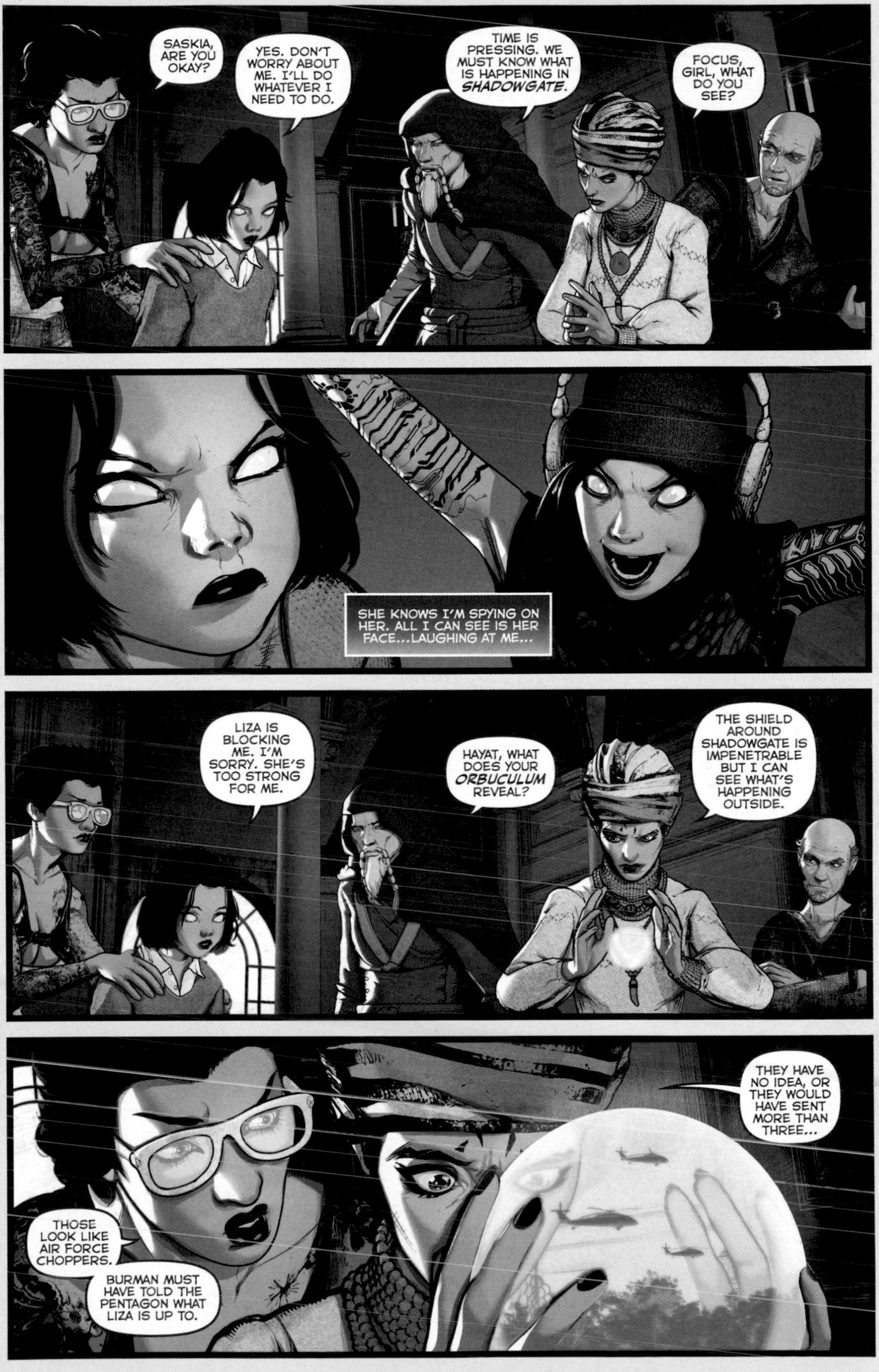
SASKIA, ARE YOU OKAY?
YES. DON'T WORRY ABOUT ME. I'LL DO WHATEVER I NEED TO DO.
TIME IS PRESSING. WE MUST KNOW WHAT IS HAPPENING IN SHADOWGATE.
FOCUS, GIRL, WHAT DO YOU SEE?
SHE KNOWS I'M SPYING ON HER. ALL I CAN SEE IS HER FACE...LAUGHING AT ME...
LIZA IS BLOCKING ME. I'M SORRY. SHE'S TOO STRONG FOR ME.
HAYAT, WHAT DOES YOUR ORBUCULUM REVEAL?
THE SHIELD AROUND SHADOWGATE IS IMPENETRABLE BUT I CAN SEE WHAT'S HAPPENING OUTSIDE.
THEY HAVE NO IDEA, OR THEY WOULD HAVE SENT MORE THAN THREE...
THOSE LOOK LIKE AIR FORCE CHOPPERS.
BURMAN MUST HAVE TOLD THE PENTAGON WHAT LIZA IS UP TO.

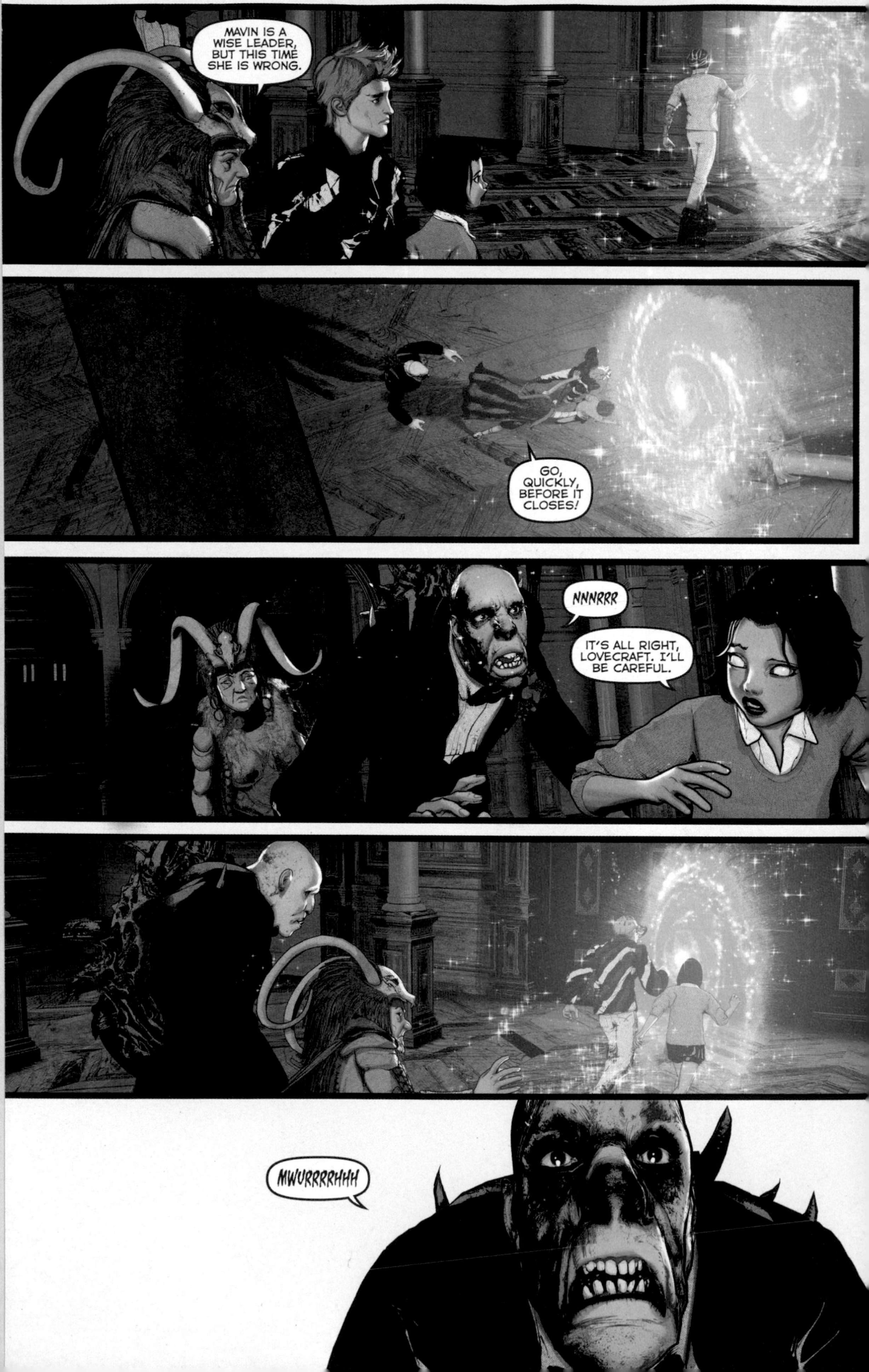
MAVIN IS A WISE LEADER, BUT THIS TIME SHE IS WRONG.
GO, QUICKLY, BEFORE IT CLOSES!
NNNRRR
IT'S ALL RIGHT, LOVECRAFT. I'LL BE CAREFUL.
MWURRRRHHH

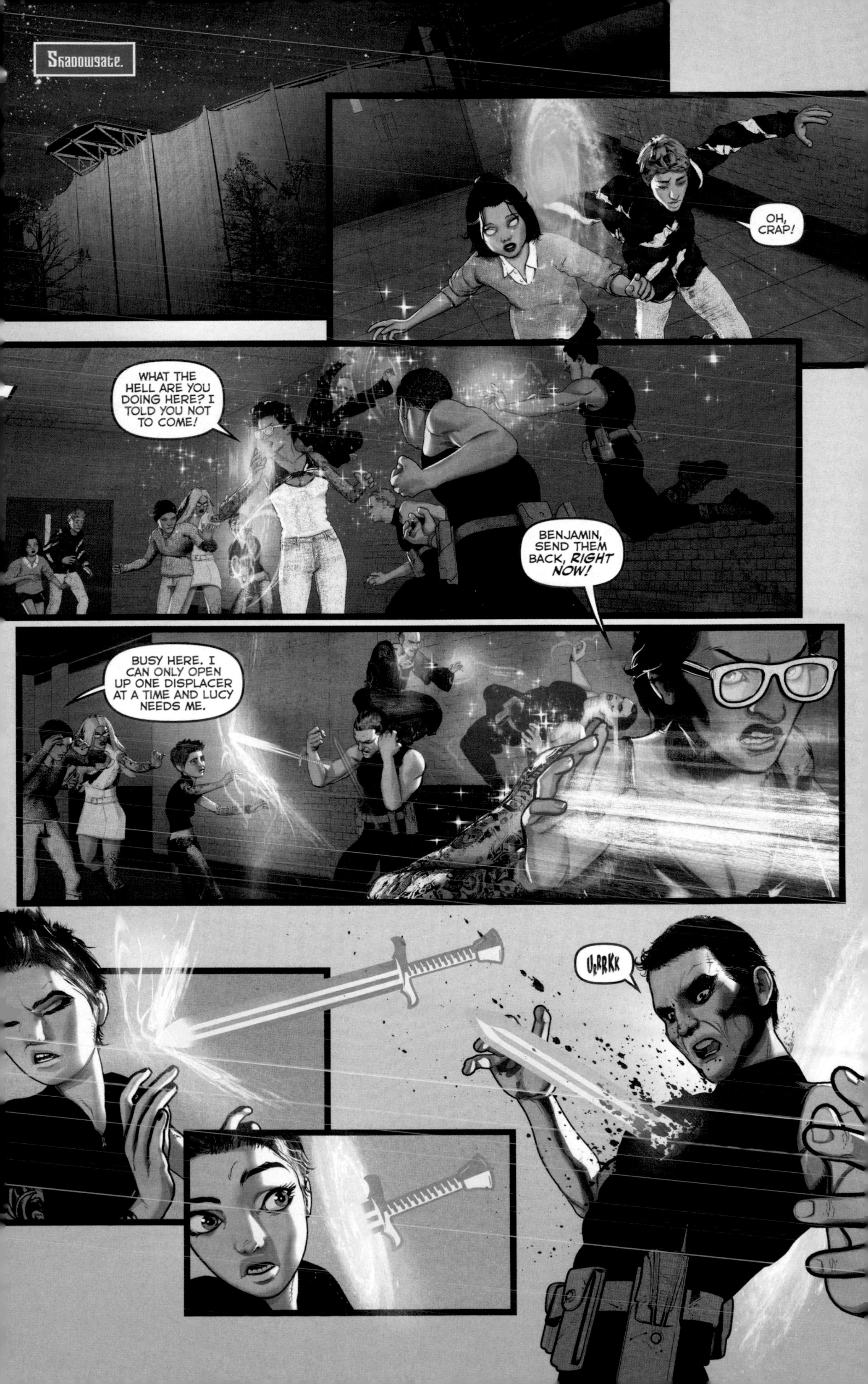
Shadowgate.
OH, CRAP!
WHAT THE HELL ARE YOU DOING HERE? I TOLD YOU NOT TO COME!
BENJAMIN, SEND THEM BACK, RIGHT NOW!
BUSY HERE. I CAN ONLY OPEN UP ONE DISPLACER AT A TIME AND LUCY NEEDS ME.
URRRKK

YOU SEE WHAT YOU'VE WALKED INTO?
I CAN'T LOOK OUT FOR YOU.
I WILL TAKE CARE OF THESE YOUNGSTERS.
THERE'S NO POINT IN US BEING HERE. WE'RE JUST GETTING IN THE WAY.
OH, YOU HAVE A PURPOSE...IF I CAN KEEP YOU ALIVE LONG ENOUGH.
WE ALL HAVE A PURPOSE!
DAMMIT, I'M SORRY, BRO! THIS IS FUCKED UP!
YOU AREN'T CHILDREN!
YOU'RE MONSTERS!
YOU SEE?! YOU'RE SAFE WITH ME...
...UNLESS I GET MYSELF KILLED. THEN YOU'RE DOOMED!

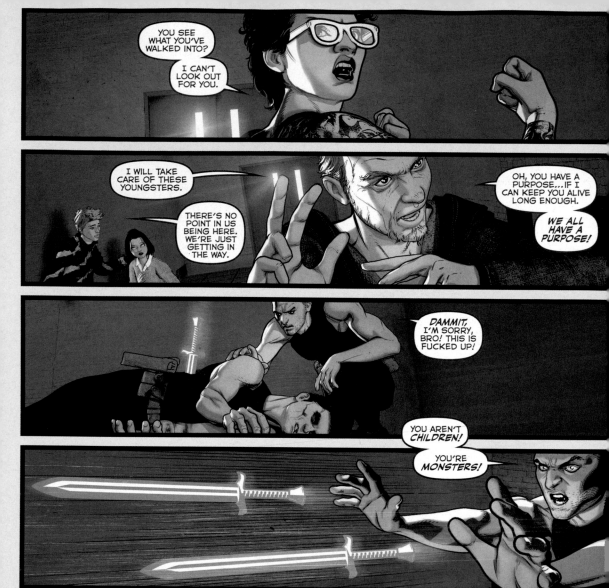

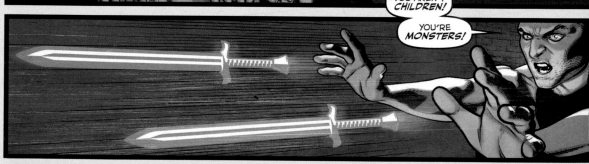

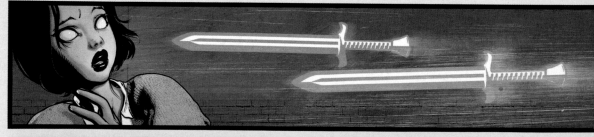

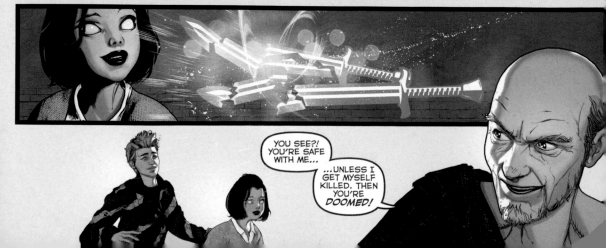

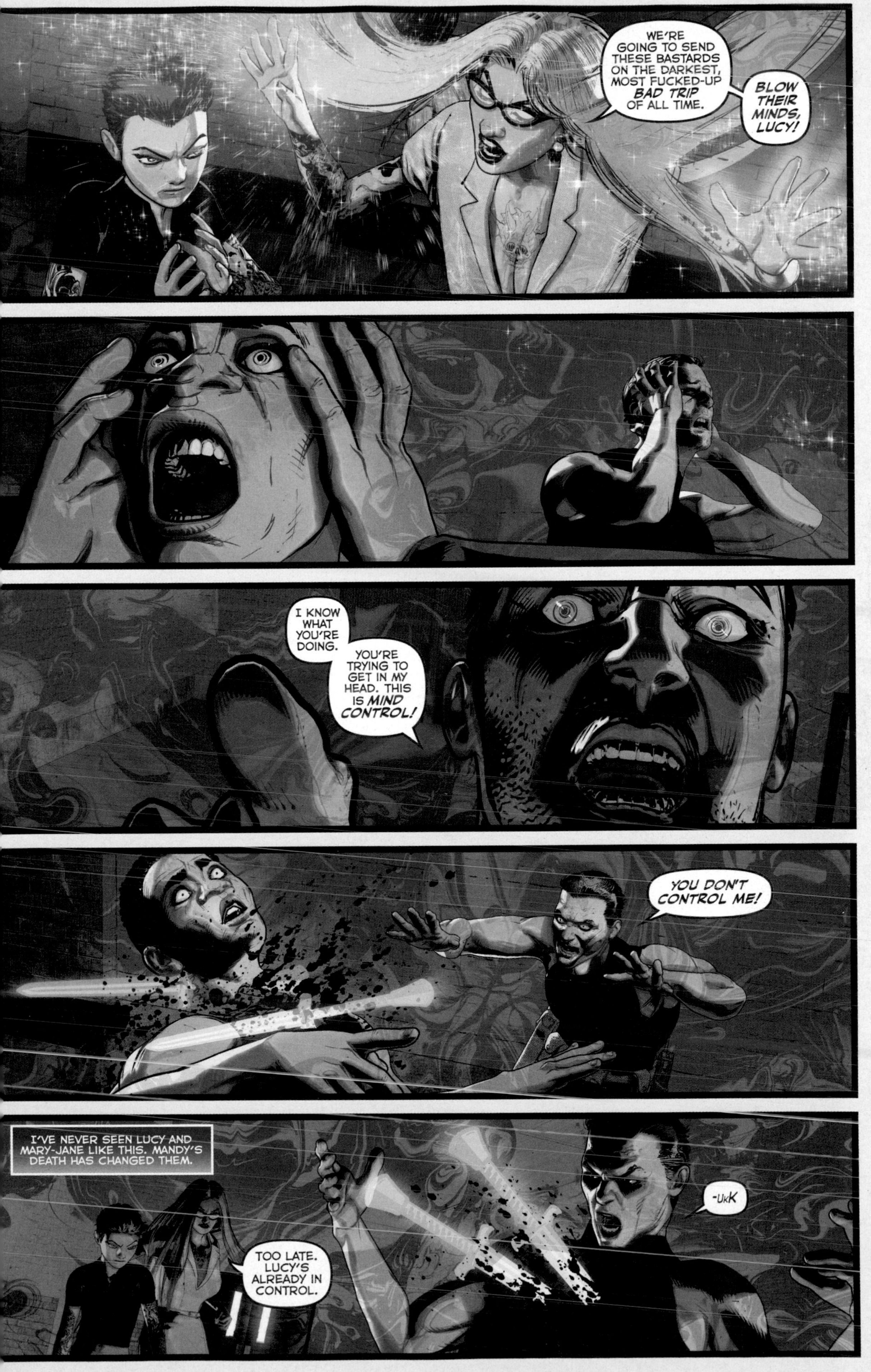
WE'RE GOING TO SEND THESE BASTARDS ON THE DARKEST, MOST FUCKED-UP BAD TRIP OF ALL TIME.
BLOW THEIR MINDS, LUCY!
I KNOW WHAT YOU'RE DOING.
YOU'RE TRYING TO GET IN MY HEAD. THIS IS MIND CONTROL!
YOU DON'T CONTROL ME!
I'VE NEVER SEEN LUCY AND MARY-JANE LIKE THIS. MANDY'S DEATH HAS CHANGED THEM.
-UKK
TOO LATE. LUCY'S ALREADY IN CONTROL.

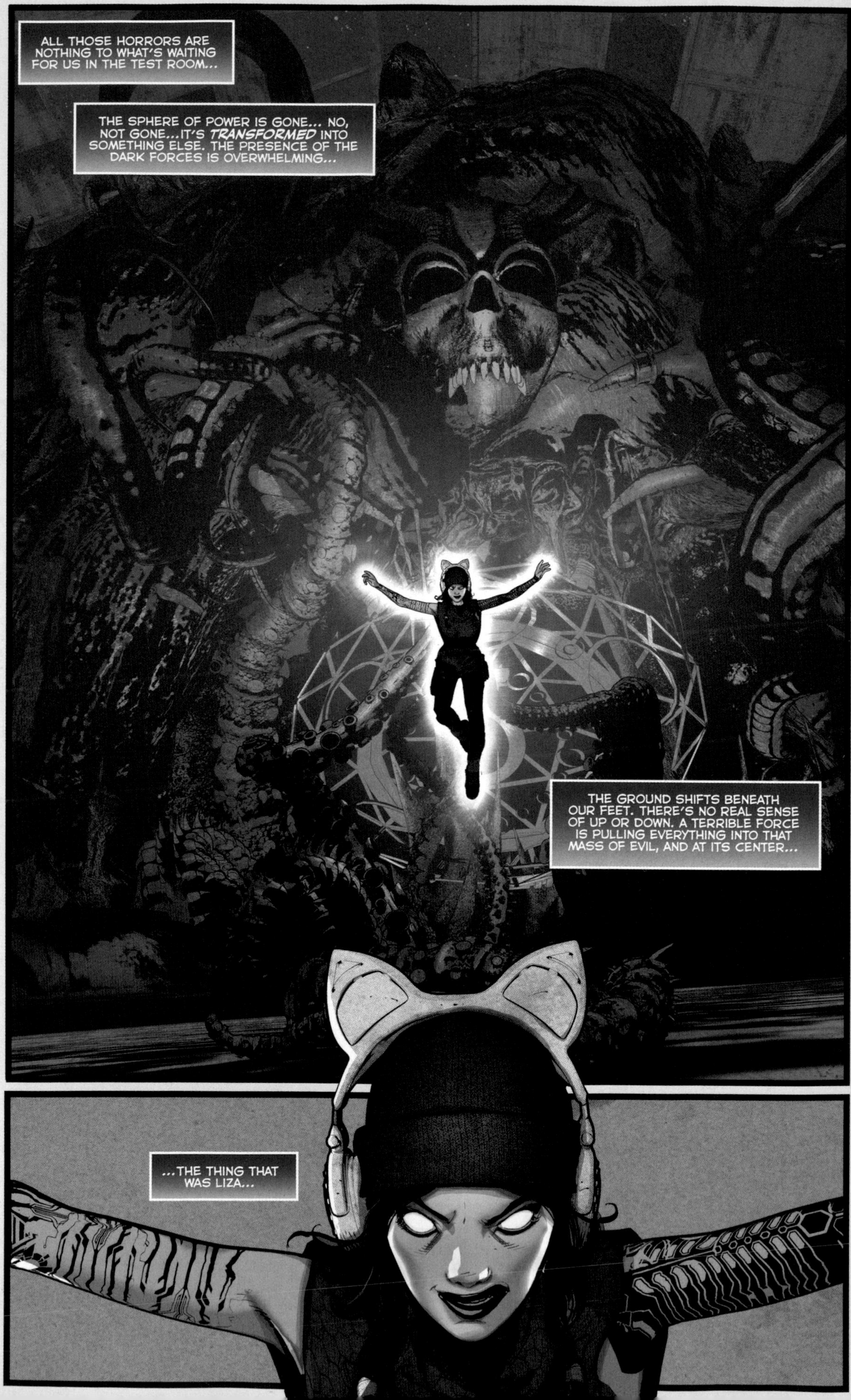
ALL THOSE HORRORS ARE NOTHING TO WHAT'S WAITING FOR US IN THE TEST ROOM...
THE SPHERE OF POWER IS GONE... NO, NOT GONE...IT'S *TRANSFORMED* INTO SOMETHING ELSE. THE PRESENCE OF THE DARK FORCES IS OVERWHELMING...
THE GROUND SHIFTS BENEATH OUR FEET. THERE'S NO REAL SENSE OF UP OR DOWN. A TERRIBLE FORCE IS PULLING EVERYTHING INTO THAT MASS OF EVIL, AND AT ITS CENTER...
...THE THING THAT WAS LIZA...

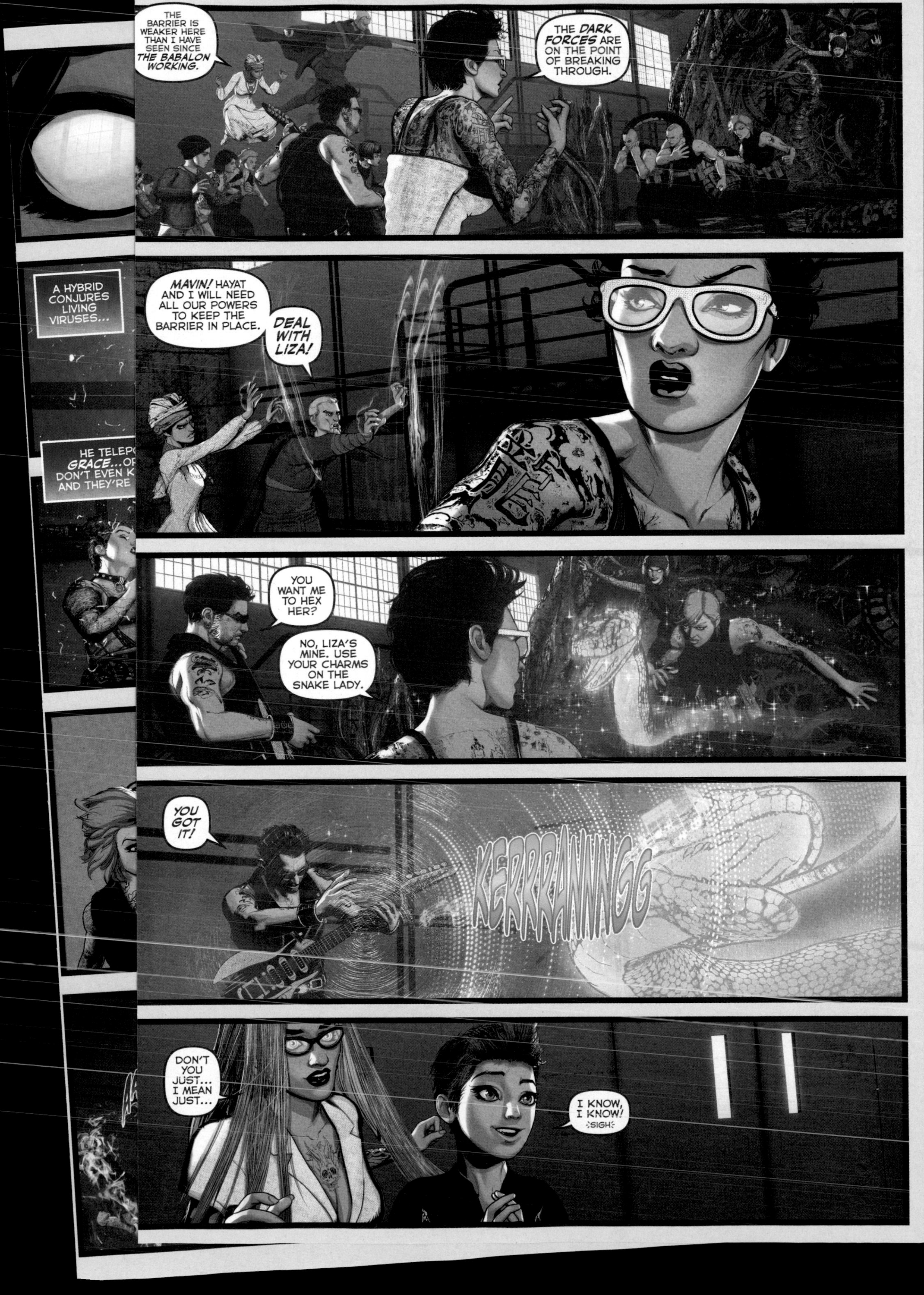
THE BARRIER IS WEAKER HERE THAN I HAVE SEEN SINCE *THE BABALON WORKING.*
THE *DARK FORCES* ARE ON THE POINT OF BREAKING THROUGH.
MAVIN! HAYAT AND I WILL NEED ALL OUR POWERS TO KEEP THE BARRIER IN PLACE.
DEAL WITH LIZA!
YOU WANT ME TO HEX HER?
NO, LIZA'S MINE. USE YOUR CHARMS ON THE SNAKE LADY.
YOU GOT IT!
KERRRANNNGG
DON'T YOU JUST... I MEAN JUST...
I KNOW, I KNOW! *SIGH*
A HYBRID CONJURES LIVING VIRUSES...

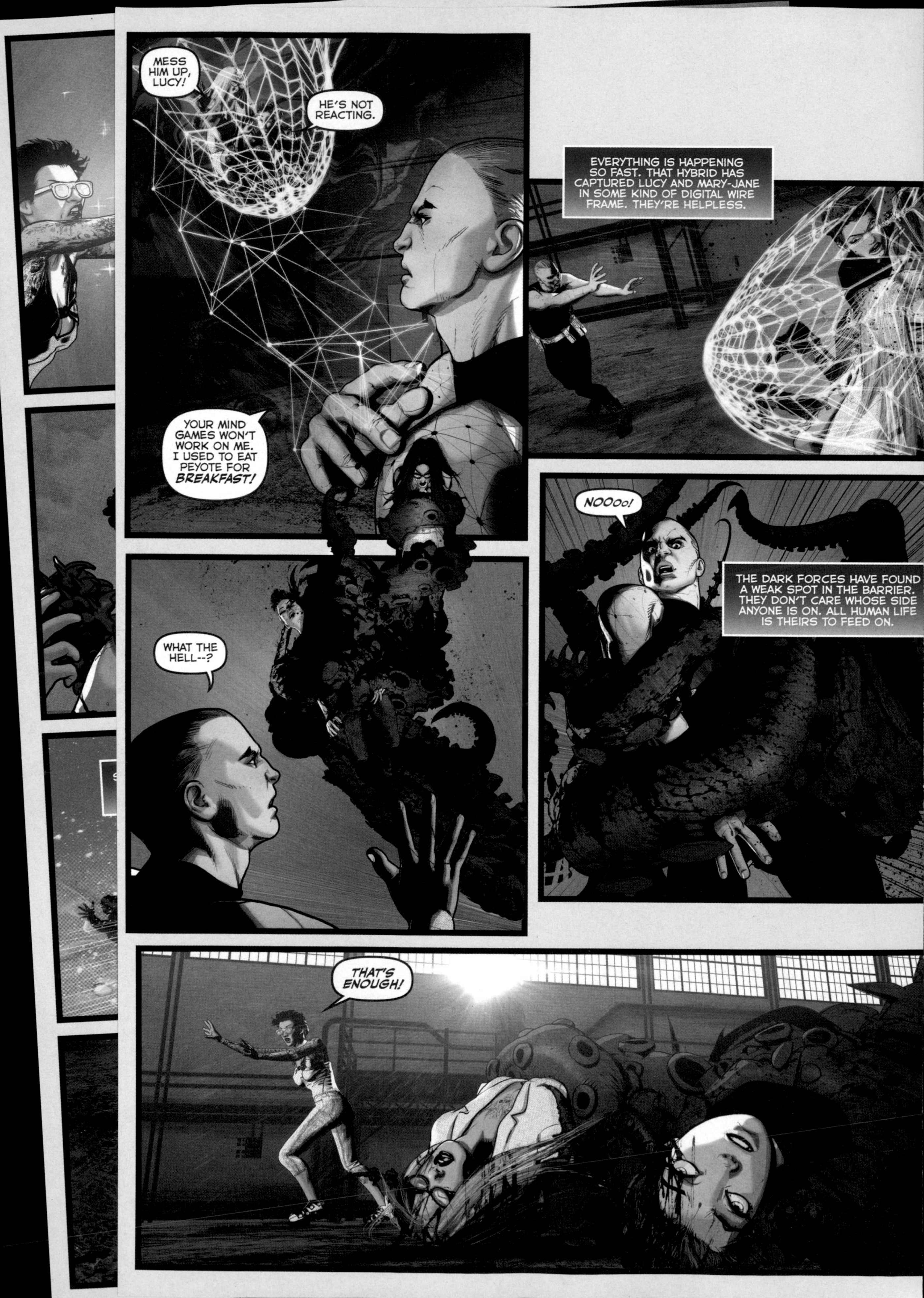

MESS HIM UP, LUCY!
HE'S NOT REACTING.
YOUR MIND GAMES WON'T WORK ON ME. I USED TO EAT PEYOTE FOR BREAKFAST!
EVERYTHING IS HAPPENING SO FAST. THAT HYBRID HAS CAPTURED LUCY AND MARY-JANE IN SOME KIND OF DIGITAL WIRE FRAME. THEY'RE HELPLESS.
WHAT THE HELL--?
NOOOo!
THE DARK FORCES HAVE FOUND A WEAK SPOT IN THE BARRIER. THEY DON'T CARE WHOSE SIDE ANYONE IS ON. ALL HUMAN LIFE IS THEIRS TO FEED ON.
THAT'S ENOUGH!

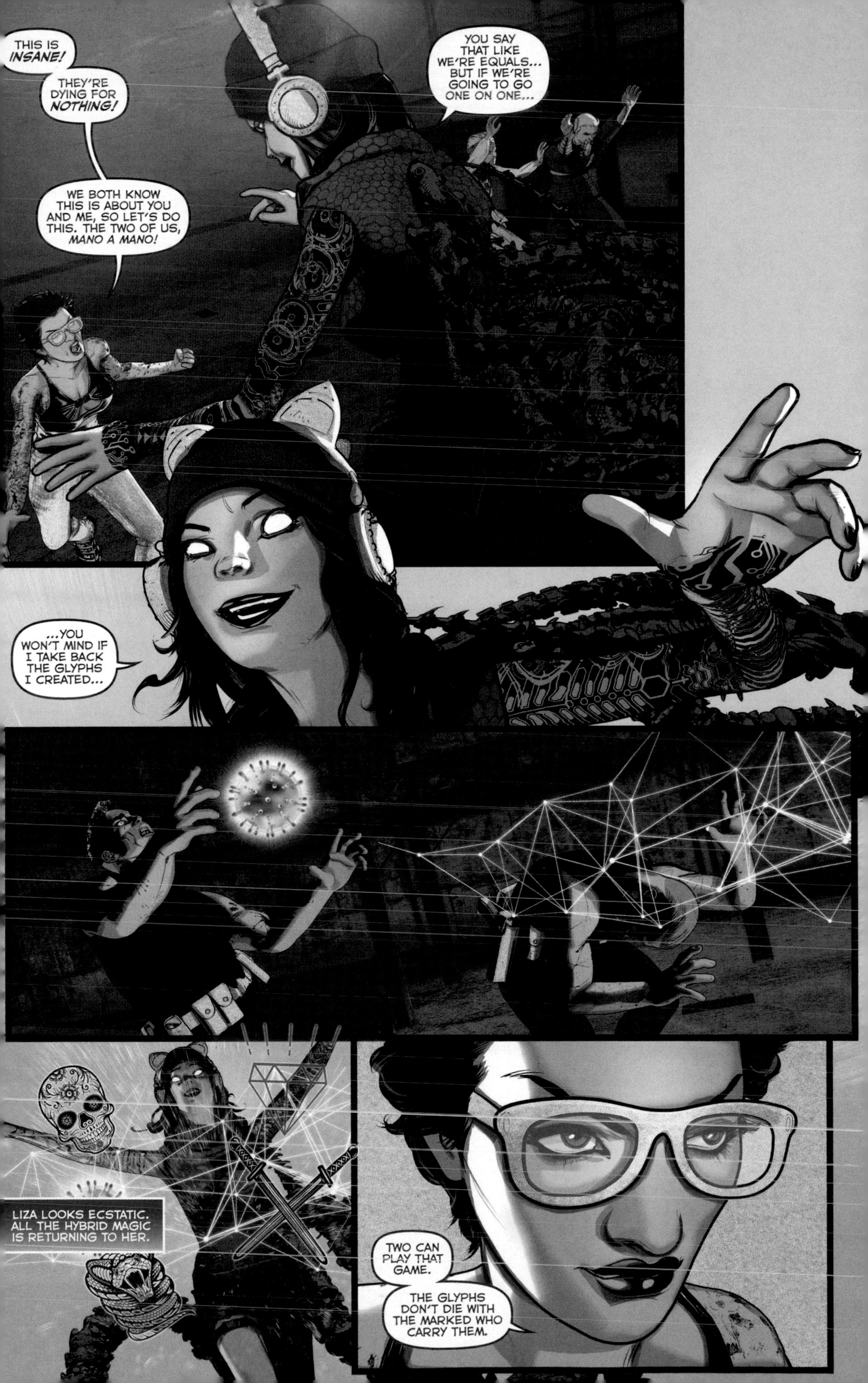
THIS IS *INSANE!*
THEY'RE DYING FOR *NOTHING!*
WE BOTH KNOW THIS IS ABOUT YOU AND ME, SO LET'S DO THIS. THE TWO OF US, *MANO A MANO!*
YOU SAY THAT LIKE WE'RE EQUALS... BUT IF WE'RE GOING TO GO ONE ON ONE...
...YOU WON'T MIND IF I TAKE BACK THE GLYPHS I CREATED...
LIZA LOOKS ECSTATIC. ALL THE HYBRID MAGIC IS RETURNING TO HER.
TWO CAN PLAY THAT GAME.
THE GLYPHS DON'T DIE WITH THE MARKED WHO CARRY THEM.

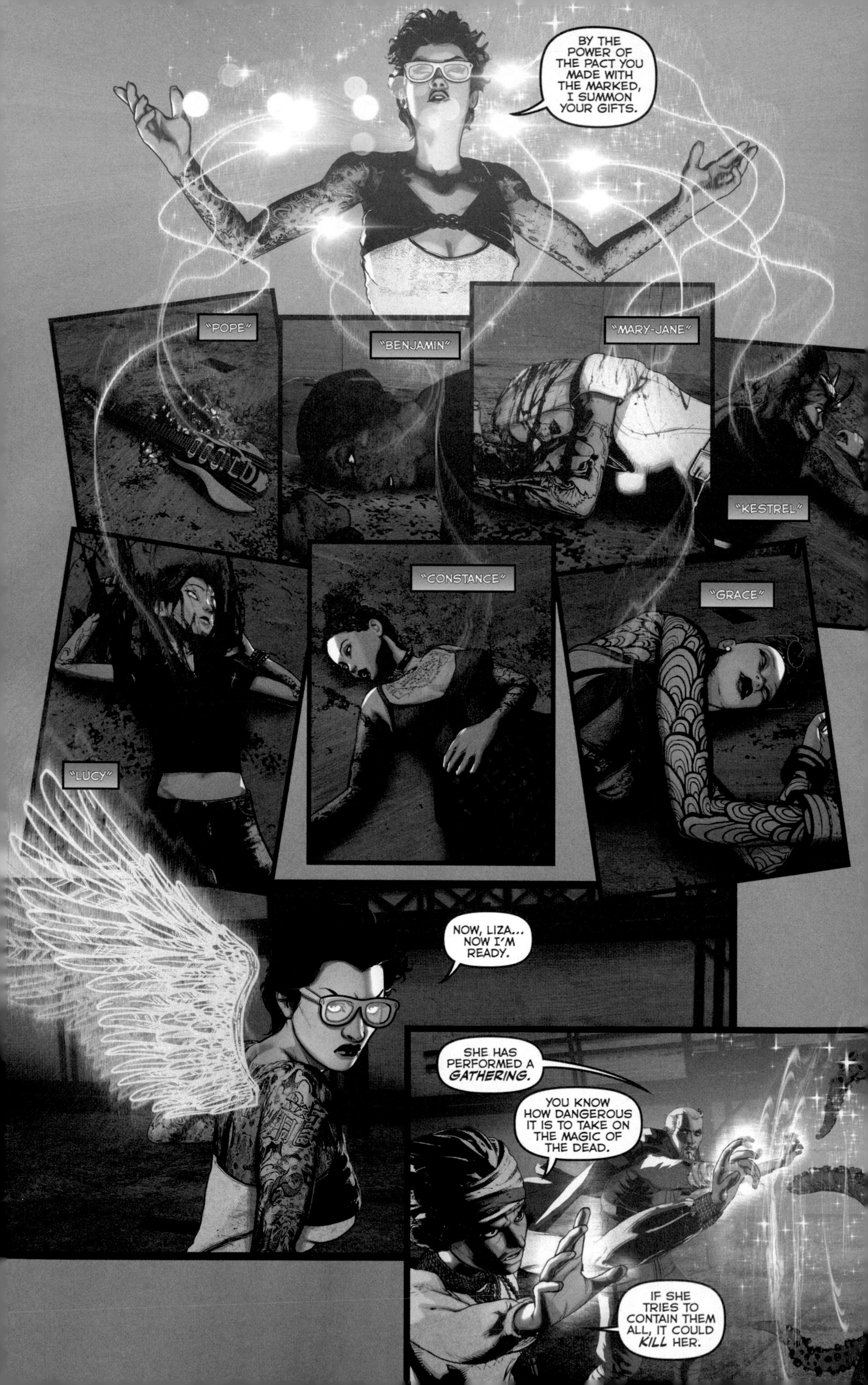
BY THE POWER OF THE PACT YOU MADE WITH THE MARKED, I SUMMON YOUR GIFTS.
"POPE"
"BENJAMIN"
"MARY-JANE"
"KESTREL"
"CONSTANCE"
"GRACE"
"LUCY"
NOW, LIZA... NOW I'M READY.
SHE HAS PERFORMED A GATHERING.
YOU KNOW HOW DANGEROUS IT IS TO TAKE ON THE MAGIC OF THE DEAD.
IF SHE TRIES TO CONTAIN THEM ALL, IT COULD KILL HER.

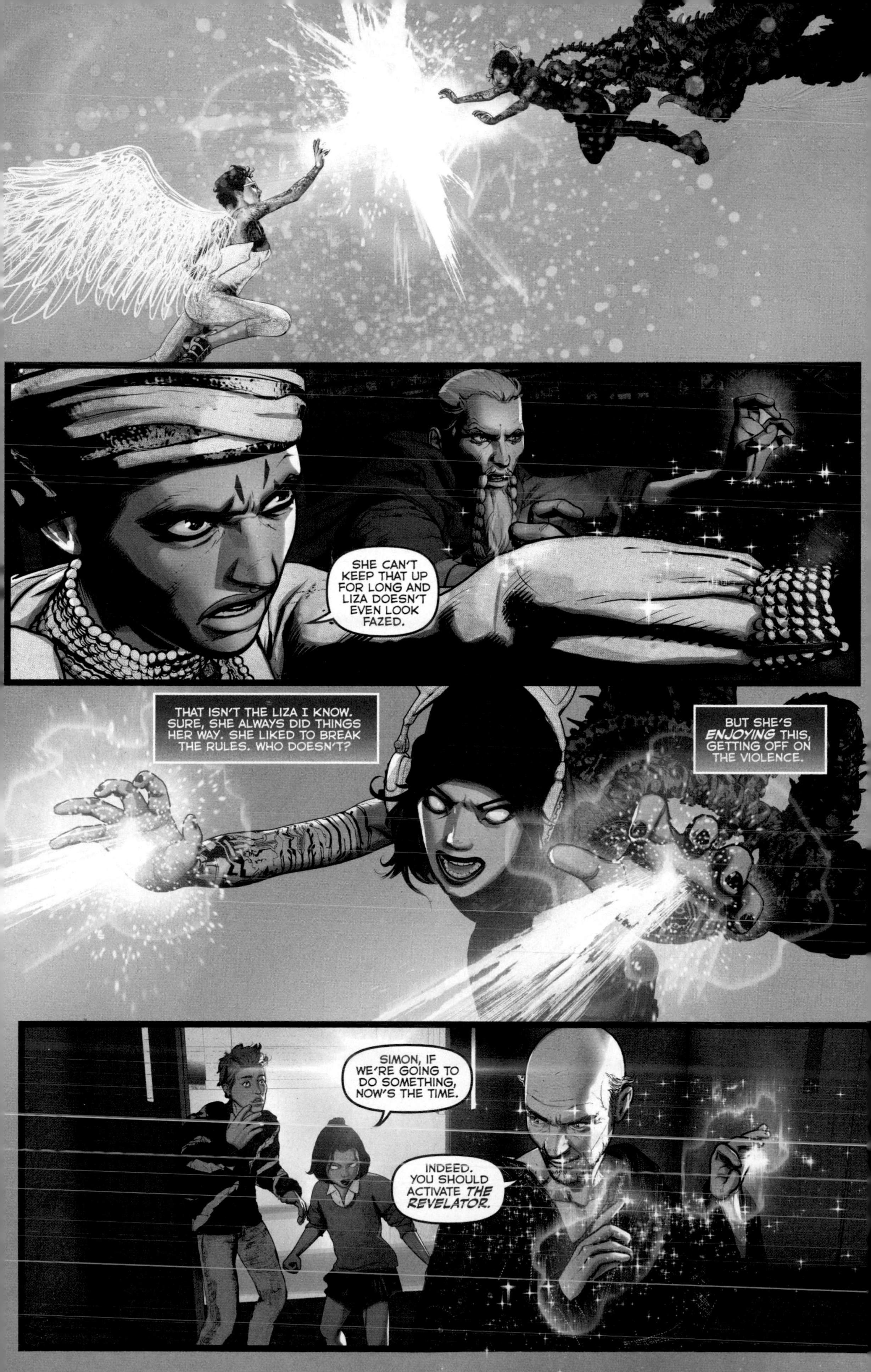
SHE CAN'T KEEP THAT UP FOR LONG AND LIZA DOESN'T EVEN LOOK FAZED.
THAT ISN'T THE LIZA I KNOW. SURE, SHE ALWAYS DID THINGS HER WAY. SHE LIKED TO BREAK THE RULES. WHO DOESN'T?
BUT SHE'S ENJOYING THIS, GETTING OFF ON THE VIOLENCE.
SIMON, IF WE'RE GOING TO DO SOMETHING, NOW'S THE TIME.
INDEED. YOU SHOULD ACTIVATE THE REVELATOR.

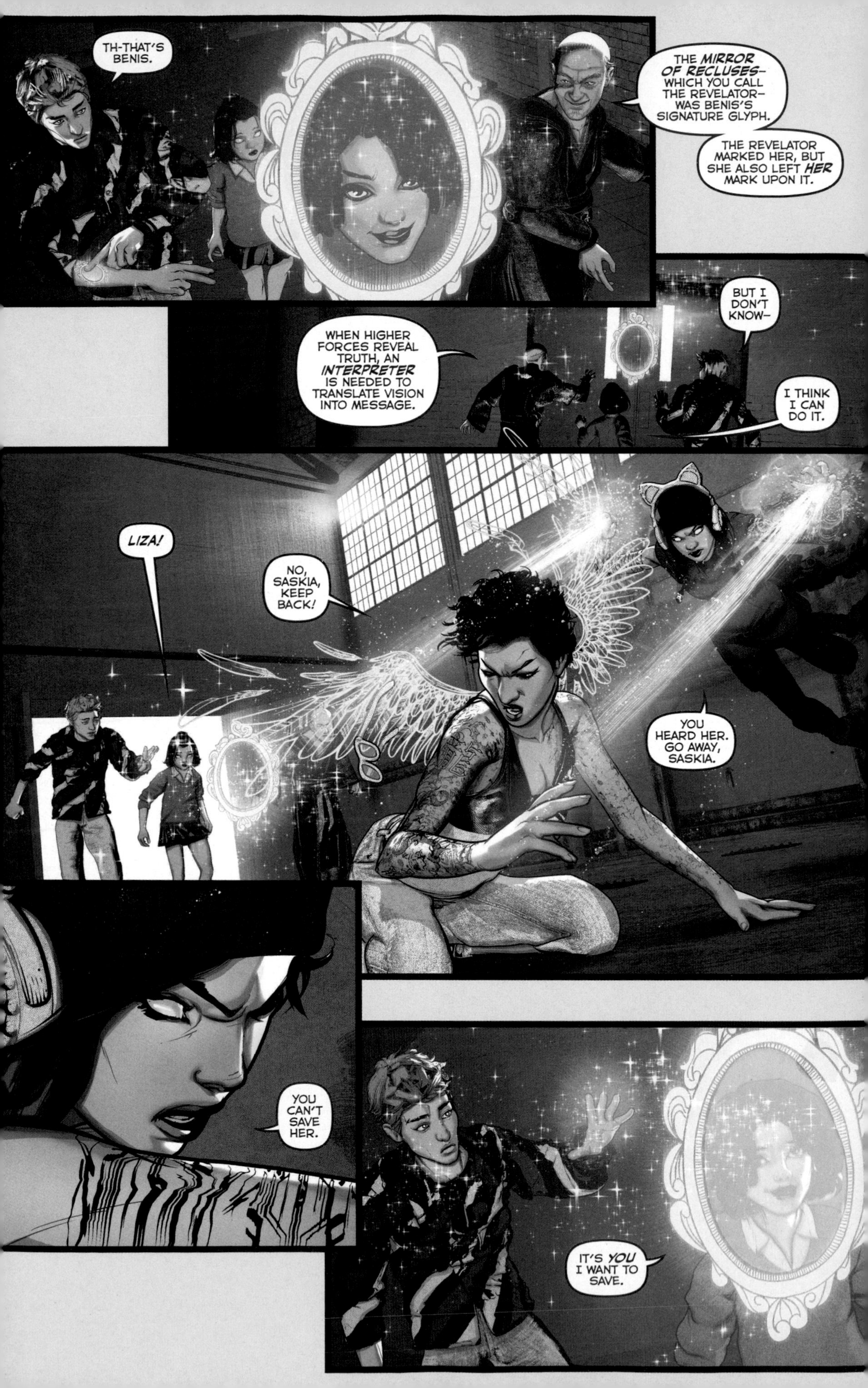
TH-THAT'S BENIS.
THE MIRROR OF RECLUSES— WHICH YOU CALL THE REVELATOR— WAS BENIS'S SIGNATURE GLYPH.
THE REVELATOR MARKED HER, BUT SHE ALSO LEFT HER MARK UPON IT.
WHEN HIGHER FORCES REVEAL TRUTH, AN INTERPRETER IS NEEDED TO TRANSLATE VISION INTO MESSAGE.
BUT I DON'T KNOW—
I THINK I CAN DO IT.
LIZA!
NO, SASKIA, KEEP BACK!
YOU HEARD HER. GO AWAY, SASKIA.
YOU CAN'T SAVE HER.
IT'S YOU I WANT TO SAVE.

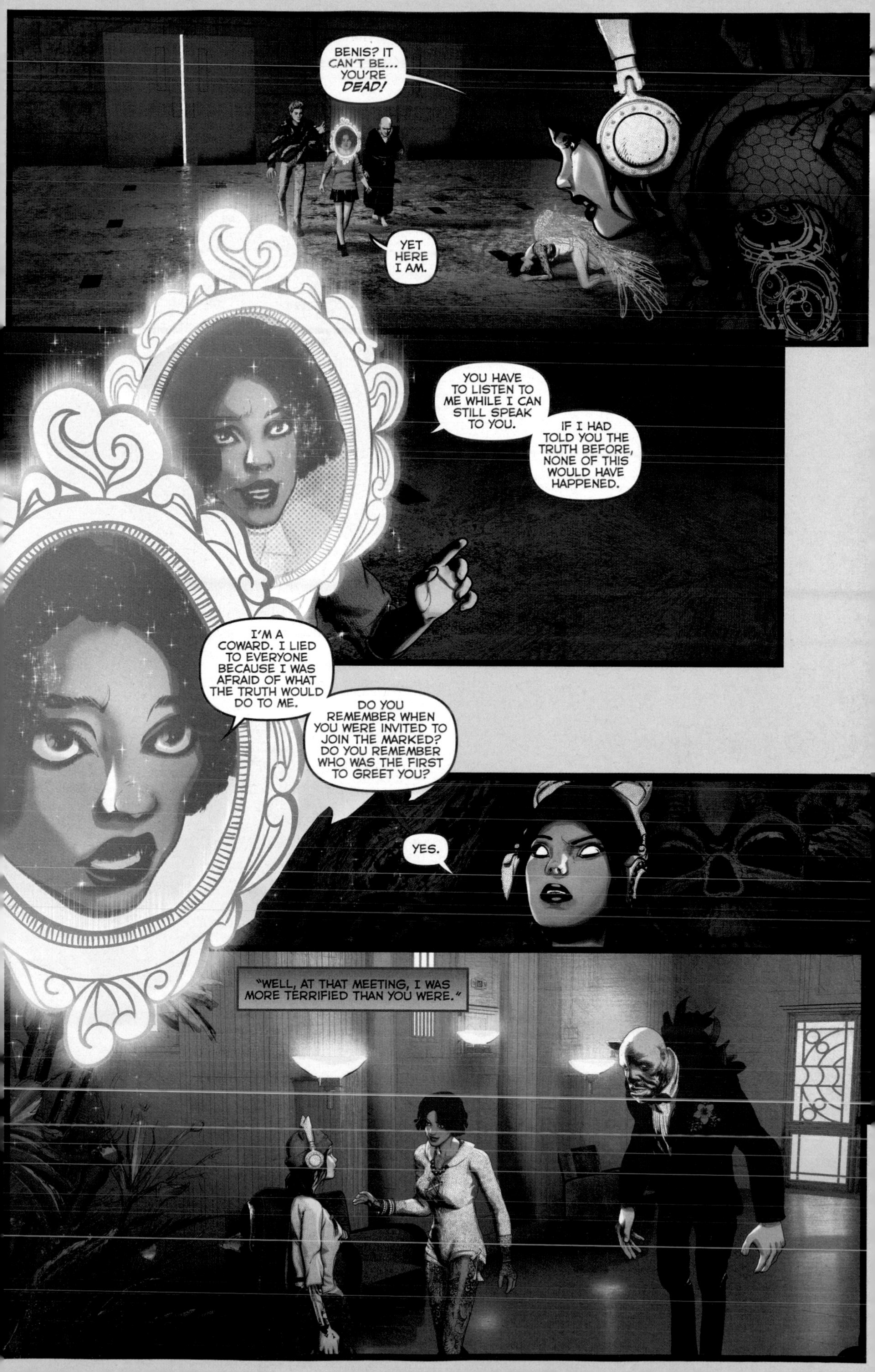
BENIS? IT CAN'T BE... YOU'RE *DEAD!*
YET HERE I AM.
YOU HAVE TO LISTEN TO ME WHILE I CAN STILL SPEAK TO YOU.
IF I HAD TOLD YOU THE TRUTH BEFORE, NONE OF THIS WOULD HAVE HAPPENED.
I'M A COWARD. I LIED TO EVERYONE BECAUSE I WAS AFRAID OF WHAT THE TRUTH WOULD DO TO ME.
DO YOU REMEMBER WHEN YOU WERE INVITED TO JOIN THE MARKED? DO YOU REMEMBER WHO WAS THE FIRST TO GREET YOU?
YES.
"WELL, AT THAT MEETING, I WAS MORE TERRIFIED THAN YOU WERE."

WHY WOULD YOU BE SCARED? I WAS JUST A KID. YOU WERE MY MENTOR. YOU TAUGHT ME EVERYTHING.

NOT EVERYTHING. IT WAS TOO LATE TO GUIDE YOU THROUGH ALL THE TROUBLES OF YOUR CHILDHOOD. YOU WERE ALREADY DAMAGED.

"YOU WERE ALWAYS THE LONER. I UNDERSTOOD THAT. I'VE LIVED ALONE MOST OF MY LIFE."

"WHATEVER FRIENDS I MADE DIED, WHILE I LIVED ON AND ON..."

DON'T PROJECT ON ME. I WAS HAPPY BY MYSELF. AND WHEN I WANTED TO BE WITH THE OTHERS, I WAS WITH THEM.

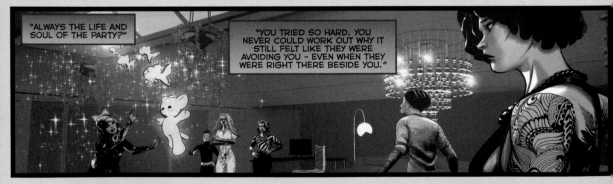

"ALWAYS THE LIFE AND SOUL OF THE PARTY?"

"YOU TRIED SO HARD. YOU NEVER COULD WORK OUT WHY IT STILL FELT LIKE THEY WERE AVOIDING YOU - EVEN WHEN THEY WERE RIGHT THERE BESIDE YOU."

YOU DIDN'T KNOW HOW TO BE PART OF A GROUP, PART OF A *FAMILY*.

YEAH, WELL I NEVER *HAD* ONE, DID I? FOSTER PARENTS ARE LIKE RENT-A-FAMILY.

THEY GO THROUGH THE MOTIONS FOR A WHILE, THEN YOU MOVE ON AND THE STATE PAYS THE BILL.

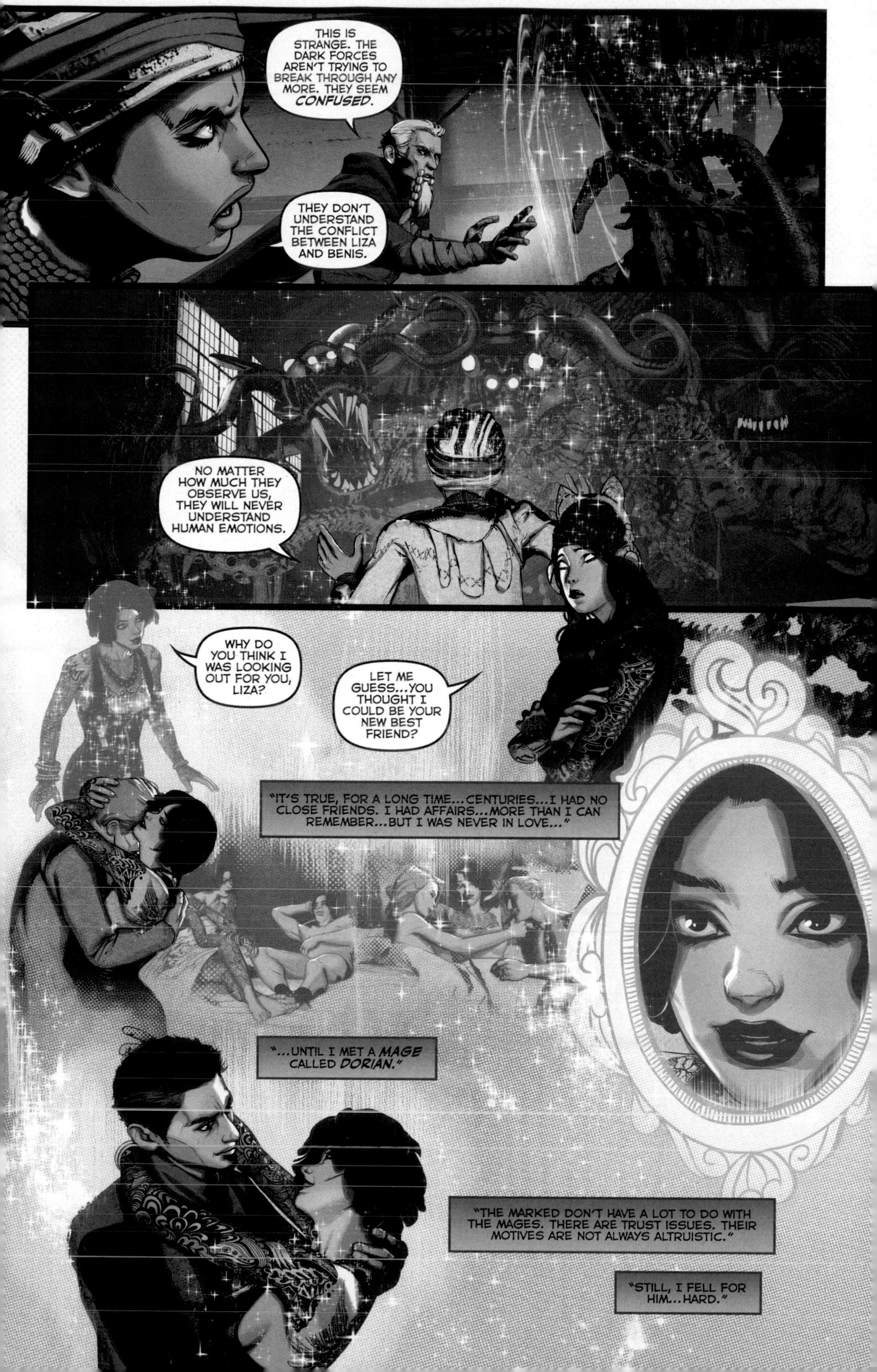
THIS IS STRANGE. THE DARK FORCES AREN'T TRYING TO BREAK THROUGH ANY MORE. THEY SEEM CONFUSED.
THEY DON'T UNDERSTAND THE CONFLICT BETWEEN LIZA AND BENIS.
NO MATTER HOW MUCH THEY OBSERVE US, THEY WILL NEVER UNDERSTAND HUMAN EMOTIONS.
WHY DO YOU THINK I WAS LOOKING OUT FOR YOU, LIZA?
LET ME GUESS...YOU THOUGHT I COULD BE YOUR NEW BEST FRIEND?
"IT'S TRUE, FOR A LONG TIME...CENTURIES...I HAD NO CLOSE FRIENDS. I HAD AFFAIRS...MORE THAN I CAN REMEMBER...BUT I WAS NEVER IN LOVE..."
"...UNTIL I MET A MAGE CALLED DORIAN."
"THE MARKED DON'T HAVE A LOT TO DO WITH THE MAGES. THERE ARE TRUST ISSUES. THEIR MOTIVES ARE NOT ALWAYS ALTRUISTIC."
"STILL, I FELL FOR HIM...HARD."

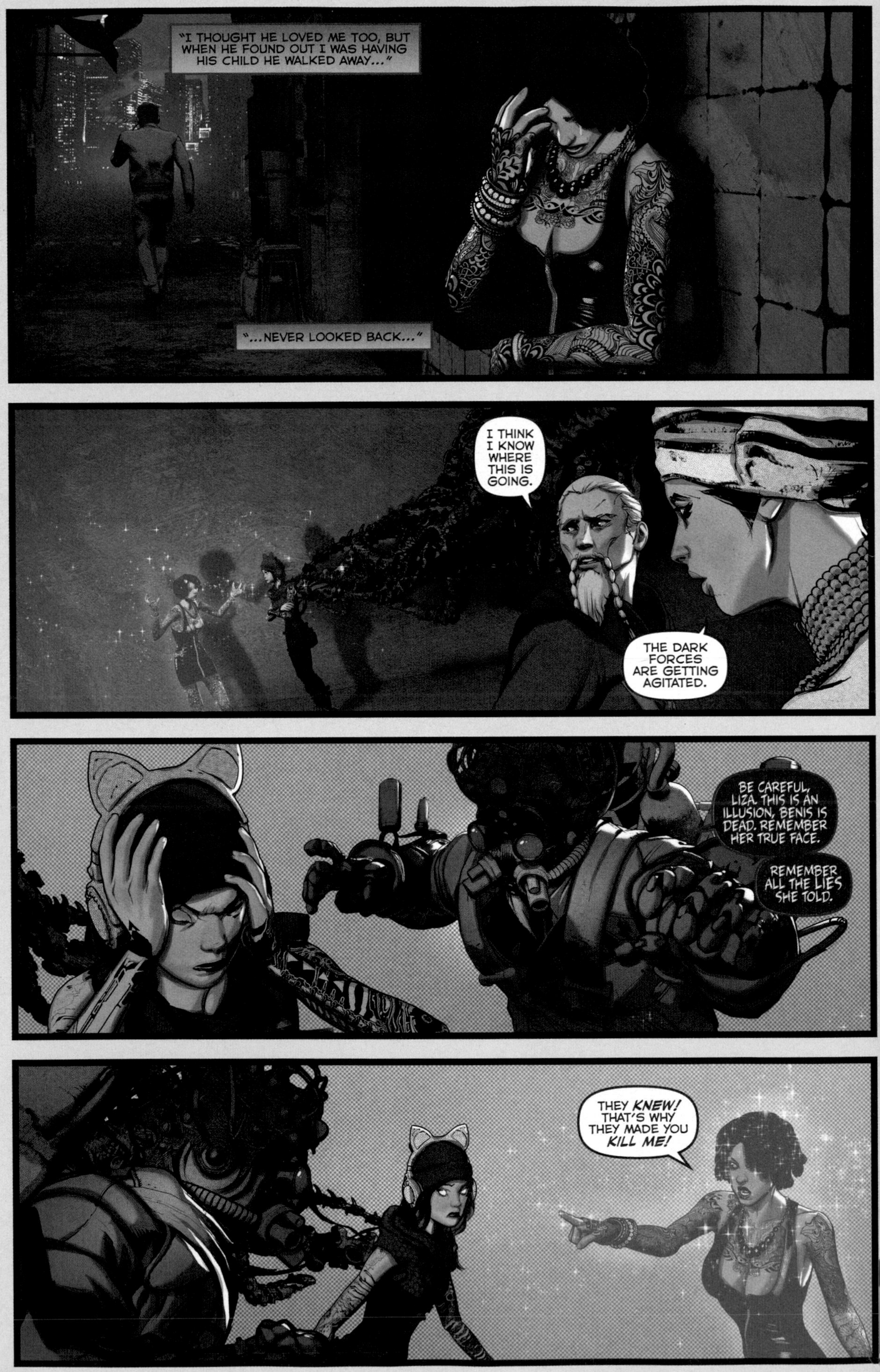
"I THOUGHT HE LOVED ME TOO, BUT WHEN HE FOUND OUT I WAS HAVING HIS CHILD HE WALKED AWAY..."
"...NEVER LOOKED BACK..."
I THINK I KNOW WHERE THIS IS GOING.
THE DARK FORCES ARE GETTING AGITATED.
BE CAREFUL, LIZA. THIS IS AN ILLUSION, BENIS IS DEAD. REMEMBER HER TRUE FACE.
REMEMBER ALL THE LIES SHE TOLD.
THEY *KNEW!* THAT'S WHY THEY MADE YOU *KILL ME!*

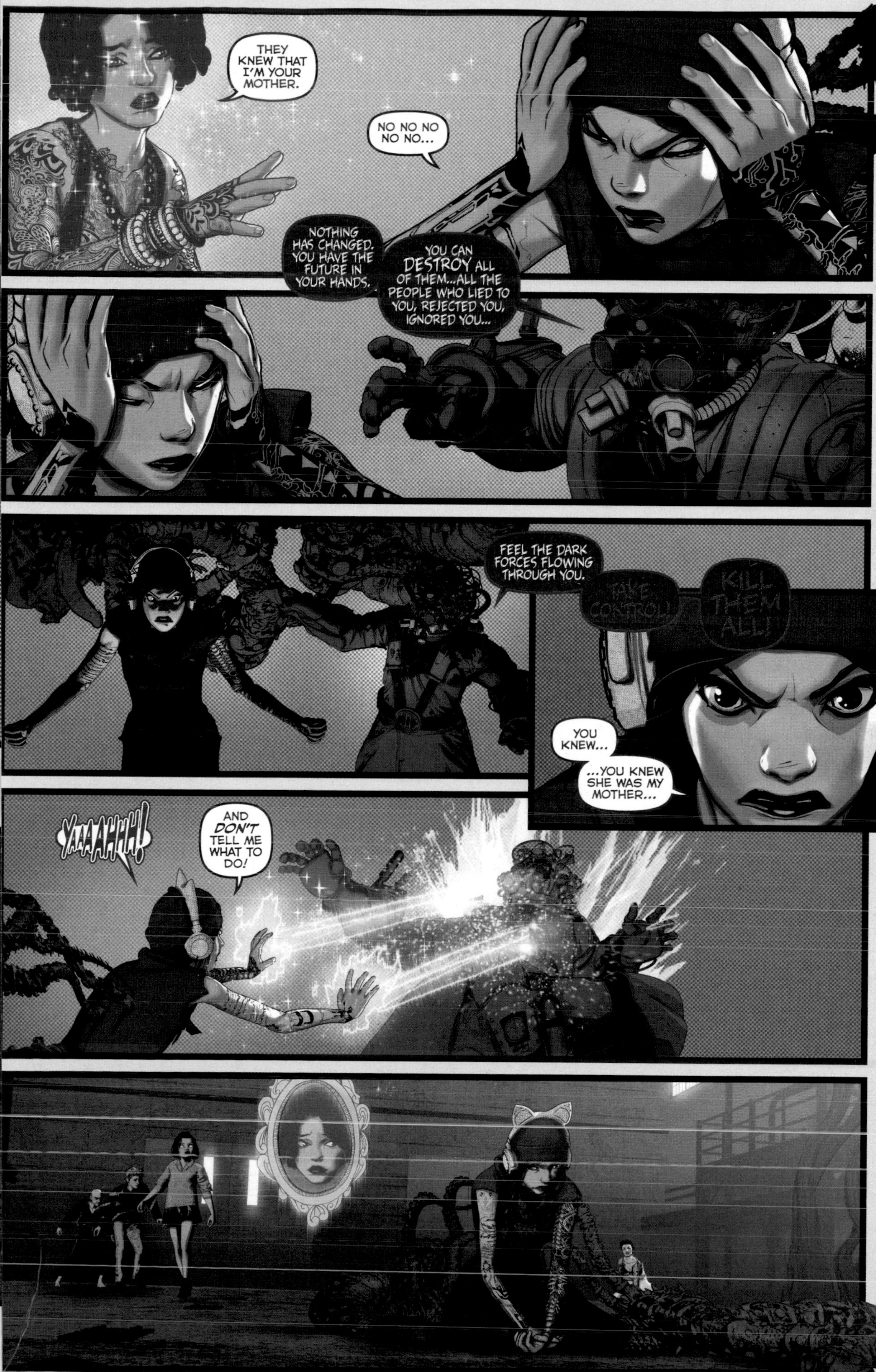
THEY KNEW THAT I'M YOUR MOTHER.
NO NO NO NO NO...
NOTHING HAS CHANGED. YOU HAVE THE FUTURE IN YOUR HANDS.
YOU CAN DESTROY ALL OF THEM...ALL THE PEOPLE WHO LIED TO YOU, REJECTED YOU, IGNORED YOU...
FEEL THE DARK FORCES FLOWING THROUGH YOU.
TAKE CONTROL!
KILL THEM ALL!
YOU KNEW...
...YOU KNEW SHE WAS MY MOTHER...
YAAAAHHH!
AND DON'T TELL ME WHAT TO DO!

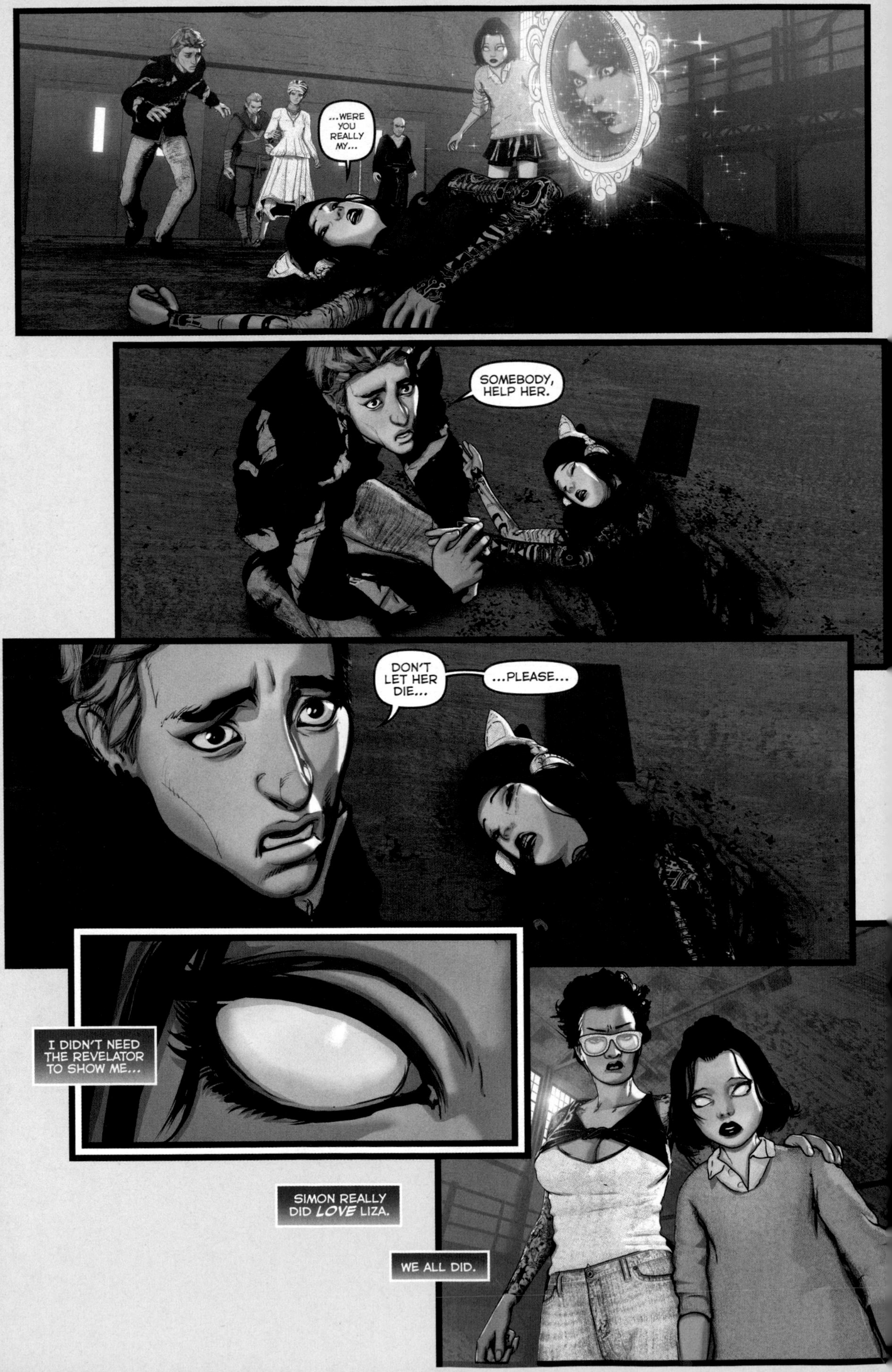
...WERE YOU REALLY MY...
SOMEBODY, HELP HER.
DON'T LET HER DIE...
...PLEASE...
I DIDN'T NEED THE REVELATOR TO SHOW ME...
SIMON REALLY DID LOVE LIZA.
WE ALL DID.

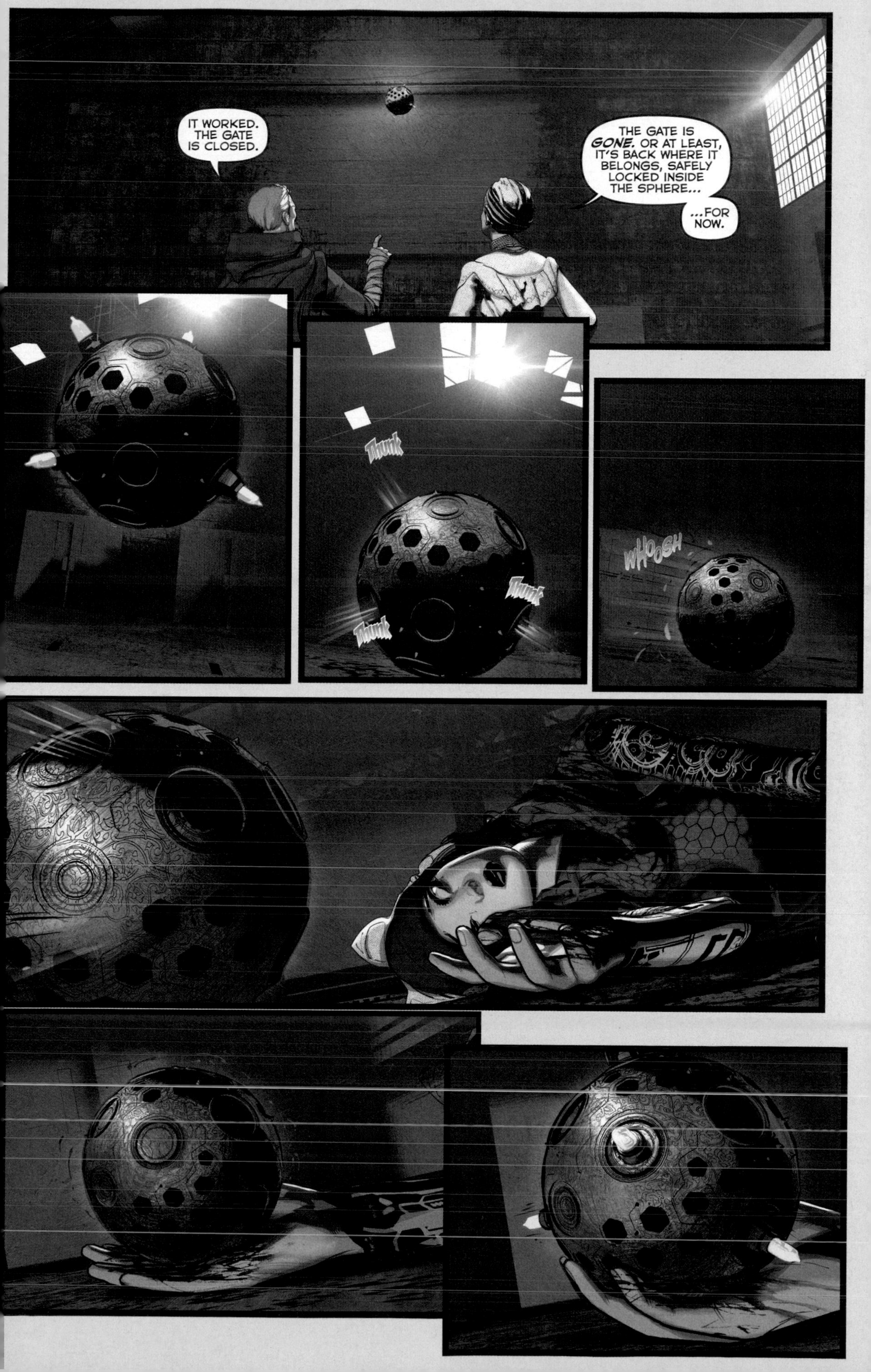
IT WORKED. THE GATE IS CLOSED.
THE GATE IS GONE. OR AT LEAST, IT'S BACK WHERE IT BELONGS, SAFELY LOCKED INSIDE THE SPHERE...
...FOR NOW.
THUNK
THUNK
THUNK
WHOOSH

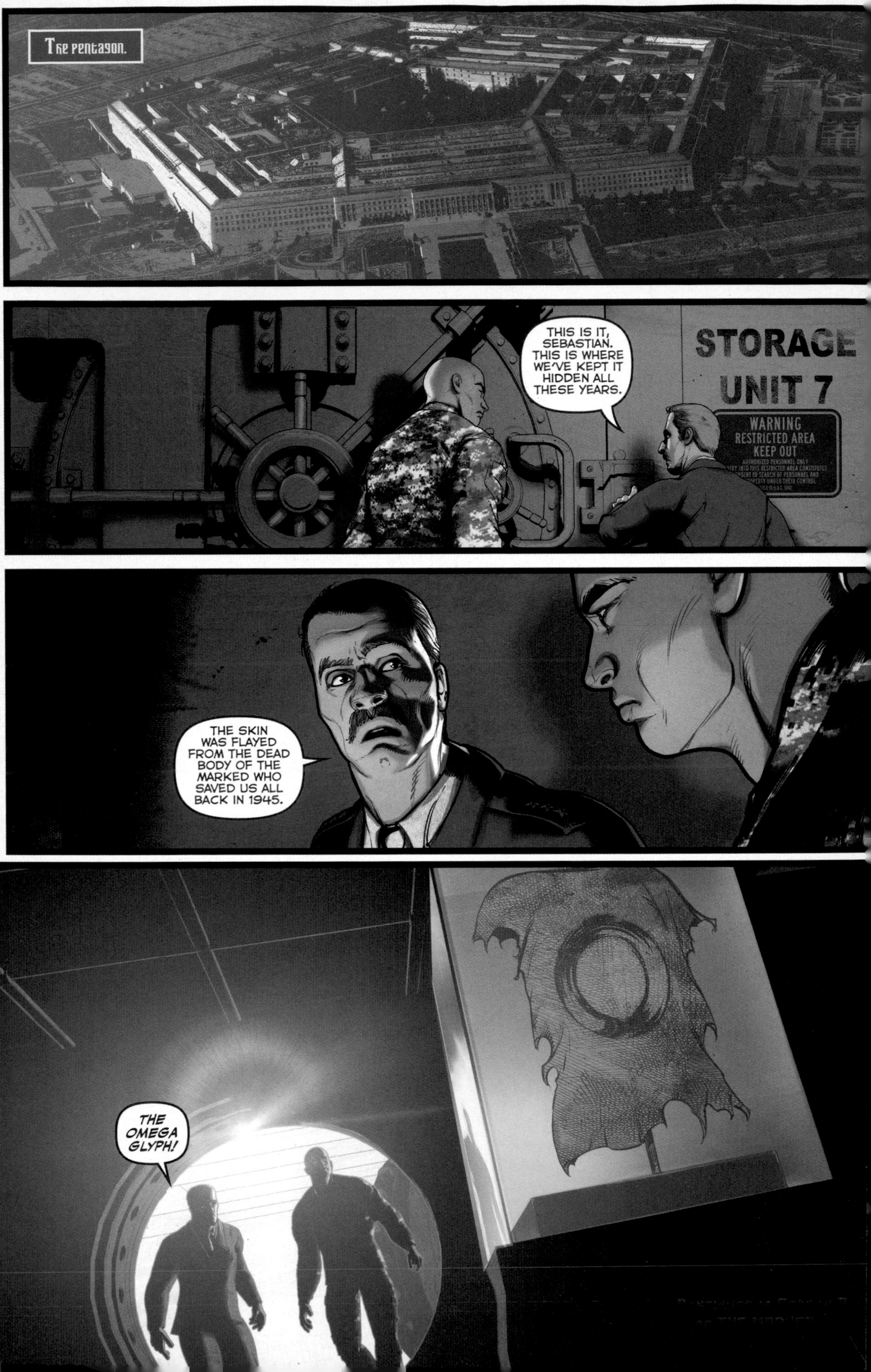
The pentagon.
THIS IS IT, SEBASTIAN. THIS IS WHERE WE'VE KEPT IT HIDDEN ALL THESE YEARS.
STORAGE UNIT 7
WARNING RESTRICTED AREA KEEP OUT
THE SKIN WAS FLAYED FROM THE DEAD BODY OF THE MARKED WHO SAVED US ALL BACK IN 1945.
THE OMEGA GLYPH!

ART GALLERY

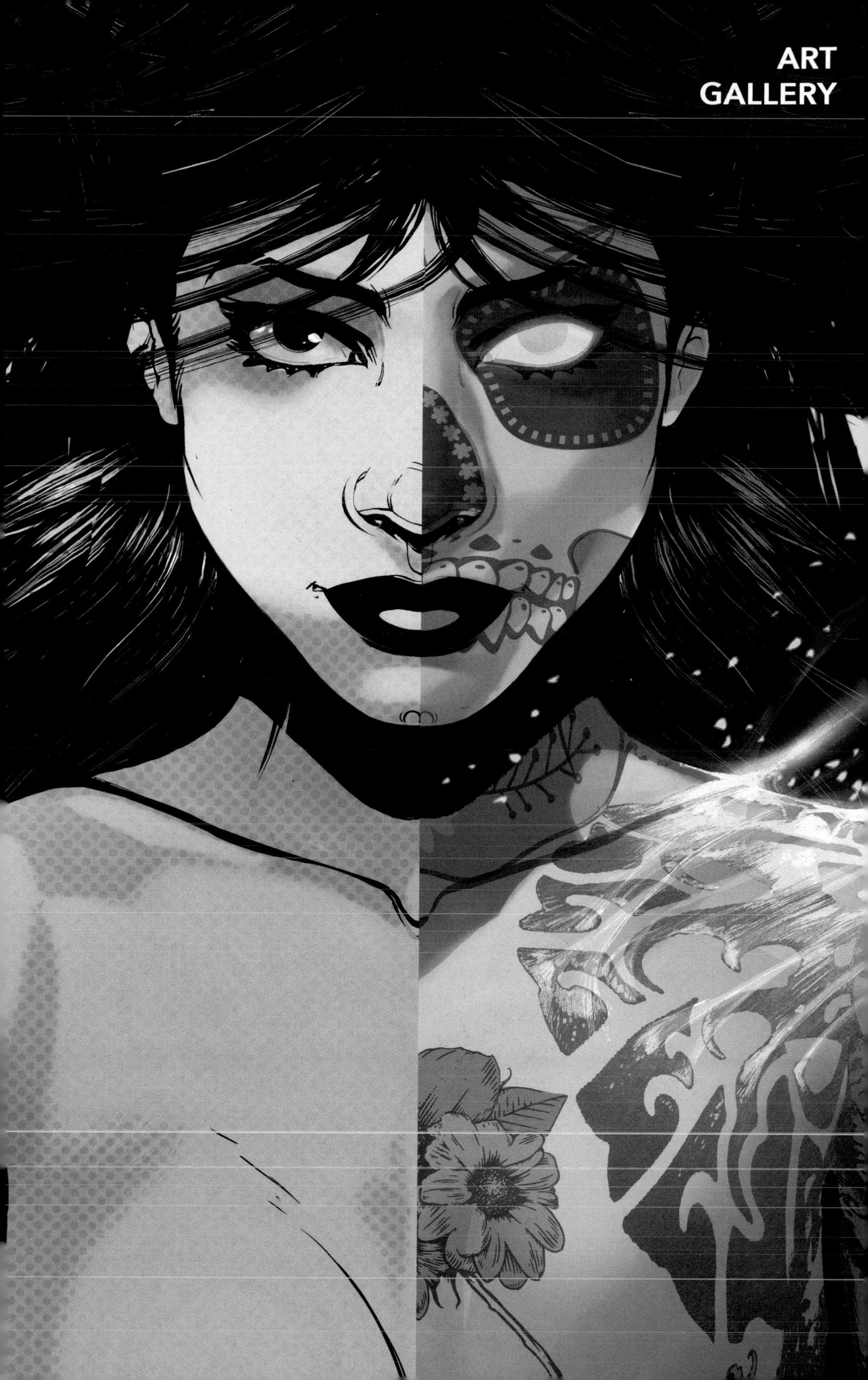

ISSUE #1 COVER B

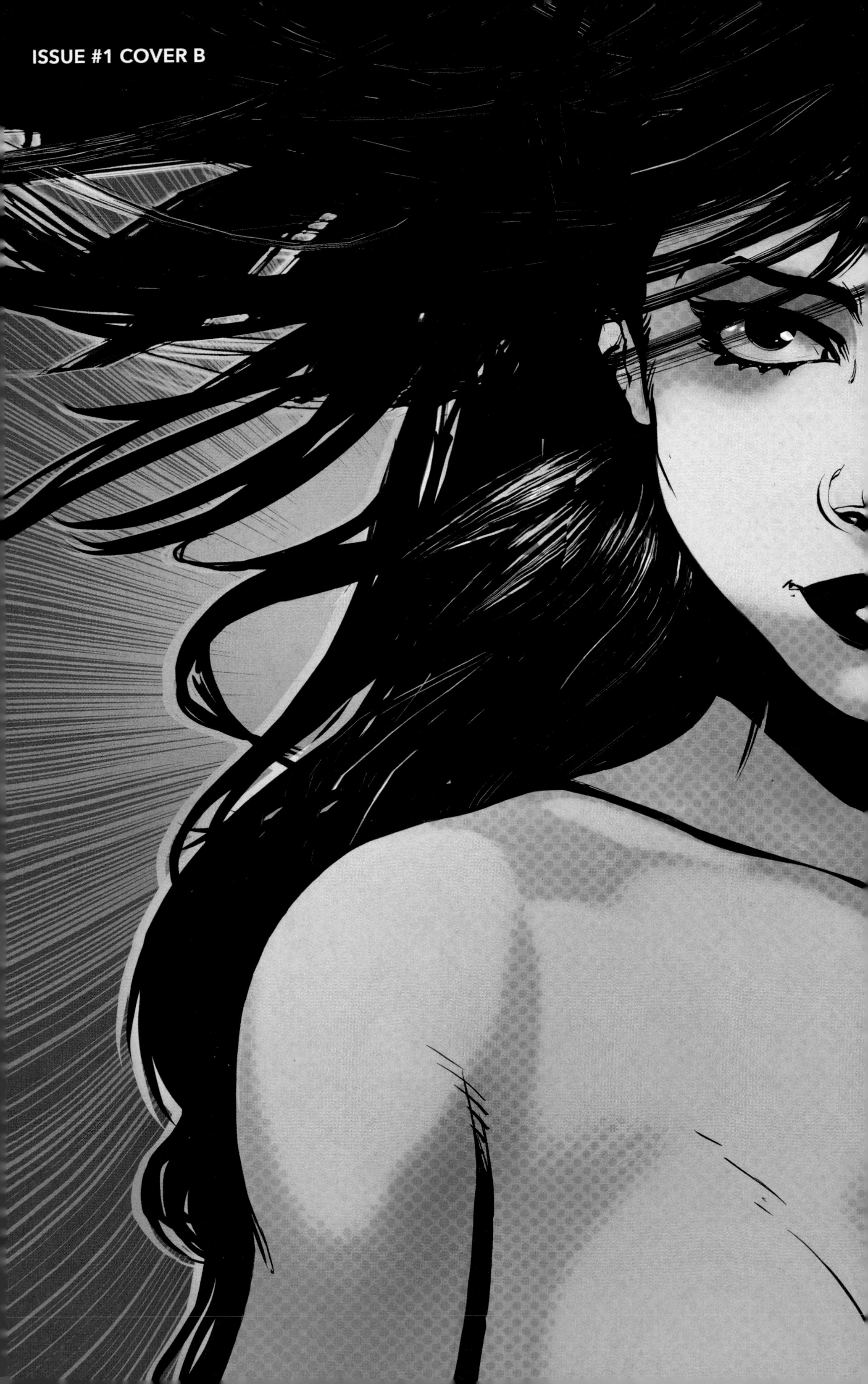

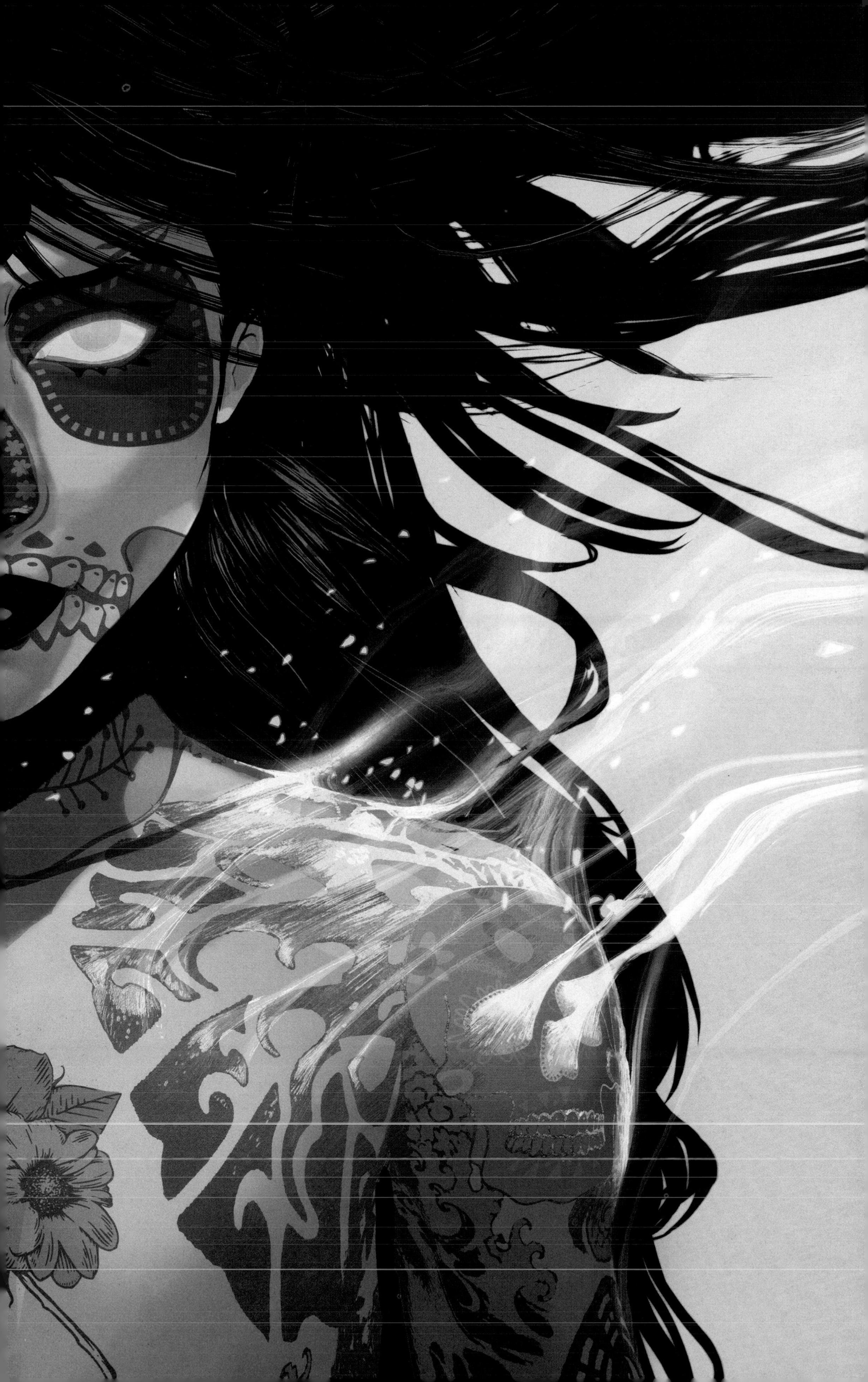

ISSUE #2 COVER B

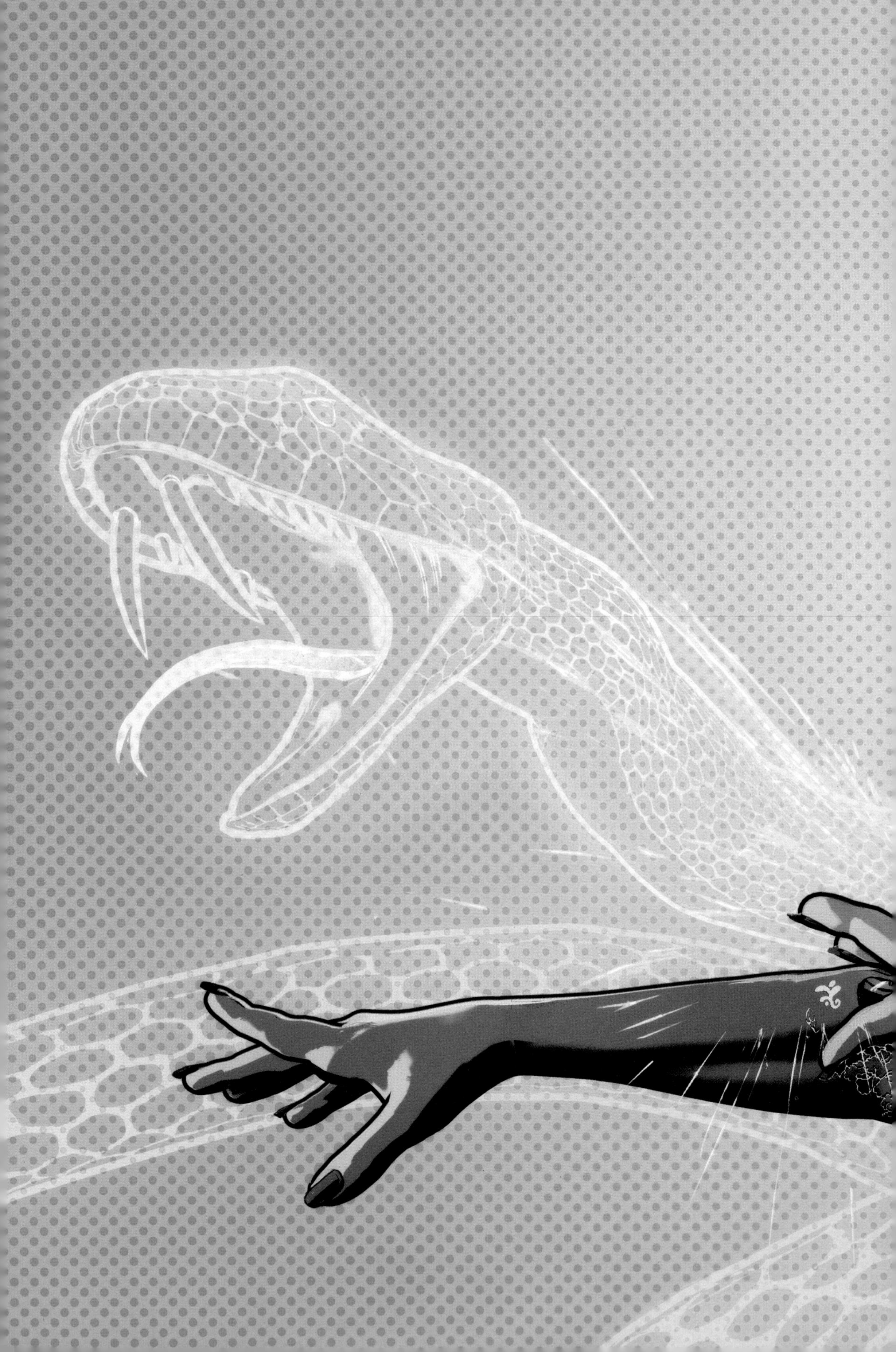

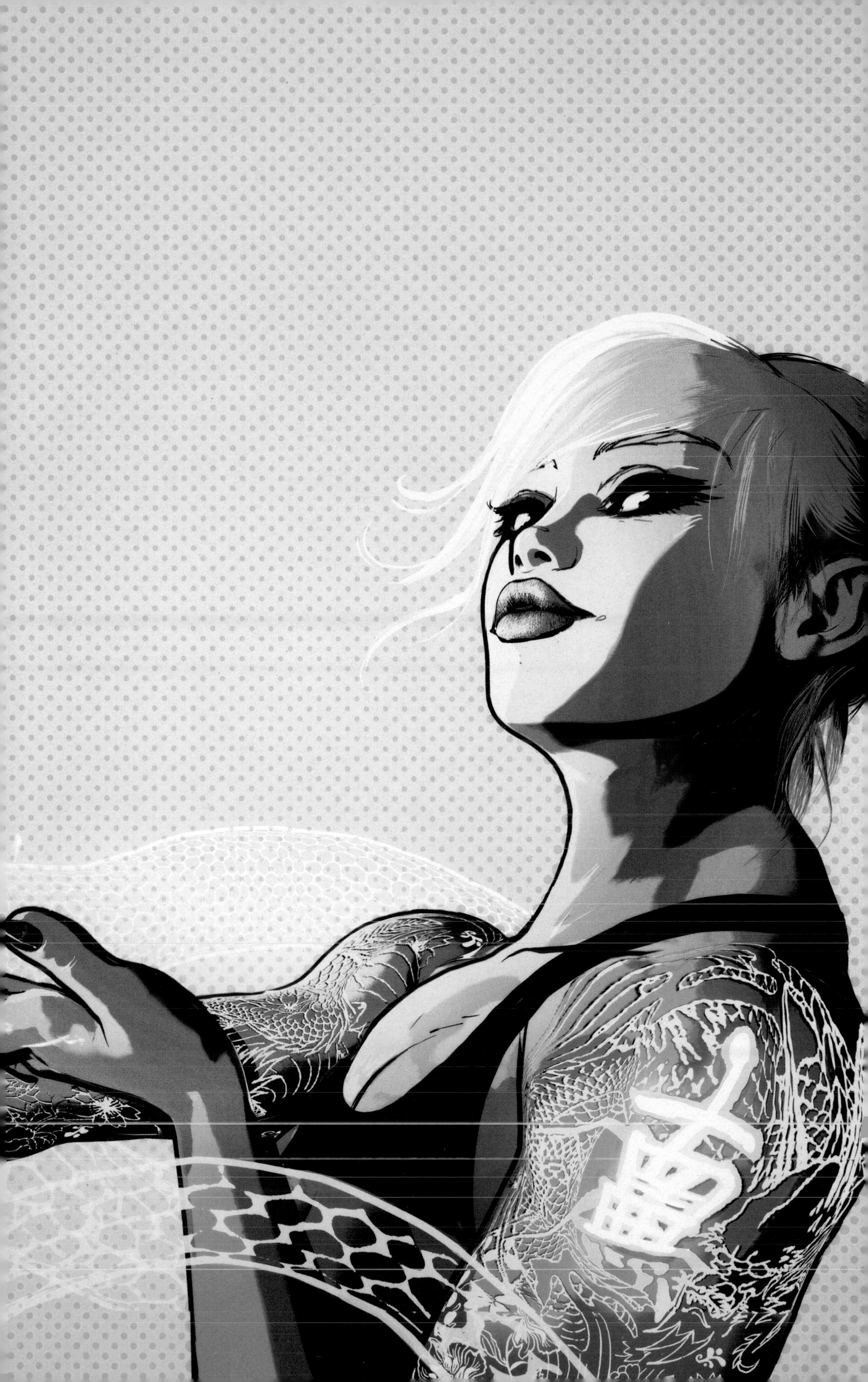

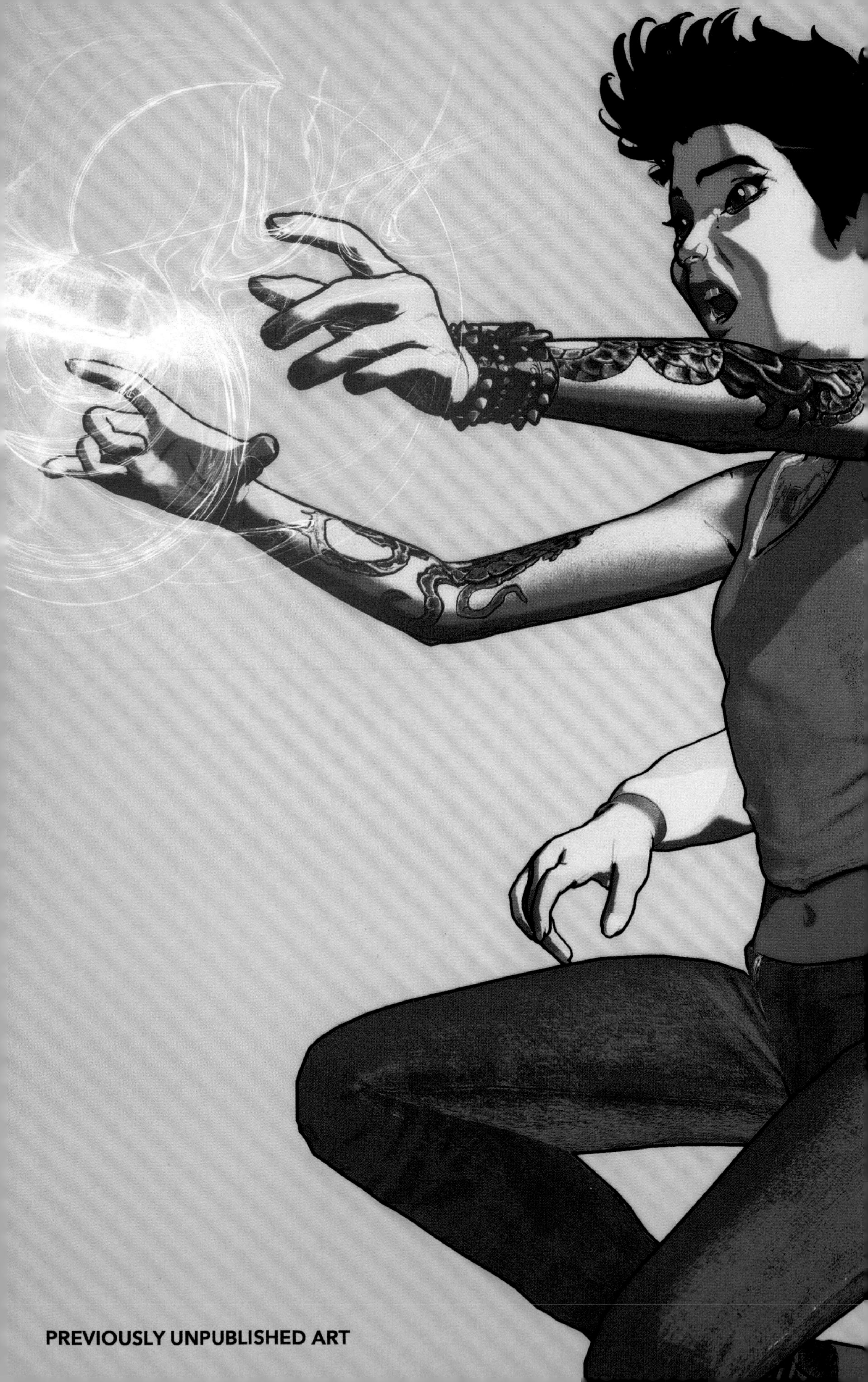

PREVIOUSLY UNPUBLISHED ART

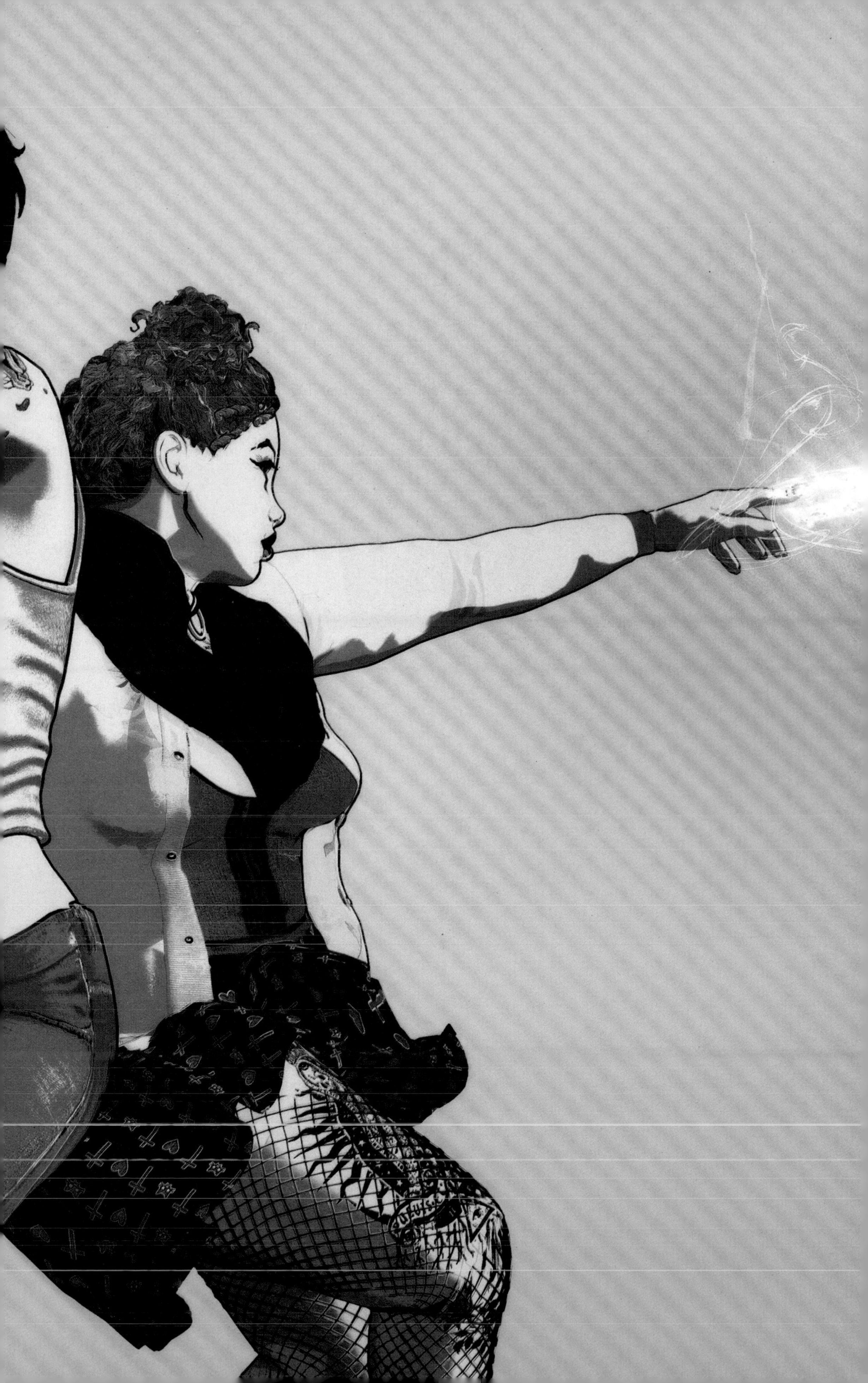

PREVIOUSLY UNPUBLISHED ART

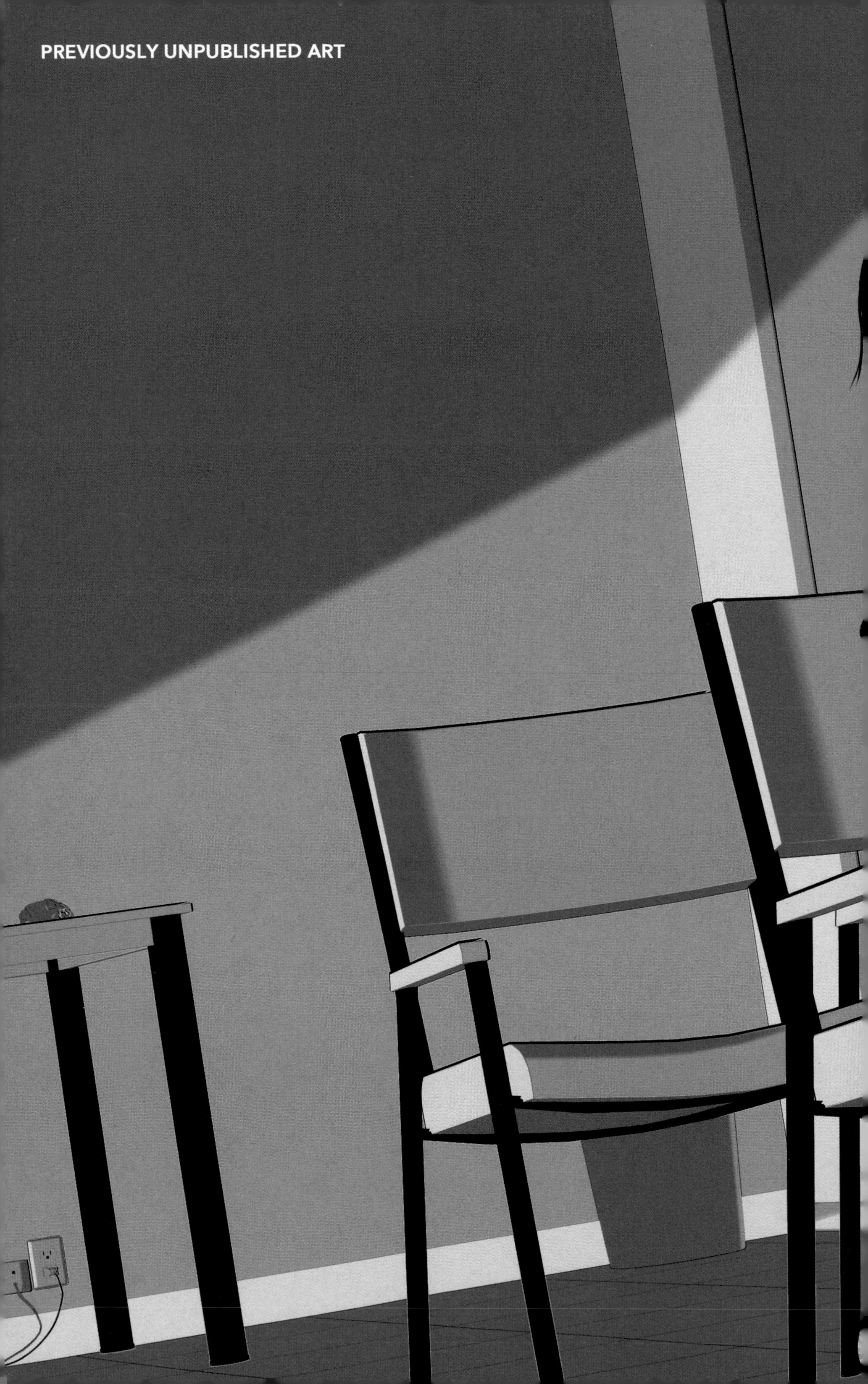

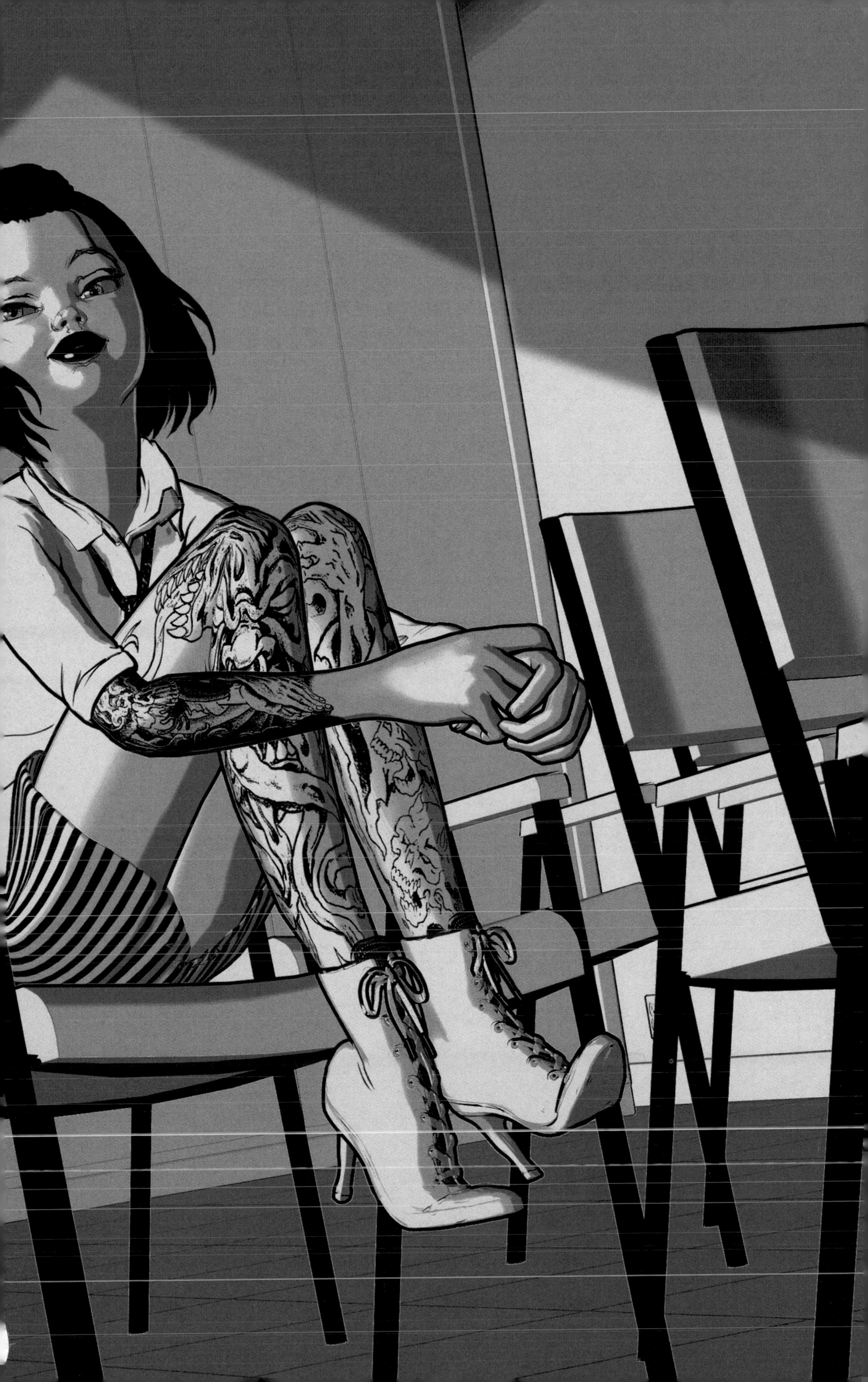

PREVIOUSLY UNPUBLISHED ART

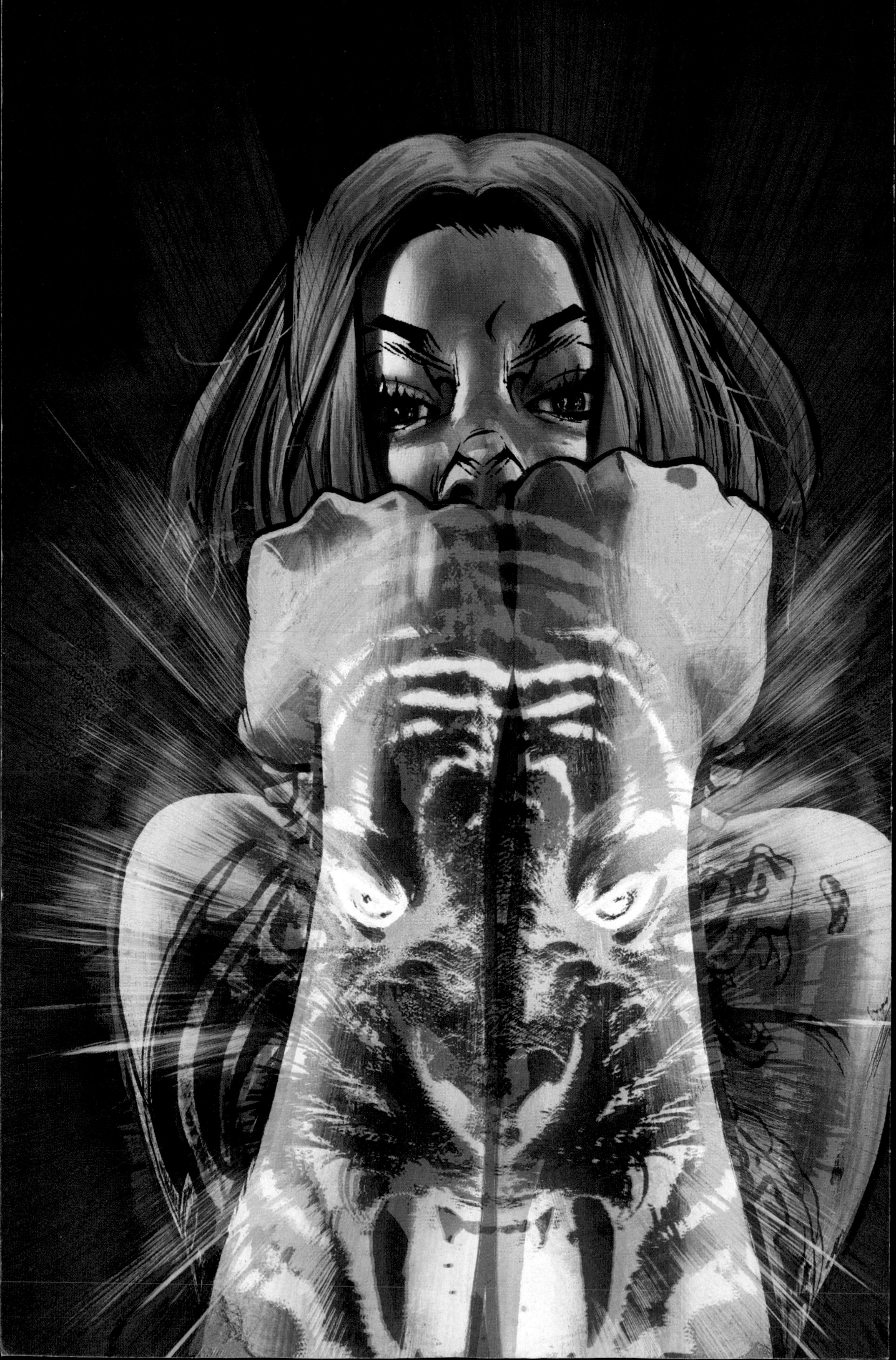

More books by Brian Haberlin you're bound to enjoy...

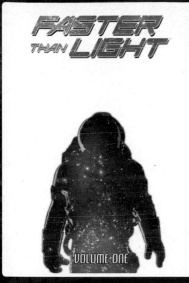

FASTER THAN LIGHT
VOLUME ONE

FASTER THAN LIGHT Volume One

In the very near future we discover the secret of faster-than-light travel. Suddenly the universe is wide open to us, but are we ready for it? With all the idealism of the original *Star Trek* and the grit and immediacy of *Gravity* and *The Martian*, the story of humanity's first thrilling and terrifying adventures to the stars takes flight! The trade also features over 25 augmented reality pages to use with your smart device.

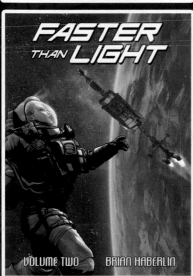

FASTER THAN LIGHT
VOLUME TWO
BRIAN HABERLIN

FASTER THAN LIGHT Volume Two

Politics and power-grabs get in the way of the mission as Captain Forest loses command of the Discovery. Can he be saved by his staunchly loyal crew? New secrets are revealed about both our benefactors and the oncoming storm of the Outsiders... and we meet a slew of new aliens and creatures along the way! Featuring an award-nominated app that makes it look like interactive holograms are coming out of the book!

HINE • HABERLIN • VAN DYKE
SONATA™
VOLUME ONE: VALLEY OF THE GODS

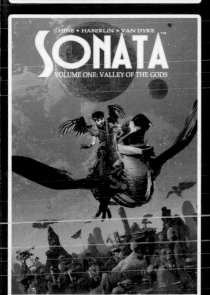

SONATA Volume One: VALLEY OF THE GODS

Two cultures clash on a planet both sides believe is their Promised Land. The Rans are a peace-loving people. The Tayans are a race of warriors who are here to colonize and control. There are the Sleeping Giants, who may be monsters or the gods of legend. Sonata is a young woman who will break all the rules to find her place in this world, and she's not about to let sleeping gods lie.

only from image® Shadowline®

A Book For Every Reader...
...A Book For Every Taste.

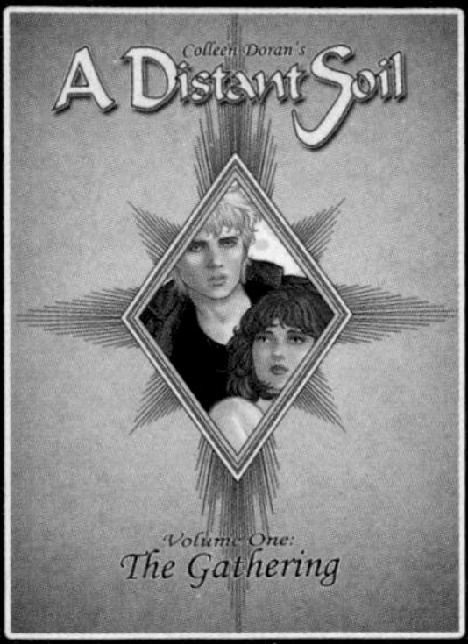
Colleen Doran's
A Distant Soil
Volume One:
The Gathering

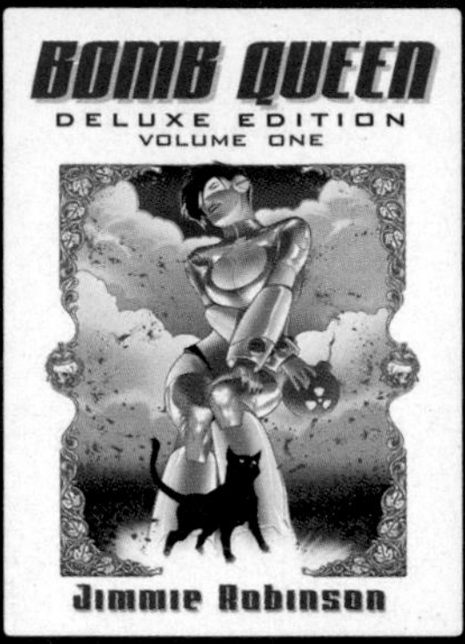
BOMB QUEEN
DELUXE EDITION
VOLUME ONE
Jimmie Robinson

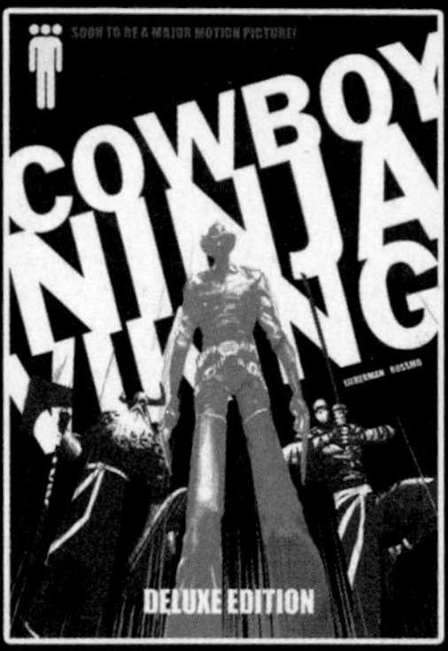
COWBOY NINJA VIKING
DELUXE EDITION

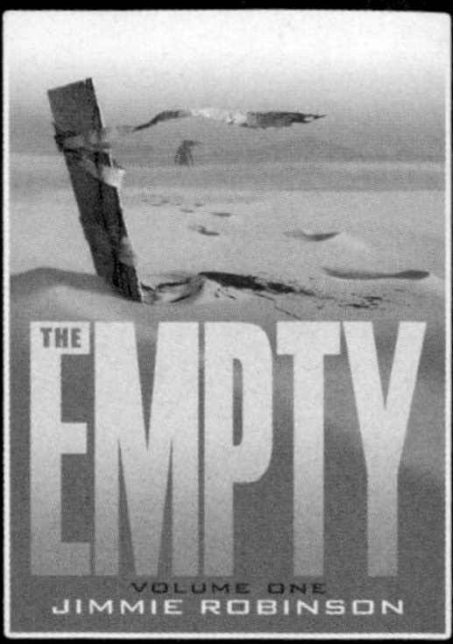
THE EMPTY
VOLUME ONE
JIMMIE ROBINSON

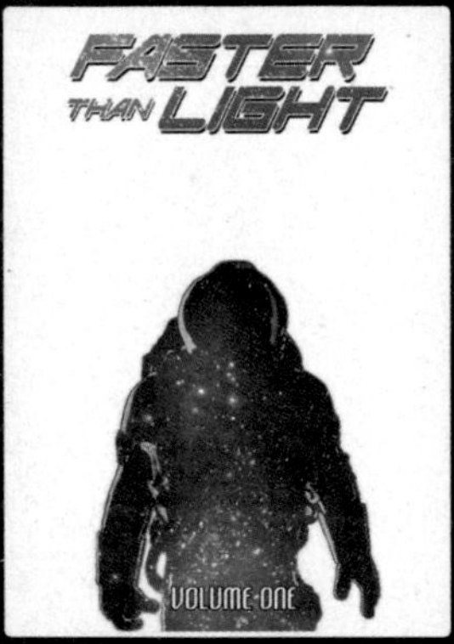
FASTER THAN LIGHT
VOLUME ONE

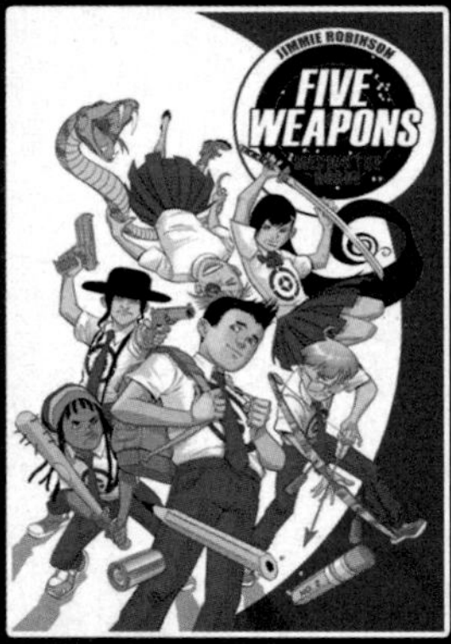
JIMMIE ROBINSON
FIVE WEAPONS

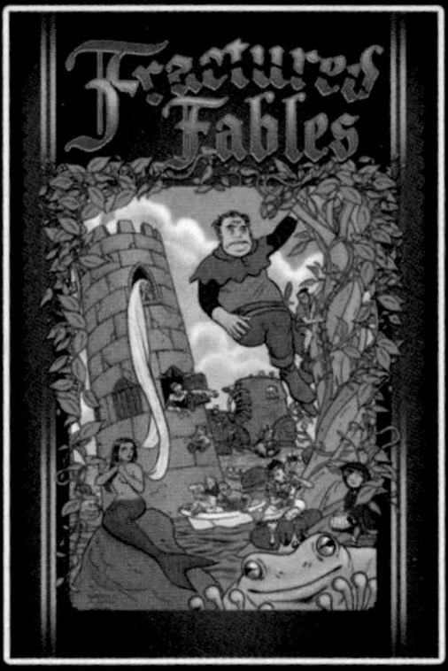
Fractured Fables

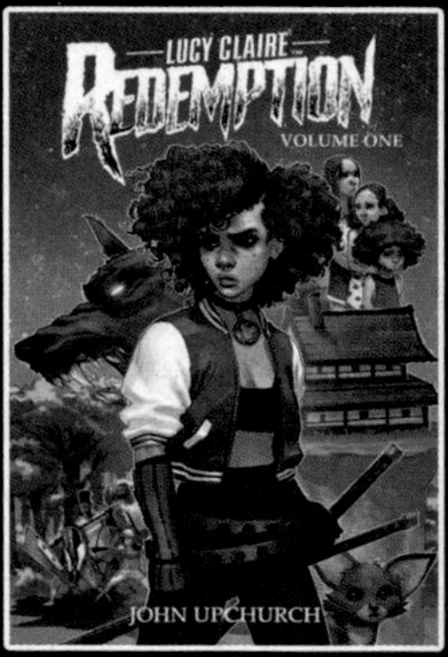
LUCY CLAIRE
REDEMPTION
VOLUME ONE
JOHN UPCHURCH

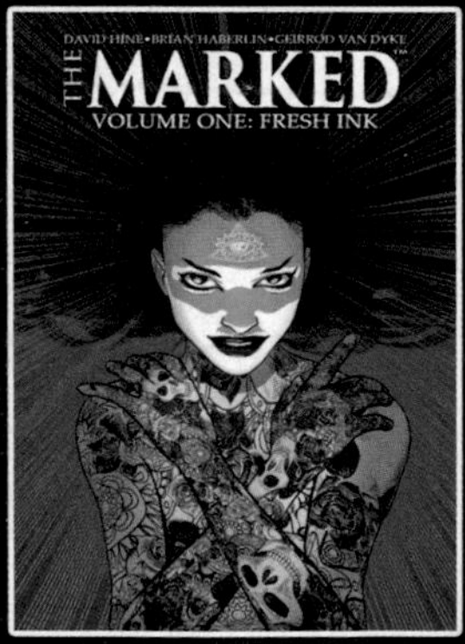
DAVID HINE • BRIAN HABERLIN • GEIRROD VAN DYKE
THE MARKED
VOLUME ONE: FRESH INK

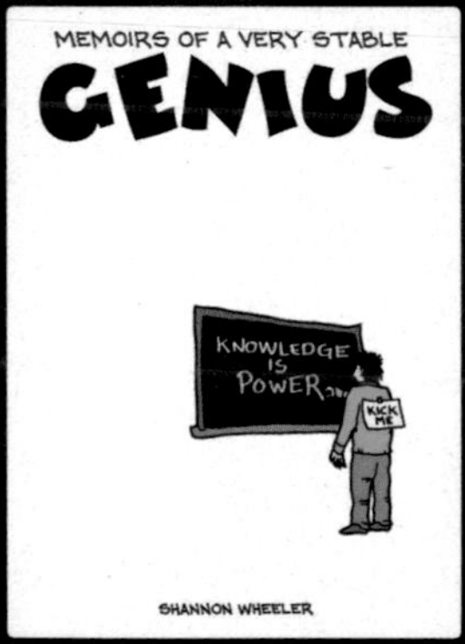
MEMOIRS OF A VERY STABLE
GENIUS
KNOWLEDGE IS POWER
KICK ME
SHANNON WHEELER

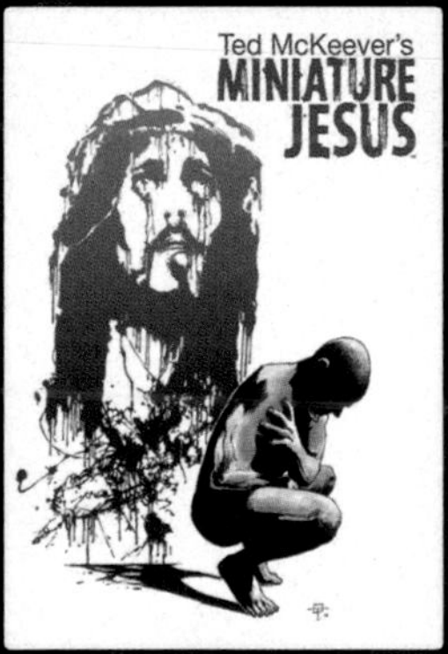
Ted McKeever's
MINIATURE JESUS

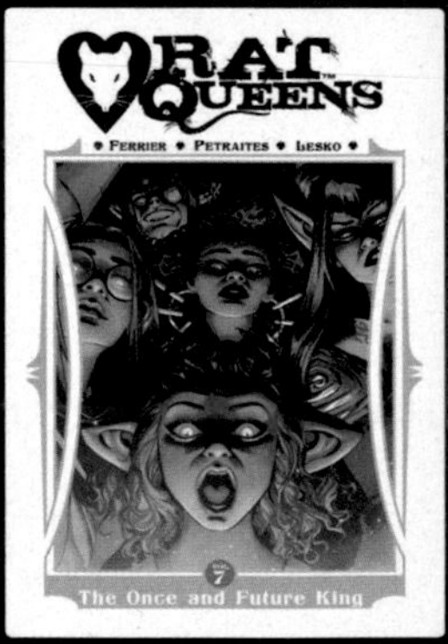
RAT QUEENS
FERRIER • PETRAITES • LESKO
7
The Once and Future King

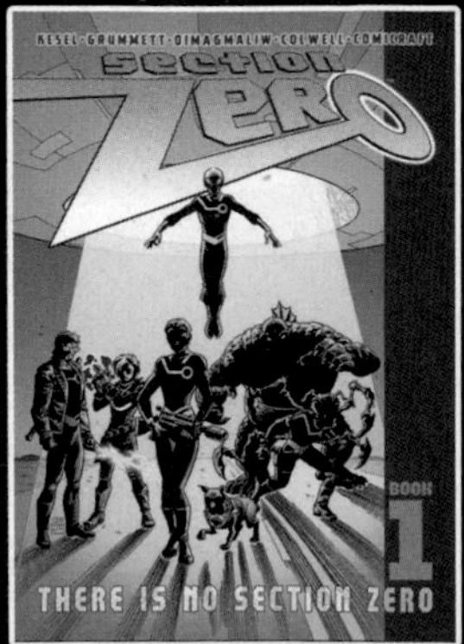
SECTION ZERO
BOOK 1
THERE IS NO SECTION ZERO

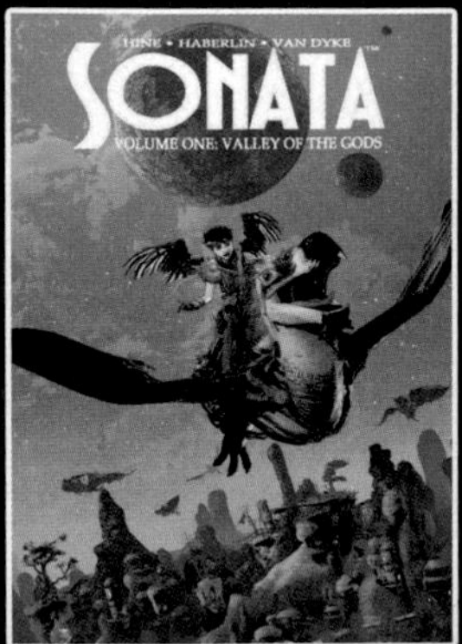
HINE • HABERLIN • VAN DYKE
SONATA
VOLUME ONE: VALLEY OF THE GODS

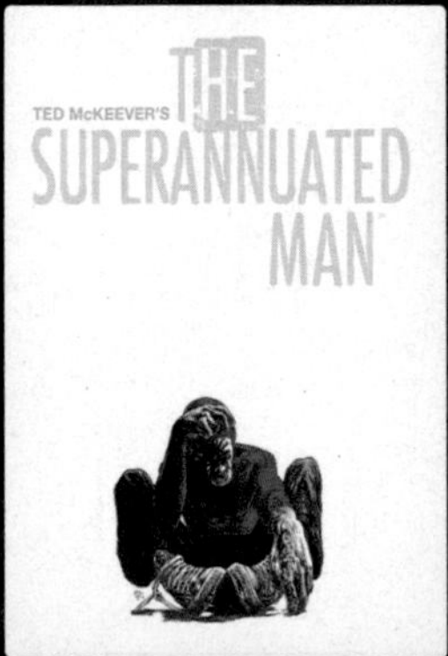
TED McKEEVER'S
THE SUPERANNUATED MAN

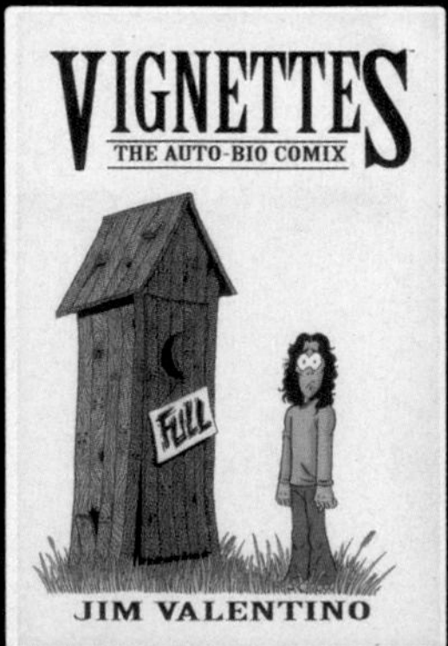
VIGNETTES
THE AUTO-BIO COMIX
FULL
JIM VALENTINO

THIS is Diversity... image® Shadowline®